SECOND
Time Around

ALSO BY NANCY HERKNESS

Second Glances Series

Second to None (novella)

Wager of Hearts Series

The CEO Buys In
The All-Star Antes Up
The VIP Doubles Down
The Irishman's Christmas Gamble (novella)

Whisper Horse Novels

Take Me Home
Country Roads
The Place I Belong
A Down-Home Country Christmas (novella)

Stand-Alone Novels

A Bridge to Love
Shower of Stars
Music of the Night

SECOND
Time Around

A *Second Glances* NOVEL

NANCY HERKNESS

Text copyright © 2018 by Nancy Herkness
All rights reserved.

Published by Montlake Romance, Seattle

www.apub.com

Amazon, the Amazon logo, and Montlake Romance are trademarks of Amazon.com, Inc., or its affiliates.

ISBN-13: 9781503902145
ISBN-10: 1503902145

Cover design by Letitia Hasser

Printed in the United States of America

To Rebecca and Loukas,
who follow their passions and
make me proud every single day.

Chapter 1

Kyra Dixon scooped her tray off the counter and headed for the one empty chair . . . at a table already occupied by a businessman engrossed in his laptop. But this was New York City, so you sat with strangers when it was unavoidable. That made the vacant chair fair game as long as she didn't attempt to converse with the man. She'd learned that when she first came to Manhattan from Macungie, Pennsylvania, eight long years ago.

It was tough threading her way through the packed-in tables at Ceres, one of the wildly successful chain of cafés, where she splurged once every two weeks. The food might be fast, but it was also fresh, with surprising ingredients. Plunking her tray onto the table, she murmured a perfunctory "Hope you don't mind" before slinging her backpack onto the floor and sitting down.

The man nodded but didn't raise his eyes from his computer, so she allowed herself a quick assessment. The waves of his blond hair appeared so natural that she knew his haircut had cost more than her week's wages. His navy-blue suit fit his broad shoulders without a wrinkle—it must have been custom-tailored. If he'd walked into Stratus, the high-end club where Kyra worked as a bartender, she would expect a big tip from him. In fact, he looked out of place wedged into the cramped tables here.

Shrugging, she picked up her lamb wrap, anticipating the creamy burst of avocado-and-yogurt spread when she bit into it. It was this combination that tempted her to spend her hard-earned money on eating out before she headed for her bartending job. She sank her teeth through the tomato-basil tortilla, relished the rich fattiness of the lamb, and then . . . no avocado, no yogurt.

She put the wrap on the plate and peeled it open. One tiny smear of the creamy spread was positioned right in the center of the tortilla. "Of all the stingy . . . !"

"Is there something wrong with your food?" A deep voice with a slight Connecticut intonation made her look up from her defective lamb wrap.

She stared. Her companion had raised his head from his laptop, and she could see that his eyes were a deep jade green. She'd only seen eyes like that once before in her life. She tried to overlay the expensively dressed executive with the lanky classics major she'd known back in college. It could be him. With ten years, a serious haircut, and a lot of success in between.

His eyes widened a fraction. "Kyra? Kyra Dixon?"

It *was* him. The man she'd wanted never to face again.

She flattened the palm of her hand against her chest in exaggerated shock. "Will Chase! Who'd have thought we'd run into each other in the seething masses of New York City?"

For a moment he seemed stunned. Then a glint of amused challenge lit his eyes. "'I count myself in nothing else so happy as in a soul remembering my good friends.'"

"Quote wars!" For a moment she was back at Brunell University, trading quotations with the gorgeous blond boy from upper-crust Connecticut. They'd pick a topic and trade quotes until one of them couldn't think of another appropriate comeback. Will had been her suitemate's boyfriend, but Babette hadn't been very faithful. So Kyra

2

was often pressed into entertaining him while Babette was getting rid of another guy. Kyra hadn't found the duty a chore. "Shakespeare is too easy," she scoffed.

"Easy but true, in this case."

Kyra dug into the dusty corners of her memory and came back with: "'There is flattery in friendship.'"

Will nodded his approval. "Back at me with the Bard. Well done."

Kyra gave a little crow of triumph as she flashed back to the heady days of college when she drank in knowledge like wine. But those days were long gone. She pulled herself back to the present and the somewhat intimidating man across from her. "Do you work near here?" she asked.

His lips twisted into a smile with an edge of irony. "I suppose you could say that I work right here."

Kyra glanced around the crowded café he claimed was his office. "Wait . . . what do you mean?"

He swept his hand in a half circle. "I own this place. The whole chain and a few miscellaneous subsidiaries, in fact."

"Oh." Surprise made her stomach flip. He'd always been out of her league, but she didn't expect him to be *that* successful. Ceres had cafés all over the world. She also didn't expect him to be in the food business. He had been headed for law school after Brunell.

She'd had to drop out of college after her sophomore year, when he'd only been a junior, so his plans must have changed. Not to mention that Brunell didn't send her alumni magazines, which contained class notes columns announcing their graduates' impressive accomplishments. They only sent bills for her student-loan payments. "Wow! Congratulations on your success," she finally managed.

"Thank you, but I seem to have a quality-control problem." He frowned at the defective lamb wrap on her tray. "Let me get you a replacement with the right amount of avocado-yogurt spread and then we'll catch up." He gave her one of those warm, dazzling smiles that highlighted the deep cleft in his chin and made her dream of things she couldn't have.

"Really, it's fine," she said.

He was already standing up with her plate in his hand and an expression on his face that made her glad she wasn't the manager on duty. He raised his eyebrows in a way that was pure CEO. "I heard you call it 'stingy.'"

"You've got me there." She gave him a wave of permission and he turned to weave through the tables. As he approached the service counter, the cashiers cast him wary looks. He strode past them and into the food prep area, where she lost sight of him.

Had he known she had a heart-stopping crush on him in college? Or had her we're-just-friends banter been convincing enough for him to believe that she was merely being courteous by making conversation while he waited for Babette?

He might have thought that, if it hadn't been for the one awful night.

Her hope had always been that he didn't remember how that had ended. Or if he did, that he was too much of a gentleman to say so. Because William Peyton Chase III was definitely a gentleman.

Still, embarrassment prickled over her skin with a hot flush. Amazing that she could feel the sting of her humiliation after all these years.

Will was headed back toward her, his blond head and fluid stride snagging the approving glance of almost every woman he passed. A little spurt of triumph jetted through her when he sat down at her table, and she caught a few of those glances turning to envy. She'd felt the same way at Brunell when Will would catch sight of her between classes and call out for her to wait so he could walk with her. For those few moments, his golden attention made her feel like she belonged.

"They'll bring the wrap to the table as soon as it's ready," he said as he slid onto the seat, his gaze skimming over her. "You look terrific."

"Thanks, and I'll return the compliment." Truthfully, she looked better than usual because she'd just had her hair done, so its long, artfully highlighted brown waves flowed over her shoulders and down her back. It was an investment for work. When she'd started at Stratus, she'd noticed that the bartenders with long hair got bigger tips, so she'd let hers grow. And she'd invested in a couple of expensive black lace push-up bras that also added to her take for the evening.

"No, I mean it about looking terrific," he said, his gaze limpid with genuine admiration.

Will's sincerity was one of the things that had disarmed her back in college. "Why do you think *I* don't mean it?"

He made a dismissive movement, his long, elegant hand capturing her gaze. "I've just got a better haircut. Although I sometimes miss the ponytail." He had always disregarded the power of his strong cheekbones and the indent in his chin, which had made him all the more magnetic. Unfortunately, she had a weakness for cleft chins.

His gesture reminded her of how she'd always pictured him in a courtroom, swaying the jury with his sincerity and his flair for the dramatic. "Why aren't you a lawyer?"

"'Two roads diverged in the wood, and I—I took the one less traveled by.'" His smile was tight.

"'And that has made all the difference.'" She finished the line of Robert Frost's poem. "Also too easy."

She waited, a trick she'd learned when negotiating down her mother's credit card debt.

He met her gaze. "The law didn't appeal to me."

"I remember you felt that way, but the family firm was there for you to claim your place in." Late one night, he'd confided his distaste for the path that had been laid out for him almost from birth: Brunell, Harvard Law, a partnership at Chase, Banfield, and Trost.

"A woman I knew back at Brunell gave me some wise advice," he said. "She told me that our parents' expectations belong to them. We need to run our lives by our own expectations."

"Did I say that? If I did, I was trying to convince myself." She didn't want him casting his mind back to college days.

"You lived it," he said. "As I remember, your parents didn't want you to go to a liberal arts college, so you got yourself a scholarship and went anyway. That made a big impression on me."

She had admitted to him that neither of her parents understood why she wanted to go to a fancy college that taught nothing practical. "Yeah, that didn't work out so well." Her partial scholarship had required her to take out a pile of loans. Now she had plenty of debt and no degree to show for it. And she'd wanted so badly to be the first person in her family to graduate from college.

"Why didn't you come back?" he inquired. "I asked around when I didn't see you the next fall, but no one seemed to know."

The disconcerting flush burned over her skin again. He was circling too close to her mortification.

"My father got sick. My mother needed help taking care of him."

Her father had told her to go back to school. She'd been so tempted to leave the terrible sight of him wasting away in the hospital bed set up in their living room. Not because she didn't love him, but because she wanted to remember him as the man with hands so strong that when he'd tossed her up in the air as a child, she never once doubted he'd catch her again. He'd worked in the nearby Mack Trucks factory, handling the inventory of heavy metal engine blocks and giant wheel rims. The job turned his wiry frame into pure tensile muscle.

Forestalling the inevitable question, she continued. "He died late that year."

"I'm sorry," Will said. "You were close to him."

"He supported my dreams, even when he didn't understand them."

rent-free apartment on the top floor of a townhouse owned by one of the center's board members. In lieu of a salary, of course.

"So you went into the food business, too." He smiled. "You used to whip up amazing dishes in that tiny kitchen in your suite."

She'd always cooked after her mother's phone calls. The meditative repetition of chopping and stirring and scrubbing the pots afterward offered an escape from the guilt and stress. The more complicated the dish, the more relaxing she found it.

"You had a knack for dropping by just as the food came out of the oven," she said.

"'After a good dinner one can forgive anybody, even one's own relations.'"

She had to think about that one. "Oscar Wilde?"

"You've still got it," he said.

"Don't ever doubt it." But she doubted it herself. As time rolled on and she still hadn't found a way to return to college, the knowledge she'd worked so hard to acquire seemed to leach away. She met his intense gaze squarely. "I'm afraid I need to say good-bye."

For good. He brought back too many yearnings that had no place in her life now.

But Will reached into his breast pocket, pulled out a pen and a business card, and scrawled something on the back of it. "This is my personal cell number. Give me a call the next time you crave a lamb wrap. I'll make sure you get a good one."

She zipped the card into a pocket in her backpack and stood, holding out her hand. "Great to see you, Will."

He stood as well. Instead of taking her hand, he walked around the table. "A handshake is too formal between old college friends." He cupped his hands over her shoulders and bent to brush his lips against her cheek.

Warm, firm lips. A whiff of something clean and woodsy from his aftershave. A tickle at her temple as his hair whispered against her skin.

She was back at Brunell, longing for him to put his arms around her and pull her in so her breasts would be crushed against that well-muscled chest, her thighs intertwined with his, her fingers buried in the golden spill of his hair.

And he had, just that once.

She stepped away and swung her backpack over her shoulder. "Rah, Brunell!"

Then she walked out of his restaurant—and his life—one more time.

Chapter 2

Will walked through heavy mahogany doors into the bar of the ultra-exclusive Bellwether Club. He scanned the brass-topped tables and leather-upholstered chairs before spotting his host, Nathan Trainor. The CEO of Trainor Electronics stood as Will approached, a smile of welcome lighting his serious face.

The men shook hands and sat as a waiter materialized beside their table.

"Take your coat and tie off. Make yourself comfortable," Nathan said after Will had ordered. The CEO had already shed his suit jacket and lounged in his rolled-up shirtsleeves. "There's no dress code at the Bellwether."

Will shrugged out of his own jacket. "Just can't resist rubbing my nose in it, can you?"

Nathan's gray eyes sparked with amusement. "It's one of the few places where I can be a member and you can't."

"Do you think Frankie would accept me if I told her my father had disinherited me?"

"Too late. You've already made your fortune."

"Without a dime from my family." Will took a swig of the Macallan single malt the waiter had placed in front of him.

"Give it up, Chase. Your father paid for your fancy boarding school and Brunell U. You graduated with a solid-gold education and no debt. Those of us who belong to the Bellwether Club had to start with nothing."

Will held up a hand in defeat. "I hope to persuade Frankie to make an exception for me." But he knew the tough Irishwoman who owned the Bellwether Club wasn't prone to breaking her own rules.

He liked the Bellwether Club's members precisely because they had made their fortunes from the ground up, the way Frankie had . . . or as Kyra said, they had earned them. His old college friend's name evoked a twinge of nostalgia.

Although technically he had built his multinational corporation on his own, Will had indeed started with major advantages, his education being the least of them. He had benefited heavily from the connections he had access to, old family friends with the kind of money that they could afford to risk on an energetic young man's start-up idea, a young man they saw as one of their own.

His father might look down his nose at Will's career choice, but he hadn't prevented his son from using other people's money to fund it. Will suspected that his father hoped Ceres would fail, and his shame at having lost the money of people he knew would drive him into the familial embrace of Chase, Banfield, and Trost.

Nathan raised his glass. "To having a hard-ass as a father."

"At least yours came around in the long run."

"Thanks to my wife," Nathan said, sipping his drink as a soft light glowed in his eyes.

"You're a lucky man, my friend." Will leaned back in his chair. "So, are we here for business or pleasure?" He and Nathan had met when he decided to explore the installation of Trainor Electronics batteries as power backup for Ceres's refrigerators. The technology was still experimental, so Will and Nathan had spent a lot of time together working out the issues.

"Refuge," Nathan said. "Tonight is Chloe's baby shower at our place." Nathan's wife was pregnant with their first child.

"I've been in your penthouse. You could hold four baby showers simultaneously without one overlapping the others."

"Chloe says I hover."

Will grinned. "Do you?"

"I express a rational concern at times." But the corners of Nathan's mouth twitched into a smile of self-mockery.

Will laughed outright. "You drive her crazy."

"That's one man's opinion."

"I'd trade you the baby shower for my mother's Spring Fling in a New York minute," Will said, grimacing into his glass at the prospect of attending his mother's annual garden party for her friends and his father's business colleagues. "Are you and Chloe coming?"

Nathan raised an eyebrow. "Since you've painted the event in such glowing colors, no. Actually, we're flying to Florida that weekend to bring Chloe's grandmother back up here for the summer."

"Damn. I was hoping for reinforcements." Will took a sip of his drink, letting the smooth burn ease his dread of the upcoming event. His father would throw verbal barbs at him. His mother would throw eligible women at him. His sister, at least, would have the good sense to disappear to the stables after making a brief appearance. "So you're leaving me to the wolves."

"It seems harsh to call your family 'wolves.'"

"You're right. Sharks would be more accurate. Larger, sharper teeth."

Nathan snorted. "Take a date to throw out as chum."

"That gets complicated." Especially since he had ended a relationship his parents approved of at that very party. On the surface, he and Petra had appeared to be a great match, but when he'd insisted on taking her away from the social scene to be alone together, it had been a disaster.

"You must have a female friend who will go with you as camouflage."

He started to shrug, but Kyra's face flashed in his mind again, her long-lashed brown eyes more guarded than they'd been in college, her dark hair flowing over her shoulders in carefully sophisticated waves, her curves more sculpted now. But she still remembered their quote wars and her slanting smile hadn't changed at all.

"Have you ever met someone who reminds you that you once were a different person?" Will asked.

"Chloe. That's why I married her." Nathan stretched out his legs. "So who makes you feel that way?"

"An old college friend. I ran into her today while I was inspecting one of my Ceres cafés."

"Ah."

Will raised his eyebrows at Nathan's tone. "We were nothing but friends." Except for one night when he had embarrassed himself. Now that he thought about it, Kyra had been there for two of his most humiliating moments in college. Which meant he should probably avoid her.

"I don't believe I said anything to the contrary." Nathan flicked a cashew crumb off his trousers. "What aspect of the 'old you' did she remind you of?"

Will shook his head. "She was my girlfriend's suitemate, and it turned out my girlfriend didn't consider our relationship exclusive. So I often ended up talking to Kyra while Babette was otherwise occupied." He grimaced. "I was under the delusion that Babette took a great deal of time getting dressed and putting on her makeup when, in fact, she was, er, entertaining another man in her room. At any rate, I got to know and respect Kyra's passion for soaking up knowledge. She used to audit extra courses just because she was interested in the subjects. No one else I knew did that."

"So now she's a college professor or something?"

"She's a bartender at Stratus and a cook at an after-school care center. She dropped out of Brunell after two years." Will shifted in his chair. "Her father got sick and died."

"It bothers you," Nathan said.

Will swirled his scotch in the cut crystal tumbler. "She had an amazing mind. She planned to be an editor and discover the next Jane Austen. I have no doubt she would do exactly that, if given the opportunity." He met Nathan's gaze. "She inspired me to use my time at Brunell to actually learn something instead of hanging out at the frat house. And now . . ." He shrugged.

"So are you going to take her to the party?"

Will made a dismissive gesture. "That would be unkind to Kyra."

"Maybe not. Maybe you also remind her of the person she used to be."

Chapter 3

Kyra picked up the scrub brush to work on one of the battered pots in the Carver After-School Care Center's kitchen. Today's so-called snack had been taco macaroni, a one-pot kid-friendly dish made from a recipe Felicia, one of the fifth graders, had brought in. That meant the child helped to prepare the meal, and Kyra posted her photo, in which Felicia was grinning with pride as she held a steaming plate heaped with the casserole, on the chef's wall of honor. The kids had wolfed down the pasta, their eyes lit with appreciation, partly because sometimes the "snacks" were the only dinner they got.

As Kyra scrubbed at the sticky remnants of the casserole, she recalled her meeting with Will . . . again. It had been a week and he kept striding into her mind—sometimes in his business suit, sometimes in his college jeans and polo shirt—at odd moments. She hadn't thought of him in years—well, not very often—but now she couldn't stop. It was like being back in college when he was the Big Man on Campus and she was the mousy girl from the boondocks with a giant crush on him.

"Unfinished business," she muttered to herself. That had to be it. For one brief, dreamlike moment, she had thought she would have the ultimate experience in Will's arms . . . but then it hadn't happened. She'd gone back to being the blue-collar girl from Nowhere, PA.

"Hey, Ms. Kyra, could I ask you something?" Diego's voice, soft as it was, made her drop the scrub brush as she spun away from the sink.

The kid's long dark hair hung to the shoulders of his gray Knicks sweatshirt, and his hands were shoved in the pockets of jeans so new they still had a crease down the leg. His recently appointed guardian, Violet Johnson, one of the center's board members, took good care of him.

Kyra used the back of her rubber-glove–covered wrist to shove a strand of hair away from her face. "Sure thing, sweetie. Ask away."

Diego was huge for his thirteen years—tall, broad, and muscular. Yet when he touched one of the motley array of rescue dogs that the kids took care of at the center, known as the K-9 Angelz, his hands moved as delicately as butterflies, and his chocolate-brown eyes were soft with concern. The local veterinarian had even given him an internship at her clinic because Diego was so good with animals.

"One of the dogs, Shaq, keeps throwing up his food. He ain't . . . isn't sick that Doc Quillen can tell, so we think he's got a sensitive stomach."

Kyra scanned her memory of the resident dogs. She didn't interact with them much because they were banned from her domain of kitchen and dining room due to health department regulations. However, she'd seen how devoted the children were to their adopted pets and how much the dogs' unconditional love meant to them.

"Isn't Shaq the giant pit-bull mix?" She was about to say that it seemed ridiculous for such a tough-looking dog to have a picky stomach when she remembered whom she was talking to. Diego was a huge, scary-looking kid—so scary, in fact, that his moneylender father had wanted to use him to intimidate his nonpaying customers, while the boy wanted to take care of every small creature he encountered.

Diego nodded. "Yeah, he's the biggest dog of the K-9 Angelz. And his kid is Felicia. Why that little girl picked such a big Angel . . ." He shook his head. "Anyways, I was wondering if you got an idea for food that might not upset his stomach so much."

"Don't they make hypoallergenic dog food?" She stripped off her gloves as she headed for her laptop to look it up.

"Yeah, but he can't tolerate that neither and it ain't . . . isn't cheap. Doc says we need to figure out what ingredient bothers him, so we need to try foods that got just a few ingredients and we know what they all are. And fresh is better 'cause the premade stuff might have some preservative or something that makes him sick."

"Huh." Kyra put her hands on her hips. "I don't know anything about dog food. Let me do some research and I'll come up with some recipes."

The worried furrows in Diego's forehead eased. "Hey, you want me to clean that pot for you? I got more muscles than you."

"You're the best, kiddo." She ruffled his long hair, making him duck away from her with a grimace that covered a smile. The staff never discussed it, but she knew that Diego used to sleep at the center because his father had thrown him out and his mother was MIA. The boy had found a happy foster home with Violet, but Kyra still tried to give him the affection a family member would, kind of like a favorite aunt.

She glanced at the clock over the kitchen door and grabbed her backpack and sweatshirt. "You saved my butt from being late to work, too. Thanks, Diego!"

After racing home to change into her "sexy bartender" outfit, she stood on the subway platform, hoping the train would arrive soon so she'd have time to grab a lamb-and-yogurt wrap at Ceres. She hadn't been back since she saw Will there, partly because she was afraid she'd run into him again, partly because she was afraid she wouldn't.

His business card lay on her dresser. Every now and then, she flipped it over to see his bold handwriting where he'd jotted down his cell number. Once she'd even run her finger over the ink, which was one of those stupid gestures people made in sappy movies.

She'd wanted him with every fiber of her body back in college, even though she knew the handsome golden boy from an upper-class family in Connecticut would never consider her as a girlfriend. And the differences between them had only gotten greater in the present, so there was no point in reviving that pipe dream.

But he had reminded her of her other dreams. The ones in which she got a master's and became a brilliantly perceptive editor, carefully cultivating the budding literary talents she would rescue from the publisher's slush pile. When she'd discovered all her mother's debts—with Kyra's name as the unwitting cosigner on the credit cards—she'd shoved those goals aside and focused on paying off the bills. Now those dreams had faded so far into the background she'd nearly forgotten them. Until yesterday.

She still had significant debts to pay off, but she also had a reliable income now. The encounter with Will had made her wonder. Was she using the debt as an excuse? Was she afraid to try again?

The thunder of the arriving subway train scattered her thoughts. When she walked into Ceres twenty minutes later and stepped into the line to order, she noticed some changes at the café.

The tables were farther apart, not crammed in for maximum seating. It made the space more inviting and quieter. The lighting seemed brighter, although she hadn't been conscious that it was dim before. The room had appeared a little dingy previously, but now it didn't. There were additional staff members in tan shirts circulating around the floor, and they were smiling. For that matter, the cashiers had more pleasant attitudes, too.

Will must have really chewed out the manager.

When she sat down to eat her lamp wrap, she peeled it open to find the pureed avocado and yogurt spread evenly in a thin layer over the inside of the tortilla. The lamb was moist with just a tiny hint of pink, since they weren't allowed to serve it rare without a warning about undercooked meat. And there were crunchy bits of carrot that had never been included before.

It was delicious and bursting with freshness. She raised her water bottle in a silent toast to Will's impressive results.

The limousine eased to a stop in front of a white canopy with a silver lining. Will smiled at the sly reference to the saying about clouds, since the canopy hovered over the entrance to the Stratus Club. He swung open the car door, only to have a white-suited doorman catch and hold it, while he stepped out onto the gray carpet that stretched across the sidewalk.

After Nathan had planted the idea of inviting Kyra to his parents' garden party, Will hadn't been able to shake it. She would be a breath of fresh air in the rarefied atmosphere of the Connecticut high-society gathering.

Not to mention staving off his mother's introductions of what she considered marriageable young women. When he went home, Will sometimes felt as though he'd slipped through a time warp into Regency England, where eligible bachelors were expected to choose a suitable wife from the assortment at the soiree.

Kyra would also provide a buffer against Petra. His ex-fiancée would be more likely to keep her distance if he had a date. He should have thought of that tactic sooner.

Most tempting of all, Kyra would carry him back to the college days when he'd been able to shrug off the weight of the world's expectations. Exhilarating days when he had studied just for the sake of knowledge. No balance sheets, no stockholders.

His meeting with Kyra had forced him to admit to the restless dissatisfaction that grumbled through the back of his mind during every meeting, every restaurant opening, and every proposed acquisition these days. His partner Greg accused him of being a champion of the status quo every time Will shot down a new product idea. When Greg really wanted to piss Will off, he claimed Will was turning into his father.

But Kyra had flooded his veins with the intoxicating elixir of carefree, potential-filled youth. He wanted to feel that again.

So he walked through the stainless steel portal the doorman swept open.

Bracing himself for a barrage of overloud music and headache-inducing strobe lights, he was pleasantly surprised by the restrained elegance of the entrance foyer's blue floor and white columns, both of solid marble. Only the ceiling hinted at the club's theme, with a painted sky that included a swath of indistinct white clouds—he assumed that was an authentic depiction of a stratus formation, since the word came from a Latin prefix meaning "layer."

"Welcome to the Stratus Club, sir." A young blonde woman with exceedingly long legs shown off by a slit in her white skirt approached him. "Is this your first visit with us?"

"It is."

"If you'll come with me, we'll make sure you are well taken care of." She clicked across the floor in her high heels, leading him through another brushed stainless steel door.

In the anteroom, a man in a dark suit scanned Will's credit card and handed him a small silver ingot stamped with a cloud and an *S*. "Just touch the server's tablet with this and it will take care of payment."

Will slipped the ingot into his breast pocket and followed the willowy blonde through the foyer and into the hum of conversation filling the main room. It was furnished in a tasteful, understated style with silver-gray upholstery and various hues of blue infusing the carpeting and walls. Projected on the ceiling was a sky with clouds of various configurations moving across it as though on a windy day. While he watched, the sky began to glow with the colors of sunset, throwing a warm light over the well-dressed patrons sipping their cocktails.

"Would you prefer a table or a booth?" the hostess asked.

"A seat at the bar."

"Of course."

She swayed between the marble-topped tables and capacious chairs, leading him to a side room where the clouds continued to wash across the ceiling. One wall of the space was occupied by a long bar of intricately grained wood. Blue marble topped it while the same stone material was inset into panels behind the shelves, which held bottles of expensive liquor.

Will scanned the decor for only a moment before his gaze snagged on the woman wielding a silver cocktail shaker like a master.

Kyra. She was wearing a fitted black sleeveless top that showed a tantalizing amount of cleavage, as well as graceful but well-toned arms. Her hair cascaded over her shoulders in ripples that caught glints of the pinks and golds of the artificial sunset. Her generous mouth was curved into a smile that hinted at some private amusement. That smile had always tempted him to kiss her as though he could somehow taste the laughter on her lips.

Awareness surged through him with an unexpected heat . . . and he remembered that night. The frat party, where he'd gone to drown the still-smarting injury Babette had inflicted on his fragile male ego. It had been a couple of days after he'd caught her screwing another guy in her bedroom. Kyra had witnessed his humiliation, offering awkward sympathy as he tried to pretend that he didn't care. Her kindness had made him feel like an even bigger idiot.

His frat brothers had attempted to console him by revealing that the slime bucket was just one of several others whom Babette screwed while she was supposedly his girlfriend. Their flawed logic had been that she couldn't be faithful to anyone, so it wasn't only him.

Earlier that day, he'd had a final confrontation with Babette, who didn't understand what his problem was. His response had been simple: "I don't share." And he'd walked away.

But he was still pissed off, so he'd headed for the party and downed several shots. He'd already switched to beer when he saw Kyra walk in with a couple of other sophomore women.

Even through the haze of alcohol, he knew he should look out for her. She wasn't accustomed to rowdy parties like this one. When two of his frat brothers eyed Kyra up and down, he decided to intervene.

Someone had gotten her a beer by the time he had wedged his way through the crush of sweaty bodies. She sipped it as though she didn't really like it, while she laughed and flirted with the two guys. He'd hesitated for a moment, thinking that maybe she wouldn't appreciate his interference. But then a third brother had come up behind her, snaking his arm around her waist and pulling her back against him. Will was sure the asshole had a hard-on that he was grinding into Kyra.

Will lost it, slamming his fellow frat brother in the shoulder to knock him away from Kyra before hurling the contents of his half-drunk beer in the cretin's face.

He'd grabbed Kyra's hand and towed her out the front door before the asshole could retaliate. He would deal with the guy later. Right then he'd just wanted to get Kyra out of there.

"Will? What brings you to Stratus?" The surprise and pleasure in Kyra's voice jerked him back from his stagger down memory lane.

He slid onto the high bar chair. "You."

Kyra nearly dropped the cocktail shaker. "Seriously?"

Will smiled, his teeth flashing in the fake sunset. "You didn't call, so I had no choice but to track you down with the only piece of information I had."

"I'm pretty sure you could just Google my address." She tried to sound cool after her very uncool first reaction to his appearance. God, he looked good in that charcoal suit. The pale gray shirt and dark tie made his eyes blaze even brighter green, and his shoulders looked even wider than she remembered.

"Where's the fun in that?" He reached up to loosen his tie and yank it out of his collar. Her internal temperature rose at least ten degrees when he unfastened the first two buttons of his shirt to expose the strong column of his neck. When he rolled his head in a stretching motion, she noticed the dusting of dark blond scruff over the cleft in his chin.

"I thought if I avoided the law profession, I wouldn't have to wear a tie," he said with a wry grimace.

"You should have gone to Silicon Valley. Those guys wear jeans and T-shirts. Designer, of course." It had taken her a while to learn the subtle differences, but now she could spot a high-fashion T-shirt from twenty paces. "What can I get you to drink?"

"Your specialty."

"I don't limit myself to one specialty. Is your favorite hard stuff still whiskey?"

"You remember that?"

She remembered more than she wanted to admit about Will Chase. "I'll make you my own personal version of a Vieux Carré."

"That's a new one to me."

She pulled down the bottles of Benedictine, rye, cognac, sweet vermouth, two kinds of bitters, and her secret ingredient, limoncello. Taking extra care to get the proportions exactly right, she poured and stirred before garnishing it with a lemon twist and setting the glass in front of him on a cloud-shaped linen cocktail napkin. "It's potent," she warned as he reached for the glass.

A tingle danced over her skin when he wrapped his long fingers around the old-fashioned glass. During their heated late-night discussions, she'd been hypnotized by his gestures, so smooth and assured, wishing he would apply that physical eloquence to her body. Now all the youthful softness had been honed away from his hands and face, and his presence had been sharpened to a pitch of sheer power by time and success.

As he raised the glass, she sucked in a breath and watched those sculpted lips touch the fine crystal in a near kiss. Desire sparked as she relived the way his mouth had felt on hers that night. Their first kiss had seared through her, making her body vibrate with arousal. When he'd brought his hand up to cup her breast through the thin gauze shirt she'd worn, she'd nearly come just from feeling his palm against her tight nipple.

"It's complex, like a great wine." His voice twined with her memory to stoke the heat flaring in her belly. He took another sip, his eyes crinkling at the corners so she could tell he was smiling as he drank. "Will I be able to get this at any other bar?"

"Not quite the same," she said, her voice gravelly with longing. "I give it my own special twist."

"That will keep me coming back."

"You've caught on to my evil plan." But he was the one giving her wicked longings.

He reached into his breast pocket and slid a Stratus pay ingot onto the bar. She waved it away, although she wanted to feel the warmth of his body that the metal would hold. "I told you the first drink's on me."

He nudged the ingot toward her. "I didn't come to take advantage of an old friendship. I came to renew it."

Excitement fluttered through her. But he was talking friendship, nothing more.

Two patrons farther down the bar looked up to catch her attention, and she inwardly cursed their timing. "Excuse me, I'll be right back," she said.

She didn't want to leave the sensual cocoon Will's presence wrapped her in, but she summoned up her sexy bartender persona and sashayed down the bar to make a martini and a Manhattan for two of her regulars. Her hips moved with an extra sway because Will was watching her. She could almost feel the heat of his gaze on the curves of her behind.

Just as she started back in Will's direction, Derek, the club's manager, beckoned her through the door that led to the various storerooms. As always, he was dressed entirely in a pale gray that matched his eyes, which made his nearly black hair stand out like a hovering shadow.

"You and Mr. Chase seem to be getting along well," Derek said.

"He's an old friend from college," she said. "He's also the CEO of Ceres."

"That I'm already aware of," Derek said, with a slight smile. "Now that I understand the connection, I'm going to assign you to be his personal bartender tonight. I'll tell Bastian and Cleo."

Of course Derek had already figured out that Will was the CEO of Ceres. Derek made it his business to know that kind of thing. He also made it his business to keep CEOs of international corporations happy, so he would pull a bartender off all other customers to take care of the important patron. Despite the fact that Derek supplemented that bartender's pay to compensate for lost tips, Kyra usually avoided those assignments. She was always trying to maximize her nightly take because every dollar earned meant another dollar of debt paid off.

However, she would give up the extra pay without a qualm in order to be able to focus on Will. She gave Derek a nod and a wide smile.

"Good news!" she said, as she returned to Will. "I'm all yours for the evening . . . as long as you keep drinking."

"As I recall, the last time I saw you at college, I had been drinking for far too long," he said with a grimace.

She hoped he didn't remember too much more about that night at Brunell. "Want to move to a booth?" she asked. Her blood was singing at the thrill of having him seek her out.

"Sounds good, but I can't stay long. I have a late conference call."

The fizz in her veins went flat at the limit on their time together.

He gestured at the display of bottles. "Can I buy you a drink?"

Patrons often wanted to treat her to something expensive, but the bartenders were discouraged from drinking on the job. "I'm good with club soda." She pulled herself a tall glass of the fizzing liquid and dropped in a slice of lime before setting it, a bowl of Stratus's famous gourmet nut mixture, and Will's drink on a silver tray. "I'll be right back." She winked at Will and headed down the long expanse of bar toward the exit at the end.

Cleo stopped her, leaning in to murmur, "How'd you get Derek to let you go private with that one? He's too good-looking to be rich."

"CEO of Ceres," Kyra murmured back. "Old college friend."

Cleo whistled. "Rah, rah for the old alma mater. I'd like to have a study session with him."

Kyra chuckled and unlatched the wooden gate to let herself out. Will stood with the tray balanced on one hand, his gaze focused on her. She did her bartender strut as she walked toward him, knowing a glimpse of bare stomach showed between her hip-hugging black trousers and her vest. When his aristocratic nostrils flared in response, a thrill of power ran through her.

"Allow me," she said, taking the tray from him. "I have to show my boss I'm still working." She led him to a booth tucked into a secluded corner.

Placing the tray on the table, she slipped onto the silver leather banquette that wrapped around all three sides. The expanse of the cushions and the privacy of the location sometimes tempted couples to get a little hot and heavy in the booth.

She didn't anticipate anything like that from Will, but disappointment still pinged at her when he settled himself opposite her, the table between them. He could have sat just a little closer.

He took another sip of his drink, making her ache to feel his mouth on hers as his lips touched the rim. He set the glass down. "You're a talented bartender—you have to be to work here—but that's not what I expected you to be doing."

A pang of regret and shame lanced through her. It wasn't what she had expected either. Despite living like a nun and hustling for tips with all she had, the total of her debts never seemed to lessen.

In fact, it felt like a boulder, grinding her into the grimy sidewalks of New York.

But she wasn't going to allow any more shadows to darken her second encounter with Will. "I have a new project," she said.

He raised his eyebrows in inquiry.

"Dog food."

That elicited a less-than-elegant snort of laughter from him.

She grinned. "I just got asked to develop limited-ingredient dog food for a huge pit-bull mix with a sensitive stomach."

"You've piqued my interest." He tilted his glass toward her. "How did this request come about?"

"The Carver After-School Care Center has a program called K-9 Angelz. The center's director, Emily Wade, came up with the idea of having the kids 'adopt' a rescue dog and be responsible for caring for it after school. She wanted the kids to feel needed and to teach them responsibility. But she also wanted them to experience the kind of unconditional love a dog offers you." Kyra gave him a sober look. "It's amazing to see how the kids light up when they're around the dogs. Even the toughest of boys turns into a marshmallow when a dog jumps on his lap or licks his hand."

He nodded.

"There's one thirteen-year-old kid—Diego—who's kind of the junior supervisor of the program. He wants to be a veterinarian. Today he came to me because the pittie mix is having stomach problems."

"Do you have any ideas about how to solve them?" Will's gaze was intent.

"Fresh, limited ingredients, according to Diego. That way you can isolate what's causing the problem. I'm thinking chicken to start with, because it's relatively bland. And it's cheap." She gave him a resigned smile. "I considered venison or bison because those would be meats the dog's ancestors would have eaten so he should be adapted to them. But they're beyond our budget."

"Rice," Will said. "Maybe brown rice. I think that would be a good fiber. No gluten, in case that's the problem."

"And pumpkin. I've read that's good for dogs prone to digestive issues." She was getting fired up now that she had someone to discuss her thoughts with. "I have to work out proportions, and then I have to see if the dog will actually eat it."

"I grew up with golden retrievers and they ate pretty much anything," Will said. "Including my mother's favorite pair of Ferragamos."

Kyra laughed. Of course, his family had owned golden retrievers, the quintessential WASP dog. With pedigrees almost as illustrious as their human masters. "Luckily, there aren't many designer shoes lying around the Carver Center."

In fact, shoes of any kind were too valuable a commodity to be treated carelessly at the center.

"I imagine not." He glanced as his watch, took a substantial swallow of his drink, and pinned his gaze on her. "Speaking of my family, I came here with an ulterior motive."

"Oh?" What on earth could Will want from her?

"My mother throws an annual spring garden party—she calls it her Spring Fling—in Connecticut, on the family farm. She invites the whole extended family, all her friends, and my father's business associates. I wondered if you might be willing to come with me. Next Sunday. Short notice, I know."

His gaze didn't waver from her face, which made it hard to respond, since she had to concentrate on not letting her mouth fall open in astonishment.

"I, um, well, that sounds like fun." Total lie. It sounded terrifying. But she had Sunday off from work, so she had no commitments to stop her.

"Fun?" He shook his head. "It's stuffy and tense and boring. My family all snap at each other when no one else is listening. That's why I'm asking you to come as a buffer."

"When you put it that way, how can I refuse?" She would be like a fish that didn't even know which way the ocean was. But the chance to see Will in his childhood environment was irresistible. In college, he'd dropped casual comments about racing his sailboat on Long Island

Sound, or his sister getting thrown from her horse in a cross-country event, or his mother winning the club's tennis championship. It sounded like *The Great Gatsby* come to life. She had to experience it just once. "I'd be happy to go with you."

The expression that crossed his face was hard to read, except for relief. "That's the best news I've had all day," he said.

"What's the dress code?"

"Casual. It's outdoors. There are tents in case it rains. Although even the weather rarely dares to displease my mother."

"'Casual' covers a lot of territory for women," she said. "Not jeans, I assume."

He thought for a minute. "Dresses, sort of colorful. Flat shoes because of the grass. Straw hats, if it's sunny."

"What are you wearing?" *That might help.*

"My uniform. Khakis and a button-down shirt. Loafers."

"No tie?"

"Hell, no!" he said. "Shirtsleeves rolled up, too."

She got the picture, and she had nothing appropriate to wear. She sighed inwardly. This was going to cost her more money than she could afford. However, she couldn't resist the opportunity to journey into the exotic country of upper-crust Connecticut. Not to mention, spending time with her college crush, who was even more crushworthy now.

"Okay, a rolled-up shirtsleeves kind of dress." She took a gulp of her club soda as she debated where to find a dress that looked expensive but was bargain priced.

"I'll pick you up at noon. We'll make a fashionably late entrance. Which means we won't have to endure the party as long."

"This sounds more and more delightful all the time."

Will finally smiled, albeit with an edge. "It won't be as bad for you. They're not your family."

"I hear you." But at least he still had his mother and father. As complicated as her parents had made her life, she sometimes felt terribly alone without them.

He sat back against the banquette. "Now I'm looking forward to the party."

"You don't have to flatter me. I've agreed to go." But she couldn't stop a smile of gratification from curling the corners of her mouth.

"You might begin to have second thoughts." He pulled out his cell phone. "May I get your number so I don't have to track you down at the Carver Center?"

He tapped at the phone's screen as she rattled off her phone number.

"Do you still have my cell number or did you chuck my card?" he asked with that self-deprecating smile that always charmed her.

"Just text me and I'll have it on my phone."

"So you chucked it."

The disappointment in his tone surprised her. "No, it's at my apartment."

His fingers flew over the keys of his phone.

A ping sounded from her back pocket, indicating she'd gotten his text, and she started to reach for her phone.

"Read it later," he said with a roguish glint in his eyes. He placed his empty glass on the tray. "My apologies, but I have to go. Overseas business makes for odd working hours."

"I guess CEOs don't get paid for overtime."

"Actually, we do. A great deal, in fact." He stood up.

She followed suit, picking up the tray to use as a barrier between them. Her comment seemed to have triggered a shift into executive mode because the lines of his face hardened and his chin took on an arrogant upward tilt, making him look less like the Will she'd known at Brunell and more like the formidable businessman he was now.

"Thanks for the invitation," she said, awkward now that they had returned to their current roles in life.

"Thanks for the drink." He leaned across the tray to give her the barest brush of his lips on her cheek. Even that made her want to close her eyes to savor the shiver of delight it sent scudding over her skin.

As he strode away, she watched the women's heads turn as they had at Ceres, some blatantly, some more subtly because they were with a date. But almost every female looked. And she was going to a party with him.

"The text," she muttered, shifting the tray to one hand so she could grab her phone and thumb her way to the message.

I would not wish any companion in the world but you.

"I know how rare that is," Will said.

She nodded, unable to force words through the clog of emotion in her throat.

"But you became an editor?" he asked. He pointed to her backpack with a smile. "Is that filled with unpublished masterpieces?"

That swept away her moment of weakness. She shook her head and gave him a wry smile. "Publishers tend to want editors with college degrees." In fact, with her two jobs, she barely had time to read a book for pleasure these days.

A server dressed in the Ceres uniform of tan polo shirt and green trousers arrived at their table, laden down with a tray and a large take-out bag. "Here you are, Mr. Chase."

"The sandwich is for my friend," Will said, taking the bag from the young man.

The tray held not just a wrap, but also a glass of lemonade, a bag of sweet-potato chips, an apple, and a giant chocolate chip cookie.

Will waved at the unexpected bounty. "To make up for the inconvenience of having to wait." He held up the take-out bag. "And some extra apology for later."

"Really, it wasn't that big a deal," she protested.

"I disagree." His tone was sharp.

She picked up the wrap and bit into it, leaning over abruptly as a glob of avocado-yogurt spread gushed from the open end of the tortilla and plopped onto the plate.

Will's jaw tightened and his eyes turned the frigid green of a winter ocean. Kyra felt another pang of sympathy for the café's unlucky, albeit incompetent, manager.

"That is unacceptable," he said, his fingers drumming an irritated beat on the tabletop.

"It's very generous," she said, trying to tilt the rolled-up tortilla so it didn't ooze spread from every crevice.

"Too much is as bad as too little. The balance of ingredients is crucial," he snapped. He flattened his palm on the table so his fingers were still. "Sorry. It's not your fault they can't get it right."

"Don't be too hard on whoever you're going to ream out. It's got to be nerve-racking to have the CEO inspect your place, so he or she may have overreacted."

"He wouldn't have anything to worry about if he hadn't short-changed a customer on an expensive ingredient. That's not how Ceres generates profits."

"'You make money the old-fashioned way. You earn it.'" She imitated a plummy British accent.

His fine blond brows drew down in thought. "If that's a quote, I can't place it."

"It's from an old commercial that my father used to repeat all the time. For some brokerage firm that doesn't exist anymore."

His scary CEO look eased. "I like to think that's true about Ceres." He leaned back in the chair. "So tell me what you're doing instead of editing."

She pointed to her mouth to indicate she was chewing.

"Sorry. It's not fair to ask you questions while you're eating." Something about his apologetic tone made her able to see past the CEO to the student she used to know.

"I took too big a bite because I have to go soon," she said. "My night job is bartending at Stratus, and I need to change into my work clothes."

A fleeting look of surprise and perhaps disappointment crossed his face. "Stratus is very high-end. You must be an excellent bartender."

"Have you ever been there?"

He shook his head.

"Well, if you decide to visit, your first drink is on me," she said. "My day job is cooking for about fifty kids at an after-school care center in South Harlem. It's a great gig." Especially since it came with a

Chapter 4

Monday afternoon, Kyra slotted dirty plates into the ancient industrial dishwasher in the Carver Center's kitchen, a task so mechanical that her mind was free to wander to Will, as it had all weekend.

She had spent the rest of her shift at Stratus trying not to interpret his gratifying text too literally. He was just continuing their Shakespearean exchange. Yet she couldn't stop a little smile from curling her lips every time she thought of it.

Then she had debated how to answer it. It had to be another line from the Bard, but she needed to dial back the overblown emotional content. Finally, she typed in, Good night, good night! Parting is such sweet sorrow.

Friendly. Noncommittal.

That was before she closed out her electronic server book, and the club's computer system showed that Will had left her a one-hundred-dollar tip for his free drink. Although she was accustomed to large tips—that was why she worked at Stratus—she'd felt awkward about how to respond. Should she thank him? Should she pretend it was all in a day's work and accept it without comment? In the end, she texted a casual Thank you for the generous tip. His response was a simple You're welcome.

She couldn't help wondering if he intended for her to use it to buy an appropriate outfit for the Spring Fling. She might have given away her lack of wardrobe by how closely she questioned him about what to wear. The thought made her close her eyes in mortification.

"Hey, Ms. Kyra." Diego's voice pulled her out of her reverie and back to the kitchen of the Carver Center. "Ms. Emily say . . . says you got the dog food ready to try."

She pivoted to see Diego and Felicia standing by the counter, the thin little girl dwarfed by Diego's height and breadth.

"Sure do." Kyra opened one of the motley collection of donated refrigerators and retrieved a plastic container. "Let me warm it up a bit to make it more appetizing," she said, plopping two tablespoons full of shredded boiled chicken, pumpkin, and brown rice into a glass bowl and popping it in the microwave.

"If Shaq thinks we going to warm up his dinner every day, he got another think coming," Diego said.

Felicia giggled in her high-pitched voice. "Shaq don't . . . doesn't care whether his food be hot or cold. He just loves to eat."

"But you can't give him treats all the time," Diego said sternly. "It ain't good for his health to get overweight."

Kyra smiled as she watched the two kids. "Did you tell your mom how much everyone liked the taco macaroni, Felicia?"

The girl nodded, her braids swinging and her huge brown eyes warm with pleasure. "She say she going to send in another recipe for next week, but I tell her I got to spend time with Shaq, so someone else will help you."

"I'd love the recipe," Kyra said. "Although I'll miss having you as my sous-chef." However, she was touched by how much the girl cared about her dog.

"I really want this food to work," Felicia said, "'cause then Shaq can come home with me for a slumber party. But Mama don't . . . doesn't want no barf or diarrhea in our apartment."

Kyra choked on a laugh. "I can't blame her for that." The canine slumber parties were the center director's latest brainstorm. With the participation of parents or guardians, the kids were allowed to take their K-9 Angelz home with them for a night or a weekend. Emily Wade believed it made them feel as though they truly owned the dogs.

When the microwave dinged, Kyra pulled out the dog food and tipped it into the gleaming stainless steel dog bowl Diego had brought. She handed the dish to the boy. "Let's see what Shaq thinks of my recipe."

Felicia poked it with her finger. "He's gonna love this."

"Since I think it looks good, he'll think it's lit," Diego said, sniffing the experimental dog food.

"That's good, right?" Kyra asked.

Diego grinned and nodded as he led the way downstairs to the "kennel" on the ground floor. When he reached the bottom of the steps, a glossy black dog leaped up from a dog bed by the wall and raced over to the boy.

"Hey, Mario," Diego said, kneeling to ruffle the dog's ears with one hand. Diego's dramatic rescue of the black dog had become a Carver Center legend. He'd interrupted Max Varela's first visit to the center and prompted Emily to commandeer Max's limousine to get the injured dog to the vet. That was before she and Max were even dating. "This ain't . . . isn't for you, though." He gave a hand signal, which made the dog look at him reproachfully before he turned to walk back with dragging steps to the bed.

"Mario doesn't have to go lay down. He and Shaq be cool with each other," Felicia said.

"We don't want Mario distracting Shaq. This is called a controlled experiment," Diego said, satisfaction shining in his eyes because he knew the terminology from his science classes.

The dogs' crates—at this time of day empty except for Shaq's—were lined up in what had once been a storage room. Now the formerly dingy walls were a warm cream, and the two windows at the back sketched rectangles of spring sunshine on the pale gray paint of the cement floor.

Emily had wisely laid down strict rules about where the dogs could eat, sleep, and play. They were always fed in the kennel area, although Kyra had seen the kids slip their adopted K-9 Angelz a treat or two upstairs in the main lounge. However, Diego obeyed all the rules, even though Mario lived with him and not at the Carver Center. The boy felt strongly about setting a good example.

Felicia walked to the giant crate at the end of the row and unlatched the door, signaling that Shaq could come out. Under the pit-bull mix's beautiful brindle coat, massive muscles rippled as he rose and walked out into the kennel area, his thick tail wagging. Kyra couldn't help thinking that Shaq would be a more appropriate dog for Diego than for skinny little Felicia, but the girl knelt and hugged him while Shaq gave her doggy kisses with his long pink-and-black tongue.

"How do his front paws stay so clean and white?" Kyra asked.

"I wash them every week," Felicia said, standing up to lead Shaq over to Kyra. "Gotta keep him looking fine."

Kyra reached down to stroke the huge head Shaq had shoved against her thigh in search of attention. He sighed in bliss when she scratched behind his ears.

Diego took the bowl to Shaq's feeding station and fitted it into the steel stand. At the sound of metal hitting metal, the dog's attention swerved to the food.

"Okay, boy, you get a special snack today," Felicia said, making the gesture that gave him permission to eat.

The dog waddled to the bowl with his distinctive muscle-bound gait. He put his nose in the dish and finished the food in one gulp. Wagging his tail, he swung his gaze between Diego and Felicia with a hopeful expression.

"He liked it," Diego said, scratching the dog's head.

"How would he know?" Kyra asked. "He swallowed it without tasting it."

"Told you he loves to eat," Felicia said.

"Now we got to mix it with his other food, and give him a bigger portion at every meal until it's all the new food," Diego said. "That way his digestive system will adjust to it easy." He looked at Felicia. "You come to me when it's feeding time. I'll help you with the mixing."

Kyra eyed Diego with new respect. The boy knew a heck of a lot about caring for dogs. Not only that, but when he spoke about it, he sounded like a trained professional.

"The container is in the green refrigerator with a label that says 'Shaq Only,'" Kyra said. "I put the calorie count per cup on it, too, so you can calculate how much he needs to eat every day."

"How'd you know we'd need that?" Diego asked.

"By reading dog food labels. The serving size is determined by the age and weight of the dog."

"Course we don't know exactly how old Shaq is," Felicia said, scratching down Shaq's spine to the dog's obvious delight. "He's a rescue like all of them."

Kyra found herself petting the pit bull's big head again. "What do you guess?"

"Doc Quillen thinks about four," Diego said.

Shaq let out a sigh of pleasure when Kyra bent slightly to scratch his chest. A startled look crossed Felicia's face. "Shaq don't usually take to people the first time he meets them," she said. "But he be down with you. I mean, he likes you."

"He just smells the food on my fingers." Kyra had not grown up with pets. Her mother had doted on a teacup Yorkie named Starlight, but the little creature had been a one-woman dog. When a young Kyra had tried to pet Starry, the little dog growled at her, so she left the Yorkie alone after that.

Shaq let out another happy sigh and leaned against Kyra's leg, making her stagger. "What a sweetheart!" Kyra surprised herself by saying, "Not your typical pit bull."

A frown drew Diego's dark brows downward. "Pitties aren't aggressive by nature. They get trained that way. They want to be loved just like any other dog."

"We all just want to be loved." Kyra ruffled his hair as usual. "It's how we go about it that can be the problem."

Diego smoothed his black hair back, but he was smiling.

"Shaq's righteous," Felicia said with great emphasis. "He don't bother nobody . . . anybody who don't want to be bothered." She surprised Kyra by throwing her arms around Kyra's waist in a hug. "Thank you for the food. I can't wait for Shaq to come home with me. It'll be almost like Mario living with Diego."

Kyra gave Felicia a squeeze on the shoulder. "Happy to help, sweetie. But we still don't know if the food will help his digestion."

"It will," Felicia said with a confidence that made Kyra's heart twist.

"You can take him outside now," Diego said. "Min-joo's waiting in the doggy playground."

"Is Min-joo Shaq's junior kid?" Kyra asked. Each dog had two children, an older and a younger one, assigned to it. The idea was to give the dogs continuity as the older kids aged out of the center.

Diego nodded. "And she's even smaller than Felicia."

"That must be a sight," Kyra said. She watched the kids go out the back door before she headed up the stairs. She'd been thinking about Will the whole time she'd worked on the dog food, so maybe she should tell him about its success. Pulling out her phone, she typed in: Chicken, pumpkin, brown rice combo passed taste test. But will it pass digestion test?

She hesitated as her thumb hovered over the send button. It was Monday afternoon. Will had more important things to do than text about dog food. She shrugged and hit the button. He didn't have to answer it.

She had gotten five steps farther down the hallway to the kitchen when her phone pinged. That couldn't be Will.

"Pass" being the key word, I assume.

She grinned, both at his joke and at the fact that he had responded to her instantly.

Not sure if it's been passing too fast or too slow, she typed back. This time she waited for the ping.

An important distinction. You need to study your test client more thoroughly.

Think I'll let someone else handle the scatological research. She leaned against the wall, staring at her phone. She wasn't disappointed.

Can't believe we're discussing this shit, came right back.

She gave a crack of laughter. She had always loved the way Will would switch from highbrow to earthiness in an instant.

Me either. Don't you have balance sheets to analyze?

The pause was longer this time. She started walking again. But the ping came right as she strolled through the kitchen door.

Nothing so interesting. I have a meeting in five.

So he was filling a few free minutes on his schedule. She was fine with that.

"Kyra, you wanted some help?"

Kyra jerked her gaze away from her phone to see Emily, the center's dynamic young director, sitting at the kitchen's long island with a mug of steaming coffee in front of her. Her dark hair was pulled back in a neat ponytail, and she wore tailored trousers, a silk blouse, and a blazer. She always dressed in business attire because she felt all the adults at the center were role models for the kids. Kyra got a pass on dressing up because cooking was messy work.

"Oh God, yes. Thank you so much for coming down."

"Happy to," Emily said. "First, I want to thank you for helping Diego with the dog food project. I know that's not exactly your job."

"I enjoyed the challenge," Kyra said. "We just did a taste test and Shaq approved. Now we have to see if his digestion improves."

"It's amazing how much time we spend discussing the dogs' poop," Emily said, making a comic grimace.

Kyra laughed, her text exchange with Will fresh in her mind. "Since they can't talk, that's one way to judge their general health."

Emily took a sip of her coffee. "I'm intrigued to find out what you need my help with."

Kyra hurried to the pantry and plucked a garment bag off the apron hook. On Saturday she'd gone shopping at her favorite deep-discount clothing store and found three possible dresses for the Chases' Spring Fling. The owner of the store trusted her enough to bend the "no returns" policy, so Kyra could bring back the two frocks she wouldn't need after her consultation with Emily.

She carried the bag to the kitchen island. "I need your advice on wardrobe since you hang out with billionaires." Emily's fiancé had recently sold his cutting-edge chemical company for a massive amount of money.

Emily laughed, her brown eyes soft. "Only one billionaire."

"That's one more than I spend time with." Kyra unzipped the bag and pulled out the dresses. "So I'm going to the Chase family's spring garden party in Connecticut. It's outdoors under tents on Sunday afternoon. Will is wearing khakis, a button-down shirt with no tie and the sleeves rolled up, and loafers. Which of these do I wear?"

"Whoa! That's a lot of information to process. Who's Will?"

Kyra left the dresses lying on the bag and plopped down on a stool across from Emily. "You know the Ceres café chain? He's the CEO of that . . . and several other companies, according to Google. I knew him in college, and we ran into each other at my favorite Ceres last week."

"And he invited you to a party already? You must have been good friends in college," Emily said. "Have you stayed in touch?"

Kyra shook her head. "He was my suitemate's boyfriend so we spent a lot of time together, just talking." She gave Emily an off-center smile. "Which didn't stop me from having a huge crush on him, but he was off-limits. Not that I could have competed with Babette anyway."

"Seems like he might have had a crush on you, too, if he asked you out after seeing you once."

Kyra sighed. "No, he just wants a buffer between him and his family. He and his parents don't get along. Since he told me all about it in college, I make the perfect fake date."

"Don't sell yourself short. You're a bright, beautiful woman." Emily got that soft expression again. "You know, billionaires are human beings just like us."

"Seriously, it's not like that. I'm from blue-collar Pennsylvania and, to compound the problem of all his money, he's Connecticut aristocracy." Kyra stood and picked up the dresses, not sure if she was trying to convince Emily or herself. His text had fanned a tiny flicker of ridiculous hope. She shook her head and held up the first dress. "Option number one."

It was a ruffled floral in soft pinks and greens. Emily tilted her head and considered it. "Maybe."

"Number two." She held up a print sheath that swirled with brilliantly colored flowers.

Emily shaded her eyes. "It's . . . lively."

Kyra laid it aside. "Not really my style either, but I figured Will's mother probably has a closet full of Lily Pulitzers and it kind of looks like one."

The third dress was a crocheted lace sheath in peach, cut away at the shoulders. The underlayer stopped just above the knee, while the lace continued down a few more inches.

Emily's face lit up. "Ooh, I like that one."

Kyra frowned at it. "You don't think the shoulder cutouts are too . . . I don't know, revealing?" Truth was she'd bought it because she felt beautiful and a little sexy in it, but that was also why she didn't think it was appropriate.

"If there was cleavage on display, it might look too overt. But this just shows off your pretty shoulders," Emily said. "Let's see how it looks on you."

Kyra took it into the walk-in pantry and closed the door, shimmying out of her jeans and into the dress. She smoothed it over her hips and returned to the dining room to stand awkwardly in front of Emily.

Emily made a circular motion with her hand, and Kyra turned around slowly.

"It's perfect," Emily said when Kyra was facing her again. "The crocheted lace makes it not too formal, and the little bit of peekaboo at the bottom adds a subtle sexiness. I wouldn't wear it with clogs, though."

"You think?" Kyra glanced down at the black rubber clogs she wore for cooking. "Will said to wear flats because the party is on the lawn. Shoes are my next project, now that I have the dress." She winced inwardly at the added cost. *This shindig had better be worth it.*

"And I think dangly earrings and some bangle bracelets. Want to raid my jewelry box after work this evening?" A blush crept up Emily's cheeks. "Max goes a little overboard on the gifts sometimes."

"That would be the best!" Kyra's mother had never wanted fine jewelry, preferring to buy faddy costume pieces that went out of style in a year. And those Connecticut ladies would know if she was wearing anything less than fourteen karat.

Emily stood and scooped up her coffee mug. "We'll make sure Will has a crush on *you* by the end of the party."

"Good job catching the zoning issue with the new location," Will said as he rose to signal the meeting was over. "Let me know when you've resolved it."

His five top executives filed out, but Greg Ebersole, his chief operating officer, remained in his chair. As the door closed, Greg pushed back from the table and swiveled toward Will. His gray eyes were sharp with interest. "You were smiling when you walked into the meeting. What's going on?"

"Was I?" Will flipped the cover closed on his tablet and took a step toward the door.

"A real smile, not the fake one you use these days."

Greg had come up with the basic idea for Ceres years ago, sharing his pie-in-the-sky dream with a teenage Will one lazy summer afternoon as they drank beer on Will's mother's sailboat. Back then Greg was a young chef without the capital to start something big. But Will hadn't forgotten the man's vision or passion. When Will had refused to go to law school, his father had challenged him to find a better career. Will had tracked down Greg and persuaded him that they could turn the chef's dream into reality.

Maybe that's why Will was so dissatisfied now. He'd borrowed someone else's dream.

Except that he'd enjoyed the early days of building Ceres, when he and Greg had worked and worried and sweated side by side, sometimes even unloading trucks of produce or baked goods themselves to get the ingredients into a café before it opened for business.

As a result, Greg wasn't at all intimidated by Will. In fact, Greg wasn't intimidated by many people.

As he thought of Kyra's texts, Will's lips twitched. "I was just shooting the shit via text with an old college friend."

Greg rolled his eyes. "Frat boy humor."

"It was scatological but not a boy." Back at Brunell, something about Kyra had allowed him to relax and let his sense of humor roam free. It seemed she still had that effect on him.

"Really?" Greg sat forward. "And she's only a 'friend'?"

"Tell me you're not one of those people who believes men and women can't be friends."

"It can happen, but there's always an undercurrent of the potential for more." Greg stood up and collected his own tablet. "Especially when she makes you smile."

Chapter 5

Kyra plucked at the coral lace hem of her dress as she stood in the foyer by the front door, waiting for Will.

"Stop fidgeting, honey," Gloria said from her living room, where she was pretending to dust some silk flowers. She'd left the door to her ground-floor apartment open to keep Kyra company. "You look perfect."

"It's not too short?"

"Even if it were, you've got the legs for it." Gloria put down the feather duster and came to the doorway. "Why are you so nervous about going to a party?"

"I had such a huge crush on Will in college that I'm starting to feel like I'm back there, obsessing over what he thinks of me." That much of her history she'd already confessed to her landlady.

Gloria chuckled. "That doesn't stop just because you've graduated. He thinks *something* about you or he wouldn't have invited you on a date."

Kyra hadn't told her the truth of why Will had issued his invitation, or what kind of a party it was. Maybe she should have, since she admired Gloria's levelheaded view of the world. "He just needed a plus-one so it's not really a date."

"Maybe that was true when he asked you, but once he sees you in this outfit, he'll be bowled right over."

Kyra took two steps across the small foyer to hug the older woman, drawing comfort from the waft of Shalimar, Gloria's signature scent. "You make me feel like a million bucks." And she needed a little positive reinforcement at that moment.

"Honey, you are worth way more than a million bucks." Gloria gave her a firm squeeze before releasing her. "Now I'm going back to my housekeeping so I don't get in your way." She winked as she picked up the duster again. "However, you can't stop me from watching out the window."

"I wouldn't dream of it," Kyra said. "I'll want to hear your opinion tonight."

"You won't even have to ask. I'll give it to you for free." Gloria whistled as she looked out her front window. "There's a long, shiny black limo slowing down right in front of our steps. You'd better scoot on out there."

Kyra blew Gloria a kiss and slipped through the door to meet Will on the stoop.

"Hey, Will," she said, the intense green of his eyes startling her all over again, even though she'd seen him only a week ago.

"Kyra." His smile had a sharp, hot edge that made a shiver run over her skin. "You look beautiful." His voice seemed to pull her toward him like a snake charmer's music.

"You're not so bad yourself." *Keep it light,* she thought, even though she wanted to brush her fingers over the golden hair that was catching glints of sunlight on his forearms. True to his word, he'd rolled up his sleeves, and the muscles displayed made her wonder about his shoulders . . . and his chest . . . and his thighs.

He bent his head and she tilted hers to present her cheek, although somehow he found her lips. It was a mere feather of a kiss but heat slid through her. She lurched back a step to break the contact, but his gaze still held hers and the heat intensified.

"Shall we?" His voice broke through her momentary daze, and she glanced down to see him holding out his arm, crooked at the elbow in an invitation. Oh, those delicious, upper-crust manners. They undermined her defenses every time. She tucked her hand under his elbow and got her wish to feel his forearm—solid and warm—under her palm.

He turned them both toward the limousine.

"I haven't ridden in one of these since my high school prom," she said.

"Yours was probably a lot fancier," Will said, waving away the driver to open the door himself. "This one has no multicolored lights or two-tone upholstery, although I did stock a bottle of champagne if you're interested."

Kyra ducked into the limo and found it plenty fancy. The seats were warm cognac leather, and the built-in storage was paneled in a swirly-grained wood in the same tones. The silver-gray carpet was so lush that she wanted to kick off her new shoes and curl her toes into it. A leather-padded privacy panel closed them away from the driver in their own little cocoon of luxury.

When Will had seated himself and closed the door, Kyra said, "I'm glad we have a long drive because I'm going to enjoy this luxury the whole way." Not to mention being able to feel the body heat radiating from him where their shoulders nearly brushed.

"We're not driving. The traffic will be god-awful, especially on the way home."

"Then how are we getting there? Transporter beam?"

Will didn't crack a smile. "Helicopter."

Kyra swallowed through the nerves that grabbed at her throat. She'd been on a plane twice in her life and liked the view, although a few stretches of turbulence had terrified her.

But she kept her reservations to herself because she noticed that Will hadn't really smiled since he'd shown up on her doorstep. She didn't count that sharklike baring of teeth after he'd surveyed her from head to toe as a smile.

"This will be my first helicopter ride," she said.

"I hope you'll enjoy it." He bent his head to rub the back of his neck in an unhappy gesture.

"You don't have to go," she said, wishing she had the guts to offer to massage his neck herself. Touching the warm, vulnerable skin there would be heaven.

"What?" His head snapped back up.

"Tell your mother you're sick or there's an urgent business matter you have to deal with."

His gaze felt heavy on her for a long moment before he shook his head, forcing a smile. "My apologies," he said. "I'm being a bad host." He flipped open one of the limo's compartments and pulled out the champagne. Dom Pérignon, of course. "May I pour you some?"

"Tempting, but I think I should be sober, at least when I arrive." She would need to keep her wits about her in order to fit in with Will's crowd.

"You may regret that." He slotted the bottle back into the compartment with a sigh. "Fortunately, if you change your mind, you can get drunk quickly once you're there."

"Is it really that awful?" Kyra had a hard time imagining that the brilliantly successful man beside her would be intimidated by anyone, even his controlling parents.

"Awful? No. Arion Farm is a beautiful place. The trees will be flowering. There will be foals cavorting in the fields. Champagne will flow like water." He gestured out the window. "The sun is shining, as per my mother's request to the Almighty."

"Not the farm. I know you love that." Back at Brunell, when he'd casually mentioned hiding in the stables or getting lost in the privet maze, she'd thought of his childhood home as a sort of enchanted castle.

"Your family. Even though you didn't go into law, your father can't argue with your success."

"My father is a lawyer. He can argue with anything."

"What about your mother?" Will had seemed to have fewer issues with her when he was in college.

"Mother is like a steady drip of water on a stone. She never raises her voice, but she wears you down." He shifted on his seat. "Schuyler will be there, too."

"Your sister? Didn't she take the pressure off you by becoming a lawyer herself?"

He rubbed the back of his neck again. "It's complicated."

"I've got a whole helicopter ride."

He snorted. "It would take longer than even the round-trip to explain all the warped twists and turns of my family."

"Well, I'll listen if you want to talk." *Maybe venting would help him relax.*

He shifted on the seat so he was facing her. "You always listened."

"You fascinated me. Like an alien from another planet." Kyra let her gaze travel over the golden hair that waved back from his high forehead, the straight, sharp lines of his nose and jaw, and the concentrated hue of his eyes. Today he seemed even more foreign and unreachable. She shook her head. "Even your clothes were exotic."

He glanced down at his green pencil-striped shirt and khaki trousers. "Not exactly haute couture."

"No, it's haute Connecticut. And I'm from low Pennsylvania." And his long, elegant body made his outfit look like it was custom-tailored.

She wondered now if he'd opened up to her in college because their worlds didn't intersect. He didn't have to worry about her spilling his secrets to someone who mattered. She'd even wondered then, if on that final humiliating night, he'd escorted her out of the frat house not to protect her but to keep her away from his friends.

The limousine eased to a stop. "We're at the heliport, sir," the chauffeur said through the intercom.

Will climbed out and ducked his head and shoulders back in to hold out his hand, his broad palm and long fingers offering support and temptation. She laid her own palm against his and he closed his fingers firmly around it.

As she stepped onto the macadam of the heliport, a blast of wind and noise made her flinch. A chopper was just taking off, its rotors beating the air at high speed.

Will turned his body to shelter her from the buffeting of the din and the stinging, grit-laden air. The gallantry of the gesture made her insides go quivery. As soon as that chopper was out over the Hudson River, Will stepped back, leaving her exposed to the dangers of the world once again. Or so it felt.

He grasped her elbow to steer her toward a glossy forest-green helicopter with Cronus Holdings and two crossed ears of corn painted on the side in gold. She'd discovered through Google that Cronus was the holding company that encompassed all of Will's enterprises, of which there were many besides Ceres.

"Hello, Roxy, nice day for flying." Will greeted a slim woman wearing black trousers, a white blouse with a pilot's epaulets, and mirrored sunglasses, who was inspecting something underneath the copter.

Roxy straightened. "Smooth as glass, so no fun at all."

"I'm not complaining," Kyra said, the tension in her throat easing at the news.

"Not a flyer?" Roxy's voice was neutral but her raised eyebrows somehow expressed her scorn.

"Her first time in a helicopter," Will said.

"So go easy on me," Kyra added, her stomach still queasy with apprehension.

Roxy smiled. "No Rambo runs today, I promise."

Will kept hold of Kyra's elbow as she climbed the few steps into the helicopter's cabin. Four large armchairs in the same cognac leather as the limo's seats were arrayed around a polished wood console. She took one that faced forward, and Will dropped into the chair beside her.

"What's a Rambo run?" she asked as she fastened her seat belt.

"A very illegal maneuver that involves flying low and fast up a river, generally between cliffs on either side. Don't worry. There's no chance of her doing it anywhere near New York City."

The helicopter shuddered and began to vibrate, so Kyra assumed that Roxy had fired up the engine. She dug her fingers into the leather armrests as the aircraft rose and sideslipped toward the sparkling waves of the Hudson River.

"You'll forget to be nervous once you look at the scenery," Will said, obviously noticing her white-knuckled grip.

Kyra shifted in her seat to peer out the window. They were skimming over the New Jersey side of the Hudson River. She swallowed a gasp at the sight of roofs whizzing past far below them before transferring her gaze to the river. The tugboats pushing barges up and down the river left distinct Vs of wake behind them, and the white canvas on the masts of sailboats seemed to glow in the bright sunshine. The George Washington Bridge surged into view, its iron cables looking like fragile cobwebs while the cars crawled across its span like brightly colored ants.

She levered herself closer to the window, her concern overcome by her fascination. "It's a map come to life."

Will nodded. "As I predicted. You always enjoyed a new perspective."

Pleasure at his words flashed through her. She turned to meet his gaze. "I did." But somehow the excitement of new discoveries had slipped away from her. She'd been at Stratus for eight years, and at the Carver Center for six. Both jobs had settled into routines. Except for an occasional diversion like the dog food challenge.

She shoved aside all her dismal thoughts and turned back to the window, exclaiming over the varied sights that passed in and out of view.

As they got closer to his home, Will grew quieter, so she filled the tense air with a barrage of enthusiastic comments. However, when they circled Arion Farm, he moved to the chair facing her and looked through the same window.

"There's the main house." He pointed to a sprawling stone structure complete with turrets and a circular driveway with the letters *AF* worked in the paving stones at the center. The lawns around it glowed emerald while a large rectangular swimming pool sparkled aquamarine blue.

It was Kyra's turn to go quiet, as the extent of his family's wealth and privilege was spread out beneath her in a way that was impossible to ignore. Her stomach felt hollow. She would never belong here.

"That's the privet maze," he said as the chopper passed over an intricate pattern of paths and hedges. "I shouldn't let you see it from above. Makes it too easy to figure out how to get to the center." The hint of a mischievous boy in his face nearly melted her. "See the oval of the riding ring? The stables are the buildings to the left of it. Schuyler will go hide there before the end of the party."

"Maybe we could join her later? Horses are so beautiful." As a child, Kyra had wanted to learn how to ride. However, she'd put that fantasy away because her parents thought it was a waste of money.

"Maybe you could borrow jeans and boots from Schuyler and go riding. I'll even join you."

Kyra sighed. Of course he could ride. He could do anything. "I don't know how. I just like to pet them."

"That's the caretaker's house. He was a nice guy, but his wife always looked like she'd just bitten into a lemon. Which meant that Schuyler and I would dare each other to play pranks on her." He actually smiled at the memory. "There were some good ones."

"Did you get in trouble?" She wanted to keep him talking about something that had happy associations for him.

He shook his head. "She never tattled to our parents, although she must have known it was us. I give her credit."

Will would have been irresistible as a child, those amazing eyes unclouded by experience, his face alight with impish laughter, his charm and intelligence endearing rather than intimidating. Even a sourpuss would have been hard-pressed to stay angry with him.

"She secretly liked you both, I bet," Kyra said.

"She hid it well. But her husband, George, snuck us her homemade cookies. Those were a high treat, partly because they were illicit." A shadow crossed his face. "We didn't get that kind of guilty pleasure at the big house."

"Wait, this woman baked cookies, and it never occurred to you that they were meant for you and Schuyler? I think she played the grouch with you guys for fun."

Will sat back in his seat, his gaze turned inward. "I never thought of that. Now I'm glad I went to her funeral two years ago."

It was the sort of thing he would do: attend the funeral of someone he thought hadn't liked him because she had worked for his family and he owed her that sign of respect.

The helicopter came to a hover and slowly lost altitude. Kyra practically smashed her face against the window to watch the aircraft ease down in the middle of a well-mowed field. She was also relieved to be back on solid ground.

The rotors slowed to a halt and Will unlocked the door, pushing it upward, while the steps dropped down. He exited before turning to hold out his hand.

It was an angle she hadn't often seen him from, so she enjoyed the view of his face tilted up. She could examine the way his hair swept back in waves from his forehead, the tiny lines at the corners of his eyes, and the dark lashes that outlined his brilliant eyes. For a long moment, she crouched in the doorway, mesmerized by his beauty.

"What did you think of the ride?" Roxy's voice sliced through the spell.

As Kyra put her hand in Will's, she grinned at the pilot and said, "Next time let's do the Rambo run."

"That's what I like to hear," Roxy said, giving her a thumbs-up.

Kyra indulged herself in leaning on Will's strength as she came down the helicopter's steps. His grip was firm and his arm was steady as a rock. A rush of longing coursed through her as she thought of how wonderful it would be to occasionally have someone to lean on. It was exhausting to fend for herself all the time.

He dropped her hand but put his palm against the small of her back to guide her toward what looked like a miniature sports car parked on the grass. It was bright red and "Will" was painted on the hood in swirling gold script.

"Honey, I shrunk the Ferrari," Kyra said.

Will gave her a pained look. "It's a golf cart. My parents gave it to me when I was a kid. Schuyler has one that looks like a classic Mustang Shelby."

"You really did grow up in Disney World," she said as he helped her into the passenger seat.

"Is that what you think?" He released her hand but didn't move.

She met his gaze. "Disney World also has rides that make people scream."

He laughed, but the sound held no joy. "No one would dare raise their voice in my family."

He walked around the cart, settled into the driver's seat, and turned the key. "It doesn't have the same pickup as a real Ferrari, but I loved it as a kid."

She grabbed the side as they bounced across the meadow before turning onto a paved lane. As the stone turrets of the house came into view, the sound of big band music wafted over the hum of the golf cart's electric motor. The muscles in her throat tensed as she faced the prospect of meeting Will's parents and a few hundred of their closest high-society friends.

She fiddled with the bracelet Emily had loaned her. It was eighteen-karat gold, set with Peruvian opals that glowed a soft, translucent aqua. She wore matching teardrop earrings as well. At least her jewelry would pass muster.

"No reason to go in the front door," Will said, swinging the cart off the lane and across the grass. He steered through an arched trellis and pulled up in the crook of a stone wall. Now the murmur of voices mingled with the music.

Kyra took a deep breath.

"You look worried." Her head snapped around to find Will leaning on the steering wheel as he watched her. "No need for it," he said. "My parents will be scrupulously polite to you."

"What are their names?" Kyra swallowed to clear the tightness in her throat.

"Twain and Betsy. My father got the nickname because he's William the second."

She would have a hard time calling them anything other than Mr. and Mrs. Chase.

He sprang out of the cart and came around just as her feet touched the ground. Her taupe patent leather sandals had wedge heels, which would prevent her from sinking into the grass. She'd gotten the idea from studying photos of Kate, the Duchess of Cambridge, at garden parties. She'd figured that the stylish young duchess would have practical experience with such events.

"Anyone else I should know about?" she asked.

"Schuyler might have a date, but I'll be meeting him for the first time, too."

Will rested his hand on the small of her back again. She was getting to like that little gesture that claimed her.

They walked around the wall and through a formal garden, where a cascading fountain glittered in the sunlight. The party sounds grew louder just before they rounded a corner of the house.

Kyra stopped to take in the swirl of brightly colored dresses and the charm of natty bow ties, the dance of white-jacketed waiters balancing silver trays filled with drinks in various hues, and the flutter of pastel tablecloths, all highlighted against the brilliant emerald of closely mowed grass.

"Having second thoughts?" Will's tone was sardonic.

"No, it's so beautiful, I want to admire it a moment." It was also way out of her league.

She glanced up at Will to find him surveying the scene before them. "I suppose it is, on the surface. But like the ocean, there's an undertow," he said.

A young woman with a tray of champagne flutes approached them. Will took two, handing Kyra one before touching her glass with his. "*Morituri te salutant.*"

"I didn't study Latin."

"The slaves who were forced to fight to the death in a staged naval battle for Emperor Claudius greeted him by saying, 'We who are about to die salute you.'" Will took a sip of his champagne, his movements stiff with tension.

"You're being dramatic." Kyra tilted her glass in the direction of the party. "There's no blood on the grass."

"Yet." Will took another gulp of champagne before offering her his arm, along with a tight smile. "Let me introduce you to my parents."

He led her past serving tables laden with platters of canapés that looked like tiny, colorful sculptures, bouquets of fresh fruit on skewers, and chocolates dusted with gold flakes. Guests called out to him as he passed, but Will just presented a dazzling, distant smile and kept walking. Finally, they reached a set of wide, shallow steps that led to the stone porch running the length of the house. As soon as they hit the top step, Will put his arm around Kyra's waist and pulled her in against his side. Startled, she stiffened, but his grip stayed firm. It was then that she understood he was using her as a shield.

An older man and woman stood by the door, greeting guests as they came out through the house. Kyra had time to see that the man had light-brown hair shot with silver while the woman's hair was pale blonde. He sported a blue-and-white seersucker suit with a yellow bow tie, while the woman wore a linen sheath dress in a vivid green-and-yellow pattern, embellished around the keyhole neckline with tiny gold beads.

"Mum," Will said, leaning down to brush a kiss on his mother's cheek. "I'd like you to meet an old college friend, Kyra Dixon." Somehow he managed to make the word "friend" sound like something much more intimate. "Kyra, my mother, Betsy."

His mother's warm smile went stiff as she pivoted to hold out her hand to Kyra. But it was her eyes that made Kyra blink. Will had gotten the deep jade color from his mother. "Lovely to meet you. You graduated from Brunell, then?"

Why did she have to phrase it that way? "I was a year behind Will," Kyra said, shaking hands. "Thank you for including me in your hospitality."

"Any friend of Will's . . ." Betsy's gaze skimmed over her, and Kyra knew the woman had accurately assessed her dress as costing $39.99, making her feel like trailer trash. "Enjoy yourself, my dear."

Will's father shook her hand. "Kyra, I'm Twain. We're delighted to have you here. Will, glad you made it."

The two men locked gazes.

"Have I ever not, Dad?" Will said.

"You've always come," his father acknowledged. "And it hasn't always been convenient for you to do so."

"Thanks," Will said. "Kyra and I are going to grab something to eat."

"I imagine it will be a bit different from what you serve at your little fast-food franchise," Betsy said, those startling eyes projecting nothing but indulgent good humor.

Kyra nearly gasped at the insult. No wonder Will hated to come home. However, his smile was unfazed. "Actually, I shared some of my recipes with your caterer."

Betsy trilled out a laugh. "Oh, dearest, you're such a hoot." She turned to Kyra. "Isn't he funny?"

"I eat at Ceres every chance I get," Kyra said, knowing she was digging her own grave. What the hell? She'd never see Will's mother again. "The food there is delicious."

Will's father made an odd sound in his throat, almost as though he were choking on something. Kyra couldn't read his expression well enough to interpret it.

"You're a sweet girl," Betsy said with utter insincerity before turning away to greet the next guest coming through the door.

"I hope you can stay afterward so we can get to know you better, Kyra." Twain smiled at Kyra in a way that reminded her of Will's smooth charm. He shifted his gaze to his son. "I'm interested in your move into organic farming. Maybe we could discuss that later. See if we could implement some of your methods here at Arion Farm."

Will nodded but said nothing as he moved away.

"The opening skirmish is behind us," he muttered, steering her back down the steps and toward one of the bars set up on the lawn. "I need something stronger than champagne."

Kyra was still sipping her bubbly, but when the bartender offered her a beautiful pink Cosmopolitan, she decided a stronger beverage was in order after being reduced to postmidnight Cinderella status by Betsy Chase. Will ordered straight scotch and swallowed half of it in one gulp.

"Will, how the hell are you?" A man dressed in plaid madras trousers, a yellow shirt, and a navy belt embroidered with lime-green martini glasses strolled up. He winked at Kyra. "Leave it to my old pal to find the prettiest gal at the party. I'm Farrington Lange. My friends call me Farr. Possibly because that's where they wish I would go."

"Farr!" For the first time, Will's expression relaxed into a real smile. "My mother didn't tell me you were coming." He shook hands with the other man. "Kyra, stay away from this guy. He's trouble. Farr, this is Kyra Dixon, an old friend from Brunell."

Farr leaned in to give her an air kiss, his breath indicating he'd had a few drinks already. "If you get tired of this stuffed corporate shirt, come find me for some fun." But the twinkle in his hazel eyes undercut the insult.

Will snorted. "Pot, meet kettle. You're an investment banker."

"IBs work hard but we play hard, too." Farr scanned Will up and down. "You look like you haven't had enough to drink."

"I'm working on it," Will said, swirling the scotch in his tumbler.

"Will's been keeping you a secret, Kyra," Farr said.

"We just reconnected," Kyra said, liking Will's genial pal. "I ran into him at a Ceres in the city."

"Will's a very conscientious CEO," Farr said. "Always checking up on the dining experience. That's what I told the fellows at work when we bid on the Ceres IPO."

"I appreciated the endorsement and the bid," Will said.

"Were you a classics major like Will?" Farr asked Kyra.

"No, English lit. The only foreign language I speak is Pennsylvanian."

"Ah, she's funny as well as lovely. I'd lure you away from Will, but he needs all his reinforcements." Farr's smile faded. "Just a heads-up: Petra is here."

Will winced. "I suppose that was inevitable."

Kyra felt comfortable enough with Farr to say, "Why is Petra bad news?"

Farr looked at Will, who said with forced disinterest, "I was engaged to her a couple of years ago. Our parting was a little . . . difficult."

"Which is to say that Petra would like to still be engaged to him," Farr elaborated.

The shock of Will's near marriage made her slosh her Cosmo over the rim of her glass. Although why should she be surprised? Women must throw themselves at him on a regular basis. That didn't stop her from feeling a sear of ridiculous jealousy, though.

She longed to know why he had broken it off but kept her questions to herself. Will was wound tightly enough as it was. He didn't need her prying into a past that seemed to disturb him.

"That's awkward," she said.

"You'll force her to keep her distance," Farr said. "It's part of the social code. Petra won't bother Will when he has a beautiful woman on his arm."

"Ooh, I like the compliment subtly hidden in there," Kyra said, trying to steer the conversation away from the source of Will's discomfort.

"Subtle is not a word that I associate with Farr." Will joined the banter but his shoulders were still rigid.

"You underestimate me, Chase. That's your fatal mistake," his friend said. "I see Leighton Davies headed in this direction. Let's bolt for the food tables."

"Dear God, yes," Will agreed, setting his hand against Kyra's back and pressing her into motion. "He'll tell us every tack and jibe of the last race he sailed in."

"I thought you sailed, too," Kyra said as they navigated through the crowd.

"Because my mother insisted. She's the sailing fanatic."

Kyra stumbled in surprise. She'd assumed it had been Will's father who forced him to sail.

"Yet you still won all the races," Farr pointed out. "Until Davies came along and gave you some real competition."

"I was glad he showed up," Will said. "It gave me an excuse to quit."

"Your mother never quite got over it," Farr mused.

Kyra was adjusting her perspective on Will's family dynamics. He'd talked about disappointing his father, but it seemed that his mother was the one who was most unhappy with Will's choices. She certainly had reacted badly to Kyra's presence.

They'd reached the buffet table. Will handed her one of the china plates—a creamy white with a blue pattern of stylized leaves and flowers around the edge, accented by a rim of gold. Her mother had collected fine china teacups, so Kyra recognized the pattern as Grenville by Royal Crown Derby. Just the stack of plates on the buffet table represented thousands of dollars.

As she served herself tea sandwiches decorated with real flowers, asparagus rolled in paper-thin bread, and sliced hard-boiled eggs topped with heaps of caviar, she noticed that all the tongs were sterling silver.

"Save room for the lobster table," Will said, nodding toward another buffet spread.

"The lobster table?"

"Technically, it's the seafood buffet, but most people load up on the lobster tails."

"Even high-and-mighty Connecticut society loves free lobster," Farr said as he piled three tenderloin crostini onto his plate.

"Are you from around here?" Kyra asked.

Farr shook his head. "Alabama born and bred. I went to boarding school with Will."

"We got assigned as roommates our first year at Marston," Will said. "Best thing that happened to me there."

Farr feigned dramatic surprise. "I never knew you felt that way."

"I've told you often enough," Will said with a grin.

Kyra encouraged the banter between the men, grateful to Farr for easing the stiffness in Will's shoulders.

As Will walked ahead in search of an empty table, Farr came up beside Kyra. "If I'm being a third wheel, just say so, and I'll wander off unoffended."

Kyra wished she could consider Farr a third wheel but she shook her head. "I'm just here as a friend like you."

"This party has bad memories for him," Farr said. "That's why I always try to show up."

"Petra?"

"And other familial disasters."

"This way." Will turned to indicate the chosen table. "What are you two colluding about?"

"Just wondering if you were going to tack or jibe," Kyra said.

Will lifted his eyes to the sky, as though praying for divine intervention.

"Hoping I will be struck dumb?" she asked.

"On the contrary, you've been too quiet. Of course, it's hard to get a word in edgewise when Farr's around." Kyra could see Will was trying to make light conversation, even as he periodically swept his gaze over the guests with a wary vigilance.

"Kyra's tired of listening to all those Connecticut lockjawed accents. She needs a little southern honey in her ear," Farr said, exaggerating his drawl.

They arrived at a table covered by a lavender tablecloth and adorned with an arrangement of lilacs and yellow daisies. Will put down his plate and held the gilded bamboo chair for Kyra. She couldn't remember the last time a man had helped her with her chair.

She popped a tea sandwich into her mouth, closing her eyes to savor the bite of the watercress with the smoothness of the cream cheese and another flavor she couldn't quite identify.

"Mum's famous recipe for watercress sandwiches," Will said. She opened her eyes to find him watching her with a slight smile playing around his lips. "She won't share the secret ingredient with me because she's afraid I'll put it on the menu at Ceres."

"There is something else there," Kyra said.

"I'm guessing it's radish."

"Could be," Kyra allowed. "However, I was thinking mint."

"Maybe it's both." Farr bit into his crostini with gusto. "I prefer some good red meat myself."

Kyra was about to take another bite for analysis when a woman walked up behind Will. She had dark-blonde hair pulled back in a low bun, sunglasses that concealed her eyes, and a strong resemblance to Betsy Chase.

"Schuyler!" Farr popped up from his chair to embrace the newcomer, her multihued plaid sundress clashing with his vivid trousers.

Will rose, too, and hugged his sister. "I thought you might have shown more guts than I have and refused to come."

Schuyler laughed without a trace of humor. "Dad's my boss so I might get fired if I didn't show up."

"Would that be so terrible?" Will asked, making Schuyler laugh. He turned to Kyra. "Kyra, my sister, Schuyler. Kyra's an old friend from Brunell whom I just reconnected with."

"And he brought you here for a date?" Schuyler took Kyra's proffered hand in a grip that verged on painfully firm. "I wouldn't blame you if you refused to ever go out with my brother again."

"I think it helps not to be related," Kyra said.

This time Schuyler's chuckle was genuine. "No doubt about it. I see you came by helicopter. Can I hitch a ride home with you?"

Will nodded. "Get some food and join us."

"I ate already," Schuyler said. She hesitated a moment before looking her brother in the eye. "Petra's here."

"Farr warned me."

"She's had too much to drink."

Will's lips flattened into a straight line. "It just gets better."

Kyra's curiosity was at fever pitch now.

"I'll be at the stables later if you want to escape," Schuyler said before she strode off in the direction of the bar and they all seated themselves again. Will chewed through a half-dozen canapés in silence while Farr entertained Kyra with stories of their escapades from boarding school.

As Kyra applauded their ingenuity in having gotten a large sow into the headmaster's office, Will turned to her. "Forgive my rudeness. You should know that Petra announced the end of our engagement very publicly at this event two years ago. She doesn't handle alcohol well, so it was an ugly scene. That's why the news that she's here and drinking has made me an appallingly bad companion."

"Hear! Hear!" Farr said, raising his martini glass. "Honesty at last."

If Will was talking about it, Kyra wanted to know one thing very badly. "Who broke it off?"

Will cleared his throat. After a moment's silence, he said, "I did."

That explained why Petra still wanted to be engaged to him. But what would make the ever-chivalrous, morally upright Will Chase dump his fiancée? It had to be pretty awful. Maybe Petra had pulled a Babette on him. That made her heart squeeze. He didn't deserve to be cheated on twice by women he was in love with. On the other hand, she could understand Petra's refusal to give him up. To win Will's love only to lose it would be like going from sunlight to fog.

"We were going to make each other miserable," Will said. "My mistake for proposing to her, so my responsibility to make it right."

"And Will still feels responsible," Farr said, an odd edge to his voice.

Chapter 6

"All right, we've done our duty. Let's head for the stables." Will steered Kyra past a tipsy older gentleman with a smile and a nod. "I saw Schuyler head in that direction about half an hour ago."

"I won't argue with you." Kyra had run out of pleasant things to say to all these people with whom she had nothing in common. Although she had to give them credit: No one had been overt about the fact that she didn't belong. Will's golden aura had surrounded her so they didn't dare question her presence. But she was tired of small talk, tired of seeing the dresses and jewelry and shoes that cost more than she made in a month, tired of trying to remember names for long enough to bid their owners farewell with a personal touch. It reminded her too much of her job at Stratus.

On the other hand, she'd loved watching Will in his natural habitat. The bone-deep confidence with which he carried himself was on display as guest after guest claimed his attention. He would bend his elegant head toward the women for a kiss on the cheek. The men he greeted with a straightforward gaze and a firm, heartfelt handshake. No matter what gender, everyone lit up when he focused his attention on them. She found herself memorizing some of his turns of phrase that said nothing but sounded meaningful. She could use them on customers.

"You've been a trooper." Will put his arm around her waist and gave her a squeeze as they wove through the guests. The strength of his grasp and the solidity of his body against her side made her want to lean into him, just to rest. But that way lay danger.

"It's been fun." She smiled as Will gave her a skeptical look. "Really. It's like a field study: the plumage and flocking habits of the Connecticut crested upper class."

Will choked on a laugh. "That's the kind of comment that's kept me sane today. Thank you again for coming."

"Will! Wait!" A woman's voice called from behind them.

Will went so rigid that he seemed made of stone, the arm around Kyra's waist like a weight. Every angle of his face sharpened and hardened. "Don't turn around," he said through gritted teeth. His grip on her tightened, and he propelled her through the crowd in the opposite direction.

"Petra, that's not a good idea." Farr's voice was lower in volume but still distinct.

It took every ounce of Kyra's willpower not to angle her head around to see what Will's ex-fiancée looked like.

"But he's leaving and I want to meet his date." Petra's voice held a hint of petulance.

"They're just going to see Schuyler at the stables." Farr's voice was receding as Will lengthened his already ground-eating stride. "They'll be back."

Will muttered a curse under his breath before he said, "Farr is going to expect a big favor in exchange for running interference."

"I don't think he'll expect anything other than a thank-you."

Will gave a mirthless laugh. "You don't know much about investment bankers, even friendly ones." He changed direction to approach one of the bars, saying, "Let's take some supplies to the stables."

He handed her three empty crystal flutes. "In case Schuyler didn't think ahead," he said before grabbing an unopened bottle of champagne from a tub of ice behind the bar.

Will had been drinking scotch most of the afternoon, so Kyra was relieved that he was switching to lighter stuff, especially since the near miss with his ex-fiancée would certainly justify a more powerful anesthetic. She couldn't say he was drunk. His balance was firm; his speech clear. However, as the afternoon progressed, he had become less careful in what he said to the other guests. He was never rude, but he slid in a barb every now and then, although the guests never realized it. A few times she'd had to cough to cover up the giggle that threatened. Because Will was very clever.

"Will!" A man's voice broke through the chatter.

"It just keeps getting better," Will ground out in an angry mutter, and Kyra turned to see Twain Chase approaching them.

The older man cast a glance at the glasses in Kyra's hand and raised an eyebrow before turning to his son. "It's impossible to hold a conversation for more than five minutes in this horde," Twain said. "Your mother and I hope you'll stay after the party for a family dinner."

"Kyra needs to get back to the city," Will said. "Next time."

Somehow she found the presence of mind to smile and nod, even though she had no pressing engagement awaiting her at home. At the same time, she tried to locate Farr and Petra among the swirling crowd without appearing to do so. It might be her only chance to find out what sort of woman had induced Will to propose.

"It would mean a lot to your mum if you'd give us an hour," Twain said, but the truth sounded in his voice: a pleading undercurrent that meant he was the one who wanted to spend time with his son. He offered Kyra an apologetic smile. "I don't mean to upset your schedule."

"Don't worry about it," she said, trying to give Will a chance to change his mind if he wanted to. She gave up on her surreptitious search for Petra and focused on the two men facing off, the proud angle of their chins and the unyielding set of their shoulders so strikingly similar.

"We'll see what we can finagle," Will said, but Kyra heard the refusal in his voice.

"I'd appreciate it, son."

Kyra caught the flash of disappointment in Twain's gray eyes. As he walked away, his movements seemed slow and tired.

"I can stay," Kyra said when she was sure Twain was out of earshot. "Your dad really wants you here."

Will ignored her offer. "I've had enough of this party." He caught her hand and towed her away from the guests, his brisk gait forcing her to trot alongside him. She'd never seen his usually impeccable manners desert him to the point that he forgot to be solicitous of her shorter legs. It was a measure of how upset he was by the conversation with his father and the near encounter with Petra. Farr said Will felt responsible for her, but maybe he was still in love with her even though he had broken off the engagement.

The thought sent her heart plummeting.

"Do we walk or drive to the stables?" Kyra asked, breathless from keeping up with Will. "I'd love to take the mini Ferrari for a spin." And instructing her on how to drive it might relax the rigidity in Will's jaw and body.

"Then we shall drive." She could hear the effort it took to make his response sound easy and casual.

They arrived at the Ferrari without further incident. Will stowed the glasses in the cart's trunk and settled the bottle between his feet. His smile was forced when he said, "Don't want it getting shaken up and exploding behind us."

He explained the simple controls to Kyra, the tension in his voice easing as he did so. She gingerly backed the cart away from the wall and then drove it onto the paved lane.

"Thank you," Will said.

"For driving?" *Keep it light.*

"For—" He seemed to be at a loss before he bit out a laugh. "For not turning around."

"That was pretty hard, to be honest."

"You wanted to meet Petra?" His tone was disbelieving.

"No, just to see her. You nearly married her so I can't help being curious."

He gave her a seductive smile. "She doesn't hold a candle to you."

Kyra wasn't buying that, but the fact that he would say it sent a warm little glow through her. She gunned the engine down the straightaway.

The breeze created by the cart's motion combed through her hair and gave her a sense of freedom. She laughed and glanced over at Will. His eyes were focused on her, hot and intense, while his dark-blond hair ruffled and fluttered around the chiseled bones of his face.

"Oh," Kyra said, the cart weaving a bit as she got caught in his look.

"Steady." Will grabbed the wheel to straighten their course. He shifted his gaze forward, but the heat of it still licked along Kyra's nerve endings, making her aware of where he brushed against her at shoulder and thigh. Maybe it hadn't been an empty compliment.

"Turn right," Will said.

She turned down another paved lane that led to a courtyard surrounded on three sides by the stone stables. About half the stalls had the top doors open and horses' glossy heads poking out of them.

"Where should I park? I don't want to scare them," she said.

"Go around to the back. That's where the trucks bring in the hay and feed."

As Kyra pulled in beside a maroon pickup truck with "Arion Farm" lettered on the side, Schuyler walked out of the wide doorway just beside it. "Hey, bro, welcome to the sanctuary."

Will raised the champagne bottle. "I've brought provisions, Sky."

"Such a Boy Scout," Schuyler said, accepting one of the flutes. "I drank mine straight out of the bottle."

Kyra laughed, and Will worked the cork out with a gentle pop, spilling golden liquid into the elegant glasses. "Kyra loves horses," he said.

Enthusiasm shone in Schuyler's eyes. "You ride?"

"Only in my dreams," Kyra said.

"We should change that," Schuyler said. "But let me introduce you to the residents. We used to leave them out to pasture during the party. Mum liked the pretty picture it made. But one year a couple of drunken guests decided to go bareback riding, and that didn't end well. For the riders, not the horses, thank God."

"Sky would have committed murder if they'd injured a horse," Will said.

"I don't blame her," Kyra said. "Animals trust us to take care of them. We shouldn't abuse that trust."

Schuyler gave her an approving nod.

As they toured the stable yard, Schuyler shared little sketches of information about each horse, her deep love for them clear in the way she touched and talked about them.

"Did you ever consider being a professional equestrian?" Kyra asked her.

"When I was a kid, sure," Schuyler said with a shrug. "But when Will ditched law school, I had to step up."

She threw her brother a teasing glance but his lips were drawn into a tense, flat line.

"Lighten up, Will," his sister said, giving him a nudge on his shoulder before she turned to Kyra. "Honestly, lawyering is in the Chase genes, so I'm happy with my chosen field. I just sometimes wish I could use my skills for something more . . . meaningful." She shrugged again. "Listen to me, sounding New Agey."

"I get it," Kyra said. "That's why I work with the kids at the Carver Center. It balances my other job." And her laser focus on paying off her debt, which made her feel mercenary at times.

A dark-brown horse stretched out his neck to lip Kyra's hair into his mouth and give it a gentle tug. "You're a playful fellow, aren't you?" she said with a startled laugh, stroking the hard, graceful curve of his neck.

"That's Will's horse, Bucephalus," Schuyler said, feeding the friendly creature a carrot.

Will shook his head. "Not mine anymore." But he stroked the horse's nose and scratched behind his ears. "How are you doing, old man?"

"Alexander the Great's steed," Kyra said. "You named him?"

"With an utter lack of modesty," Will said, still petting his former mount.

"Do you ever ride him?" Kyra asked.

"No, and I feel guilty about it. The grooms exercise him," Will admitted. "But I'm too sentimental to sell him. Horses aren't always treated well when they get sold on. I owe Buccy a happy life, even if I can't be part of it."

She'd never seen Will around an animal before. His affection for the horse made her heart twist.

Schuyler took a sip of champagne. "I didn't hear any explosions so I assume you managed to avoid Petra."

"Only by Farr's intervention," Will said, the muscles in his face tightening again.

"Headed her off at the pass, did he?" Schuyler said. "He's a good friend."

"One of the best," Will agreed. "Why don't you go out with him, Sky?"

Schuyler gave her brother an odd look. "He's not interested in me." She tossed back the rest of her drink. "I'm going to return to the fray. The stable office is unlocked but I recommend lounging on the hay bales in the feed storage room. It smells nicer."

"Office or hay bales?" Will asked Kyra, as Schuyler climbed into her Mustang golf cart.

"Definitely hay bales," Kyra said. "I can pretend I'm a horsewoman."

"First stop, the tack room then. I've learned that rolling in the hay isn't as comfortable as it looks."

Will led her into a room filled with racks of gleaming saddles and neatly hung bridles with shiny bits, all overlaid by the rich smell of leather polish. Handing her his champagne glass, he flipped open a trunk and pulled out a couple of burgundy horse blankets. "This is where they keep the clean ones," he said, a glint of humor in his eyes.

He seemed to have recovered from his sister's mention of Petra, much to Kyra's relief. Strolling back through the stable yard, she inhaled deeply and looked around with avid attention. She didn't belong here, would never belong here, but she wanted to remember it as vividly as she could.

"No wonder Schuyler likes the stables," she said.

"It was her escape when the parental pressure got too overwhelming," Will said. "Jump on a horse and ride away from it."

"Did you try to sail away from it?"

He shook his head. "My heart wasn't in sailing. My escape was books. Mostly my parents were impressed with my reading, which meant I could do so with impunity."

"You were lucky. My parents thought I was wasting my time reading Victorian novels."

Will put down the champagne bottle and shook out the horse blankets, settling them over a mound of loose hay. "That's why I chose the Greek and Roman classics; I could claim I was prepping for reading them in Latin, so Dad left me alone." He held out his hand. "Have a seat."

As she took his hand and folded her legs under her to sit on one of the blankets, she felt that shiver of awareness run over her skin again. Enclosed in the dim fragrant space of the barn, Will's presence seemed magnified. Then he dropped onto the blanket next to her and stretched out on his side, propped on one elbow with his champagne glass in the other hand.

He was so close that she could see the pale hair glinting where his shirt was unbuttoned at the neck. She caught a whiff of the woodsy soap he used. His face was level with hers so the texture of the skin over his cheekbones and jawline tempted her fingers to explore.

She gulped a swig of champagne to quell the longing that seared through her. "You know, your father respects you. It's your mother who doesn't approve of what you do."

Will actually rocked back an inch as he frowned. "My father has never forgiven me for not being a lawyer at Chase, Banfield, and Trost."

"You're wrong. There's pride in his eyes when he looks at you. He really wanted to discuss organic farming with you. That was sincere."

Will shook his head.

"Your mother called Ceres a 'little fast-food franchise.'"

His frown eased somewhat. "Mum calls everything little. The women she plays tennis with are 'her little group of gals,' and they're nationally ranked amateur players. The Spring Fling is just a 'casual little gathering.' You've seen it."

"She insulted Ceres. Your father didn't." Kyra started to take another swallow of champagne when she realized her glass was empty. "But it's none of my business."

She reached for the bottle between them just as Will did, so their fingers brushed. She pulled her hand back more abruptly than she meant to, but he made no comment as he refilled her glass.

"It's your business because I dragged you to this party." Will refilled his glass as well. "You always pegged people exactly right at Brunell."

"I've spent all of five minutes with your parents, so take my comments with a grain of salt." She could hardly judge his family's inner workings based on such a brief acquaintance.

He drank down his glassful of champagne in two swallows, drawing Kyra's gaze to the ripple of muscles in his neck. She was grateful when he flipped onto his back and closed those hypnotic eyes. "God, this feels good."

What felt good? The hay? Lying down? Being with her?

Kyra didn't copy his position. She didn't want to give up the chance to drink in the length of him laid on the blanket like a feast. She'd always known he was tall, but when he was on her level like this, she was aware of how solid he was. He had one arm tucked under his head so the cotton of his shirt pulled tight over the bulge of his triceps. The expanse of striped fabric that covered his shoulders and chest was impressive, as was the flat plane of his abdomen. She followed the stretch of his legs all the way down to where they extended beyond the horse blanket, his ankles crossed so she could see the shine of his loafers.

She squinted at his socks, a medium blue with red silhouettes of sharks circling on them. "Are your socks a comment on the party guests?" she asked.

He opened his eyes and flexed one foot as he glanced down with a crooked smile. "It was that or T. rexes. Either would work."

Kyra laughed and flopped back on her horse blanket to gaze at the rafters of the barn as lust sparked through her. She needed a moment to quell that reaction.

"Kyra, I've had just enough to drink to ask you this." His deep, cultured voice shimmered over her skin. "What happened that night after the frat party?"

Embarrassment sent a stinging flush over her cheeks. He'd lulled her into a false sense of security, hadn't he? "Nothing. You feel asleep on the couch." That was true, and she hoped it would end the conversation.

"I remember more than that." His voice sounded closer, and she made the mistake of turning her head. He'd rolled onto his side again. Now he was nearly touching her, his gaze on her face while heat flickered in the depths of his eyes. "But not enough more."

She should sit up and scoot away from him, but she didn't have the self-discipline. "We got a little hot and heavy, but before anything, um, serious happened, you started snoring."

"Thank God, because I would hate to think that I didn't remember making love to you."

Kyra couldn't breathe as Will leaned in toward her, his eyes fastened on her lips. His words had wiped away the deep-seated sense of inadequacy, the mortifying conviction that she had been too dull to keep him awake. Now all she could think about was finishing what they had started all those years ago. She tilted her head so their mouths could meet, at first a light, teasing pressure, but then Will threaded his fingers into her hair and cupped the back of her neck to deepen the kiss. She whimpered at the pleasure of his lips against hers, and he touched their seam with his tongue, not demanding she open to him, but just tracing along it.

She reached blindly for him, her hand finding his shoulder and tugging him closer. She wanted to feel her breasts against his chest. He shifted so he was braced over her. "Will," she breathed, arching upward. And then she got her wish as he cradled her head between both hands and let his weight press her into the springy hay.

He angled her head to kiss her neck just behind her earlobe, sending shivers of delight streaking down to tighten her nipples. He nibbled at her sensitive skin, and she gasped and shuddered, her hands like talons curving over the muscles of his shoulders. Her hips rocked and he again gave her what she wanted by driving his leg between hers, so she had the friction of his muscled thigh to push against. She could feel him harden against her, ratcheting up her longing.

His body was so solid and warm, his shirt smelled of the woods and Will, and the heat and motion of his lips made her insides soften and ache on a hot glide down between her legs.

"Not in a barn," he said, rolling off her. He picked a piece of straw out of her hair. "We're doing it right this time."

Still in a daze of arousal, Kyra said, "Not in your childhood bedroom either."

"Spoilsport." He smiled but looked away from her for a few moments before he gave a decisive nod. He came to his knees and offered his hand to her, rising and pulling her up with him. "You don't get seasick, do you?"

He tugged her along by the hand, that one point of contact sending a ripple of arousal through her.

"I don't know."

That put a hitch in his long stride. "You've never been on a boat?"

"Just a kayak," she said. "Not a lot of oceans where I grew up."

He dropped a hot kiss on her lips. "I'm beginning to enjoy being your first."

Heat bloomed low in her belly. "Hate to break it to you, but you're not my first." She gave him a wry look as he helped her into the golf cart.

"Your first helicopter ride." He spun the cart away from the barn. "Your first sailboat ride." He gave her a wicked glance. "Your first sailboat sex."

"Don't even think about the helicopter," she said, grabbing the side of the cart as he sped over the grass.

"You've never wanted to join the mile-high club in a jet?"

The suggestive purr in his voice seemed to stroke over her skin.

"In one of those teeny, tiny bathrooms? You'd have to be a contortionist." But her imagination kicked into overdrive, painting a picture of her perched on the tiny steel sink, thighs spread, while Will drove into her.

"That's what makes it so satisfying," he said. "You have to work hard to find the right position."

They skidded to a stop on a cobblestone apron in front of a multidoored garage. Will leaped out of the cart and tapped a code into the keypad on the garage wall, while Kyra tried to ignore the ache of yearning between her legs. The wooden door with its beveled glass windows glided upward to reveal a sports car in British racing green with a curved, elongated hood. She caught sight of the distinctive chrome ornament shaped like a leaping cat. "A Jaguar!"

He ran his long fingers along the car's roof in a way that made her feel as though he was tracing the curves of her own body. "A classic E-type. My seventeenth-birthday gift."

He walked to the passenger door and swung it open for her.

"It's a sexy car," Kyra said, slipping onto the tan leather seat and almost gasping at the friction against her sensitized clit.

"Wait until you hear the engine." His voice went low with a hint of extra meaning.

Inside the garage, the engine throbbed like one of the longest pipes in an organ. As he shifted up, the car's exhaust added an extra bass note.

"Top down?" he asked.

"Why not? It'll blow the hay out of my hair." And cool off some of the steam she'd worked up.

He hit a button and the ragtop folded back behind them. Then he punched the accelerator and Kyra sank back into the seat like a fighter pilot. By the time they pulled onto a wharf twenty minutes later, adrenaline and anticipation were surging through her, making laughter spill out of her throat. "That might have been better than sex," she teased.

Will bent to rumble into her ear. "I'll have to do my best to convince you otherwise." He took her hand in his strong grip to lead her through a gate marked "Private—Boat Owners Only." The creaking wooden docks held an assortment of sleek motor yachts and elegant sailboats, but Will drew her down a ramp to a float where small skiffs were tied up. A teenage boy in a sky-blue polo shirt, khaki shorts, and boat shoes leaped off the milk crate he'd been seated on, swiping away at his cell phone. "Hey, Mr. Chase, where to?"

"The *Royal Wave*," Will said before turning to Kyra. "It's moored out in the harbor. Easier to get in and out that way."

"You got it," the young man said, heading for one of the runabouts. He held the boat steady at the dock while Will helped Kyra in and then followed her, his balance as secure on the sea as it was on land. For some reason, that fanned the flames smoldering inside her even higher. When they were settled side by side on the metal seat, the kid cast off and stepped into the boat before it drifted away from the dock.

"I'm betting you were just like that when you were young," Kyra said by Will's ear, as the outboard motor roared to life. "Knew exactly what you were doing on a boat."

He lifted his head and sniffed the air as they headed away from the dock. "I worked here several summers when I was around his age. I liked running people out to their yachts. The tips were good, too."

She flushed as she remembered Will's over-the-top gratuity to her, but he was turned into the sea wind that flattened his shirt against the firm curves of his pecs, curves her palms itched to press against. Her embarrassment transmuted into pure desire.

Their youthful skipper wove through the marina, dodging a couple of yachts just coming in, and gunned the motor when they got out into the harbor. Although it was dotted with moored boats, the craft were farther apart, so he had their skiff skimming over the waves. Kyra realized they were headed for a graceful single-masted sailboat with a dark-blue hull and wooden trim.

"My mother's beloved Hinckley," Will said, standing to flip down a wooden ladder while their young captain held the skiff against the sailboat's hull. "You might want to take your shoes off."

"I'm more worried about climbing that in my dress," Kyra said, surveying the ladder that rose and fell with the rocking of the boat.

"I'll give you a little boost," Will said, a roguish twinkle in his eyes.

"Yeah, thanks." She unstrapped and handed him her sandals, along with her clutch, all of which he tossed onto the cockpit's cushioned bench. She stood carefully, bracing her legs as he held the ladder with one hand and her elbow with the other. She took a deep breath, grabbed the ladder, and waited for the skiff to ride up a wave before thrusting her foot onto the first step. Will's hand shifted to her bottom and he gave her a lift so powerful that she practically flew up the ladder.

Her step down on the deck wasn't graceful, but somehow she plunked onto the bench without ripping her dress or twisting her ankle.

Will was there beside her almost immediately, bending to retrieve her handbag. "Sorry, I didn't think through the whole tight skirt angle. Are you all right?"

"I'm a little worried about getting back in the skiff, but for now I'm fine." She heard the skiff's engine grumble away from the sailboat.

Now that they were alone on the boat, Kyra was frozen by a sudden shyness. Back at the barn, Will's mouth and hands had stopped her from thinking, but the fog of arousal had dissipated on the journey to the boat.

"Are we sailing somewhere?" she asked, glancing around to avoid looking at Will.

"No, we've got all the privacy we need right here." He slid open the door—no, it was called a hatch, she remembered—that led into the interior cabin. "More steps but these aren't moving. Much," he said, slanting a smile over his shoulder. Something in her face or posture must have alerted him to her change of mood because he came back to hold out both his hands, palms up. When she placed hers in them, he pulled her upright to stand, an inch or so of space between them. "I want you. Very much," he said. "But you can say no. No harm, no foul."

He wanted her. A bald statement, but somehow it made her heart squeeze. His eyes burned greener than the grass at his parents' farm and the fire in them reignited the desire in her veins.

Yet she found it hard to answer him with her own words, so she fell back on their quote swapping. "'In delay there lies no plenty; Then come kiss me, sweet-and-twenty.'"

She had expected him to respond with another line from Shakespeare, but he let go of her hands and swept his arms around her, holding her against him from knee to shoulder. He bent and found her lips in a kiss that sent tendrils of need curling through her. Her shyness evaporated like dew in July, and she wound her fingers into the hair at the nape of his neck. When he released her lips, his face was tight with desire. "Not so sweet-and-twenty," he said. "More like dirty-and-thirty-something."

A laugh rasped up from deep in her throat. He touched his lips to the hollow at the base of her neck, almost as though he wanted to kiss the source of the sound. She felt it as a bolt of lightning straight to her breasts.

He kept his arm around her waist and walked toward the open hatch. "No more delays then," he said. "I'll go first."

He ran lightly down the few steps and pivoted, reaching toward her. She leaned in to take his hands but he seized her waist and lifted her down, letting her slide along his body until her feet touched the floor. She let out a long sigh at how wonderful he felt against her.

"Hold that thought," he said, flipping open a storage compartment to pull out a couple of plaid comforters. Tossing them on one of the built-in benches, he fiddled with something under the cushion of another bench so that it extended out over the galley table, making a capacious bed.

Kyra laid the comforters out while Will opened a porthole, creating a delicious cross breeze of tangy sea air.

As he came up to her, she laid her palm on his chest, holding him at a distance. "Fair warning: if you fall asleep on me again, I will finish without you."

"Sleep is the farthest thing from my mind right now," he said, his fingers drifting up her bare arms in delicious, exploring strokes. She could feel the tiny hairs on her skin dance and tingle.

"This time we start with you," she said.

"A gentleman is taught that ladies should go—or come—first." His voice was a slow pour of seduction.

She lifted her hands to the first button on his shirt and flicked it open. "I didn't say anything about coming. I just want to see you naked."

The hiss of his inhale was audible in the boat's enclosed cabin. He toed off his loafers and gave her a heavy-lidded smile. "A gentleman is also taught that he should do everything in his power to make a lady's wishes come true." He started to unbuckle his belt, but Kyra grabbed his hands.

"The lady wishes to undress you herself." She might only have this one chance to enjoy his body, and she planned to savor it.

"As long as the wish is reciprocal, the gentleman is willing, although a bit impatient." He let his hands fall to his sides.

Kyra finished unbuttoning his shirt, yanking the tails out of his waistband and dragging the shirt down his arms before tossing it across the cabin. Now she sucked in a long breath because he was more than she expected. The lanky college boy's body had been transformed into the muscle and sinew of a man who exuded control over himself and those around him. It was a heady experience to have all that leashed power at her command.

She ran one fingertip over the swell of muscle that joined his neck to his shoulder, then trailed back along the sharp edge of his clavicle. His skin was warm and smooth as silk until she reached the center of his chest where a patch of gilded hair tickled her fingers.

"You're doing this to torture me," he said, his voice tight.

She smiled up into his eyes. "I'm doing this because I didn't get to ten years ago."

"Revenge is a dish best served cold, but it's having the opposite effect on me," he said, cupping a hand over her backside and pulling her against him to feel his erection.

The delicious ache inside her turned to a furnace of need. But she wasn't going to rush this . . . yet. "Does a gentleman hurry a lady?"

"I'm losing my grip on gentleman and regressing to caveman." He brought his hand back to his side, although it was curled into a fist.

She shifted her exploration to his arm, following the line of muscle from his shoulder, over his biceps, to his forearm. He must work out regularly. His well-defined abs caught her eye so she trailed her fingers over them, following the line of blond hair down his center to his waist.

"Finally," he rasped.

Just to bother him, she skimmed her hand back up his chest to stroke his cheek. He groaned and let his head fall backward, the tendons of his neck standing out as he fought his frustration.

She smiled at her ability to affect him, and went back to his belt. Unbuckling the leather tab, she noticed that the brown fabric of the belt had a pattern of knives, forks, and spoons woven into it, a subtle reminder that he hadn't followed the path his parents had chosen for him. As soon as she had run the zipper of his khakis down, he shoved his trousers to his ankles, ripping them and his socks off before straightening to stand in his black silk boxer briefs, tented by his straining cock.

His powerful thighs and calves glistened with blond hair, and she stooped to glide her hands over the swells and indents above his knees. She looked up to see his chest rising and falling in an accelerated rhythm.

"Turn around," she said.

A sound that was very primitive indeed tore from his throat, but he obeyed, pivoting on one bare heel. He put his hands on his hips and bent his head, making his triceps bulge outward.

"Ooh, this is amazing," she said, following the straight line of his spine down to his tight butt and cupping it briefly through the silk before letting her palms flutter over all the hills and valleys of his back.

Her nipples had hardened already, and the dampness between her legs grew hotter and more liquid. She wound her arms around his waist, pulling herself against the expanse of sculpted muscle and tendon. Pinpoints of sensation streaked from her breasts to her core and she moaned.

The sound seemed to break his control because he turned like a striking snake in her arms, reaching around to run her zipper down the back of her dress. He pushed the peach-colored fabric down her arms, over her hips, and to the floor. For a moment his gaze drifted over her lacy bra and bikini panties. Then he stripped both flimsy pieces of lingerie off her, hurling them across the cabin.

"So beautiful," he murmured. "More so even than I remembered."

"You remember?" She stepped into him, closing her eyes as her bare skin came in contact with his, the wanting inside her flaming like a bonfire. She leaned into him to feel her breasts crushed against the living wall of his chest.

"I fought hard against the damned alcohol." He wound his arm around her waist and splayed his hand over her buttock. "You felt so right in my arms because we knew each other in other ways first." He put his lips against hers. "Now we'll know each other in all ways."

His hands were everywhere, stroking, kneading, cupping. She seized his shoulders and held on as he built her longing to a fever pitch, arching into him and begging with incoherent sounds. He walked her backward and lowered her onto the bed before he came down on one knee beside her thigh. She lifted her hips in an invitation, and he slid his hand between her thighs to rub his thumb against her clit. She mewed with pleasure, but it wasn't enough.

"Inside me," she said.

He slipped one finger into the wet heat of her, making her muscles ripple in near orgasm.

"Another," she begged, needing to be filled.

He pulled out and used the moisture on his finger to glide over her clit before easing two fingers inside her, and she felt herself open farther.

"Yes!"

As she rocked with him, he worked his fingers in and out, driving her arousal higher and higher. Her eyes were closed, her focus on the fire low in her body, so it shocked her when she felt the warm, wet touch of his lips on one nipple, making her cry out and grab at his head to hold it there. He sucked at her breast, and lightning seemed to ricochet through her until it coiled in her belly.

His mouth pulling on her and his fingers sliding in and out of her had her teetering on the verge of climax, but she wanted him to come with her the first time they made love.

"Will, stop!"

He released her nipple and withdrew his hand from between her legs, his eyes clouded with concern as he bent over her. "Did I hurt you?"

"No, no . . . God, no! I want you inside me when I come." She fumbled at the waistband of his briefs, but her angle and his erection made it hard to yank them down. Will brushed her hands aside and had the briefs off in an instant. He picked up one of the condoms he'd dropped on the bed earlier and ripped open the foil envelope.

"Let me," Kyra said, wanting to touch him. She took the condom but then stroked her fingers down the hard length of his cock without it. She glanced up to see his gaze on her fingers where they encircled him, so she rubbed her thumb against the head where it was wet.

"Kyra," he breathed. "Yes, that."

She stroked him twice more, feeling the pulse of him under her hand.

"The condom," he said in a strangled voice. "Now."

She rolled it on and then he tumbled her back on the bed, his hips wedged between her thighs, the tip of him poised just outside her. He positioned himself, then laced his fingers between hers and pinned their hands to the bed on either side of her head.

He flexed his hips and thrust all the way inside her in one motion, and they both cried out. And then it was all about the feel of him filling her, moving in her, moving against her, murmuring in her ear, as he drove her relentlessly up toward her climax. Everything in her body centered on him, every feeling, every thought, every sensation. He held her hands so all she could do was angle her hips to offer him more.

And then he released one hand to reach down between them, to touch her on the small sensitive spot that detonated the explosion inside her, sending light and pleasure and relief bursting through her as her muscles clenched around him.

He stilled, letting her enjoy her release without distraction. As she quieted, he began to move again, slowly at first. But she freed both hands to run them down his back and curl her fingers into his buttocks, urging him on. His motion, the friction of skin on skin, the brush of his chest against her breasts, twisted the longing inside her tight again. As her name seemed to wrench itself from his throat and he began to pulse inside her, another orgasm blossomed, a gentler pleasure but still sending waves of ecstasy crashing through her.

Then they both sank down into the cushions as though their bones had melted. Will's heart pounded against her chest and his breath sounded loud by her ear. He shifted to settle his weight mostly on the bed, but one of his arms was still slung over her waist, and one of his legs remained between hers.

As the fizz in her blood quieted, she became aware of the boat rocking gently, the breeze fluttering the curtains of the porthole, and the freshness of salt air. And Will. The heat of his body, the scent of his shampoo and of sex, the heavy feel of his arm on her, the scuff of his lightly furred thigh against the sensitive inner skin of her legs.

She blew out a long sigh. She'd finally gotten what she'd dreamed of all those years ago, and that was a treacherous thing. Because she wanted more.

"Waiting ten years paid off," he said.

She choked on a laugh. "Is that how you're spinning it? That it was better to wait?"

"Couldn't sell you on that excuse, eh?"

"No, but you could sell me on almost anything else right now."

"Then I've succeeded." He rose up on his elbow and looked down at her, his expression a strange mix of satisfaction and longing. "Probably better than I would have done in college, to be honest."

"Youth and enthusiasm can overcome a lack of finesse," she said. "But I can't picture you ever being awkward, even back then."

He snorted. "Catching Babette in bed with another guy was awkward. Especially since you were there to witness it."

"You never came to our suite again after that. Not that I blamed you, but I missed our conversations," Kyra said. And her fantasy of Will suddenly pulling her into his arms to say, *I've just used Babette as a way to get to you. You're the one I really want,* before he kissed her.

"My ego was too wrecked to revisit the scene of my humiliation. Didn't you notice that I casually ran into you on campus more often than usual after the fiasco?"

Surprise jolted through her. "You mean that was intentional? I thought you'd switched classes or something." That was the rationale she'd used to keep her fantasies in check because she *had* noticed how often they seemed to encounter each other after the incident.

"I was going to ask you out, but I needed to lick my wounded pride a little longer. And then you were gone."

Her thoughts tripped over one another at the revelation that he had considered dating her. But that was college, where most students tended to overlook differences in social and financial backgrounds. Being smart was more important than being rich for those four—or in her case, two—years of ivory-tower seclusion. That was one reason she'd loved Brunell so much; it was a democracy of the mind, completely different from the real world.

But she and Will lived in a different reality now. He was a billionaire with a pedigree. She was exactly the opposite. She needed to remember that before she started building castles in the air. Regret settled on her like a lead weight.

She nestled closer to him to shrug off the burden. She could float among the clouds for just a little longer.

Will tightened his arm around Kyra's waist as she wiggled against his side. He felt . . . good. Like he hadn't just spent three hours at the dreadful Spring Fling with the muscles in his neck and shoulders tied in knots. Or nearly missed an encounter with Petra. He splayed his fingers over Kyra's rib cage to savor more of the warm, silky texture of her skin. She twitched with a muffled giggle. Ticklish. That made him smile.

Making love to Kyra had been so easy. Also exciting, satisfying, and uncomplicated. They took pleasure in the same things, in the same ways. No drama, no undercurrents. Just a beautiful, intelligent woman who responded to him with straightforward enthusiasm. No wonder he felt like he was twenty again.

He turned his head to inhale her fragrance. It was a clean, almost lemony scent, warmed seductively by their exertions. Hunger for her flared again, but he tamped it down, wanting to savor the relaxed pleasure of her body pressed to his. If he moved, he might be forced back into the present instead of living in this moment out of time.

Even the party hadn't been as bad as he anticipated. Kyra had stayed at his side, throwing little slanted glances of secret, shared amusement at him. Sometimes it had been when a party guest approached, wearing a particularly clashing outfit. Sometimes it had been over an especially clueless remark. She hadn't been mean, just entertained. She had shifted his perspective, so he could view the situation with some of her detachment and humor.

Except when it involved his parents or Petra.

He shoved the thought of them all into a dark corner of his mind, refusing to allow them to ruin his mood of mellow semi-arousal. It was a surprisingly nice state to drift in. Wanting her but feeling no urgency to act on his desire.

He considered untying the *Royal Wave* from her mooring and sailing to a private cove where they would drop anchor. Then he could remain in this suspension of reality and make love to Kyra for the rest of the day and night.

He huffed out a breath, making Kyra giggle again. Pipe dreams. So many people expected so many things of him.

There was no escape.

Chapter 7

Kyra came awake with a sense of panic because her bed seemed to be rocking violently beneath her. As she registered the weight of Will's arm over her waist and the feel of his bare skin against hers, her awareness came surging back. The bed *was* rocking. She could hear the rumbling sound of a powerful engine and guessed they'd been hit by the wake of a large boat.

Will slept through it without a twitch, but he was accustomed to being on the water. She tried to gauge the time by the slant of light through the porthole. She guessed they'd dozed off for nearly an hour.

Which meant she needed to wake Will. But she closed her eyes again, imprinting on her memory how the muscles and tendons of his arm felt against the softness of her waist, how the tickle of his slow, steady breathing whispered over her skin, how the heat of his big body on her one side contrasted with the brush of the cooling breeze on the other.

She ran her fingertips up a ridge in his arm and shook his shoulder gently. "Will, we fell asleep."

He stirred, muttering something she couldn't understand, and pulled her into him. She felt his cock harden and push against her hip.

"Are you awake?" she asked, shaking him again.

"I was trying not to be."

"I think it's late," she said, even as he skimmed his hand up to cup her breast. And suddenly a liquid wave of desire rolled through her to settle low in her belly. But she caught his wrist and pulled it away. "I like the way your mind works, but we don't have time."

He let her move his hand before he looked straight up at the ceiling. "I don't want to leave this bed."

"I'd be flattered except I know you just dread going back to your family."

"You'd be wrong. There are many more important reasons I want to stay." He turned his head back toward her so she could see the seriousness in his eyes. "All of them are about you."

Happiness shimmered through her like a mirage of clear, cool water on hot asphalt. "Okay, I'm flattered."

"No flattery, just truth. You're something special. I knew that at Brunell."

After those words, Kyra couldn't lie still. She levered herself up on one elbow, wanting to get a better view of his face to judge his sincerity. "You sure didn't let on that you felt that way." She winced at her slip into the country phrasing but she was shocked all over again.

"What do you mean? I came by the suite every chance I could."

"To see Babette."

"I always hoped Babette would be busy for at least half an hour." He gave her a bone-melting smile.

So their conversations hadn't just been holding patterns for him, as she'd always thought. Why hadn't he ever given any sign that he wanted more from her? But she knew. He couldn't have taken her to his frat parties and been comfortable that she would fit in with his friends. She didn't have the right clothes or the right attitude about drinking or the right social graces. Those were things she'd taught herself later, when she came to New York and her survival depended on it. He probably didn't even realize that was why he hadn't asked her out.

"Lucky for me, Babette was a popular girl," Kyra said, her comment holding an edge she couldn't keep in.

"Lucky for me, too, in the long run." Will contracted the magnificent set of muscles in his torso to sit up on the bed. "Duty calls."

"Does that mean we're staying for dinner after all?"

He shook his head. "Just a quick stop to say good-bye. Maybe a little longer if they behave themselves."

"At least you're not quoting dying gladiators now," Kyra pointed out.

"Proving that you have done wonders for my mental state," he said. Standing, he began to gather up their scattered clothing, while she admired the play of muscles moving under his skin. She felt her center go liquid again as she remembered what all the power had felt like over and inside her.

He dropped the clothes on the bed beside her and began to sort them into his and hers. "If you'd like to freshen up, the head is through that door." He nodded toward the front of the boat.

She didn't want to wash the feel of him from her body, but she should. "My purse. It's still outside."

He pulled on his trousers and ran lightly up the steps, the arches of his bare feet as strong and elegant as the rest of him. "Here you go," he said, returning with her clutch and her sandals dangling from his fingers.

She stood and stretched up onto her toes to brush a kiss on his cheek. "My knight in khaki armor." The fact that her breast brushed his chest did nothing to reduce her yearning for him.

The head was roomier than she expected and fitted out with scented soap, fluffy white towels, and a well-lit mirror that made her gasp at the disarray of her hair and makeup. She used a washcloth to clean up and then did her best to redo her face with the minimum of cosmetics in her purse. She hadn't been prepared for an afternoon of uninhibited sex.

The "uninhibited" part had surprised her the most. She thought she'd be nervous or worried about what Will thought of her, but the chemistry had burned so fast and intensely that any concerns had been consumed by the fire.

Which didn't mean she wouldn't second-guess everything tomorrow and the next day.

She heard water running and realized that Will must be using the galley sink to clean up. She dragged her little purse brush through the tangles of her hair and vacated the bathroom to find Will leaning over the sink as he splashed water over his face.

"All yours," she said, feeling very naked compared to Will, who was now dressed from the waist down. She scooped her panties off the bed and tugged them on.

He straightened and finger combed his damp hair away from his face. "Maybe I could use a mirror," he said, with a wry smile.

"Trust me, you look perfect." She fastened her bra.

He crossed the space between them in two steps. "You looked more perfect without these." He hooked a finger in the lace of her panties and snapped the waistband in a playful gesture before giving her bottom a quick squeeze. "Mmm, love those curves."

"We have to go," Kyra said, smacking his arm.

She hated the way his mouth flattened into a straight line of unhappiness. He released her, grabbed his shirt, and shut himself into the bathroom. No, the head.

Kyra dressed, checking that she still wore all the pieces of Emily's jewelry. She searched the sleeping quarters to find a small mirror so she could do a more thorough job on her hair. When Will came out of the head, he was fully clothed and rerolling his shirtsleeves.

"You know Ceres started here," he said, coaxing a precise fold into the shirt fabric. "I was working as a waiter at the yacht club."

"I thought you chauffeured people to their boats."

He looked up at her. "I did that in the morning when the boat traffic was busiest. I waited tables at night."

"Nothing wrong with your work ethic," Kyra said. She knew he was stalling because he didn't want to face his family, but she wanted to hear the story. She plunked down on the bed.

"Yours either," he said, provoking Kyra to give a wave of dismissal. "Why do you deny it? You work two jobs."

"I suppose I don't think of cooking at the Carver Center as a job, exactly." Besides, she worked two jobs out of necessity, not choice. "But go on. I want to hear about the creation of Ceres."

"The head chef at the country club, Greg Ebersole, reamed me out the first night I worked there because I screwed something up. He reamed me out the second night for another mistake. And it went on like that for about a week. Since I didn't quit, he decided maybe I was okay. When a group of us from the club went out on my mother's boat on our day off, he came along. I wanted to keep my job so I stocked the fridge with his favorite kind of beer."

Will's voice warmed as he looked into the past.

"We got pretty drunk and he started talking about this idea he had that people wanted healthy fast food. Not only that, the food sources should be organic and local. I was only a teenager but something about his passion made me pay attention, and the idea stuck with me all through college."

"Is that why you took the business minor at Brunell?"

He nodded and sat down beside her. "I wanted to escape the law but I needed an alternative."

He took her hand and placed it on his thigh, idly running his fingers over her knuckles. The warm pads of his fingertips brushing her skin made it hard to focus on his story.

"When I graduated and was staring the prospect of Harvard Law in its grim face, I called Greg and asked him if he wanted to partner with a know-nothing, inexperienced kid fresh out of college who happened to have some great connections." Will shook his head in reminiscent disbelief. "I don't know why the hell he said yes, except that all great chefs are a little crazy."

"He said yes because you're brilliant, hardworking, trustworthy . . . and well connected."

Will stared straight ahead, lost in the past.

"So how did you get started?" she prompted.

His lips twisted into a smile that derided his younger self. "I wanted to open ten locations all at once to make a significant splash. Greg explained that my idea was insane and whittled it down to four. So I scouted sites and raised funds while he found suppliers and worked on the menu." Will smiled. "I remember the late-night taste tests. God, some of his recipes were bad. That was my only talent with the food: being the target customer."

"You certainly knew that my lamb wrap was out of balance," Kyra said.

Will snorted. "Your dog Shaq would have known that." He flexed his fingers around Kyra's. "We opened four Ceres at the same time. It's a miracle the whole thing wasn't a total fiasco."

Kyra could picture Will dashing from one restaurant to the next, making sure everything went smoothly. "Did you still have your pony-tail then?"

"No, I needed to look respectable when I went begging for money." He ran his hand over the back of his head where the ponytail once was. "Did you know that my father wouldn't invest a penny in Ceres?" Will's tone was bitter. "But he didn't tell his friends not to invest, so I guess I should be grateful for that." He turned to her. "I've never told anyone but Greg that. Didn't want them to know that my own father had no confidence in me."

Kyra turned her hand to twine her fingers with his. "He might have wanted you to be able to say you succeeded on your own. You showed everyone, including yourself, that you didn't need his help."

"You're attributing far more paternal sensitivity to him than he has ever demonstrated." But she could see the stubborn denial in the set of his jaw soften. "Maybe I'll give him the benefit of the doubt." He stood and helped her up with their joined hands. "Back to the salt mines."

Will swiped an app that hailed the water taxi. While they waited on deck, he pointed out the especially interesting boats. No more sharing of secrets from the past because he was putting the protective walls back up again. Kyra missed the raw, vulnerable Will.

As the skiff bounced over the waves toward them, Kyra interrupted the flow of smooth chitchat. "Your secrets are safe with me. I won't betray them or you."

He brushed the back of his fingers down her cheek. "That's why I told you."

Then their cheery skipper was maneuvering the skiff up to the ladder. Kyra had left her feet bare and managed not to rip any seams or fall into the harbor as she clambered into the small craft.

"Had a nice afternoon aboard the *Royal Wave*?" the boy asked, as he eased the skiff away from the sailboat.

Kyra choked on a giggle when Will grinned and said, "It was very satisfying."

She nudged his ankle, which made him grin more. Then the kid gunned the motor so that speaking became too difficult. But Will's fingers were still interwoven with hers, which wrapped her in a haze of contentment.

All too soon, they were in the Jaguar, headed back to Arion Farm. The closer they got, the more frequently Will lifted a hand to rub at the back of his neck.

"Maybe we should just head for the helicopter," Kyra said.

Will's laugh held no mirth. "Don't tempt me, Circe."

"Hey, she turned men into pigs, although I think that was metaphorical. I would never do that to you. What a terrible waste it would be."

He chuckled with actual amusement. "I see you are on the side of those who believe that men revealed their bestial side when in Circe's company. She enslaved even the brave ones, the lions and wolves, with her sexuality."

"As I remember, Odysseus, who was supposedly so determined to get home to Penelope, hung around with Circe for a year or so. She must have been amazing in the sack."

"So you're like Circe in that way, too."

"A backhanded compliment if ever I heard one." But a smug smile curled the corners of her mouth.

"And now we have arrived at the passage between Scylla and Charybdis," Will murmured, steering the car through the gateposts that marked the entrance to his parents' estate.

"Do you always revert to Greek mythology when you're stressed?" Kyra asked, but she knew the answer. She had escaped into Charlotte Brontë and Jane Austen. Will went farther back into the past.

"The Greeks understood the bloody side of family dynamics." Will swung the Jaguar around the circle in front of the house that now held only about a dozen parked cars.

Kyra snorted. "They did have a tendency to kill their immediate relatives . . . when they weren't sleeping with their mothers. Not that I'm implying anything like that about your family."

"I'm relieved." He put his arm around her waist and steered her up the wide stone steps and through the unlocked front door.

"Oh. My. God," Kyra said on one long breath as they stepped into the entrance hall. Warm oak paneling covered the walls, and a huge pastel Oriental rug lay on the polished plank floor. Centered on it was a circular leather-topped oak table bearing an enormous china vase of fresh flowers. Paintings of horses and gilt-framed mirrors hung on the panels, and a staircase of the same highly grained oak rose to a wide landing before it joined with a gallery that ran around three sides of the hallway. "It's not Disney World. It's a real, live castle."

Will shrugged. "Birds in gilded cages." Settling his arm more firmly around her waist, he turned them through a wide arch and into a room that stretched from the front to the back of the mansion. Kyra had a quick impression of more oak paneling, a fireplace, and a ceiling with intricate plaster designs. Then she confronted the daunting array of faces turned toward her, their owners scattered around the various chintz-covered chairs and sofas with glasses in their hands. The hum of conversation came to a sudden halt.

Kyra felt a shudder run through Will while his grip on her hardened into a vise. It was so similar to his earlier reaction to Petra's voice that Kyra got a bad feeling.

"Will!" His mother floated up from the chair in which she sat. "So glad you could rejoin us. Let's get you and Kyra drinks."

The conversations began again, but Kyra caught people casting surreptitious glances at Will and her.

Betsy Chase beckoned them over to the built-in bar. "What can I offer you?"

"White wine would be great," Kyra said, keeping it simple. What she really wanted was a double shot of vodka because the tension in the room was so thick she could cut it with the proverbial knife. *Was Petra here?*

"I'll take care of it, Mum," Will said, his voice so cold it made Kyra shiver.

"I know Schuyler went to the stables, but where did you wander off to?" Betsy asked, appearing oblivious to her son's mood as she handed him a wineglass.

Kyra felt a blush creep up her cheeks, but Will's composure shifted not a millimeter as he said, "Kyra had never been on a sailboat so I took her aboard the *Royal Wave*."

"Isn't she a little beauty?" Betsy asked, her face lit with enthusiasm. "And she handles like a dream."

"She's gorgeous," Kyra agreed. "I'm not a sailor so I wouldn't know about handling."

"Next time, let Kyra take the helm," Betsy admonished Will. "That will be a treat for her."

Kyra didn't know how he managed it, but Will kept pouring scotch into the crystal tumbler without a waver or a drop spilled. "I'll make sure to do that," he said.

Only the volume of scotch he swallowed all at once betrayed any discomfort.

Betsy linked her arm through Kyra's. "Let me introduce you to everyone."

"I'll handle it, Mum," Will said, reaching for Kyra.

"It will be my pleasure." Betsy smiled at her son but her arm was like a steel bar holding Kyra prisoner. Will lowered his hand, although his face was tight with anger.

Farr sauntered up at that moment. "I'll keep you company, William."

Kyra refused to let her dismay show, even to Will. Finding the strength to smile with enthusiasm at both men, she said, "I can't wait to meet everyone."

As Betsy drew her toward the other guests, Kyra heard Will mutter, "You don't have to babysit me, Farr."

"Oh, the ingratitude after what I did for you earlier," his friend shot back.

Now Kyra had to focus on the lions she was being thrown to. Betsy swept her by Schuyler and Twain, saying she knew them already. After that it was a mad blur of names and faces, but Kyra just put on her friendly bartender persona and made it through. Until Betsy stopped in front of two women sitting side by side on a plaid love seat.

"Kyra, I'd like you to meet Petra Bradenton-Crosby and Katie Phipps. Kyra's an old college chum of Will's," she said to the ladies.

Kyra felt like she'd been socked in the stomach. Petra Bradenton-Crosby was stunningly beautiful but not in the way she'd expected. Kyra had pictured blonde hair, blue eyes, an English rose complexion, and the angular, athletic figure that so many of Will's female acquaintances seemed to have.

Petra was darkly exotic with short-cropped nearly black hair, huge brown eyes, skin like cream, and a figure that would make Kyra's customers at Stratus fall over themselves. She wore a beige linen sheath with tiny pleated details that screamed designer.

Even more startling, Petra smiled at her with what looked like genuine warmth and stood to shake hands. "Kyra, how lovely! Will so enjoyed his days at Brunell. It's a pleasure to meet someone who was part of that."

Kyra had been prepared to dislike Petra on sight but it was impossible. The woman radiated interest and attentiveness. "Glad to meet you, too," Kyra managed to say, but it wasn't easy when her jaw kept trying to drop.

Katie and Betsy strolled away together, so Kyra was left alone with the woman whose heart Will was reputed to have broken. Her friendly bartender persona deserted her.

"Let's sit and be comfortable," Petra said, sinking onto the love seat with perfect grace.

Kyra wished someone would rescue her, but she didn't want to drag Will into conversation with Petra, so she kept her gaze resolutely away from his vicinity. "Are you from around here?" she asked Petra.

"Originally, but now I live in Manhattan. On the Upper West Side."

Great, she was on the same small island with Will.

Petra continued, "But I travel a great deal, so my condo is almost a waste of money. However, having three major airports to choose from makes the travel easier."

"What takes you away from New York so often?" Kyra asked, her curiosity getting the better of her.

"My work. I'm a fund-raiser for Doctors Abroad."

Of course she was. Kyra wanted to groan. "What a worthwhile organization to work for!" she said instead. "I admire what they do so much. How did you get started with them?" She didn't want Petra to ask what Kyra did to make a living.

"I began as a volunteer at a fund-raising event they held when I was in college." Petra shook her head with a self-deprecating smile. "I only did it because the boy I was dating back then had organized it. But I got bowled over by the cause, and became more and more involved. When I graduated, it seemed natural to move into a job with them. And I've been there ever since."

Kyra could see by the way Petra leaned toward her that she was going to ask a question, so she cast around for another way to throw her off. "Where have you traveled recently?"

"Oh, all over." She held up the strand of carved wooden beads that cascaded down from her slender neck. "Some lovely ladies made this for me when I was in Kenya a couple of months ago. Wasn't that the sweetest thing?" She let the necklace fall, her gaze fastened on Kyra as though seeking her agreement. "Last week I was in Los Angeles and Seattle. I'm trying to set up some highly visible events around the country to raise our profile."

"You must be succeeding because it's certainly a well-known and well-respected charity," Kyra said.

"You are so kind to say that," Petra said, but it was automatic. She expected the compliment. "I'm very passionate about the cause, so I tend to talk too much about it. Tell me more about you. Where do you live?"

Since Petra lived in New York, she'd insist on a specific locale. "South Harlem, on the top floor of a wonderful old townhouse from the eighteen hundreds. The heat is a little unreliable, but it has great charm."

"That area is very popular now," Petra said, nodding. "There are some real architectural gems for almost reasonable prices."

Like Kyra could buy any of them.

"I work at an after-school care center nearby as the chief cook and bottle washer. And I do some bartending." There, she'd told the truth and it hadn't sounded so bad.

"I love kids." Again it sounded a little rote, but her eyes were warm. "What ages do you work with?"

"What we call the in-between kids, eight through thirteen with some wiggle room. They're too old for the preschool programs and too young for the teen programs, so they can get kind of lost. We offer them a safe, stable place with healthy food and quiet study facilities. And they can adopt rescue dogs in the K-9 Angelz program." Kyra stopped with a short laugh. "I get passionate about my cause, too, I guess."

Just then, Will walked up with Farr trailing behind him. "Petra. This is unexpected." He bent and kissed the air beside her cheek.

A look of longing crossed Petra's face and she tilted her head toward him, as though she hoped to have his lips actually touch her skin. "How have you been, Will?"

"Good," he said. "And you?" His voice was polite but distant.

"Busy as ever," she said. "Lots of traveling."

Will nodded, the motion a curt jerk of his head. "I'm afraid Kyra and I need to head back to the city."

Petra started to say something, then pressed her lips together and nodded. "Safe travels."

"And to you," Will responded, holding out his hand to Kyra. His grip was almost crushing as he helped her rise from the cushy love seat.

"Great meeting you," Kyra said to Petra. "Good luck with your fund-raising."

Petra nodded but her eyes were on the man beside Kyra. Even her body angled toward him, despite the fact that Farr took the seat Kyra had just vacated.

No matter what had happened between them, Petra still wanted Will.

Will tucked Kyra's hand into his elbow and stalked across the room, forcing her to jog to keep up with him for the first few steps. When he noticed, he muttered an apology and shortened his stride. She could feel anger sizzling off him in waves.

His father and mother glanced their way and then left their guests to follow them into the entrance hall.

"Son, your mother wants to say good-bye." His father's voice crackled with command.

Kyra was afraid Will would keep on walking, but he halted just a few steps from the front door. He dipped his head to Kyra and murmured, "I'm sorry about this disaster. I'll make it up to you."

She gave his elbow a reassuring squeeze as he turned them both to face his parents. Twain stood with his arm around Betsy's shoulders. Kyra couldn't decide if he was showing solidarity or holding her back.

"I've asked you not to invite Petra to private family gatherings," Will said.

Betsy made a graceful but dismissive gesture. "It wasn't a family gathering. Just a few special friends lingering after the party. You needn't have rushed off so rudely."

Kyra felt Will stiffen. "You are not doing Petra any favors," he said. "You lead her to think I want her here."

"Why shouldn't you want her here?" his mother said. "She's a lovely girl, and she still cares about you."

Kyra smothered a gasp. His mother had no idea how serious her relationship with Will was, and yet she was praising another woman in Kyra's presence. Betsy was putting her on notice that she had other plans for Will.

Will took Kyra's hand from his arm and lifted it to brush his lips over her knuckles. "I offer my mother's sincerest regrets for her words," he said, his eyes blazing with fury as he smiled down at her. The intensity of it made her shiver.

"It won't happen again." Twain spoke with authority and a hint of apology. "You've made your position clear and we should honor it."

"Next, hell will freeze over," Will said in an oddly conversational tone, given the fraught atmosphere. "But I appreciate your support, sir." He returned Kyra's hand to the crook of his elbow.

Betsy opened her mouth, but Kyra saw Twain's fingers tighten on his wife's shoulder in a warning. Will's mother looked annoyed but she clamped her lips shut.

Kyra tried to think of an innocuous social phrase to extricate them all, but each one that came to mind—it was a pleasure, nice to meet you, thank you for your hospitality—rang with such irony she couldn't bring herself to mouth any of them.

Will solved the problem. "I'll try to get home for Christmas," he said before he pivoted to march out the door.

Kyra heard Betsy's strangled cry of dismay, and then Will was hurrying her to the Jaguar, handing her in, and closing her door with a snap.

He slipped into the driver's seat, revved the engine, and peeled out over the cobblestones, tires squealing. His knuckles were white as he gripped the steering wheel, his chin jutting with anger.

"Don't worry about it," she said, reaching over to touch his upper arm. "You warned me." She tried to make her smile reassuring, but she could feel the tremor in her muscles.

"My mother went beyond the pale," he said, his voice taut with rage. "You think she's done her worst and then . . ."

"You're not responsible for what your parents do," Kyra said. Although she'd learned the hard way that wasn't always true.

He took his eyes off the road to glance at her. "I knew I was taking you into a pit of vipers. It was inexcusable on my part."

"You're being dramatic again. I've dealt with far worse, believe me."

He swung the Jaguar off the road and bumped to a halt at the edge of the field where the helicopter stood waiting. "But I invited you to a party, not a soap opera." He hit the button that closed the car's ragtop over them again.

Kyra shrugged. "Things happen. Don't sweat it."

"Are you really that tough? Or do you just talk a good game?" He surveyed her with a piercing gaze.

"A little of both." She heard the chopper's engine whine to life. "Wait, didn't Schuyler want a ride with us?"

"Oh, hell, you're right." He yanked his phone out of his pocket and typed a rapid message. "She has fifteen minutes."

Wedging his wide shoulders against the driver's-side window, he finally smiled at her. "I planned to spend the whole ride back to New York apologizing, but it looks like we'll have an audience. When do you have another day off?"

Excitement burbled up inside her, even as she tried to tamp it down. He only wanted to see her again because he felt guilty. "Tomorrow night. I work at the center until six. After that I work every night until next Sunday."

But his smile widened with what seemed to be genuine pleasure. "Tomorrow. Is seven too early to pick you up?"

"Depends on how dressed up I have to be." Her blood was racing in her veins at the prospect of seeing him again so soon.

"Personally, I'd rather you weren't dressed at all." Wicked delight glinted in his eyes.

"There are laws about that." Her insides were melting in the most delicious way.

"Only in public. In private, your state of undress is no one's business but mine. And I consider it very serious business." His voice had dropped to a seductive rumble, its vibration echoing in her belly.

"You haven't answered my question," she said on an exhale.

"I got distracted with picturing you naked and lying across the leather seats in the limo."

"Will!" She shifted as heat and moisture pooled between her legs.

He reached across the console to lay his palm on the bare skin just above her knee. "If I go higher, will I find you wet?"

The hollow between her legs seemed to pulse with longing. "Schuyler is coming," she ground out.

"Just a quick dip so I can lick your taste from my finger," he coaxed.

Need overcame good sense. She nodded and he leaned over to slide his hand under her skirt, bunching it on his wrist as she spread her thighs to give him better access. He found the edge of her panties and pushed aside the lace, seeking the hot center of her and driving his finger in. Her hips bucked and he sucked in a breath. "I want to make you come so badly."

She gasped and opened her legs wider, desire making her shameless. "If you watch for Schuyler."

Before her last word was spoken, he had slipped two fingers inside her and turned his hand so his thumb could tease her clit. His first stroke had her head slamming back into the headrest as pleasure shot through her. "Like that. Again," she demanded.

He obliged, but rotated his wrist at the same time, adding an extra angle to the press of his fingers within her. The surprise of the delicious new sensation nearly made her scream. She pushed her pelvis upward to offer more. He did it again and her arousal coiled tighter.

"God, I want to put my mouth between your thighs," he rasped as he worked his fingers in and out of her. "I want to lick into you and taste it when you come."

And she was there, her muscles clamping down hard before everything inside her exploded into hot, liquid orgasm. "Will, yes!" she gasped before a long, inarticulate cry tore from her throat as her muscles convulsed again and again around his thrusting fingers. When the orgasm faded to tiny shudders, she sagged down onto the seat and he slid out of her, lifting his fingers to his mouth and sucking on them as he hummed deep in his throat.

"You taste like chocolate and the sea," he said.

"Mmm." Kyra was lost in the afterglow, her eyes closed, her head tilted back against the soft leather of the Jag's seat. She felt a tug on her dress and looked down to see Will smoothing it down over her thighs. "Such a gentleman," she said.

"No, just making sure there's a next time. And Schuyler is about to arrive."

Kyra bolted upright in her seat, jerking her dress down even farther.

Will laid a calming hand on her frantic ones. "She would applaud, not judge."

"That's what *you* think." Not that she had direct knowledge, since she was an only child, but in her observations, siblings were protective of each other when it came to love interests.

There was a tap at Will's window, and Schuyler peered through the slightly steamy glass. Will swung his door open slowly and hauled himself out of the car. Kyra took a deep breath, checked her dress again, and climbed out just as Will came around to hold her door.

"Thanks for waiting," Schuyler said, but she had a funny smile on her face while she eyed the two of them, as though she suspected them of doing exactly what they had been doing. "The traffic report is appalling."

They trooped across the field to the chopper, Will acting as escort between them, Schuyler keeping up a running commentary about the party guests.

A wave of exhaustion swept over Kyra. She hadn't realized how stressful it had been to smile and nod and make conversation with a whole party of total strangers. Not to mention sex with Will. It had been incredible, but the intensity and unexpectedness had drained her.

Even the thrilling thought that he wanted to see her again so soon couldn't boost her sagging energy.

As they climbed into the helicopter, she found herself hoping Schuyler would talk all the way back to New York.

Will watched Kyra stare out the helicopter's window, while his sister babbled on about who'd done what at the party. Fury seethed in his chest as he thought of his mother's unspeakable rudeness to Kyra—who was now so much more than just a buffer in a difficult situation. He hated that their day had nearly ended on such a sour note.

Thank God she had let him give her an orgasm in the car, even though it had left him with a hard-on that still pressed against his briefs. She had looked so glorious with her thighs spread and his hand buried between them. Her little pants of arousal and the wet heat inside her had made him want to drag her over to straddle his lap so he could thrust his cock into her over and over again. But first he wanted to taste her directly instead of just on his fingers.

He yanked his imagination away from sex with Kyra. Tomorrow night wasn't that far away. Then he could turn his fantasies into reality.

But the next picture that rose up in his mind was the sight of Kyra and Petra sitting on the love seat, chatting. What the hell was his mother trying to accomplish? If she thought Petra would somehow eclipse Kyra, she was dead wrong. Kyra was so strong, so wise, so sexy—his mind began to wander again so he pulled it up short. Beside her, Petra seemed shallow and bland.

He'd been fooled by Petra's exotic beauty and her outward poise at first, just like everyone else. However, Petra was nothing but a pretty facade that covered a boundless concern for herself and her image.

Kyra was a woman of depths and passion.

His gaze traced over the tilt of her head propped on her hand, the crescent of her eyelashes against her smooth cheeks, her generous mouth, and the curve of her breasts under the lace, before slipping down her legs to the subtle nude polish on her toenails. He'd heard his mother make a snarky comment about Kyra's clothes coming from Macy's, but he admired her the more for looking exquisite without having to pay exorbitant prices for clothes.

A sudden movement drew his gaze back up to her face. She must have fallen asleep, and her chin had slipped off her hand. Now she blinked dazedly in the sunlight slanting through the window.

He leaned forward to touch her knee. "Tilt the seat back so you can sleep," he said. "You've had a rough day."

She gave him that slightly crooked smile he had come to enjoy. "I didn't run into my ex-fiancée."

"But I knew all the guests at the party and you met them all for the first time."

Schuyler nodded. "You should have pushed him overboard when you had the chance on the *Royal Wave*. It would have been fitting punishment for dragging you into the family drama."

Kyra raised her hand to cover a yawn. "I think all the fresh air made me sleepy. I'm used to nice, unhealthy pollution. Keeps you alert."

"Fresh air?" His sister raised her eyebrows. "I thought it was all the, um, *exercise.*"

"Schuyler." Will shot her a warning look.

She smirked at him. "If you disappear for several hours with your lovely date, people know what you're doing. And they're envious."

Kyra made a choking sound as color glowed in her cheeks. Her gaze met Will's. "She called me lovely so I'm okay with it."

Schuyler laughed. "You should keep her, Will."

Chapter 8

Kyra found room for the last bunch of carrots in one of the Carver's Center's mismatched refrigerators. The kids called Mondays "veggie day" with varying degrees of enthusiasm because in the morning, Kyra made the rounds of local grocery stores, which donated fresh produce that hadn't sold over the weekend. She would sort through it, choosing things that would last another day and cooking the rest before it wilted. In her opinion, these were the most interesting meals of the week because they required creativity to entice the kids into eating them. And they allowed her to stretch her food budget. Thank goodness she'd helped her old boss with ordering at the restaurant back in Macungie. He'd taught her how to combine inexpensive ingredients to make food that tasted gourmet.

Today she was making veggie pizzas. Turn anything into a pizza and the kids would fall on it like ravening wolves. She had dumped her piles of vegetables in the sink and begun to wash them when Emily Wade walked in with her habitual mug of coffee.

"Oh, good," Kyra said. "I have your jewelry to return. It was perfect for the party. Made me feel like a million bucks."

"I'm so glad." Emily settled on a stool at the island. "Tell me about the party. Was it fun?"

Kyra dried her hands on a dish towel as she considered how to answer that. "Not fun, but fascinating. For one thing, we flew up there in a helicopter." She slid onto a stool opposite Emily's. "Of course you're probably accustomed to traveling like that."

"Not really. It still seems extravagant to me."

"The farm Will grew up on is amazing. Horses and formal gardens and a swimming pool. He has a golf cart that looks like a Ferrari from when he was a kid."

"It's hard to imagine that kind of life," Emily said. "Max didn't grow up rich."

"I don't think it was as magical as it looks. There's a lot of family tension." Kyra made a wry face as she thought of her own mother. "Of course, we poor families have plenty of that, too. But it kind of depresses me that all that beauty and breeding doesn't make people behave better."

"What about Will? Did you enjoy his company after all these years?" Emily watched her over the rim of her mug as she took a sip.

Kyra swallowed a laugh. She'd enjoyed him all right. "We got along so well that we're having dinner together—alone—tonight."

"I'm so glad. Sometimes the second time around is better because you have a shared history."

"You would know." Emily had met her fiancé, Max, eight years before, when he was a newly graduated PhD working as a civilian consultant with the Marine Corps. But she'd been happily married to another man then, and Max had never let on that he was in love with her—Emily had no idea. But Emily's husband, a captain in the Marines, had been killed in action four years ago, so when she and Max reconnected last Christmas, he had wooed her into marrying him. Everyone at the center felt Emily deserved to be happy, and Max certainly did a good job of that.

In fact, he was slated to be officially inducted as a director on the center's board next week, and Kyra was planning a splurge buffet of special hors d'oeuvres to celebrate.

"What do you think of Will now?" Emily asked. "Has he changed?"

She thought Will had an incredible body and very skillful hands, but that wasn't appropriate to share with her boss. She flattened her palms on the stainless steel countertop. "I'd guess it's a little like your Max. I knew Will when he was a college student. Now he runs a billion-dollar company. That kind of power and responsibility has to change you, but I don't understand in what ways yet." She shrugged. "Being at a large party with people you've never met before isn't the best venue for getting to know someone better."

Emily smiled. "I'm glad you're giving him a chance."

"I feel like it's more that he's giving me a chance." Kyra shook her head. "He's handsome and rich and charming and smart. He could have any woman he wants."

And a woman he didn't want. Petra still threw a shadow over Will, whether he acknowledged it or not.

"But he chose you to take to a family party. That says something."

"It says that he wanted someone undemanding so there would be no extra stress."

"I don't think that's the only reason he asked you," Emily said. "But I'll let you figure that out for yourself."

Kyra jumped off the stool. "Let me get your jewelry. That way I won't be nervous about losing it any longer."

She retrieved the velvet bag from the half-empty cereal box in the pantry where she'd stashed it, checking that all three pieces were still there.

"I appreciate your trusting me with these," Kyra said, as she placed the bag carefully on the counter beside Emily.

"Feel free to borrow them any time." Emily dropped the bag in her blazer pocket and stood. "Diego says Shaq's new diet is a success. Thank you again for cooking for a whole new species."

"It wasn't much of a challenge as far as taste buds go. That dog will eat anything. But I'm happy that it helped his digestion settle down."

"You'll probably get more requests for custom dog food." Emily looked concerned. "Every kid thinks his or her dog is special."

"I don't mind since the dogs don't complain about the menu," Kyra said. "I'm already working on how to get canned pumpkin by the case because Diego says it would help all the K-9 Angelz."

"Don't feel obligated to do that. You've already found so many innovative ways to stretch the food budget. I don't know how you do it."

"Honestly, it's an interesting task. Many of the local merchants *want* to help out the center, so this is the perfect way for them to do that without having to part with cash that they can't really afford to give up. It's a win-win." Kyra wrinkled her nose. "I sound like some kind of obnoxious MBA."

"You sound dedicated and passionate, two qualities I treasure in the folks who work here." Emily gave her a brief hug and left Kyra to her pizza making.

Unfortunately, the repetitive washing and chopping allowed her mind to drift, and as always it chose Will as its destination.

There had been no opportunity to talk about what had happened between them because of Schuyler's presence. Maybe that was for the best. Kyra needed time to absorb the sudden intimacy of their relationship and the fact that Will wanted to see her again.

She felt out of her depth, especially now that she'd had a glimpse into Will's personal world. It was a long way from her family's tiny prefab ranch house in the sticks of Pennsylvania, where her father worked in the Mack Trucks factory and her mother was a part-time school secretary. Not that her childhood had been hard in the material sense, but she had no need for a fancy golf cart to tool around the family estate.

Did growing up with Will's kind of privilege make him a different person? He had seemed so approachable in college. It was only his extraordinary attractiveness that appeared to set him above her then. Now that she'd seen where he came from, the distance between them looked like the Grand Canyon. Not to mention the fact that he was insanely wealthy, a feat he'd accomplished by himself.

Damn, he was intimidating.

She would be crazy to think he wanted anything more than some fun sex from her, no matter what Emily said. Kyra wished she could do casual because, God knows, the sex had been terrific. But for her, physical intimacy always led to emotional involvement. Since she had been halfway in love with Will in college, it would be all too easy to fall down that rabbit hole now.

And when he dumped her—very politely, of course—it would hurt like hell. Why set herself up for the certainty of that kind of pain? She had enough stress between juggling two jobs and reducing her debt. Sometimes she was too exhausted even to read, her greatest and most affordable pleasure. No, she needed to stay focused, instead of day-dreaming about what might have been.

Her cell phone dinged with an arriving text. She glanced down at the screen. Despite telling herself not to feel this way, excitement flooded her veins just from seeing Will's name on her phone.

Would Perseus suit you for dinner tonight? I owe you food without tension.

Because billionaires could get reservations at the city's hottest and most expensive restaurant any time they wanted them. Proving every-thing she'd been thinking about their lack of common ground was true. So why was she smiling at her phone like a besotted idiot.

A thought struck her and she typed: Isn't it closed on Mondays?

There was a pause before his text came back. No. Are we on?

yes I said yes I will Yes. She'd never actually read *Ulysses*, but one of her English professors liked to quote it at odd moments.

Ah, now you've got my mind moving in an interesting direction. I'll pick you up at 7.

She Googled the entire quotation from *Ulysses* and discovered that it was a seduction scene. Well, that worked for her.

Perseus was fancy, which made Kyra decide to go with black. So what if it was spring and the city was bursting with color? In New York, black was the standard for every season.

She had two little black dresses—one for summer, one for winter. She pulled out the summer one, a close-fitting column dress overlaid with black cotton lace, along with a pair of high-heeled black sandals, whose tiny straps crisscrossed her feet and ankles in a way that added a little edge to the ensemble. She rooted through her underwear drawer to find her barely-there black silk-and-lace lingerie. She might have to say good-bye to Will after tonight, but there was no reason not to enjoy herself one last time.

After dressing, she piled her hair up on top of her head in a series of complex twists to add some sophistication. She hoped. Out of all the jewelry her mother had ordered during her television shopping binges, Kyra had kept one pair of real pearl-and-gold chandelier earrings. They'd served her well in the city so she fastened them to her earlobes, tilting her head to make them dance. She added a turquoise silk stole that a friend had brought her from India and nodded at herself in the mirror.

The labels might not say Chanel or Versace, but she looked darned good. At the very least, she wouldn't embarrass herself or Will.

When the limo pulled up in front of her building, she was peering out the small barred window set in the front door. As Will emerged from the car, the low-slanting rays of the late-day sun set his hair agleam and outlined his face and shoulders in a rim of gold.

How could a man be so beautiful yet so entirely masculine?

Maybe it was the way his gray suit highlighted the breadth of his shoulders. Or the powerful motion of his long stride. It could be the sharp planes of his face that seemed sculpted in stone. Or how he carried himself with a confidence that came close to arrogance without ever crossing that boundary.

Her question to herself had been rhetorical, an excuse to drink him in as he crossed the sidewalk and trod lightly up the steps to her door. She swung it open before he could ring the bell. No reason to alert her kind but very inquisitive landlady to Will's presence. Although the limo was pretty conspicuous in this neighborhood.

Will's attention was focused on her as she walked through the door and pulled it shut behind her. His eyes were lit by the same sunshine that set his hair ablaze. He took her shoulders and held her away from him for a moment, his gaze traveling over her face, before bending to kiss her on the mouth in a way that made her want to drag him up the three flights of stairs to her bedroom.

When he lifted his head, he said, "'She walks in beauty, like the night.'"

The kiss had seared through her all the way down to her toes, and they curled into the soles of her sandals. That was bad. "Byron? Really?" she scoffed to remind herself that she shouldn't go there.

"Sometimes he got it right," Will said, unruffled by her lack of appreciation for his compliment.

"As I recall, the poem goes downhill rapidly after that first line."

Will thought for a minute. "'All that's best of dark and bright meet in her aspect and her eyes' isn't so bad. But after that first stanza I can't argue with you."

"Byron's more my time period than yours. The Romans didn't have anything you could use?"

His eyes burned hotter. "Catullus is for later tonight."

"No quoting in foreign languages."

He smiled with a slow, sensual curve of his lips. "I'll make sure you understand every word I'm saying." He slid his arm around her waist. "But dinner first."

As she scooted across the seat of the limo, his words about her being spread naked across the leather popped into her head. That made liquid heat pool low inside her.

When Will folded himself onto the seat beside her and closed the car door, the air in the dim, enclosed space seemed to vibrate with desire. But he did nothing more than take her hand, holding it on the seat between them. "I don't want yesterday's unpleasant moments to color tonight, so I will apologize only once for my family. It is, however, a sincere apology."

Kyra gave his fingers a reassuring squeeze. "I never hold people responsible for their parents." Although as she knew all too well, others did.

He kissed the back of her hand and released it. "Another reason I like you." Reaching into his breast pocket, he pulled out a business card and pen. "Before I get distracted, will you give me the Carver Center's phone number?"

Kyra took the card and jotted Emily's direct line on the back of it. "You and Farr weren't just being polite about coming to visit?"

"Why would you think that?" Will sounded almost offended.

"Because we were at a party making conversation." When Farr had found out she worked at the Carver Center, he had surprised her by questioning her at length about its programs. Will explained that Farr was chairman of the Thalia Foundation, the charitable organization Cronus Holdings funded, and he was on the lookout for worthy new projects to support.

"Farr is always serious when money is involved," Will said.

"Good to know." Kyra handed the card back to Will. "Our director will be delighted to show you the facility."

Will frowned. "You'll join us, too."

"Sure, but Emily is the driving force behind the center. She's the one who can answer all your questions and tell you what the center needs." But glee danced through her at the thought that Will wanted her on the tour.

He relaxed back against the seat, stretching out his long legs so she could see his whimsical socks. Today they were navy blue, dotted with tiny sailboats. She sucked in her breath as she wondered if he had been thinking of yesterday's tryst on the *Royal Wave*.

"That reminds me of the dog food project," Will said, squashing her little hum of sexual speculation. "Has it been declared a success?"

"A resounding one. I've been warned that I may be pressed into developing more custom canine cuisine." Kyra grinned. "Every kid thinks their dog deserves special treatment."

He didn't return her smile. "Won't that add to your workload?"

"Not so much. Dog food is pretty simple stuff. The hardest part is always the budget. I'm working on a source for low-cost canned pumpkin because it turns out all the dogs would benefit from adding that to their food."

"I can help you with that. I could even find you organic pumpkin."

She felt herself becoming more entangled in Will's world and knew she couldn't agree for her own peace of mind. "That's really nice but I have to run it by Emily. She likes to use local sources."

"Ceres is committed to using local sources as well." Once again she seemed to have offended him.

"Right, I know that. I meant really local, as in South Harlem."

"Ah, I understand." The edge of affront faded from his voice. "That makes it more of a challenge but I'll see what I can do."

Kyra sighed. She should have remembered that Will could not be stopped once he fixed on a goal.

"I have some ideas for other flavors in dog food for sensitive stomachs," Will continued.

She could hear the fervor in his voice. He'd devoted serious thought to the topic. She felt a flush of pleasure that he'd focused his considerable mental resources on her problem. "Let's hear them," she said.

For the rest of the trip, they discussed dog food. When the limo pulled into an underground garage and came to a stop, Will made a wry face. "I guess that wasn't the most romantic topic of conversation."

"There's nothing more romantic than solving a problem for someone you care about." She might be going out on a limb with that last part.

He traced his index finger along the side of her face. "You're an unusual woman." Then he leaned in and kissed her, a promise that he would do more soon.

They stepped off the elevator into a burgundy-carpeted lounge with huge glass windows that framed a view of Central Park. The taupe velvet sofas and chairs were empty and there was no sound of conversation. Only the mouth-watering scent of food drifted through the air.

"This way," Will said, guiding her across the lounge and through a glass-and-steel door.

"Mr. Chase, Ms. Dixon." The maître d', a young man dressed in a fitted black suit, stepped from behind his podium. "Welcome to Perseus, Ms. Dixon. It's a pleasure to have you back, Mr. Chase. Please follow me."

Kyra's suspicions were confirmed as they entered a soaring space filled with beautifully set but unoccupied tables. She halted. "It *is* closed tonight."

"Not if you know the chef," Will said.

"There was no need to do this," Kyra said to Will. "We could have gone somewhere else."

"I wanted to take you to the best restaurant in New York," Will said. "You deserve it after yesterday."

She flashed back to the sailboat again. "Yesterday wasn't all bad," she said with a half smile.

No matter how much he'd paid to have it opened just for them, Kyra couldn't help feeling bad about the staff who counted on their day of rest. She treasured her free Monday evenings, although she always volunteered to work when there was a special event at Stratus, so she supposed some employees here might be in a similar situation. She turned to the maître d'. "I'm sorry you had to come in on your day off."

"I'm happy to be here," the man said, his tone earnest. "Mr. Chase has been most generous."

"Everyone is here voluntarily. Relax and enjoy it," Will said in a way that reminded her he was a CEO who was accustomed to being in command.

He moved her toward a table for two set right in front of the window. Two huge arrangements of flowers graced stands on either side, their fragrance mingling with the food's, while an array of white pillar candles flickered on the taupe linen tablecloth. Will took Kyra's chair from the maître d' and waited for her to sit.

As she took her place, he whispered beside her ear, "M. F. K. Fisher said that sharing food with another human being is an intimate act. I wanted our first dinner to be perfect . . . and private."

The flutter of his breath on her cheek and the purr of his words made her shiver with desire. "It's not exactly private." She gestured to the wall of glass beside their table. Below it, a swirling kaleidoscope of taxis, pedestrians, and horse-drawn carriages ebbed and surged along the avenue that edged the leafy, green park.

Will seated himself in the chair across from her with a wicked glint in his eyes. "No one ever looks up."

She was sure he wouldn't really do anything improper in the restaurant, but it still made flickers of heat lick along her skin to imagine it.

The sommelier arrived with a bottle of vintage champagne, displayed the label to Will, and then removed the cork with a muted pop. The sparkling wine spilled into the tall, slender flutes like flowing sunlight. When she picked up her glass, Will stretched his arm across the table to touch his flute to hers. "'Champagne! In victory one deserves it, in defeat one needs it.'"

"I like that one. Who said it?"

"Napoleon, who experienced the extremes of victory and defeat in his lifetime."

"Which one are we drinking to now?"

"Survival," Will said, before he lifted the glass to his lips and took a long swallow.

Kyra sipped the fizzing liquid and closed her eyes. The champagne tasted like sunlight, too: bright, vibrant, and golden. "Champagne always seems celebratory to me."

"We are celebrating the fact that there are three hundred sixty-four days before the next Spring Fling," Will said. "That makes this the best day of the year."

"Seriously, if you hate it so much, schedule a trip to Hong Kong next spring," Kyra said, holding up the glass to watch the miniscule bubbles drawing lines straight up through the champagne.

"As the guests were leaving yesterday, Mum handed out 'save the date' cards for next year."

"Then schedule an *emergency* business trip to Hong Kong."

Will bit out a startled laugh. "Ceres doesn't have a presence there."

"You have a year to build one." Kyra lowered her glass to look at him. "It's just a party. Not a wedding or a funeral."

"For my mother, it's a command performance."

Kyra considered whether she should voice her thoughts on this. With a tiny shrug, she went ahead. "In my opinion, your mother gave up the right to expect your presence when she ambushed you with Petra. Since you specifically asked that Petra not be included and your mother flouted that request, she has expressed her disregard for your wishes. Therefore you are free to disregard hers."

"You're the one who should have been the lawyer," Will said.

She shook her head. "If your parents don't respect your boundaries, you have to enforce them somehow."

"Did yours?"

Kyra took a large swallow of the champagne. She didn't want to discuss her parents, but she owed Will some part of the truth because it might help him. "My father was old-school blue collar. He felt that mothers should guide their daughters because that was woman stuff, so he didn't intervene much in my life. If he'd had a son, he would have been involved with him. That's just the way Pop was."

"And your mother?" Will leaned back in his chair, but pinned her with his gaze.

Just then the maître d' and two waiters arrived, presenting small plates of oysters in their shells. "Our amuse-bouche is Kiwa oysters with green apple mignonette, green apple foam, radish, and pink peppercorns. Bon appétit!" the maître d' said in hushed, mellifluous tones.

Relieved by the interruption, Kyra picked up one of the two oyster shells from the bed of salt on her plate. First she inhaled, catching the apple scent. Then she held the shell to her lips and sucked the oyster into her mouth. It had a velvety texture, a fresh burst of brine, and then an almost coppery aftertaste, accented by the burn of pepper. Swallowing, she opened her eyes wide. "Wow! That was intense."

"They're from New Zealand," Will said, his lips closing over the end of the shell before he drew the oyster in.

She couldn't tear her eyes away from his mouth, remembering the way he'd licked his fingers after he'd made her come in the Jaguar. Desire slithered through her, flicking at her nipples before coiling between her thighs, and the sailboats on his socks glided through her mind.

"You didn't like it?" Will asked, gesturing toward the oyster remaining on her plate.

"No, no, I just wanted to give myself time to absorb the flavor." She scooped up the second oyster, which was covered in a cloud of pale gold foam atop a paper-thin slice of radish. The alternate flavor accents gave the oyster's intensity a different twist. "Amazing," she said, placing the empty shell back on the plate.

Once again she watched Will's mouth touch the shell, imagining his lips on her. She shifted on her chair as the wanting pulsed inside her.

This meal was going to be torture if every time he put food in his mouth, she thought of what else that mouth might be doing. She finished off her champagne and put the empty glass on the table. Before the sommelier could approach, Will twisted the champagne bottle out of its silver bucket and refilled her flute.

Waiters whisked their plates away, leaving the tablecloth clear for a new dish to be served.

"Prawn and avocado roulade," the maître d' explained. The waiters set down white plates showcasing a beautifully rich, green cylinder of layered avocado slices with a garnish of leaves and tiny yellow flowers. She cut into it and brought a forkful to her mouth. The flavors were cool, smooth, and subtle. "Mmm, unbelievable," she murmured, slicing off the next bite.

"So how well did your mother respect your boundaries?" Will asked. Clearly, the fantastic food was old hat to him because he chewed and swallowed without a noticeable reaction.

She grimaced. "Not well at all. She didn't want me to go to college because it meant I wouldn't be home to keep her company while Dad worked the late shift. But she did sign the financial aid forms for my application, so I give her credit for that." As it turned out, her mother was all too willing to sign financial forms that involved Kyra.

Will refilled his own glass and settled back in his chair, waiting.

Kyra gave in. "Once I left, she hated my absence. Every phone call, she did her best to persuade me to come home. Sometimes it was an enticement, like a trip somewhere with her, but more often she wielded guilt. She missed me so much, was so lonely without me. Her friends didn't understand her." Kyra felt the pinch of guilt even now. "Those were the phone calls that made me cook gourmet meals. I had to work off the terrible stew of emotions that she stirred up."

She'd learned how cooking warded off stress in Macungie. The chef at the restaurant where she worked let her chop all his vegetables when she came in fretting about something her mother had done. Slashing a razor-sharp knife through crisp veggies worked wonders.

She took a gulp of champagne before she looked at Will. "I held out for two years, knowing that this was my only chance to become myself."

"And then your father got sick." Will's voice was gentle with understanding.

The familiar sadness and loss welled in her chest. "Lung cancer. He'd smoked all his life. I wanted to be there for him, so I stayed home as long as he lived. My mother couldn't cope with his illness, and she leaned on me heavily. I always felt like I wasn't doing enough for either one of them. Now I understand that it was a lot to expect of a nineteen-year-old."

Will stretched his arm out on the table with his hand palm up. She put hers in it and found a surprising comfort in the warm, strong cage of his fingers.

"That's a lot to expect of anyone at any age," he said. "No wonder you're so strong."

"I didn't feel strong. I felt exhausted and wrung out. A failure." She'd never admitted that to anyone else. "After Pop died, I wanted to go to bed and sleep for about a month. But my mother needed me."

She took a deep breath. "I wrote the date that Brunell started again the following year on my calendar. Every time I thought I was going to collapse under the weight of her demands, I pulled out the calendar and counted how many months were left. Then it was weeks. I never got down to days because Mother was diagnosed with breast cancer." She still remembered how guilty she felt, because after she'd cried with her mother at the terror of the news, she'd cried for herself that she would never go back to Brunell.

"You had to put your dreams on hold again," Will said.

"I gave up on my dreams." Or maybe that had come later, when she'd discovered all the credit card bills her mother had accumulated in her efforts to ward off the terror of her impending death.

"We all need dreams," he said. "Or life becomes drudgery."

Her dream was to write "paid in full" on all her mother's debts. Then she could begin to build her own life again. She shook her head. "I'm happy. I have two good jobs and a cozy place to live. What more does anyone need?"

He raised his eyebrows. "Some people might find that satisfying."

"And I'm one of them." She said it firmly so that he knew the topic was closed on her end. "What's *your* dream? You've already become a titan of industry."

He picked up a clean fork and twirled it between his fingers, his gaze on the spinning tines. "That was never my dream. It was just a giant middle finger to my father and the law."

"Interesting motivation, but it carried you to the top."

"But now that I'm there"—he lifted his eyes to hers, letting her see the dissatisfaction in them—"the top feels empty. Because it was not my real destination."

"The good news is that you can do anything you want to now. You have all the resources."

"I'm responsible for thousands of people's jobs in multiple countries. I can't just walk away."

"You have a management team, don't you? Can't they run the company?"

His lips curled in a dark smile. "No one's irreplaceable? Of course they can and do run the company day to day. They just can't grow it. I have access to the financial resources. And companies are like great white sharks . . . if they aren't moving, they die." He flipped the fork again. "I'm trying to get Cronus Holdings into a position where the cash flow will fund future expansion. It's just not there yet."

"But you have a plan." In some ways, his predicament wasn't all that different from hers. It was just on a much larger scale.

"Several," he said. "But they take time, and I find myself suddenly impatient."

"Why suddenly?"

She was annoyed by the interruption as another course was served.

"Chicken poached with black truffle and asparagus," the maître d' intoned.

The rich, earthy aroma of truffles caught her attention, and she closed her eyes to inhale the expensive fragrance.

"You know truffles are considered an aphrodisiac." Will's voice held a note of provocation.

She opened her eyes to find his gaze focused on her. "Did you request that they be included on the menu?" she asked.

"I don't need an aphrodisiac when I'm with you."

"Aphrodisiacs aren't just for men." Arousal rippled through her but it had nothing to do with food. She took a bite of the chicken and groaned out loud as the tender poultry melted in her mouth and released a cloud of earthy, sexy truffle. "This is so good I never want to eat anything else for the rest of my life."

"The chef will be very disappointed since there are eight more courses with the appropriate wines to come." He took his own first taste and nodded. "I see what you mean."

Kyra ate another bite, enjoying it just as much as the first. "It's hard to concentrate on conversation when the food is so distractingly delicious. However, I haven't forgotten my question."

"I haven't either. I'm just not sure I want to answer it." His tone was dry.

"Aha! A secret to pry out of you. Let me think of what leverage I might have." She dipped her fingertip in the small smear of sauce that remained on her plate and licked the exquisite flavor from her skin. It was so good, she forgot that she was teasing him and did it again.

"Stop!" he commanded. "Unless you don't want to taste any more courses."

She looked at him to find his jaw tight and his gaze fastened on her mouth. She ran her tongue over her lips and was rewarded by a guttural noise deep in his throat. "Will you answer my question?"

"That depends on what I'll get for it," he said.

She'd had too much champagne. That was the only explanation for the thought that struck her and the fact that she spoke it out loud. She leaned toward him and dropped her voice. "If you answer honestly, I'll go to the ladies' room, take off my panties, and slip them in your pocket on my way back to my seat."

She heard him inhale sharply. Then his eyelids hooded the blaze in his eyes. "Who judges whether my answer is honest?"

"I do." She gave him a sidelong smile.

"That seems like a conflict of interest, but I'm counting on your integrity."

"Okay, let's hear it." She wasn't sure what she expected, but she figured it would be interesting.

"You."

She straightened in her chair. "Wait, what?"

"*You* make me impatient."

"That requires clarification." She had no idea what he was going to say next.

"You reminded me of my younger self. Before I became a titan of industry." He repeated her phrase with an edge of sarcasm. "Before I made the decision to sell out."

127

"You didn't sell out."

He waved a hand in dismissal. "I won't deny that I enjoyed the challenge of building Ceres but it wasn't my passion. You've made that clear to me."

"I have?"

"You fought for what you wanted against the most difficult of opponents. Your parents."

"You didn't go to law school."

"No, but what I did, I did to impress my father, to show him I could succeed without him. I was still playing by his rules, following his definition of success." He leaned in. "You didn't allow your parents to warp your vision."

"But you won. I lost."

"You made it to Brunell for two years. That is a victory."

All she'd been able to see was the debt it had added to her suffocating load, but maybe he wasn't completely wrong. Those two years at college had opened the world to her. If she hadn't left Macungie before her parents fell ill, she might never have considered living anywhere else. Brunell had given her the idea of striking out for the big city . . . and the confidence to take the risk.

Her world seemed to tilt and then right itself, but with a new perspective, one where she saw herself as a bold adventurer rather than as a debt-ridden failure. She had gotten herself out of Macungie. She had survived in one of the world's most demanding cities. She was eating dinner with a billionaire CEO.

"Thank you," she said, feeling dizzy with a sense of her own power. "I needed that."

Now she just had to hold on to this new idea of herself.

"No matter what success I claim for myself, I began with more than most people. You remind me that if a dream was easy, it wouldn't be worth dreaming." Will dropped his gaze to his hands where they lay

128

on the table. "I have too many regrets. It's time to replace them with new dreams."

The waiters arrived with a new course, and Kyra was reminded that this conversation had started as a sort of dare. Somehow it had turned into something real, something that had changed her.

She'd missed most of what the maître d' said, retaining only that it involved lobster, which was fine with her.

As soon the waiters left, Will leaned forward. "I believe I upheld my end of the bargain."

His eyes glittered hotter than the candle flames, and she sucked in a breath. She'd never done anything like this before. The idea had come from a story her fellow bartender, Cleo, had told her late one night when they were cleaning up. Kyra had thought it sounded hot and sophisticated, but she'd never imagined a situation where she might carry it out in reality. However, a deal was a deal.

"Your answer lacked specific detail but it was honest," Kyra said, putting her napkin on the table and picking up her purse. "I'll be back in a few minutes. If you eat my lobster, you forfeit the panties."

Will laughed, a low rasp of amusement and anticipation. "I won't even eat my own until you return."

She stood and glanced around to see where the restrooms might be. The maître d' glided over immediately. "The ladies' room?" he asked. When she nodded, he turned toward the lounge. "I'll show you."

The bathroom was in keeping with the restaurant. Every detail was subtle but beautiful. The sinks were square white bowls set on a counter made of a gray stone with white veins. The hand towels were white linen embroidered with a snake-haired woman, Medusa, the Gorgon Perseus had killed. She smiled at the thought that Will would appreciate the mythological reference.

Each toilet was enclosed in a spacious stall tiled from floor to ceiling with a mosaic of silver, gray, and taupe glass squares. She walked into one and locked the door, then laughed at herself. She was the only one who would be using this ladies' room tonight. She bunched her dress up to her hips and hooked her fingers into her panties, pulling them down so they dropped to her ankles. Bracing her hand against the wall, she lifted one foot and then the other to free the black lace.

Fortunately, the fabric was flimsy and there wasn't much of it, so she could crumple it up in one fist.

She unlocked the door and walked out to stand in front of the full-length mirror, smoothing her dress down over her thighs. Nothing in her reflected image betrayed the fact that she wasn't wearing panties, but she felt so naked that she was sure anyone who looked at her would figure it out somehow.

"Only if they have X-ray vision," she reassured her image. But Will would know. She would be sitting across the table from him, but he would know that if she opened her thighs, nothing covered her.

A wave of desire and nerves washed through her, leaving her skin flushed. She blotted her face with one of the fancy towels, repainted her lips, and washed her hands.

There was no other reason to delay, so she smoothed her skirt down one more time before picking up her purse and the panties and pulling open the bathroom door.

The stretchy cotton fabric of her dress seemed to caress her bare buttocks with every step she took. As she walked from the lounge into the restaurant, she made the mistake of looking at Will. He sat sideways in his chair, his gaze locked on her as she came toward him.

It seemed as though he could see right through her dress to her nakedness underneath. She felt the flush rising on her skin again, but it was heady and thrilling this time. She could imagine his hand between her legs, the way it had been in the Jaguar. She felt a tiny surge of liquid heat on the insides of her upper thighs.

Now she had to get the panties into his jacket pocket. She hadn't thought through the logistics of how to manage that under the watchful eye of the maître d'.

But Will was ever a gentleman. As she approached, he stood and came around to pull out her chair. When she was beside him, he turned to put his body between her and the rest of the room. He even held his pocket flap open, so she could easily slip in the handful of lace.

"I admire a woman who pays her debts," he said, waiting for her to sit down before he pushed in her chair.

For the rest of the multicourse meal, he never said another word about their dare. However, every now and then he slid his left hand into his pocket. She could tell by the flex of his wrist that he was rubbing the lace between his fingers. Which sent a phantom touch between her legs.

The dinner passed in a sensual haze of delicious flavors on her tongue and embers of desire glowing low in her body. Watching Will across the table—the drama of his jewel-green eyes, the waves of his hair glinting with candlelight, the shadow painting the cleft in his chin, the shift of muscles under the drape of his suit—everything twined together and coiled inside her. When Perseus's celebrity chef came out to meet her, Kyra could barely put a coherent compliment together because her brain was so fogged by wanting.

And then they were walking through the lounge on the way to the limo, Will carrying in one hand a box of tiny pastries that neither one of them had the patience to stay and eat. The other hand rested on the small of her back just above the curve of her bottom. She felt it like a brand, burning through her dress to spread heat where she wore nothing at all.

The elevator doors closed and Kyra waited, expecting his hand to drift lower.

"There's a security camera," he said, his voice tight. "Otherwise . . ."

She nodded, slanting a glance up to find him staring straight forward.

The doors opened and the limo stood right where it had dropped them. Will waved off the driver and opened the door for her. She slid across the seat, feeling every puff and roll stitched into the leather cushion as it brushed against the sensitized spot between her legs. Will folded himself into the car and tossed the box of sweets onto the facing seat without any care about damaging the exquisitely decorated confections.

"I thought we'd go to my house in Manhattan," he said. "I hope that's all right with you."

"I'd love to see it," she said, her desire ratcheting up at the thought of what they would do there.

"We'll wait if you want to, but . . ." He turned the burn of his gaze on her.

The limo's privacy screen made her bold. "No waiting," she said, curling her hand around the nape of his neck and pulling his mouth to hers.

His arms went around her, one cradling her head, one around her shoulders. As their mouths met, he lowered her slowly to the seat so she lay on her back with him braced over her. Freeing his hands, he skimmed one up her thigh, pushing her dress up with his wrist, and then his finger was sliding in her.

He moaned. "You're so ready."

She bucked and mewed a protest as he withdrew his hand.

"I need to be inside you," he said, yanking a condom out of his pocket and ripping the envelope open with his teeth.

She unbuckled his belt and unfastened his trousers, knowing that he watched her as she did it. When she pulled down his boxer briefs to free his cock, it sprang up hard and long. She circled her fingers around it and stroked once before he slapped the condom on. He bunched her dress up to her waist and settled between her thighs, positioning himself and then thrusting into her with one swift stroke.

"Yes-s-s-s," he hissed between clenched teeth, his head thrown back.

"Oh, dear God, yes!" she gasped as he finally filled the ache that had built to a near scream inside her.

And then he was moving, fast and hard, so she had to brace her hand against the door to keep her head from slamming into it. She wrapped her legs around his waist to give him a better angle, and his speed accelerated. The scuff of fine wool against her inner thighs added an extra touch of friction to the overload of sensations.

She felt the first ripple of orgasm, tried to fight it off, but his rhythm was relentless. As her inner muscles clenched, he growled. Then her insides exploded, gripping and releasing him as he drove her climax to another peak and another. Then he went still and, with a wrench of her name from his throat, pumped into her, flexing his hips to hold himself deep.

Time suspended itself as she lay under him, the glow of her orgasm suffusing every inch of her body from her fingertips to her toes. He softened inside her, but still neither of them moved, the only sound, their breath slowly changing from panting to normal.

Finally, he slid out of her and sat up to dispose of the condom. She drew in her legs and pulled her dress down over her thighs.

He offered her his hand to sit up. "You could have stayed right where you were and I wouldn't have complained."

"I felt a little exposed." But her insides were still pulsing with remembered pleasure.

"Exactly how I like you." He looped an arm around her waist to scoot her against his side.

She snuggled into him, sliding one hand under his jacket so she could feel his heart beating against her palm. "There's nothing like having an eight-course dinner as foreplay."

"You are the world's most delicious dessert," he said, his mouth moving against her temple before he kissed her.

She considered pointing out that he hadn't actually tasted her but decided that might be interpreted as a challenge. Right now she needed time to come down from the intensity of their joining. "I'd put you right up there with chocolate soufflé slathered with fresh whipped cream," she said instead.

"Now you've given me an idea." He nuzzled her temple again.

"Not an original one."

He laughed and settled back against the seat.

"Where do you live?" she asked, too lazy to look out the window to see where they were going.

"East Sixty-Ninth Street. Off Fifth Avenue."

"Exactly where you'd expect a billionaire to live. A penthouse?"

"Just a house."

She laughed. "In Manhattan, that's even more amazing than a penthouse. Do you have a garden? That's what I miss most about living here, having my own bit of the outdoors. One of my favorite things about the Carver Center is the empty lot next door that they recently bought. It's been turned into a garden–slash–doggy playground. The kids adore it."

"Then I shall take you to the garden first thing." He was quiet a moment. "I think that's one reason I bought the house. After growing up on the farm, I needed the outdoors, too."

"Well, your penthouse could have had a terrace with planters full of trees and flowers."

"Not the same. I need to feel the earth under my feet."

"All I need is sunlight on my face. Sometimes I sit on my fire escape but it's not very comfortable."

A few more minutes and the limousine pulled over to the curb.

"Um, may I have my undies back before I get out of the car?" Kyra asked.

He drew the little bundle of lace out of his pocket and let it dangle from his fingertips. "Only because I will enjoy removing them again later."

Chapter 9

Kyra stood on the sidewalk, gaping at his house. "I know what else appealed to you about this place," she said. "It's the antithesis of Arion Farm."

He looked at his home as though he'd never seen it before. "I thought it was just a bold statement."

"Exactly. A bold statement that you are totally different from your parents."

The house stood in a row of beaux arts townhomes with ornately embellished facades. His, however, was starkly modern, an outlier of straight, clean lines with no decoration other than its elegant proportions, glowing windows, and the surface that was flecked with some material that picked up glints of light from the streetlamps.

"It's beautiful in a totally different way," she said. "What is the glittery stuff?"

"Quartz. The facade is terrazzo, concrete embedded with chips of marble and quartz and then polished smooth."

"Did you design it?"

"No, I bought it from a venture capitalist who moved to his own private island near Tenerife. He said the weather is perfect there all year round." He led her up the steps to the front door, a smooth slab of some warm, golden wood, which clicked open at a wave of his free hand.

"That's nifty," she said. "Like a magic wand."

"My very smart watch," he said, shaking back his cuff to show a simple stainless steel band.

"So you can just walk in your own front door with no worries. I thought rich people needed all kinds of security." Then she forgot about her question as they stepped into an entry space that glowed with light and a sense of soaring height because it was open all the way up to the ceiling of the second floor. A wood-and-glass staircase slashed up through the space in two bold flights, while a chandelier of crystal starbursts cascaded down from far above.

"Wow!" she said in a near whisper.

"You asked about security. I won't go into the details, but you are quite safe here, I promise."

She dragged her gaze away from his house and huffed out a laugh. "No one would bother to kidnap me. It was you I was worried about."

Something flickered across his face, a softening. "Very few people worry about me."

"Because you're rich? That doesn't make you any less human."

"Maybe it's because you knew me when I wasn't rich. Or less rich," he added with a wry smile. "Just a fellow student."

He had never been "just" anything to her. But she wasn't sharing that. He already had a dangerous hold on her feelings.

"Well, I'm pretty sure if a kidnapper shot you, you would bleed like the rest of us."

"You're right. Money can buy protection but not invulnerability." He shook his head. "Sometimes I forget that. And then I'm surprised when I feel pain."

He wasn't talking about physical pain now. She reached up to lay her hand against his cheek. "If you didn't, I would worry even more about you."

He lifted his hand to cover hers and stood like that for a moment, leaning his head lightly against her touch. Then he closed his fingers around hers and guided her past the staircase, through a hall with rooms opening off it on either side, and into an inviting living room, paneled in a pale blond wood on three walls while the fourth was all glass. In the light spilling out from it, she could see a patio that glittered like the house's facade, dotted with boxy modern wicker furniture with deep cushions, a fire pit, and what looked like a wall of copper with water streaming down it in sheets. Tree branches flickered in and out of the light as the breeze moved them, their shadows waltzing over the patio.

"My garden," Will said, heading for a sliding door.

As they passed through it, subtle lights glimmered to life around the patio, under the trees, within the fountain, and along paths winding through planted beds. "Fairyland," Kyra breathed, knowing her eyes were wide with the wonder of it.

"I seem to dwell in theme parks." Will's tone was amused.

"What?" She looked up to find him gazing down at her, the lights painting intriguing shadows over the angles of his face.

"You said Arion Farm was Disney World, and now we're in Fairyland."

"You're lucky to always be surrounded by beauty," she said. "Brunell was beautiful, too. Macungie, not so much."

"You never talked about it. Macungie."

She shrugged. "I wanted to leave it behind me when I was at college. I could become someone else. Actually, I felt like I was more truly myself at Brunell than at home. I didn't have to hide my brains because everyone at college was smart. I didn't have to hide my aspirations because everyone aspired, generally much higher than I did. I felt like I could unfurl myself there."

"'Unfurl yourself.' That's a good way of describing it. I thought of it more as throwing off the shackles but we both experienced a sense of freedom."

"I guess you can never go back." Kyra knew she sounded wistful. "It wouldn't be the same now. We're older and so much more experienced. The world no longer offers endless possibilities like it did then."

"Christ, we're not that old," Will said.

"Sometimes I feel ancient."

He took her shoulders and gave her the tiniest shake. "You have too much to offer the world to give up already."

She shook her head. "There's a lot you don't know."

"So tell me."

"My stories don't belong in Fairyland," she said. "There's no magic in them. Not even black magic."

"Kyra." His grip on her turned into a caress, his palms warm as they stroked up and down her bare upper arms. "*You* are magic, an enchantress."

"Back to Circe again, are we?"

"You see, that's what enchants me about you. Or one of the many things." He ran his hands up to frame her face as he bent to touch her lips with his. "This is another," he whispered against her mouth.

She was happy to avoid talking about her dingy home in industrial Pennsylvania, especially if the alternative was being kissed by Will. She threaded her hands through his hair at the nape of his neck, feeling the silky waves curling around her fingers. She rubbed her thumbs against the skin just above his collar, loving the soft, vulnerable texture as it curved over his muscles. She leaned into him, loving the pressure of him against her breasts, the contrast of hard and soft sparking little thrills that raced through her.

Then he was pulling her back into his house, striding into the hallway to a sliding wooden panel that revealed an elevator, the inside of which was embellished with the same wood. "My bedroom is on the fourth floor," he said, gesturing for her to precede him.

"Have you ever done it in the elevator?" Kyra asked with a grin as the car lifted upward.

"I'll take the Fifth on that," he said. And then the door was sliding open again.

"You'd have to be quick," she said, stepping onto the velvety carpeting of another hallway.

"There's always the emergency stop button. But I have something different in mind." He took her hand and led her into an enormous bedroom done in soft taupes and creams with rich, glossy brown wood furniture and trim. On one wall, flames flickered in a rectangular fireplace set in a surround of polished chocolate-colored granite. A king-size bed, covered in taupe linens so wrinkle free they looked almost military, backed up against a wall padded in a soft, slubby fabric. The bed faced a wall of glass that looked out onto a softly lit terrace.

"You keep a fire going all the time?" Kyra asked, although she loved the sense of cozy warmth it brought into the room.

"No, my watch told it I was coming, so it turned itself on."

"Can your watch turn down the bed?"

"I prefer to do that myself. Let me show you." He took her wrist and walked backward toward the bed, his thumb circling warm and firm in the center of her palm while his eyes picked up little gleams from the fire.

She went willingly, his touch on her palm setting up an echo between her legs. When they made it to the bed, he reached down with his free hand and ripped the coverlet and top sheet to nearly the foot. A wide expanse of cream linen invited her to hurl herself onto it.

"Turn around," he said. She did and felt his fingers at the zipper of her dress. It sang downward, and air brushed against her back. When he drew a line down her spine with his fingertip, she gasped and arched. He slipped his hands under the shoulders of her dress and eased it down over her arms and her hips where she gave a quick shimmy so it dropped to her feet.

His lips were on the side of her neck, and his hands were on her hips, pulling her bottom against him so she could feel the ridge of his erection. Then his hand was gliding over her stomach and underneath the front of her panties. He slipped between her thighs and slid a finger into the wet center of her. "Ahh," he said, his breath moist against her skin while he stroked in and out of her. That sent more heat and liquid around his questing finger, and she began to flex her hips in rhythm with him, making his erection swell harder.

She reached behind her, pushing her hand between them to massage his cock.

"Kyra," he breathed beside her ear and inserted a second finger inside her. The extra stretch and pressure made her moan in ecstasy and pushed her yearning higher.

"Not yet," he said, withdrawing his fingers and leaving her empty and wanting.

She let her head fall back against his shoulder. "It had better be soon."

He turned her in his arms, a feral smile baring his teeth. "Undress me like you did on the sailboat."

"Yes, sir." She yanked the knot out of his tie and ripped it out from under his collar. Then she jerked his jacket off his shoulders and down his arms before working loose the buttons of his shirt. The fabrics he wore were so rich and soft under her fingers that she wanted to caress them, but she needed him moving inside her more. She stripped him with swift, efficient movements until he stood naked, his skin glowing in the firelight.

"Now to finish the job I started," he said, unhooking her bra and dropping it on the floor. He cupped her breasts for a brief moment, his thumbs brushing over her hardened nipples before he stepped away. "You do your panties. I want to see what you looked like when you took them off in the ladies' room."

"I had more clothes on then," she said, but she watched his face grow taut as she deliberately worked the black lace down her hips and thighs with slow swaying movements. His gaze fastened between her legs as she let her panties fall to her ankles and stepped out of them.

Before she could react, he seized her by the waist and flipped her onto the bed, coming down beside her.

As Kyra caught her breath, Will rolled onto his back, bringing her over on top of him. "I want to watch you," he said.

She pushed herself up from his chest. "Watch me?"

"Above me," he said. He wrapped his fingers around her hips and shifted her onto his thighs. He reached up to pull out a drawer built into the bed's headboard—his motion giving her a quick thrill as his thighs flexed against her—and retrieved a condom. "Kneel over me," he said, rolling the condom on with brisk efficiency.

Excitement and molten desire coursed through her. She rose onto her knees and scooted forward so she was poised over the jut of his cock. Reaching between her legs, she guided the tip of him inside her before she slowly folded down at her knees, taking him in little by little so she could feel herself stretch around him in slow motion. His eyes were half closed, his head angled back so the tendons of his neck stood out. His fingers dug into her thighs as he told her how good it was to feel her around him.

When her thighs touched the sculpted muscles of his groin and she thought she could go no lower, he grasped her hips again, working himself in even farther. Then he ran his hands up her torso to cup her breasts, thumbing her nipples to send bolts of electricity down to where their bodies were joined. His eyes followed his hands and then lifted to her face with fierce concentration. She gasped and bowed back, her eyes closed, shutting out the intensity of his gaze as sensation buffeted her in a sensual storm.

He teased her breasts, pulling, stroking, circling, until she was mindless with pleasure, the heat pulsing in her core where he impaled her. "Please, Will." She ground herself against the springy hair at the base of his cock.

He drew a line down her center with one finger until he reached her clit. Before he touched her there, he slipped his finger up inside her beside his cock, the extra stretch making her buck against him.

"Just getting it slick for you," he said, the moisture allowing his finger to glide over the bundle of sensitized nerve endings.

Somehow he knew exactly how to touch her. She lifted onto the crest of the wave, hanging there in exquisite balance until her orgasm crashed through her, pulling her body so taut that she braced her hands on Will's thighs and screamed with pleasure.

Through the convulsions of her muscles around him, Will remained still, his finger driving her up to another climax before she collapsed forward on top of his chest. Her breath came in gasps, her heart seemed determined to pound itself out of her chest, her muscles sagged in the afterglow of release.

Yet his stiff cock was still embedded in the softness inside her, the contrast sending a shivery thrill dancing through her.

His fingers played in her hair. "You looked like you were going to take flight." His voice was tight and hoarse. "But I was inside you, anchoring you to the earth. Watching you and feeling you at the same time was so intense."

"Yes." She couldn't formulate more of an answer. "Intense."

He cupped her shoulders and rolled to lie on top of her, her thighs spread on either side of his hips. He stared down at her so she felt his gaze as heat on her skin. "I won't move until you're ready," he said.

But she was ready, his words stoking the embers back to flames. "Now," she said, squeezing her inner muscles. "Do it now."

He dropped his forehead to her shoulder. "Are you sure?"

"I've never been this sure of anything."

A shudder ran through his body and he reared up to brace himself above her on his forearms. His hips flexed as he withdrew almost entirely from her and then slowly reentered her.

"Again," she demanded. She stretched her hands over her head and opened her thighs wider, offering herself completely.

A long moan tore from his throat, and he began a steady but relentless rhythm of thrusts and withdrawals. Their gazes were locked together, so she could see the strain in his face and neck as he fought against his climax. "No!" he shouted as his eyelids slammed shut and he stopped abruptly. Then a groan racked his body and he drove deep into her before she felt the first pulse of his release, and he shouted her name over and over again while his cock pumped.

His weight came down on her. She reveled in being crushed into the mattress under him until finally she needed to breathe. "Will," she gasped.

He made an incoherent sound.

"My lungs are collapsing," she said with a wispy laugh.

A grunt and then his weight shifted sideways and he flopped onto his back, his free arm flung out beside him. "'Nothing is left of me each time I see her.'"

"Is that a quote?" Kyra didn't recognize it but something about the way he said it tipped her off.

"Catullus. He must have known you in an earlier life." Will swiveled his head toward her, his eyelids heavy and a smile curling the corners of his lips. "It goes on: 'tongue numbed; arms, legs melting, on fire; drum drumming in ears; head lights gone black.' That's pretty much how I feel right now. In a good way."

"I definitely feel melted," she said, her insides still thrumming with satisfaction. She stretched luxuriously, relishing the silky feel of the fine cotton sheets and the brush of Will's skin against hers.

"God, you're beautiful." His voice was rough with desire still.

But she wasn't. He was besotted with her . . . for the moment. She was a novelty, a memory from a different time of his life. She shouldn't fool herself into believing it was anything more than that.

"It's the afterglow," she said. She turned her head to look at him, causing one of the hairpins in her updo to jab her. "Ow!" She started to pull at the already loosened strands.

"Let me," Will said, rolling onto his side and burying his fingers in the coils of hair in search of pins. "I've been wanting to set it loose the whole evening." He grinned. "But I got sidetracked."

His touch was gentle as he carefully pulled out pin after pin, spreading the freed locks over her shoulders and the sheets. The slight shift and pull made delicious tingles dance over her scalp and down her neck. She sighed. "Would you do this every night?"

"Gladly," he said, running his palm over the spread tresses. "As long as you're naked."

She chuckled. "Deal."

He propped himself up on his elbow and continued to play with her hair, using one curl to feather over her breasts so that the tingles spread across the skin there, too.

His gaze was on her chest, so she was free to drink in the clean, masculine lines and angles of his face. She wanted to file it away for a lonely night when she needed a good memory. As she traced the half smile that curved his lips, her heart twisted and she knew she had to end this soon. Or she would become the one waiting for him to end it . . . and it would hurt like hell.

And she knew just how to do it. "I know it's bad form to bring up an ex-fiancée at a moment like this but I want to be honest about something."

His lips lost their relaxed curve, compressing to a tight, hard line. "Then why would you?"

"Because I wanted to hate her and I couldn't."

He dropped her hair and looked away. "She can be quite charming when the occasion calls for it."

Kyra felt a guilty satisfaction in Will's lackluster comment about Petra. "She's still in love with you. I could see it in the way she watched you."

He sat up, his arms resting on his drawn-up knees. "She's in love with her idea of me."

She wanted to run her hand over the gorgeous muscles of his back, but that would be counterproductive. "What's the difference between her idea and you?"

"She wants a husband who goes to work twelve hours a day at an impressive job before donning a tuxedo to escort her to her latest charity affair. And occasionally brings her home an expensive gift that she can show off to her friends."

"She's working for a good cause."

He lifted a shoulder in denial. "She has the designer-decorated condo in Manhattan. She has the high-visibility position at a sympathetic but glamorous charity. Now she just needs a husband and two perfect children to complete the picture. I was the husband component."

"But you asked her to marry you. You must have felt something for her because I know you wouldn't have proposed unless you did."

"Thank you." His tone was sardonic. "She was very persistent in her attentions, and she's very beautiful. And different from other women in my parents' social circle, or so I thought." He shrugged again. "I'm as susceptible to flattery as the next man. We had a whirlwind relationship, mostly conducted at events requiring a tuxedo. Which should have been my first clue that this wasn't a match made in heaven."

"I'll bet you look dashing in a tux." His blond hair and jade eyes against the stark black and white would be striking.

He ignored her. "And, of course, my mother engineered every opportunity she could for us to be together. That should have been my second clue."

"Why does your mother like her so much?"

"Because Petra would bring me back into the fold of proper society." His tone could have cut stone.

"How did you discover that Petra wasn't who you thought she was?"

"I took her to Italy, rented a villa in the countryside built in the thirteenth century—modern by Roman standards—near one of my favorite ancient ruins." His shoulders lifted and fell. "I had a sense that she didn't really know who I was. This trip was meant to remedy that."

"It sounds unbelievably romantic." Kyra would sell her soul to go on a trip like that with Will.

"Petra was bored after the first twenty-four hours."

"Ouch." Kyra couldn't imagine that.

His laugh held no amusement. "She begged me to take her to Rome where she had friends we could visit and stores she could shop in. So I did. As soon as we got back to the States, I asked her to break our engagement." He turned to look out the window, but Kyra was sure he didn't see anything on the terrace. "She was shocked and devastated. She didn't understand why, which told me more than anything else about her."

"And she made a scene at the Spring Fling."

He winced. "I wanted her to announce that she was the person who had chosen to end the relationship. To save her dignity. She did that originally, but then she got drunk at the party and told everyone it had been me."

Now she laid a comforting hand on the back of his shoulder. "That was her choice."

"Only because she'd had a martini too many."

"Her drinking was not your fault."

He turned to look at her. "She was drinking too much because I broke the engagement."

"What was the alternative? To marry a woman who didn't love the person you are?" Kyra held the sheet to her chest and sat up to meet his gaze on the same level. "You did the right thing. For both of you."

He shook his head. "How do you do it?"

"Do what?"

"I've told you things that I've never said to anyone else. Why?"

"I'm safe." Honesty that she should probably have kept to herself.

"Safe? You're dragging my innermost secrets out into the open."

"Because I'm not part of your world, so I can't do any damage to you, even if I didn't keep your secrets to myself."

She needed to remember that.

He stared at her for a long moment, appalled at her answer. "You're wrong. I told you because I trust you with a confidence that goes back years." He'd known even as a college student that this woman had a bone-deep integrity. Maybe it was the contrast to her cheating room-mate that made her stand out, but she always had.

"Thanks," she said with a brief smile, but he could tell she didn't believe him. And he realized something else. She didn't trust him in the same way. There was something holding her back from the future she'd imagined, but she wasn't willing to share it with him.

That sent a surprising spike of hurt through his chest.

What made women conceal themselves from him?

He cupped his hands over her shoulders, loving the silk of her skin, and brought her back down onto the bed with him. Rolling onto his side so he could see her face, he feathered his fingers over her temples and traced along her eyebrows. "Entrust me with your secrets."

Her smile was nervous, as he continued to whisper his fingers over her cheekbones and jawline. "Are you attempting a Vulcan mind meld?" she asked.

"You know my past. I want to understand yours."

"I told you I dropped out of Brunell and my parents both died. Those were the big events."

He suddenly saw the hole in her story. "But after your mother died, you could have gone back to school and you didn't."

"It's nothing mysterious, just a lack of funds."

"So you came to New York to make your fortune."

She huffed out a breath, clearly frustrated by his persistence. "A friend from home who'd moved here told me how much she was making as a bartender at Stratus. She offered to put in a good word for me with Derek, the manager. I got a crash course in mixing cocktails from the manager at the restaurant in Macungie where I'd worked part-time and filled out the application for Stratus. I had to send pictures, too. That was kind of weird, but once I came for the interview, I understood." She snorted. "Even then, Derek assigned one of the other bartenders to take me shopping." She picked up a lock of her shining hair, dangling it from her fingertips. "I learned fast and grew my hair long for the tips."

"And I had to cut mine short for the venture capitalists." He thought of her arriving in a city that could eat you alive with nothing but her intelligence and an introduction to a bar manager and something twisted in his chest. For all his struggles with his parents, he at least had never been entirely alone. Maybe that was the difference he saw in her. The toughness necessary to cope with being orphaned so young.

"So you got the job."

"And here I am," she said, sweeping her slender arm around in a graceful gesture. "In bed with a billionaire."

"Ah, so you're only sleeping with me for my money," he joked. When she flinched, his attention sharpened. "I was kidding."

"I know. It's just a sensitive topic with me. One of the bartenders at Stratus really did go after wealthy customers for the gifts they would give her."

"And it shocked you."

"You can take the girl out of Macungie but you can't take Macungie out of the girl."

"I'm glad it shocked you." He combed his fingers through her hair where it spread on the pillow. "So you've made your fortune?"

She snorted. "I'm working on my second million because I hear the second one is easier than the first."

"Smart-ass." And then he waited, letting the silence draw out.

Finally she looked at him, her brown eyes snapping with anger. "Would I be bartending at Stratus if I'd made my fortune?"

"That would be a rhetorical question," he said. "What are you leaving out?"

"Why does it matter?" She started to roll away from him, but he snaked his arm around her waist to keep her close to him.

"Because I want to know you. Not like Petra."

She went still, her body tense, her face turned away. He thought she wasn't going to answer him, but she suddenly looked back at him, her eyes liquid with unshed tears. "My mother tried to build a barricade against death by buying things. Jewelry. Clothes. Shoes. China. Crystal. She ran up astronomical credit card bills. I'm still paying them off."

"You're not responsible for her debts."

She looked away again. "She took out new cards with my name on them when hers hit their limits. I didn't know."

"A good lawyer could get you out of those." But shock rippled through him at the betrayal of a mother using her daughter's name without telling her. And then crushing her daughter under a mountain of debt. The monumental selfishness of it brought on a wave of fury.

"Oh, I've done everything I could to reduce it," she said, her voice utterly flat. "The house went because she'd taken out a second mortgage. The car, gone. I returned everything I could. I negotiated payment schedules. I got interest rates lowered." An ironic smile twisted the soft curves of her lips. "I'm quite an expert on credit card debt. But the truth is that she bought all the stuff, so it needs to be paid for."

Another wave of fury washed over him, followed by the unaccustomed sense of being powerless. For all his vast fortune, he couldn't help her, even though whatever debt she had would be just a drop in the bucket for him. But she would never accept his money.

She must have read his silence as disapproval because she said, "My mother was terrified of dying. I can't blame her for that."

His answer was to gather her up in his arms and cradle her against his chest. "I'm sorry," he said.

He felt her resistance soften until she relaxed into him with a tiny hitch in her breathing. "I felt horrible for being angry with her even as I mourned her."

"You had every right to be angry." He stroked her hair as though she were a child. Maybe at that moment she was one, a child betrayed by her mother.

"I've never admitted that to anyone before, so we're even," she said, her breath whispering over his chest.

He wanted to shelter her in his arms and fend off the world for her, a protectiveness he'd never experienced before. Ironic, since she clearly didn't need or want him to.

Even more ironic that Petra would have welcomed his newly discovered desire to play the male defender but he had felt the compulsion to escape from her.

Maybe it all boiled down to the fact that he didn't really want to commit himself. He was too restless, too dissatisfied with his life to allow another person to share it.

"What time do you have to be at work tomorrow?" he asked before he thought too much about his flaws.

"Ten," she said, surprise evident in her voice.

"Then you can stay the night here. My limo is at your disposal to go home in the morning."

He felt her start and wondered what the hell he was doing.

"I . . . I'm not sure," she said. "I have things I need to do before work. Errands."

She didn't want to stay with him. Now he wanted it more than ever. "You can leave at whatever hour you need to."

"What time do you go to work?" She crossed her hands on his chest and propped her chin on them. The movement pressed her breasts against him in a way that made his cock stir.

"Whenever I feel like it." He tucked his chin down to meet her gaze with a smile. "Sometimes it pays to be the CEO."

"But when do you usually go?"

"Around seven."

"I knew you were a workaholic," she crowed. "You always pretended not to be in college, but you didn't fool me. No one makes the dean's list without doing the work."

"Writing college essays was pleasure, not work. Most of the time." He loved to dive into a piece of literature and roll around in it until it would reveal itself to him in some new and breathtaking way.

"Because you knew how to BS."

"I'm offended. My essays were based on hours of research and analysis," he said with a lifted eyebrow.

"You forget that I took a couple of the same classes you did. I could tell when you hadn't read the material and were winging it in class discussions."

"I'm pretty sure the professor could, too," he admitted.

"But you had such a glib tongue that they let you get away with it."

"Allow me to use my glib tongue to persuade you to stay until morning," he said.

"Okay. Go ahead and tell me why I should stay." Her expression was one of exaggerated anticipation.

"Oh, I'm not going to persuade you by talking." And then he rolled them both over and slid down her body.

Chapter 10

Will strolled into his COO's office, an exact duplicate of his own, only reversed so the two walls of windows looked over the Hudson River and uptown while Will's shared the river view but faced downtown. Greg was on the phone, so Will went over to watch a tugboat shoving two barges upriver. He realized that when he was in his own office, he almost never looked at the view.

Today, though, the view was less compelling than his memories of the night before. And the morning after. It wasn't just the sex, though. Kyra kept turning his perspective on end, making him examine new possibilities. Forcing him—no, leading him—into honesty about himself. He wasn't sure he was entirely comfortable with all of his revelations to her.

But he'd hated helping her climb into the limo this morning, her hair braided into a thick rope that swung over her shoulder. She wouldn't even commit to seeing him tonight because of her damned bartending job. She said it would be late when she got out, as if he cared what time she came back to his bed.

So he'd fired off a text with a John Donne quote that popped into his head.

Licence my roving hands, and let them go,
Before, behind, between, above, below.

He felt a flash of heat as he remembered her response, some lines from Algernon Swinburne, which she confessed were really about a woman but she felt described him just as well.

The long lithe arms and hotter hands than fire,
The quivering flanks, hair smelling of the south,
The bright light feet, the splendid supple thighs
And glittering eyelids of my soul's desire.

He'd expected sass and she had given him passion. He'd been knocked off-balance.

Will's attention was jerked away from Kyra as Greg finished his call and leaned back in his ergonomic chair. The gray in his salt-and-pepper hair caught gleams of morning sunlight. "I can tell you want me to do something."

Will dropped into a chair in front of the desk and stretched out his legs. "If I want you to do something, I ask you into my office. When I have an idea, I come to yours."

"The fine points of your upper-crust etiquette are too subtle for me. I'm just a blue-collar kind of guy."

"Yet you're wearing a suit and tie."

"I've sold out." Greg grinned. "What's your idea?"

"Dog food."

That startled a crack of laughter from Greg. When Will didn't smile, his COO lifted an eyebrow. "What kind of dog food?"

"Food for dogs with delicate digestion. It has to be limited to a few fresh ingredients with no preservatives. I was thinking it could be Ceres for Canines."

"May I ask where you got this idea?"

"An after-school care center in South Harlem. They have a program called K-9 Angelz where the kids are responsible for dogs as part of their education. One of the dogs had digestive problems, so an old college friend of mine came up with a recipe that solved them." Will saw reservations forming on Greg's face. "We would offer it only in upscale locations where dog owners pamper their pets. But I see a real market with plenty of margin there."

"I'm worried about putting the Ceres brand on dog food. Might freak out some human customers."

"I think it will add cachet to the dog food and some warm fuzzies to the human food, but we can let the marketing wizards figure that out."

Greg looked as though a thought had just struck him. "This college friend of yours. Would it be the same one who made you smile last week?"

Now things got delicate. "One and the same. I think we should hire her to work on the dog food project."

Greg tilted the chair back to look up at the ceiling. "How do I ask this politely? Oh, right, I can't." He brought his gaze to Will's face. "Are you sleeping with her?"

"Yes." Will never lied to his partner. "But that has no effect on my evaluation of her abilities."

"I'll buy that. You've never let pleasure get in the way of business. But it could become awkward with HR."

"Why the hell would I tell HR?"

"You wouldn't but she might. Sexual harassment in the workplace and all that." Greg spread his hands and shrugged.

"She's not that type." Will rubbed the back of his neck in irritation. "I don't even know that she'll accept the job."

Greg looked relieved. "So you haven't discussed it with her yet."

"I would never make that kind of decision without running it by you first. You know that damn well."

"Sex can cloud even the strongest man's judgment," Greg said. He grinned again. "Especially the kind of sex that makes you smile."

"I wasn't having sex when I . . . never mind," Will said, realizing that Greg was baiting him.

Greg's grin widened, then faded. "Give me a couple of hours to think about this and do some research," he said. "But I gotta admit that I've never known you to have a bad idea."

"You're forgetting my insistence that we open ten locations on the same day." Will stood.

"You were younger then."

"People keep reminding me of my age," Will complained.

"You just need to get old like me and then people are afraid to comment on your age."

Will chuckled and returned to his own office. After his night with Kyra, he felt relaxed enough not to rush around but energized enough to start a whole new pet division of Ceres. He'd been toying with the idea since the evening at Stratus, so he trusted his instincts about its viability. However, it was Kyra's revelation about her financial situation that had kicked him into gear. This was the only way that he could think to help her with her money problems. The person in charge of launching Ceres for Canines would command an impressive salary.

He grimaced. He hadn't lied about his concern that Kyra would refuse the position. He would have to get Greg to make her the offer. Otherwise, she would never accept.

But he had to try because he hated the defeat in Kyra's eyes. And the waste of her potential.

He didn't want to think about the other reasons he felt such a compulsion.

Two hours later, Greg sat down in a chair in front of Will's desk. "I think you're onto something with the dog food. Turns out people are pretty wacko about their pets and willing to spend money when they live in more urban centers. It won't play in Peoria, though."

Satisfaction surged through Will. He nodded. "Agreed about the much-maligned Peoria. Limited locations will make it even more appealing to the upscale pet owner."

"Are we doing cats, too?"

"As far as I know, cats also have sensitive stomachs."

"Gerbils?"

Will laughed. "No rodents."

"That's a relief." Greg folded his hands over his stomach. "Now tell me about this college friend of yours."

"I think you should interview her and draw your own conclusions," Will said. "I'll give you her contact information."

"Do I get a résumé to review?" Greg's tone verged on skeptical.

"Her experience is nontraditional, so her résumé won't really help your evaluation."

Greg rolled his eyes. "MBA jargon."

"Not all jargon is meaningless. She's not corporate, but she's extremely bright and hardworking. And she's already developed the dog food." Inspiration sparked in his brain. "We could tie the dog food launch into benefiting the K-9 Angelz program. We could even use their dogs as beta testers. The PR would be incredible." And it would be extra leverage to get Kyra to take the job.

"I'd like to see this place first," Greg said.

"Not a problem." Will wanted to see it, too, since he was basing a new venture on it.

"I have to ask you another question." Greg sat forward. "If your friend doesn't want the position, do you still plan to go forward with the project?"

Anger flashed hot. "Do you really think I would waste the company's money on a product I didn't believe in?"

"No." Greg kept his eyes locked on Will. "But you've killed two other new proposals in the last six months, so I have to ask myself what makes this one special."

"You agreed with me on rejecting those proposals." Will kept his voice even, although he wanted to curse at Greg.

"I could see your heart wasn't in them."

"Ceres for Canines will move forward, no matter who is at the helm," Will said, his voice ice-cold with fury.

Greg lifted a hand in surrender. "Don't get pissy. I'm on board. Send me your friend's contact info."

Will picked up his cell phone and swiped Kyra's phone number to Greg's e-mail. "Try not to scare her away by being an asshole."

Greg grinned. "If she's gone out with you already, then nothing I can do will make it any worse."

"Go find a spreadsheet to screw up," Will said, but his anger was fading. He had to admit that he should have asked himself the same question.

Kyra slapped a lime on the bar's cutting board and whacked it into paper-thin slices.

She shouldn't have stayed all night, wrapped in the luxury of Will's million-thread-count sheets and the even greater luxury of his large, powerful body. But he'd sapped her willpower with his mouth and his hands and, yes, his words. She'd let herself drift off to sleep and awakened only to make love again in the slant of early morning sunlight.

Now she had to live with the longing to do it again . . . and again.

She cut a radius in each slice, laid them in a crystal dish, and slid it onto the counter.

"Thanks," Bastian said, twisting a slice into a helix before impaling it on a stainless steel swizzle stick and dropping it into a rocks glass. "Didn't get a chance to replenish the supply earlier."

"No worries," Kyra said. She saw a customer drain his martini to the dregs and strutted down the bar to get him a refill.

The men were all smiling at her tonight, and she knew it was because her body still glowed with deep sexual satisfaction. She felt more fluid in her movements, felt her hips swaying naturally, knew her skin was suffused with a sensual flush. If it brought in more tips, she didn't have a problem with that.

What she did have a problem with was how she felt about Will. All the yearning of her college crush had returned with a vengeance, magnified by the reality of the man he'd become and the fact that she'd finally gotten her wish to make love with him.

She almost wished he'd been a disappointment in bed . . . selfish or unimaginative or cold. But no, Will had to be as brilliant at sex as he was at everything else. And then he'd had the lack of consideration to send her texts at odd moments all day with quotations from various racy poems. So she had no chance of banishing him from her thoughts. Not to mention that she'd had to rack her brain to come up with answering quotes. Which had been a hell of a lot of fun.

He'd finished his barrage of seduction with an invitation to his place after she finished work. He would send his limo to pick her up at any hour. And he would be in it.

Yep, she hated him in a big way.

She put down a linen cloud napkin and placed the fresh martini on it. "Shaken, not stirred," she said with a smile. Men were always flattered by the reference to James Bond. It made them feel dashing and dangerous.

"You have a license to kill," the man said with a wink as he took a sip.

"Kyra! How wonderful to see you again!"

Startled by the vaguely familiar woman's voice calling her name, Kyra pivoted to find Petra and Farr sliding onto bar chairs several feet away. Petra gave her a wide, friendly smile while Farr looked as though he would prefer not to be there. As soon as he met her gaze, his expression smoothed into one of affability, but she'd caught his discomfort. So it had been Petra's idea to come. Unease rippled through Kyra.

"Petra. Farr." It was strange to see the two of them in her environment instead of Will's. "Is this your first time at Stratus?"

"Oh, no, I've been several times," Petra said. "That's why I think it would be the perfect venue for a fund-raiser. I've come to take another look at the facilities."

The dress she wore made Kyra sigh with envy. Sheer cream fabric was embroidered with graceful, flowing branches in shades of pale pink. Three-quarter-length sleeves showed off Petra's slim wrists, on one of which she wore a tiny gold watch that glittered with diamonds. Long, swinging earrings of polished pink coral hung on gold chains. Kyra flinched at the sheer gorgeousness of the woman.

"I have the pleasure of experiencing Stratus for the first time," Farr said in his southern drawl. He looked very Wall Street in a tailored gray suit, a striped blue shirt with a white collar, and a red-and-blue striped tie. "Most impressive."

"Wait until you taste my cocktails," Kyra said with her well-rehearsed grin. "What would you like?"

"A Cosmopolitan," Petra said. "I love the color."

It would match her outfit, too.

"May I recommend Snow Queen Vodka from Kazakhstan?" Kyra said. "It's organic and smooth as velvet. And may I add a surprise of ginger to your Cosmo? I think you'll enjoy both."

Petra actually clapped her hands together. "Oh, yes! I love a little adventure." Her huge, dark eyes were lit with excitement. Will wasn't wrong about her ability to charm.

"Farr?" Kyra asked.

"Bourbon, straight up," he said. "What have you got?" He was scanning the display of bottles.

"A special treat. Michter's twenty year. I only offer it to those who understand it should not be diluted even with ice."

"I am in heaven and you are an angel," Farr said, laying his palms together as though in prayer and casting his eyes upward. "Give me a double."

Kyra laughed and pulled out a muddler and fresh gingerroot, whipping up the ginger Cosmopolitan at high speed. Then she poured a generous double of Michter's in a crystal rocks glass. When both Petra and Farr made sounds of pleasure after their first sip, she felt a glow of satisfaction.

Farr put his silver Stratus ingot on the bar, but Kyra shook her head. "First round's on me."

"Sugar, I know what Michter's goes for, and I'm not letting you pay for it," Farr said, nudging his ingot toward her.

"I get it at cost," Kyra said with a smile and ignored the ingot.

Petra took another sip of her Cosmo. "If we have our fund-raiser here, could this be our signature drink? It's yummy."

"I'd be honored," Kyra said. "Have you spoken with Derek about all our private party services? They're pretty amazing."

A fleeting look of guilt crossed Petra's face. "Not yet. I'm just starting the process of choosing a venue."

"I'd be happy to put you in touch with him." And she'd get a nice commission if Petra chose to have her party here. "He's a wizard at party planning."

Petra waved her hand in an airy gesture. "Not tonight. I just want to soak up the atmosphere."

"And I want to soak up this bourbon of the gods," Farr said, toasting Kyra.

"Excuse me for a moment," she said. "I've got another thirsty customer who needs my attention."

As she mixed a Vesper martini and a Negroni, Kyra puzzled over Petra's appearance at Stratus. She'd obviously gone to the trouble of finding out where Kyra worked and persuading Farr to come with her despite some reluctance on his part. Given the circumstances, it was a little disturbing to find Petra on a bar chair in her place of employment. Maybe Petra wanted to make it clear that Kyra was a worker bee and she was the customer whose business was to be courted. Not that Petra had given any sign of that. She was the epitome of graciousness.

Kyra served up the drinks, refilled another customer's glass with Prosecco, and rejoined Petra and Farr.

"You work very hard here," Petra said, her tone admiring. "And you're really good at it." She gestured to her cocktail.

"Thanks. I do my best." Kyra couldn't help being flattered, even though she suspected a hidden agenda behind Petra's presence. "Would you like anything to eat? We have some delicious tapas." She laid two menus of thick handmade paper, sky blue with clouds scudding across them, on the bar.

"No, no, we had dinner already," Petra said.

Farr picked up a menu. "I might be persuaded to soak up the bourbon with some chive blini with quail eggs. And add some of those Glidden Point oysters."

"For soaking up alcohol, I would also recommend the gruyère-and-parmesan beignets," Kyra said. "Light as a feather but with excellent bourbon-absorption properties."

"Oh, all right," Petra said, looking at the menu Farr was holding. "I'll have the wasabi spring rolls with asparagus and shiitake mushrooms."

Kyra tapped their order into her tablet, this time accepting Farr's proffered ingot. Once again, she had to leave to serve other customers. When she got back, the food had arrived and Petra was ready for another Cosmo.

"How did you learn to bartend?" she asked Kyra.

"I trained at a restaurant in my hometown in Pennsylvania." It was Kyra's oft-repeated answer. "And then I learned the fancy stuff from the pros here." She nodded to Bastian and Cleo, who were on with her that night.

"It looks like a fun job," Petra said, a little disingenuously.

"You get to meet a lot of nice people," Kyra said, putting the drink in front of Petra. Another pat answer.

"And a lot of jerks, too." Farr's tone was tart. "Especially after a few drinks."

Kyra laughed. "A few, but management has diplomatic yet firm ways to deal with them."

"Have you worked here long?" Petra continued her quiz.

"Eight years." For some reason, that suddenly sounded like a long time, as though bartending had become her career choice.

"And the same at the after-care center?"

"Not quite as long there. It took me a couple of years to find them." Or rather to find the ad offering a free apartment in South Harlem in return for cooking for kids on a tiny budget. "I consider myself lucky to have that job. The kids bring me such joy." And occasionally broke her heart with their life stories. But at least she felt like she was helping them in a very concrete way. "Now I'm even getting to love their dogs."

"The K-9 Angelz," Farr said, popping a beignet into his mouth and making appreciative noises.

"You were paying attention at the party," Kyra said, pleased. She explained the program to Petra, who was instantly enthusiastic.

"Now I'm even cooking for the dogs," Kyra joked. "This giant pit bull who looks like he could eat an entire cow has a sensitive stomach. Go figure!"

Farr and Petra laughed, and then Kyra got busy with a surge of customers, so she didn't have a chance to do more than briefly check in with them for half an hour.

But she had been watching the two of them as she worked, something she did as a bartender anyway to see whether her customers needed another drink, as well as to gauge their satisfaction and how inebriated they were. Her body language skills had been honed to a fine edge behind the bar at Stratus.

Farr felt more than friendship for Petra. It showed in the tiny, solicitous touches he gave her, in the way he bent his head close to listen to her, and in the protective way he draped his arm over the back of her bar chair. Kyra's heart twisted. She didn't know Farr well, but she respected Will's judgment when it came to friends, so she hated to see him suffer unrequited devotion. Why did Petra continue to chase after a man who didn't want her when there was one who clearly did?

Will had given Kyra the answer. Farr was only of average height, had medium-brown hair that had begun to recede, and tended toward pudginess. His career in investment banking was impressive by most standards but couldn't compete with Will's stratospheric wealth and position. For Petra, Farr's honeyed southern accent and utter devotion wouldn't make up for his perceived shortcomings.

Petra was an idiot.

When she finally got back to them, Petra had finished her second Cosmo, so she ordered another.

Farr tried to talk her out of it, but his date insisted. "They taste so-o-o-o good."

Kyra met Farr's gaze with a rueful shrug. She couldn't stop adult customers from drinking more than they should unless they became a nuisance. But this indicated that Petra's excessive drinking at the Spring Fling couldn't be laid entirely at Will's door, which should relieve him.

As Kyra muddled more ginger, Petra leaned forward, her chin propped on one graceful hand, her eyes slightly clouded with alcohol. "I have a question for you."

Kyra looked up with a smile. Petra had been peppering her with questions all evening, but it was kind of flattering. "Shoot."

"Are you in love with Will?"

The muddler hit the cocktail shaker with a loud clank as it slipped from Kyra's fingers. "Um, I've only seen him twice since college, so I'd say not."

"You can fall in love instantly," Petra said, nodding vigorously so that her hand moved with her chin. "And Will is so easy to love."

Without meaning to, Kyra glanced at Farr and saw the pain in his eyes before he looked down into his drink. "Will's a great guy. Always has been," Kyra said, finding her poise again and pouring vodka into the shaker with a flourish.

"He brought you to the party," Petra said. "The last time he brought a date to the party, it was me." A tear slid over her perfect cheekbone.

Petra got emotional when she drank. Or maybe she drank when she was emotional.

"Petra, sugar, I think it's time to go home," Farr said. "You're leaving for San Francisco early in the morning, remember?"

"Oh, Farr, you're so sweet to worry about me," Petra said, patting his hand. "But I came to talk to Kyra and she's been so busy."

"She's working," Farr said, rebuke in his voice. "We should not be taking up her time."

"But I need to speak with her about Will. And I'm leaving tomorrow, so I need to do it now." A steely testiness put an edge on Petra's usually melodious voice. "Maybe Kyra could spare a few minutes to give me a quick peek at the private party room. Just the two of us."

The lady knew how to use leverage.

Kyra looked at Farr, his usual courtly manners unraveling at the edges. "Of course," Kyra said, signaling Bastian to take over her section of the bar and explaining Petra's request in a low voice.

"I've got it covered," her fellow bartender said. "Get that party commission!"

"Working on it." Kyra let herself out from behind the bar and came around to collect Petra. Farr stood to help her off the stool, steadying her when she wobbled on her Jimmy Choo stilettos.

Farr shook his head. "Not sure this is a good idea."

"Possibly not," Kyra said. But Petra was determined, and Kyra's boss would be unhappy with her if a lucrative private event went elsewhere because of her personal issues. She didn't trust Petra not to drop some mention of Kyra's part in tonight's meeting, when Petra spoke with Derek.

The room used for private parties was up a short flight of glass-and-chrome stairs. Kyra flicked the switch for the ceiling projection before she opened the door to usher Petra inside.

Because it was evening, the ceiling displayed the night sky with the Milky Way spread across its high vault, an occasional star sending out sparkling rays at random intervals. The room was set up for a cocktail party, with tall circular tables covered in blue velvet that glinted with silver threads. The polished marble floor was inlaid with lines of silver that gleamed in the low light.

Petra gave it all a cursory glance before she headed for a silver leather divan, her high heels clicking on the stone floor. "Why don't we sit for a minute?" she said over her shoulder, with a slight wobble in her gait.

Kyra had no choice but to follow as Petra sank onto the sofa with a graceful folding of her long, elegant legs. A pang of envy pricked at Kyra. Even drunk, Petra couldn't be less than gorgeous.

Kyra perched on an ottoman facing Petra and gestured toward the room. "The decor is very flexible. This is a late-night party setup, but we can do one for any time of day. We've even done storms."

Petra ignored her sales spiel and leaned forward. Kyra could smell the vodka and cranberry on the woman's breath. "I didn't want to talk in front of Farr because he and Will are such good friends."

"About the party?"

Petra made a vague gesture of dismissal. "About Will. And you. And me."

Kyra almost laughed as she pictured some sort of weird ménage à trois. But Petra was bent on having the conversation. "You know that Will and I were engaged?" she asked. "Just a few years ago. He wanted me to say that I broke the engagement, but he did it."

"I'm not sure you should be telling me this," Kyra said, shifting on the ottoman.

"I saw how you looked at him at the Spring Fling," Petra said. "And I wanted to warn you."

So she'd been watching Will and Kyra at the party. Of course, Kyra didn't know who Petra was then, so she hadn't noticed the other woman's attention. "Warn me?" Kyra straightened her spine, trying to look more confident than she felt.

"Will isn't really capable of love," Petra said, her eyes dark, unreadable pools in the dim lighting. "I was perfect for him. I move in the same circles and have the right connections. Our mothers are tennis partners, so I know his whole family. But he couldn't commit to me." Incredulity rang in her voice before she lowered it as though telling Kyra a shameful secret. "He's in love with his job. He insisted that we go to this falling-down villa in Italy where we could *get to know each other better*." Petra made air quotes around the last phrase. "It was bad enough that he dragged me there, where there were no stores or friends to visit, but after two days of sitting around, he got on his computer to answer e-mails."

That must have been after Petra insisted that he take her to Rome. "That seems kind of unromantic," Kyra said to placate the indignant woman in front of her.

"Well, the sex was really good," Petra said, making Kyra's cheeks go hot with discomfort. "At the beginning. Then he went back to his first love . . . Ceres. I couldn't compete with a giant corporation. I don't think his partner, Greg Ebersole, liked me either." She looked bewildered by that.

Kyra was beginning to understand Will's dislike of Petra. For all her outward warmth and understanding, the woman refused to take any responsibility for the end of their relationship. She was spreading the blame around wherever she could lay it. Announcing to the Spring Fling guests that *Will* had ended the engagement was just another way to shift the onus away from herself. Kyra had seen this before. In her mother.

Petra reached out to lay a hand on Kyra's knee, her tone softening. "You're not part of Will's world, so you can't understand a man like him. I can tell you're a nice person, and I don't want to see you get hurt like I was."

Kyra felt like Petra had hauled off and punched her in the stomach. She had told herself repeatedly that she didn't fit into Will's environment, but to have someone say it out loud made her lose her breath. Did everyone at the Spring Fling think Will was just slumming it with her?

Petra was still going. "If he couldn't bring himself to marry me, well, you know what I'm trying to say."

Pride made Kyra force a laugh. "You don't have to worry about me. I've known Will a long time. I'm well aware of who he is."

"But that was in college," Petra said. "He's changed. I just didn't realize it until too late."

Hadn't Kyra said the same thing to Emily earlier? Money and power had an effect on the people who wielded them. But she'd seen Will's pain when he talked about his engagement to Petra. It was real.

"We've all changed since college," Kyra said with what she hoped was a wry shrug. She pushed up from the ottoman. "I've got to get back to the bar. My boss will wonder where I am."

"Oh my gosh, that's right! You're working. I hope you won't get in trouble." Petra unfolded her legs to rise gracefully from the divan like Venus out of the sea-foam. "I'll talk to your boss and explain that you were showing me the party room."

"It's okay. My boss likes me."

"I like you, too." Petra shocked Kyra by pulling her in for a hug, Petra's sweetly exotic floral perfume enveloping them both.

Kyra gave Petra a quick, awkward squeeze and extricated herself from the other woman's grasp. "Thanks. That's nice of you."

Petra linked her arm through Kyra's. "Some night when you're not working, we'll have to go out together."

Kyra was trying to steer Petra's slightly tottering footsteps toward the door. "That would be great," she said, knowing the invitation wasn't real.

"When could you do it?" Petra stopped right in the doorway.

"Do what?" Kyra tried to keep her moving without letting the door swing shut on both of them.

"Have a girls' night out. I bet you know all the best clubs."

Kyra nearly laughed. She knew exactly one club: Stratus. "I don't get out much because of my job. But we'll figure out a time." In the next century maybe.

Farr saw them coming down the stairs and leaped off his stool to take Petra's other arm. She smiled at him. "Such a gentleman."

"So I'm told," he said, but his face lit with pleasure. "Now this gentleman would like to see you home safely."

Petra leaned in to murmur in Kyra's ear. "Don't tell Will we talked about him. It's between us girls."

"Right," Kyra said noncommittally. She had no idea what she was going to say to Will about this evening. She could barely figure out what she thought herself.

"Kyra, it's been delightful," Farr said, brushing his lips against her cheek. "This is my kind of place. I'll be bringing some work associates here because I know they'll appreciate it."

That would please Derek. The IB guys threw around money to impress each other.

She watched Farr guide Petra out of the room before she went back to the bar, her composure shaken to the core. Bastian pulled a folded bill out of his pocket and handed it to her. "He left a hell of a tip for you. In cash."

She glanced down. It was a one-hundred-dollar bill. "Wow." She slipped it into her pocket with an odd sense of resentment. Did Farr think she needed the money?

"He took care of me as well, even though all I did was give him a glass of seltzer. A class act," Bastian said.

Or maybe he was just what Bastian described, a nice guy who did the right thing.

"To top it all off, he says he's coming back," Kyra said, trying to shake off Petra's poison as she surveyed the customers on her section of the bar. No one needed a refill.

"And the woman." He whistled softly. "She's a model, right?"

"No, just looks like one. She's a Connecticut blue blood, so no need to lower herself to object status."

"Is she throwing the private party here?" He looked hopeful.

"She might." Although Kyra suspected that had been merely an excuse for coming to talk to her.

"I'll make sure I'm available to work it." Bastian glided away to check on his customers.

Since he was darkly handsome in a chiseled, male-model way, Kyra was sure that Petra would be happy to have him on the waitstaff.

As she picked up her bartending duties again, she had to force herself to focus and smile at the customers because she was still reeling from the conversation with Petra. She'd thought . . . no, she'd deluded herself into believing that the people at the Spring Fling had liked her as a person. That the majority didn't care how much her dress had cost or that she worked as a bartender. Not that she'd volunteered that information. She'd enjoyed the party except for the encounters with Betsy Chase. Now Petra had thrown a pall over that pleasure as Kyra wondered how many people had murmured *Not our class, dear*, when she walked away.

The most humiliating realization was that Petra had warned her out of a genuine concern for Kyra's feelings. It was clear that the other woman didn't consider Kyra a threat to her designs on Will because Kyra offered no real competition. That galled her more than anything.

As she poured out a Negroni, she felt her cell phone vibrate in her back pocket. No visible cell phones were allowed at the bar, so she had to wait fifteen minutes until she found a reason to go to the wine cellar to check the text. Pulling the requested bottle from the rack and setting it down on a shelf, she yanked out her phone.

Will's name showed on the display and a thrill of anticipation quivered in her chest. She closed her eyes to fight it down. Petra's words pinged around in her brain, but they couldn't quell the exhilaration that frothed through her from just seeing Will's ID on her phone. She looked down at the screen.

At my back I always hear Time's wingèd chariot hurrying near. What time will you be done with your duties at Stratus?

Andrew Marvell's "To His Coy Mistress." She loved that poem and knew it by heart. It was funny, passionate, and amazingly powerful. She typed, Patience! An hundred years should go to praise thine eyes, and on thy forehead gaze. Will finish up in an hour.

She'd get Cleo and Bastian to take any lingering customers. She'd often done it for them when they had dates. She didn't want to miss any time with Will, since Petra had reminded her that it would be limited.

His text came back at light speed. I look forward to spending two hundred to adore each breast. For, lady, you deserve this state, nor would I love at lower rate. But now let us sport us while we may, like amorous birds of prey.

She laughed at his mash-up of the lines, even as the irony of them struck her. I always had a problem with that vulture image . . . sharp beaks tearing at bare flesh and all that. Kind of gory. Have to go back to work.

As she walked up the stairs, another text pinged. One hour. I'll be waiting.

Heat flashed through her like a lightning strike at the image of Will, all the muscled length and breadth and power of him, waiting for *her*.

Chapter 11

Outside Stratus, the limousine's glossy black paint gleamed under the club's entrance lights. Kyra's step hitched slightly when she saw it. Desire had been simmering inside her ever since Will's text message and now it was ready to boil over.

The back door swung open as soon as she got within ten feet of the car, and Will unfolded himself from the interior. He was dressed in jeans and a moss-green polo shirt, the most casual she'd seen him since college. Closing the space between them in two strides, he pulled her against him and brought his mouth down on hers for a kiss like a furnace blast. She let the heat inside her rise to meet his so their tongues touched and twisted in a dance that promised far more.

"Hey, get a room," a passerby called out, but his tone was admiring, rather than grumpy.

Kyra had forgotten they were still standing on the sidewalk and she tried to pull away, but Will had splayed his hands on her bottom to hold her tight to his erection and he didn't ease the pressure. He lifted his head a fraction of an inch, and she could see the flare of his nostrils as he breathed hard. "It's New York," he said. "We could do it in an alleyway and no one would care."

"Yes, but I work here." Kyra braced her elbows against his chest and pushed. "Also, I have to tell you something first."

"That sounds ominous," Will said, taking her backpack before he helped her into the limo.

She'd decided not to let Petra get into her head with her subtle disdain. Possibly easier said than done. So she was going to tell Will that Petra and Farr had visited Stratus without divulging the underlying reason.

Tossing the pack onto the seat facing them, he slid in beside her and hauled her onto his lap. She could feel his cock pressing against the juncture of her thighs, and her eyes nearly rolled back in her head. "I can't focus when I'm sitting on your lap," she said.

"You have no choice." He gathered up her hair to kiss the nape of her neck, sending shivers careening over her skin. "I've been waiting all day to have you here."

"Fine, I'll make it fast." She took a breath. "Petra and Farr stopped by Stratus this evening."

He dropped her hair and sat back so she could see his frown in the dim light. "Petra and Farr? Did they know you would be there?"

Kyra had thought about just how much she should tell him. "They did. Petra is considering throwing a fund-raiser there so she wanted to get my thoughts on it. Farr was being a good friend and escorting her. You know he really likes her, right?" She was trying to distract him from thinking too hard about Petra's presence.

He looked surprised. "Farr likes Petra? You mean in more than a friendly way?"

"I'm pretty sure."

Will brushed off her tangent. "Petra didn't go there to plan a party," he said. "She has a rotating list of venues she uses. I know because I've been to every one of them."

There it was, the world that Petra and Will moved in together, while Kyra was merely an employee in one of those venues. She shoved the thought away because right now she was with Will in their own little world.

"Maybe she feels the need for a fresh location. Shake things up." Kyra didn't want him brooding on the topic because she preferred not to answer any additional questions. She'd told him enough to stave off trouble later on, but not enough to cause trouble now. "Anyway, we all had a nice chat while Petra drank one Cosmo too many before Farr took her home."

Will looked pained when she mentioned the Cosmo. "I hope she didn't embarrass you."

"Actually, my fellow bartender Bastian is desperately hoping she will return. He was quite smitten."

"Another one in her long string." Will's tone was sardonic. Then his mood turned severe, and she glimpsed the streak of ruthlessness that had propelled him to the top. "I'm not happy that she tracked you down at your workplace."

"She was just a customer," Kyra said, wishing he would let it drop. "Not a big deal."

"Your life should not be troubled by my past. I'll make sure it doesn't happen again."

Kyra felt a thrill of primitive exhilaration at Will's protectiveness, especially when he wound his hand into her hair, his eyes glittering in the passing city lights, saying, "I have zero interest in discussing Petra any further."

"Then my job here is done." She'd dodged that bullet.

He used his grip on her hair to tilt her head so he could go back to kissing her neck. His other hand came up to cup her breast through the black silk blouse she wore. She felt both of his touches like brands, scorching her skin and marking her as his. Beneath her, his erection grew harder. She shifted so it hit her right between the legs, and she breathed out a wordless exclamation of pleasure.

"Kyra," Will growled against her neck. "I want you now. *Right* now."

"Yes!" she said, and suddenly she was being lifted upward by strong hands on her hips.

"Thank God you wore a skirt," Will said. "Straddle me."

She'd worn the short, black skirt for exactly this reason. And red lace lingerie, since she'd used her only set of fancy black lingerie last night. If this fling with Will continued much longer, she'd have to go shopping for more sexy undies. She knelt over him, one knee on either side of his thighs. He yanked her skirt up to her waist, his breath hissing in appreciation when he saw her panties.

"Sorry not to enjoy these more, but they need to come off," he said, jerking them down over her hips.

"I'll handle this part," she said, maneuvering so she got one leg free, leaving them around the other knee.

At the same time, he had unzipped his jeans and rolled on a condom.

"Guess you like it when I'm on top," she said, remembering the night before.

He slid a finger inside her, making her contract with pleasure. "You do, too." He pulled out his finger and sucked it into his mouth. "God, that just makes me harder."

She braced her hands on the leather upholstery on either side of his head, while he positioned his cock at her opening and curved his fingers around her hips. In one explosive motion, he pulled her down while he thrust upward, seating himself inside her with swift efficiency. Nothing like the slow sensual entrance of the night before, but just as insanely arousing.

And then he held her while he drove into her in a relentless, ever-accelerating rhythm, his breath blowing sharp and fast against her cheek. All she could do was dig her fingers into the leather and hold on as his motion sent tendrils of arousal whirling through her to wind together in her belly.

"Ahh!" He threw back his head against the seat cushion and pumped inside her, the force of his orgasm pushing her toward the limo's ceiling. She tightened her inner muscles, giving both of them an extra boost of pleasure. "Ahh," he murmured more quietly, lowering his hips as he came down from the high of his climax.

She was so close to finishing that she considered reaching down to touch herself. But she'd rather have Will's clever fingers on her, so she waited while his breathing slowed. It was hot to feel him soften inside her while he idly stroked over her hip bones with his thumbs.

"Sorry," he mumbled. "It wasn't gentlemanly to come first."

"I liked it," she whispered into his ear. "I made you forget your manners." She took great satisfaction in her ability to unravel his smooth, polished control. It struck her that maybe she was making a mistake. Maybe he didn't like what she did, since he'd been brought up not to give in to his feelings.

"It was the waiting," he said, his eyes still closed. "Waiting and thinking about you. That would bring out the caveman in anyone." So he recognized the primitive side of himself.

"Delayed gratification is good for the soul."

His eyes opened and something wicked lurked in them. "Then your soul must be very noble at this moment. Time to change that."

His grip on her hips tightened, lifting her so he could slip out. He set her beside him on the seat, her skirt still rucked up to her waist, before he stripped off and disposed of his condom. Then he pivoted and came down on his knees on the limo's plush carpeting. He hooked his hands behind her knees and spread her thighs so he could kneel between them.

"A delicious chaser for me," he said, pressing her back against the seat while he pulled her knees up onto his shoulders.

"Will!" Her position opened her to his gaze and she felt a flush of shyness.

"I want to taste you when you come," he said. And then his mouth was on her. It took only a few strokes of his tongue on her clit before her muscles convulsed with a wrenching burst of release, sending her arching up off the seat. She felt his tongue spear inside her as she clenched and eased, his touch driving her to another mind-bending orgasm.

As she relaxed down again, her body still rippling with aftershocks, she felt the palms of his hands against her bottom, supporting her. He lowered her to the seat and then gave her buttocks a lingering squeeze before sliding his hands out from underneath her. The feel of his palms against the rarely touched flesh sent another flickering response through her glowing insides.

Will slipped her knees off his shoulders, so she sprawled on the seat, her legs still on either side of his thighs. Sitting back on his heels, he licked his lips and gave her a lazy, satisfied smile. "Andrew Marvell would be proud," he said. "'Thy willing soul transpires at every pore with instant fires.'"

"'Let us roll all our strength and all our sweetness up into one ball,'" she quoted back. "'And tear our pleasures with rough strife through the iron gates of life.'"

"Was I too rough?" He sounded concerned.

"I'm quoting Marvell, not commenting on your technique."

"In that case, 'Thus, though we cannot make our sun stand still, yet we will make him run.'" He moved to the seat beside her, pulling her onto his lap once more. "Marvell had an interesting idea about using sex as a defense against time."

"The little death to ward off the big death," Kyra said, snuggling in against the soft cotton of his polo shirt. "I'm not sure that threatening her with worms and the grave sets quite the right mood for hot sex, though."

"It speaks to the most basic human instinct, the survival of the species. When faced with imminent death, we are driven to have sex one last time. It's a powerful persuasion."

"I feel like I'm back in lit class. I miss those days when we threw around words with wild abandon."

"You'll do it again," he said, his voice ringing with certainty.

She felt too mellow to argue with him, but that dream had slipped away. She banished the niggle of sadness that threatened to make her eyes tear up. Or maybe that was just the postcoital blues.

"I miss it, too." He sounded surprised.

The limo stopped and the driver's voice sounded through the intercom. "We're home, sir."

Kyra sat up and realized that her panties were still looped around one knee. "Oops, gotta get these back in place," she said, reaching for them.

But Will was quicker, his arm snaking out to pull them down to her foot. "You won't need these anyway," he said, working the red lace over her ankle boot. He stuffed the panties into his jeans pocket with a wicked smile. "It was your idea, after all."

"That was a one-time offer." But her body prickled with awareness that she was naked under her skirt.

"You can ransom them inside." He pushed open the car door.

Kyra swung her legs out the door with knees pressed together like a movie star at the Oscars. Of course, no one was wandering down the sidewalk in front of Will's ultraexpensive address at this hour. But she felt the watchful eyes of security cameras, even though she had no idea where they were hidden.

Will waved his magic wristband and they were inside the spectacular foyer. As they walked toward the back of the house, every step brought a brush of air that reminded Kyra of where her panties weren't.

"Would you like a drink?" Will asked when they reached what Kyra thought of as the garden room.

"Point me to the bar and I'll make you whatever you want, if you have the ingredients," Kyra said. That was one skill she could bring to the table.

Will shook his head. "You are off duty." He swung open a panel to reveal a wet bar. "What's your pleasure?"

"I'd love a really crisp, dry white wine."

"I have the perfect bottle but it's in the wine cellar. Excuse me for a moment." He strode out of the room.

Kyra walked to the garden door, sliding it open so the soft spring air wafted over her skin, bringing the splash of falling water from the fountain and the scent of earth and growing things. She closed her eyes and inhaled. The empty lot next to the Carver Center exuded the same aroma, especially after the grass had just been mowed. With the raised beds nearly finished, they would soon be planting vegetables and herbs to use in the center's kitchen. A couple of the kids' parents turned out to be enthusiastic gardeners and had worked with her to choose what to plant, since they knew what would thrive in the New York City climate. Their excitement at having a place to grow things was infectious.

Melancholy seeped through her as she stood in the doorway of Will's extraordinary home. She'd been happy with her life until she'd sat down at his table in Ceres. The kids at the center amazed her. Emily was a wonderful boss who was becoming a friend. Kyra's hard-won expertise as a bartender gave her satisfaction. And the debt diminished every month, even if the pace seemed glacial.

But Will made her long for things she thought she'd put behind her. Things she no longer believed she could have.

"Sorry to leave you alone." His voice made her turn to see him striding to the bar with a bottle in his hand. His usually well-groomed hair was still tousled from their lovemaking in the car, but that just made him look sexier. He walked with such confident grace that even in his faded jeans he personified power, decisiveness, and intelligence.

The simmer of dissatisfaction with her life boiled into a haze of yearning. She didn't just want to go back to school. She wanted this man. Wanted him to be waiting for her outside Stratus every night. Craved his brilliant conversation. Ached to watch the color of his eyes shift with his emotions. Hungered to have the right to touch him wherever and whenever she chose.

She must have made a sound because Will looked up from pouring the wine. "Do you want to take it outside?" he asked, finishing his task and picking up the two glasses.

As he walked toward her, his eyes glittering in the low light, his sculpted lips curved in a seductive smile, the muscles in his thighs propelling him forward with an easy strength, she just plain *wanted*.

"Kyra? Are you all right?"

She jumped. He was holding the glass of wine out to her, but she'd been too absorbed in her longing to reach for it. "Sorry, just wondering what kind of wine it is," she blithered.

His smile turned anticipatory. "Taste it first and then I'll tell you."

She lifted the glass to the light and swirled it gently as she'd been trained to do in the wine class she'd taken for Stratus. "Beautiful color and nice legs." She held it under her nose and took several quick sniffs. "Lovely but powerful. Definitely aged in oak." Will's gaze locked on her as she took the first sip. When the flavor swirled over her palate, she forgot all her fancy training, closing her eyes as she swallowed the nectar. "Oh God, this is unbelievably fantastic. What is it?"

"Le Montrachet. The wine of kings." Will took a sip from his glass and closed his eyes. "My favorite."

Of course Will would have what was arguably the world's greatest dry white wine in his cellar. That he had chosen to share it with her made her heart do somersaults. "I've never had a white wine with this kind of complexity. It's like a great red, only better."

"I knew you'd appreciate it." He kissed her, his lips cool from the wine. "I suggest we take the bottle upstairs so I can lap it out of your navel."

Kyra hissed in a breath as his words drew trails of heat through her. "I'm not sure you should treat great wine that way."

"Your body deserves nothing less than the finest." He kissed her neck just under her earlobe.

Arousal flared in her belly, as much from his words as his kisses. "As long as I get the same privileges."

He dipped his finger in the wine and drew a line down between her collarbones, then bent to lick it off, the heat of his tongue contrasting with the coolness of the wine. "Something like that?" he purred.

She nodded, her throat clenched against the moan that tried to work its way out.

"Privileges granted," he said. "Maybe I should get another bottle out of the cellar. Because I want to lick it off every inch of you."

Even as pure desire rolled through her, something else twined with it, something sweeter but much, much more dangerous.

Something that even Petra had seen in Kyra's eyes when she looked at Will.

Chapter 12

Kyra put down the knife on the kitchen island at the Carver Center and rested her pounding forehead on the back of her hand for a moment. Last night seemed surreal in the cold light of day. She'd poured several thousand dollars of wine on the naked body of a billionaire CEO and then lapped it off him, all while cavorting on a giant bed in his multimillion-dollar Manhattan townhouse. Not to mention what he'd done to her body with the other bottle of wine. Yes, they'd drunk two bottles of Le Montrachet, although drinking was a term she had to use loosely in this scenario.

The wine-infused lovemaking was only the tip of the iceberg. Early this morning she woke up wrapped in his arms with his long, strong body pressed against her.

She'd held herself still so she could drink in the beautiful planes and angles of his face while he slept. With the attention-grabbing hue of his eyes hidden behind his eyelids, she could focus on the different shades of gold in his hair and the shadow in the cleft of his chin. Generations of breeding had created a perfect bone structure that was elegant yet utterly masculine.

Finally, she could restrain herself no longer and traced her finger along one sharp cheekbone. His eyelids flickered open, and the brilliance of them speared her. "I like waking up to find you staring at me," he said, his voice raspy with morning and seduction.

"I was just thinking that your DNA should be put in a vault for future cloning."

"I, er, will take that as a compliment. I think." He rolled so that she lay on top of him. She felt his cock stir against her stomach while he stroked down to caress the curve of her backside. And she'd forgotten her hangover headache for a while.

He'd insisted on fixing her breakfast, so they'd sat across from each other at a granite-topped table in his sleek, modern kitchen, she with her oatmeal, he with his omelet, sipping coffee and sharing the newspaper.

Now she moaned out loud at how right, how comfortable, how perfect it had felt. But it wasn't Kyra's world. It was the castle in the clouds that Will strode through with exquisite, well-bred women like Petra gliding along beside him.

Lifting her head, she forced herself to concentrate on cutting the cantaloupe into uniform bite-size chunks. The kids would help her wrap the chunks in thin slices of prosciutto and skewer them with colorful toothpicks. They were part of the array of hors d'oeuvres she'd planned for Max Varela's official induction into the Carver Center's board of trustees tonight.

She'd come up with recipes that offered the children a chance to contribute since the whole Carver Center community—children, parents, staff, and trustees—was invited to attend. She was also offering deviled eggs garnished with little swirls of smoked salmon, fresh fruit skewers, and figs stuffed with robiola cheese, all things that required lots of assembly that amateur hands could provide this afternoon. Emily had authorized extra funds to purchase the ingredients, so the celebration would be especially festive.

Thank goodness she'd taken the entire evening off from bartending because of the party. Maybe she could go to bed early. Of course, Will appeared to expect her to spend every night with him now. His casual assumption was both thrilling and unnerving. She wondered if she should insist on a night to herself to actually sleep.

Who was she kidding? She was going to take every minute she could get with Will. Because there wouldn't be that many more.

She finished the cantaloupe and sliced open another one with her favorite large supersharp knife that only she was permitted to touch. The kids were not allowed to slice and dice for their own safety and to protect the center from liability.

"Wow, what did that melon do to you?" Emily strolled in as Kyra started speed chopping a slice into chunks.

"Just trying to get things ready for when the kids arrive. We have a lot of goodies to put together for the reception."

Emily plunked the shopping bag she was carrying onto the counter. "A gift from Max. He said you mentioned something about crab not being in the budget, even with the supplemental funding."

Kyra dropped the knife and reached into the bag, pulling out a container of premium lump crabmeat. "Oh my God! Tell Max he's the best." She hugged the plastic tub before peering into the bag to find five more. "Should I make crab cake bites or crab salad on minibuns or crab and artichoke dip? I can't decide."

"They all sound scrumptious, so go with your instinct." Emily sat down on a stool and held up her phone. "I got an e-mail from a Farrington Lange—who prefers to be called Farr—about a fact-finding visit here for the Thalia Foundation. Which just happens to be funded by Cronus Holdings, which just happens to own Ceres. Any connection between you and Farr?" Emily was grinning.

"I was afraid he was being polite about his interest in the Carver Center, so I didn't want to get your hopes up," Kyra said. "But yes, he's a friend of Will's and heads up the foundation's trustees. I saw him at Stratus last night, which must have prompted him to get in touch."

"Thank you." Emily stood to give her a hug. "A personal connection is the best." A light flush showed on her cheeks. "Something I counted on as well."

"Is it true that you shoved aside Max's secretary, burst into his office, and forced him to give you the money to buy the empty lot? He claims it is, but I can't picture it." Max liked to tease his fiancée, which was really cute in such a brilliant, intense man.

The flush brightened but Emily snorted. "*Shoved* is too strong a word. *Brushed* would be more accurate. I wanted that lot for the kids and the dogs, and we were running out of time and options. But no one can *force* Max Varela to do anything he doesn't want to, trust me."

"You're pretty fierce when it comes to the kids." Kyra admired Emily's devotion to the center, a devotion that had led not only to the founding of the K-9 Angelz program but a fairy-tale second chance at love. Someone should write a book about it.

"Back to Farr. I'd like you to join the tour, if possible, since you know him. Do you have a preference on the date?"

"You know my schedule better than I do. I'm fine with any day we aren't having a special meal."

"I appreciate all your work on the food for Max's induction. Your fancy hors d'oeuvres will make it so joyful." Emily swiped a chunk of cantaloupe and popped it in her mouth. "Mmm, how do you find such sweet ones?"

"I thump a lot of melons. And sniff them."

"You'll have to teach me sometime. But I'll let you get back to work."

As Emily exited, Kyra pulled out her cell phone. She texted Will: Did you lean on Farr to set up a visit to the Carver Center? If so, thank you.

She'd finished cutting up the melon when her phone pinged again. The only time I discussed it with him was at the party with you. He asked for the Carver Center's number himself.

Pinkie swear?

He texted back a graphic of the Boy Scout salute of three fingers held upright.

She chuckled. Were you really a Boy Scout? Doesn't seem the prepster thing to do.

Eagle Scout, thank you very much.

Beefing up your college application then.

That implies it needed beefing up. I'm offended.

Kyra thought for a moment. Better to be slapped with the truth than kissed with a lie. —Old Russian proverb. Gotta go back to work. Some of us don't have minions.

Veritas lux mea.

Truth is my light. She snorted and shoved her phone back in her jeans pocket. Just because it was in Latin didn't make it smarter.

The guests were still lingering as Kyra consolidated the remnants of the hors d'oeuvres onto a couple of half-empty platters. Max strolled up, his brown-and-white rescue dog, Rocco, trotting along beside him. Emily had presented Max with the puppy last Christmas, and the two were now inseparable. Rumor had it that Max even took Rocco to work when he wasn't experimenting with hazardous chemicals. The contrast between the tall man in an elegant custom-tailored suit and the little street dog with the lopsided ears was utterly endearing. No wonder Emily had fallen so hard for her billionaire chemist.

"I wanted to thank you for the impressive spread of food," he said. "The crab bites were small miracles of deliciousness. I admit to eating more than my fair share."

"You were the guest of honor, so we'll forgive you," Kyra said, glowing at the compliment. "Without your gift of the magic ingredient, no miracles would have been possible. Even more important, thank you for joining the board of trustees. It means a lot to all of us."

"I didn't join it just because Emily is the director," Max said. "I believe in what the Carver Center does for the kids . . . and the dogs. I hope to support more programs like this one, so seeing it in action firsthand will broaden my knowledge."

"Mr. Max!" Felicia dashed up, followed at a more dignified pace by Shaq, who was wearing a black bow tie for the occasion. "Did you ask her yet?"

"I was getting to it." Max smiled down at the child before lifting his gaze back to Kyra. "Rocco's been having some stomach troubles so I was wondering if you could give me some guidance."

"Ms. Kyra made Shaq so much better." Felicia stooped to hug the dog. "Pretty soon he's going to be able to come home with me for a slumber party. I can't wait."

The dog licked the girl's face, making Kyra laugh and reach down to stroke the animal's big, solid head. His eyelids drooped in an expression of canine ecstasy. "Shaq's looking very handsome this evening," Kyra said.

Felicia beamed. "My mama made the bow tie so he'd be stylin'."

Kyra turned to Max. "I'll give you some of Shaq's special blend to take home." She explained about slowly increasing the proportion of new food to old.

Max bent down to pick up Rocco, tucking him under his arm as he stroked his short, wiry coat. "Now you've got a personal chef on top of everything else," he said to the dog. "You are spoiled rotten."

Felicia straightened up. "Ms. Emily says our dogs deserve to be spoiled because they give us their love and that's the best gift of all."

"Ms. Emily is a very wise woman," Max said solemnly.

"You got to say that 'cause she's wearing your ring," Felicia said.

"Out of the mouths of babes . . . ," Kyra murmured.

Max smiled. "You've got it backward. I put a ring on her finger because she's so wise."

Felicia cocked an eyebrow at him. "She ain't here listening, you know."

"Felicia, I was looking all over for you." A slender woman dressed in a bright red suit and heels walked up to them.

"Sorry, Mama," the girl said. "Mama, this here's Ms. Kyra, the chef, and Mr. Max, the trustee."

"I'm Davina Gibson. Good to meet you." She nodded to Kyra, making her elaborate braids swing gracefully.

"Your taco macaroni recipe was a big hit here. Felicia says you might have another dish for me," Kyra said.

Davina nodded again. "My grandmother cooked for ten kids and passed her recipes down to me. I'm glad to share them." She turned to Max. "I hear you got us the K-9 Angelz yard. Felicia sure loves that dog, so I have to thank you."

"Emily had far more to do with creating the program than I did," Max said. "But you're welcome."

"Ms. Emily makes a lot of things happen," Davina said.

"She works hard because the kids are her passion," Kyra said.

Max gave them the flashing smile that all the female staff members tried to elicit. It had less effect on her now that Will had claimed her thoughts but it was still gorgeous. Davina seemed dazzled by it, too, because she blinked a few times.

"Mama, will you come with me to put Shaq in his crate? You haven't seen where he sleeps." Felicia tugged on her mother's hand.

"Sure, honey," the woman said. She looked back at Max and Kyra. "Thanks for the party. Felicia loved the crab. That's a real treat."

Emily joined them as Davina departed. "I didn't get a chance to tell you, Kyra. Farr Lange is coming tomorrow at three o'clock. I hope that works for you."

Max looked surprised. "Isn't he a trustee of the Thalia Foundation?"

Kyra noticed that he slipped his arm around his fiancée's waist and drew her closer to his side.

"I forgot to tell you, too," Emily said with a rueful smile, her face soft as she met his gaze. "I was so focused on the big event tonight. Kyra met him at a party and obviously impressed the heck out of him."

"I went to college with Will Chase, who introduced me to Farr." That sounded innocuous enough.

Emily's eyes were dancing with amusement but she didn't add to Kyra's minimal description.

"It would be great to get more foundation money behind the center, since you insist on limiting what my Catalyst Foundation can give you." Max's voice held a touch of irritation.

"Your foundation supports many other very worthy causes that count on the money," Emily said in a way that made Kyra think they'd had this discussion a few times before.

"I'm going to let you two duke this out alone," Kyra said with a smile.

As she carried a stack of empty platters downstairs to the kitchen, her cell phone vibrated in her pocket. She slid the dirty dishes onto the center island to read Will's message: I'm free to pick you up any time now.

Pleasure hummed through her at his impatience. She glanced at the time and the state of the kitchen. I'll meet you out front in an hour.

A gentleman always comes to the door, he texted back.

But she didn't want people to see him. Max would recognize him for sure. That would require some awkward explanations. She'd just have to make sure to be outside already.

A gentleman is nothing but a wolf in sheep's clothing, Kyra texted.

No argument here, he shot back.

She laughed and stuck her phone back in her pocket. She had a lot to do if she was going to keep everyone from seeing her golden lover.

Kyra was sitting on the front steps, actually enjoying the balmy spring evening, when the limo floated up the street, the glossy black paint catching the streetlights. She jumped up and ran down the steps and across the sidewalk before Will could do more than push open the door.

She pitched herself into the car's interior, landing almost on his lap.

"I like an eager woman," he said, pulling her in for a mind-bending kiss. "But I suspect I'm being kept away from the Carver Center." Amusement and hurt colored his voice.

"I just needed some air and quiet after a crazy day." True as far as it went.

He cradled her against his side, and she noticed that he wore jeans and a T-shirt, not a suit. "How does a hot Jacuzzi and a glass of wine sound?" he asked.

"Will you be in the Jacuzzi with me?"

"If you'd like, but just as company. You're tired."

"We'll see what comes up." She grinned at him.

He groaned. "Frat house humor."

As she relaxed into him, exhaustion swept over her in a wave and she yawned. "I think you'll need to be in the Jacuzzi to keep me from falling asleep and drowning."

His arm tightened. "Before you fall asleep, I want to ask you something. Farr is visiting the Carver Center tomorrow, and I had planned to come with him. However, I don't want to cause you any discomfort."

She lifted her hand to touch his cheek. "You're sweet to ask instead of just showing up. Our director, Emily, knows that I see you, um, socially. So as long as you don't ravish me on the kitchen counter, it will be okay."

"I'll save that for my own kitchen counter." He dropped a kiss on top of her head.

She closed her eyes, rocked into drowsiness by the motion of the limousine.

"One more thing," Will said, his voice rumbling in her ear where it was pressed against his chest. "I was talking to my COO, Greg Ebersole, about your limited-ingredient fresh dog food. He thought that might be something Ceres could expand into. He wants to discuss it with you, if you wouldn't mind."

Kyra's eyes flew open and she sat up. "He doesn't need to talk with me. I just Googled it. There's no secret recipe or anything."

"He sees some strong marketing opportunities by tying it in with the K-9 Angelz project. There could be some real money in it for the Carver Center."

"Wow! That would be great." Emily wanted to expand the program and had her eye on another building and adjacent lot farther north in Harlem where the prices were still reasonable. A corporate tie-in could generate the kind of cash that would make it possible to buy the properties. "But he should really talk to Emily about that sort of thing. I'm just the cook."

"You're the creator of the dog food."

"Well, sure, I'll be happy to tell him everything I know. That should take about ten minutes, tops."

"Don't undersell yourself."

He sounded annoyed. Maybe he'd talked her up to his colleague and didn't want her to undermine his glowing description. "Don't mind me. I'm just tired."

He stroked her hair. "I wouldn't have brought it up except that Greg is gung ho about the idea."

She didn't want to think about dog food right now. She nestled her head on his shoulder, yawned until her jaw creaked, and slid down into sleep.

Will felt her relax and pulled her closer against him to hold her steady as they bounced through potholes and swayed around corners. Her body felt small and trusting, almost like a child, in his arms. Strange how the tough, independent Kyra stirred his protective instincts in such a powerful way.

So powerful that he'd hired a private investigator to look into her debt load. Now he understood why she had given up the idea of going back to school, because the amount had surprised him. Frustration made his jaw clench. He could wipe out the debt in a millisecond using only his personal checking account—and had even considered doing so anonymously—but she would know he was behind the payment. And she would not be happy about it. In fact, she might be offended enough to end their relationship.

The prospect of not seeing her again made his chest go hollow. She stirred and muttered something. He eased the grip that he had unconsciously tightened on her.

He already had to battle her perception that there was some great abyss between them because of his money and background. Ironic that the self-reliance he admired so much about her made him want to shake her at the same time. He could tell from her response that the conversation with Greg was not going to accomplish what he had hoped. Kyra would either see right through it or decide that she wasn't qualified for the job.

Now he had to come up with an alternative strategy because he wanted her to make more money and he hated her job at Stratus. Bartending kept her away from him until late at night, when he couldn't stop himself from making love to her. Guilt ate at him that he was driving her to exhaustion, especially since she had fallen asleep at eight o'clock.

Not to mention that even at a high-end bar, he knew how male customers were looking at her and calculating the odds of taking her to bed with them. Her sex appeal was part of her success at her job. But it made him crazy to imagine other men ogling the opulent curves of her breasts in the V of her vest or the flash of smooth stomach between her jeans and her top. Those were his private property now.

Yet he couldn't ask her to make changes in her life just to accommodate him. Their relationship was too new, too undefined. Which bothered him. He found himself looking into the future and wanting her there with him.

She made him understand that he wasn't being true to himself. But he didn't know what *was* true, so he needed her to help him. She saw things—including him—so clearly and honestly.

He stroked his palm lightly down her back, and she snuggled into him. A strange fear tightened his throat. The things he could offer her were things she'd made clear that she didn't need. He was at the mercy of whatever she felt for him.

And he wasn't at all confident about what that might be.

Chapter 13

Last night Will had been true to his word. He had filled the Jacuzzi tub in his enormous master bathroom, helped her into it, and then perched beside her as she floated among the swirling, fragrant bubbles, sipping a glass of Le Montrachet. He'd even stripped to his waist so he could wash her hair, his long, clever fingers massaging her scalp in a way that made her moan with pleasure. Then he'd wrapped her in a thick, fluffy towel before tucking her into his bed. Naked, but untouched.

The feel of the soft linen sheets against her clean, bare skin had been close to orgasmic. When he had finished undressing and slid under the bedclothes beside her, she rolled into him, wanting more. He gathered her against his chest, kissed her gently, and said, "Sleep, sweetheart. I can tell you need it."

How could that be even sexier than having sex with him? Yet it was. Last night, at any rate. Today, she was hungry for him again.

Now she fussed around the Carver Center's kitchen. The children's snack was prepared, the big casserole dishes ready to pop into the ovens to be baked. She rearranged a few of the hanging pots, put out a fresh dish towel, and wiped an errant fingerprint off the stainless steel counter. Because Will was coming to visit in ten minutes.

Her worlds were about to collide.

Emily arrived and saved her from more nervous fidgeting. "Everything's ready upstairs," the director said before she glanced around the kitchen. "Wow! This place looks like one of those television kitchens."

Kyra laughed. "Maybe if we had a granite countertop and a couple of Viking ranges. But I gave everything an extra polish this morning." She smoothed down the top she had changed into after cooking and cleaning. It was a soft, silky robin's-egg–blue fabric, sleeveless with a draped neckline. She'd also added dangly silver earrings.

"And you came in early, I noticed." She gave Kyra's shoulder a squeeze. "Thank you for helping to put our best foot forward, even though I think you've already given us a leg up."

"Nice body part metaphors," Kyra said.

"I thought so." Emily winked before checking her reflection in the countertop and adjusting her ponytail.

"I guess we shouldn't have a swig of the cooking sherry before we're about to entertain possible donors," Kyra said with a wry smile.

Emily's eyes were warm with concern. "What worries you about the visit?"

"That's a good question." Kyra shrugged. "I guess that Will is coming into *my* world for a change, and I'm not sure what will happen."

Would he fit in or disrupt it? Would his opinion of her change? His arrival at Stratus hadn't thrown her into a tizzy, but that was because the high-end bar was really his world. She just worked there.

"He will admire you even more for the wonderful work you do here," Emily said. "How could he not?"

"Thanks." Kyra tried to draw confidence from Emily's words but her nerves were still taut with tension.

She heard the front door open and the deep voice of Powell, the guard at the front desk. She and Emily exchanged a glance and stepped out into the entrance hallway.

Farr walked toward them, wearing a power suit and an expression of cordial interest. Although Kyra introduced Emily to Farr, her gaze strayed to the man behind him.

Will was leaning slightly over the desk as he exchanged pleasantries with Powell. The sun slanting through the front window turned his hair brilliant gold, and his profile displayed his aristocratic breeding in the high forehead, straight nose, and strong chin. His pale gray suit outlined the expanse of his shoulders and the length of his legs in a way that made Kyra's mouth go dry.

He turned his head, and his eyes met hers. It was like being hit by a thousand volts of electricity. Her nerve endings sizzled with awareness. His charming smile turned into something intimate and intense. "Hello, Kyra," was all he said, and yet his voice sent tremors shimmering through her.

"Will. So glad that you could come." She did her best to keep her voice normal as he drew nearer. However, a slight quaver snuck in as she went through the initial courtesies again.

Emily went into her director-sweet-talking-donors mode and asked them if they'd like any beverages before she gave them the tour.

But all Kyra could do was watch Will, his bespoke suit and elegant presence contrasting with the worn brown linoleum floor and the cream-painted walls smudged by carelessly worn backpacks and grubby hands. He looked at ease but out of place. She wanted to kiss him in the worst way.

As Emily and Farr started up the stairs, Will moved to Kyra's side and skimmed a quick kiss over her cheek. "I just needed to touch you," he murmured beside her ear.

His lips had barely brushed her skin, but her knees went shaky and she wanted to collapse against the heat and strength of his body.

This was bad.

She allowed herself a quick graze of her fingertips over the back of his hand. "Pay attention. There will be a quiz later," she murmured back.

He had the nerve to pat her on the behind . . . and she couldn't even get mad because she enjoyed it.

♥ ♥ ♥

In his role as the Thalia Foundation's founder, Will had toured many facilities that helped others but he'd never been so impressed. The Carver Center offered computers, homework help, basic medical care, and nutritious food, but the K-9 Angelz program added a whole new dimension of both responsibility and love. He noted that the space was now packed to the gills with kids and dogs. Kyra explained in a murmur that Emily couldn't turn away a child in need. Will found that admirable but it also strained their resources. They needed to expand.

Part of his pleasure in walking through the center, though, was in having Kyra at his side in the daylight with other people around. Watching her interact with Farr, Emily, the kids, and the dogs gave him an odd sense of pride. Her trademark combination of caring and resilience fit right into the center's spirit. He understood why she chose to work there. What he didn't understand was why he felt some owner-ship of her accomplishments.

"Hey, Will, you might be able to help with this." Kyra's voice scat-tered his reflections. "Isaiah needs to name his K-9 Angel and he's look-ing for a classical reference." She smiled a challenge at him.

Will looked at the couch beside them to find three boys staring up at him with skeptical curiosity. He judged them to be about ten or eleven years old, although he was far from expert on children's ages.

"I say Anubis. It be savage," one boy said.

"And appropriate since Anubis was the jackal-headed god," Will said.

"You deadass?" another boy asked. "I mean, is that facts?"

Will nodded and added, "Anubis is the Egyptian god of the dead, so maybe not the most uplifting name."

"That be poppin'," the first boy said, bouncing on the sofa with excitement. "You gotta use that, yo."

"I don't gotta use nothin'," the boy who was evidently Isaiah scoffed. "He be *my* dog. He just gotta get his shots and sh . . . stuff." He turned to Will. "You know any other gods?"

"Greek, Roman, Norse, or Egyptian?" Will asked.

"Show-off," Kyra muttered.

"Any of them god of dogs?" the boy asked, unimpressed.

Will considered this. "Not that I can think of, although some of them hunted with hounds. Maybe if you showed me a picture of your dog, it might prompt a name to suit him."

"Dope," Isaiah said, tapping at his cell phone before holding it up.

Will took the phone and tilted it so Kyra could also see the photo of a medium-sized black dog. The dog's ancestry was so mixed that Will couldn't have hazarded a guess as to the combination of breeds, but his large, upright, pointed ears made him resemble a bat.

"That crescent-shaped white mark on his forehead kind of looks like a moon," Kyra said, a lock of her silky hair brushing the back of Will's hand as she leaned in to look. "Got anything for that?"

He reined in his desire to wind his fingers into her hair and focused on the task at hand. "You could name him after the Egyptian god of the moon, Khonsu. His name means 'traveler.'"

"That be more dope than some death god," Isaiah said, throwing a glance at the Anubis proponent. "How you spell that?"

Will spelled it. "If you'd like, I'll send you a book on the Egyptian gods, so you can learn more about Khonsu. He was a big name in Egypt."

"That'd be lit," Isaiah said. "Who are you anyway?"

"Will Chase." Will offered his hand to Isaiah and then to the other two boys who were Jayden and Zion.

"You the reason we got to be clean and quiet today?" Jayden asked.

Will heard Kyra choke on a laugh.

"You mean you aren't always?" Will lifted an eyebrow.

Zion grinned. "We got to be *extra* clean and quiet."

Isaiah waved that topic aside. "How you know so much about gods?"

Kyra jumped in. "He was a classics major in college, so he studied ancient history."

"Like Julius Caesar and those homies?" Jayden asked. "What good is that? You gotta know tech stuff now."

Will sat on the arm of the sofa. "There's a saying that those who cannot remember the past are condemned to repeat it. You want to avoid the mistakes your ancestors made, don't you?"

"I guess," Jayden said.

"Besides the stories are great. Lots of blood and guts." Will smiled.

"Like video games," Zion said, making explosive sound effects that were surprisingly realistic.

"Except with spears and swords," Kyra said, slashing through the air as though she held a blade.

Jayden looked skeptical. "Spears and swords are lame."

"Have you heard of the Spartans?" Will asked.

"Ain't that a movie? *Three Hundred Fighters* or something?" Isaiah said.

"Something like that." Will looked at Kyra. "Do we have a minute?"

"You're here to help us, so you have all the minutes you want," she said. "Although I may have to duck out to put the snack in the oven."

Will settled more comfortably and began to describe Spartan society in which the boys trained as soldiers from the time they were seven. His audience soon stopped interrupting as he went on to the legend of the three hundred at the battle of Thermopylae.

Kyra slipped away without stopping the flow of his narration. He started to rise as he saw her begin to leave, but she waved him back onto the sofa arm.

Just as he got to the exchange of messages when Xerxes demands that the Greeks hand over their arms and the Spartan king Leonidas fires back with, "Come and take them," Farr and Emily walked up.

"Are you terrifying these young men with tales of ancient violence?" Farr drawled.

Will looked at the three young faces, eyes fixed on him, bodies leaning in, enthralled by the story of men who had died thousands of years ago. He wanted to stay, to share his passion for the glorious past with them, but he smiled and stood. "I think today's video games surpass anything I can describe."

"Hey!" Jayden said. "You didn't finish the story."

"How about if I come back next week and tell you the rest?" As he turned to Emily, Will caught a look of surprise on Farr's face. "If that's all right with Ms. Emily."

"We'd love to have you any time," the director said, her smile like the sun.

He could hang out in the kitchen, too, drinking in the sight of Kyra in her element.

A feeling flowed through him like a clear, buoyant Caribbean Sea tide. He wasn't sure if it was happiness or peace.

Tearing herself away from Will had been hard, and not just because she enjoyed the chance to let her eyes rove over his long, suit-clad body. She'd been as spellbound by his stories about the Spartans as the three boys were. She'd known that he could play with words in brilliant ways but this was the first time she'd seen him share his knowledge with an audience. A very appreciative one, too.

But she'd had to get the casseroles in the oven and now she was finishing up the fresh salad to accompany them. As she scattered halved cherry tomatoes over the freshly washed lettuce, she heard footsteps behind her.

She knew it was Will before she turned. The air around her felt different when he was in the room.

As soon as she pivoted, he took her face between both of his hands and kissed her with a strange tenderness that spoke of gratitude. When he lifted his head, the angles of his face seemed less sharp somehow. "May I watch you cook?" he asked.

"Do you have a fetish I don't know about?" She rested her palms on his chest, savoring the steady beat of his heart under the smooth cotton of his dress shirt and wondering what the strange kiss meant. "Doesn't matter because you have no choice. I have to finish the snack. In fact"—she eyed his expensive suit—"I could use some help. The tour messed up my schedule."

He shucked off his jacket and tossed it over a stool. "Put me to work."

"How do you feel about wearing a chef's apron? I don't want to get spots on those million-dollar duds."

"I could take them all off." His eyes danced.

"Keep it in your pants. There are forty kids upstairs." But she loved his playful mood, so she snapped his butt with a dish towel.

"You shall pay for that later, woman," he said. "In the most sinful of ways."

"You promise?" She grinned as she grabbed a clean white apron and handed it to him. "I wish I had one with ruffles."

He wrapped it around himself with an expertise that surprised her. He noticed her reaction. "You forget that I make my living selling food," he said. "I used to spend a lot of time in the test kitchen."

"I thought all you did was taste." She handed him a pair of heat-resistant gloves. "Would you pull the casseroles out of the ovens and put them on the counter, please?"

"Tasting can be messy work." He opened an oven door and reached in for the first dish. Kyra gave herself a few seconds to enjoy the way his shirt pulled over the flex of his shoulder muscles and his gray trousers hugged his tight butt.

Then she grabbed a giant serving spoon and began to transfer the chicken, spinach, and pasta bake to capacious serving bowls. She never put hot cooking pans on the dining table because the kids weren't that careful when reaching for food.

Will set out the heavy casseroles with such efficiency that Kyra wished she always had his assistance. "If you ever want to quit your day job, let me know," she said. "You're a pretty decent sous-chef."

He went still in a way that made her look up from her task. He was gazing out the kitchen door, his oven-mitt–covered hands still wrapped around the last casserole dish.

He shook his head and went back to dishing out food. "I understand why you like working with the kids so much. They're like sponges, absorbing everything you can give them."

She'd been surprised by how comfortable he was with the three boys. He'd been entirely himself, yet they weren't at all intimidated. He'd established an easy rapport with them. And he hadn't talked down to them. Maybe that was his secret.

Just then the thunder of forty sets of feet pounding down the stairs rumbled through the kitchen. The first kids began pouring into the dining room with a screech of chairs being moved and the clamor of young voices anticipating food.

She shoved a bowl into his hands. "If you think they absorbed the Spartans like sponges, wait until you see how they absorb chicken penne."

The meal passed in its usual mad swirl of serving and cleaning up. The kids had to load their own dishes into the industrial dishwasher, but their technique required a lot of repositioning of plates. Will put his hands on Kyra's waist and set her aside, saying, "I was a busboy once so I know how this works."

Which freed up Kyra to tackle other tasks, resulting in a spotless kitchen in less than half the usual time.

"The limo's outside," Will said, untying his soiled apron. Some water had soaked through to his shirt, making it cling to the washboard of his abs. He saw the direction of her glance and lifted an eyebrow. "Maybe you have a little free time before you have to get to your next job?"

Kyra felt heat flush through her. She considered for a long moment before saying, "Want to come and see my etchings?"

Will gave her a narrow-eyed look of pure lust. "I thought you'd never ask."

They hustled out the door like two teenagers and practically fell onto the limousine's back seat. Will had her laid out under him, his mouth open on hers, his hands kneading her breasts, so that she moaned and writhed with pleasure . . . as much as she could with his hips pressing her into the leather of the seat.

He lifted his mouth an inch from hers. "When we were working in the kitchen, I couldn't decide if I wanted to bend you over the counter and take you from behind, or sit you on top of the counter with your thighs spread so I could taste you before I drove myself into you."

His words sank deep, sliding through her hot and fast to burn low in her belly. Two could play this game, though. "When you were at the dishwasher, I wanted to slip my arms under your apron from behind you so I could stroke your cock through your trousers and feel it grow hard. I wanted to make you groan out loud."

She laughed low in her throat as she felt his cock do exactly that against the V of her legs. And he groaned exactly the way she had imagined.

Then he sat up, pulling her with him. "I want to see your etchings first."

"You started it," she pointed out, rubbing her palm over his erection.

He groaned again and grabbed her wrist to pull her hand away. "Only because I was desperate to cop a feel."

Her nipples were tight with arousal and ached against her bra. "That was more than a feel."

"You didn't seem to mind," he murmured against her neck.

She turned her head, threading her fingers into his hair and holding him so she could slant her mouth against his.

Thank God the ride to her apartment wasn't long because the yearning between her legs was almost unbearable by the time they arrived. She unlocked the purple door, painted that color because it was her landlady's favorite. She was about to take Will's hand to lead him up the narrow wooden stairs when she noticed that Gloria's apartment door was open.

Her landlady stood in her favorite place by the front window, her feather duster waving gently over the silk plant. Kyra swallowed a groan of frustration, but she knew Gloria was there to meet Will. She veered away from the stairs and into her landlady's living room, towing Will with her. "Gloria, this is my old college friend Will Chase. Will, my wonderful landlady, Gloria Woods."

Her landlady tucked the feather duster under her arm before she held out her hand. "Good to meet you, Will."

"A pleasure." Will shook her hand and gave her one of his charming smiles, even though Kyra knew he was as eager to get upstairs as she was. "You have a beautiful home, a perfect turn-of-the-century Victorian."

That was exactly the right thing to say. Gloria loved her house with its polished oak woodwork, floral wallpaper, and solid brass sconces.

Pride shone in the landlady's eyes. "They built them right back then." She gestured toward the window. "That's quite a car you drive."

Will shook his head with a glint of humor in his eyes. "Jason would never allow me to drive it. He believes only a trained professional like himself can handle it."

"Gotta be tough to park," Gloria observed before fixing her gaze on him. "I hear you're taking a look at the Carver Center. Maybe I'm a little biased as a board member, but there's no place your Thalia Foundation's money would be put to better use."

"It's an impressive place. The K-9 Angelz program is truly innovative," Will said.

"But dog food costs money," Gloria said.

"Especially if it's made with limited, fresh ingredients." Will's voice held an undertone of amusement.

"Whoever heard of a pit bull who can't eat regular old dog food?" Gloria shook her head. "But leave it to Kyra to figure out how to keep him happy. Not to mention the meals she gives the kids, food they eat with pleasure but that's healthy for them and doesn't break the budget. Not so easy to find that balance."

Kyra felt a flush of gratification. "The kids make it fun."

Will surprised her by putting his hand on the small of her back in an almost possessive gesture. "I saw her in action today, so I understand what an asset she is to the center."

He sounded almost as though he was proud of her. A weird thrill ran through her at the thought.

Gloria gave Kyra a sly look. "I need to get back to my dusting, so you two go on along now."

Kyra grinned before she leaned in to give Gloria a peck on the cheek. "You dusted that plant the last time Will came here," she whispered by her landlady's ear.

"With all the pollution in this city, you can't dust too often," Gloria said, unabashed. "Now take your young man and scoot."

Kyra nearly burst out laughing at the idea of the tall, patrician CEO in his custom-tailored clothes being called her young man. Although his shirt still had a damp spot on it from washing the dishes.

"I hope to see you again soon," Will said to Gloria, his tone warm and sincere.

"You bring him by for the Sunday monthly," Gloria said to Kyra as they started toward the stairs.

"The Sunday monthly?" Will asked when they reached the second-floor landing.

The landing's stained glass window threw brilliant blues, greens, and reds across his hair and shirt. The effect made Kyra think of a Picasso painting.

"She fixes a massive and delicious Sunday dinner once a month and invites a select group of guests to join her," Kyra said. "You have been given the Gloria Woods seal of approval with that invitation."

"Happy to know that I passed muster." Will's lips quirked in a crooked smile. "I can't remember the last time I was called someone's young man."

"Gloria's old-school in some ways and really modern in others."

"I like her," Will said. He put his finger under Kyra's chin to tilt it up as he smiled. "And I like being your young man." He dipped his head to drop a quick kiss on her lips.

The kiss unleashed all the pent-up desire she'd tamped down for the meeting with Gloria. But his words lit a softer glow somewhere in her chest. She'd been afraid that he'd find Gloria's reference absurd or overreaching. "I'm glad." Emotion made it impossible to say more, so she continued up the stairs.

From behind her, Will said, "It's good that you have Gloria looking out for you."

"She's kind of like a cool aunt," Kyra said, touched that he understood what Gloria meant to her. The Carver Center community had given her a family in the city.

When she reached the third-floor landing, Kyra unlocked her apartment door and pushed it open. "Welcome to my humble abode." Luckily, she kept the place pretty tidy on most days.

Will's gaze swept her living room and she saw admiration in it. Like him, she'd opted for modern furniture but hers was in the context of a late 1800s structure. And her pieces were cheap knockoffs of the kind of stuff he had in his house. Gloria had loaned her the maroon-and-blue

Oriental rug, which Kyra felt built a bridge between the old and new elements. Her sectional sofa had clean, squared-off lines in a blue imitation-suede fabric that picked up the rug's tone. She'd cut up some fake Oriental rugs and made pillows out of them. The two front windows were hung with simple pleated cream shades to allow in the maximum amount of sunshine. The working fireplace with its white marble mantel was filled with an array of pillar candles that she lit in the summer for coziness without heat.

He walked over to the bookcases built in between the windows, reading the titles and pulling out a volume. "*Chaucer's World.* That's from Lit 302 with Professor Fleming, one of my favorite classes."

"Mine, too. That's why I kept it."

He ran his fingers over the cover before replacing it.

Earlier she had wanted him in her bedroom as quickly as possible, but now she felt hesitant about inviting him into the most private part of her world. He looked too comfortable, too right in her living room, just as he had at the Carver Center and with Gloria. She wanted him to seem awkward or out of place, but Will Chase could fit in wherever he went with an effortless grace that was dangerous to her peace of mind.

"Would you like some wine?" she asked, then winced at the thought of the fifteen-dollar bottle of Chardonnay she had in contrast to the spectacular Le Montrachet they'd been drinking at his house.

He crossed the room in three strides to cup her face in his hands. "All I want right now is you," he said.

She nodded within his grasp. "Let me show you where I keep my etchings."

He wrapped one arm around her waist to walk down the narrow hallway to her bedroom at the back of the house. The room was small so the queen-size bed took up most of the floor space. But it looked inviting covered with its geometric-patterned duvet in tones of terracotta, pale blue, and cream, accented by solid-colored pillow shams in matching shades.

Will met her eyes with a solemn gaze. "Thank you for letting me come here."

Then his eyes turned hot and he lowered his mouth to hers, teasing her lips with his tongue as he cupped her behind and brought her in against his erection.

Desire roared back to life. She ran her hands up his back, loving the swell and flex of his muscles under her touch. She traced the straight line of his spine through the fine cotton of his shirt right down to his belt and then curved her palms over the tight arcs of his buttocks.

"Ahh," he breathed into her mouth. "I need you naked on that bed." He stepped back and tugged the hem of her top upward until she lifted her arms to let him pull it over her head. Her bra seemed to come unhooked almost by magic under his deft fingers. He knelt in front of her to unzip her trousers and pull them down to her ankles before he kissed the lace of her panties at the juncture of her thighs. The press of his lips so close to the focus of her yearning had her hissing with anticipation.

Then he slowly traced his fingertips along all the edges of her panties, first around the top, then around each leg, skimming near the wet ache between her legs so that she held her breath, waiting.

He leaned in and inhaled before he blew out a breath that feathered over her sensitized skin, making her shiver. "You smell good enough to eat," he said, tossing a wicked glance up at her. "Kitchen spices and aroused woman."

Then his fingers were hooked in the side of her panties and he drew them downward. She braced one hand on his solid shoulder and stepped out of her shoes and the bundle of clothing at her ankles. He stood and grasped her shoulders so he could lower her back onto the bed. He towered above her, his eyes raking over her bare skin. "Put your hands up over your head," he rasped.

A shiver of arousal ran through her, making her nipples tighten even more as she lifted her arms and stretched them out on the duvet.

He sucked in a breath. "Circe, Helen of Troy, and Cleopatra all in one."

A purely feminine power surged through her. She arched her back to tempt his hands onto her breasts.

Instead he yanked open his belt and fly, pushed down his boxer briefs, and rolled on a condom. Putting his hands on her thighs, he pushed them wide open and stood between them. He slipped his hands under her bottom to tilt her pelvis upward before he drove his cock deep into her. The delicious shock of being filled abruptly made her body bow upward so her head was pressed back into the mattress. She bent her knees and braced her feet on either side of him to angle her pelvis even higher.

His fingers curled into her buttocks, holding her in the position he wanted as he withdrew and thrust in again. She looked up to see his eyes focused on the place their bodies joined, watching himself move in and out of her. The contrast of her total nakedness with his tailored business clothes fanned her arousal even higher.

His rhythm accelerated, making her hips buck against his grip. She caught the moment he lost control, his eyes slamming shut, his head falling back, his grasp tightening so he could plunge in and out of her straight and hard. As her body grew taut with desire, he shouted her name and he seated himself deep inside her where she could feel the pumping of his orgasm.

He held them like that until the last pulse of his climax died. Then he banded one forearm under her behind and slipped his finger down over her clit, hitting just the right spot to release her pent-up energy in a convulsion of sheer pleasure. She arched and bucked and screamed under the persuasion of his finger and his embedded cock, her muscles squeezing and relaxing over and over again until she went limp in his grip.

He slipped out of her and lowered her gently to the bed before disposing of his condom. He lay down on the bed on his side and gathered her into him, the fine fabrics of his clothing soft against her skin. "I don't suppose Gloria is hard of hearing," he said.

Surprise made her laugh. "I was expecting something more along the lines of, 'That was amazing!' or 'You're sexy as hell.'"

An answering laugh rumbled in his chest. "I was getting to that." He nuzzled up to her ear. "You wrenched my orgasm all the way up from my toes. I lost control."

Satisfaction glowed through her, stoking her physical contentment. "Gloria is not hard of hearing, but she would applaud the fact that I made you lose control."

"I got that impression when I met her."

He'd met too many people she knew. She didn't want him to become braided into her real life. When the end came, disentangling herself from him would be that much harder.

She glanced at the vintage Bakelite clock on her bedside table. She had forty-five minutes before she had to get ready for her night job. She pulled the corner of the duvet up from the bottom of the bed to wrap it around herself. Will heaved a sigh of regret but, after kissing her bare shoulder, let her sit up.

"I've been thinking about your job and the kids," she said, brushing a stray lock of hair off his forehead as he lay on his back, his eyes so deep she felt like she could drown in them.

He levered himself up on his elbow and gave her a quizzical smile. "Such a serious topic just after sex."

"It was serious sex, so it seems appropriate." She laid her palm against the sharp line of his jaw. "Have you ever thought about teaching? You were amazing with those three boys. Even I could barely tear myself away from your lesson in Spartan history."

He shook his head against her hand, but then smiled ruefully. "The look on those kids' faces when I was telling them about the Spartans made me feel . . . 'lit,' as Isaiah would say. Like electricity was crackling between me and them."

"You're a natural teacher." She smiled with a wry edge. "Although I warn you that there are also days when you want to strangle them."

"They can't be any more difficult than managing my sales force."

"It would be a big change from being a CEO," she said. "No corner office, no power suits, no minions kowtowing to you. I guess you could grow back your ponytail, though."

"The ponytail is a definite point in favor of becoming a teacher," he said. "But my minions would miss me."

"You could just teach a class once a week or something."

He appeared to consider it before he shook his head again. "It wouldn't be fair for me to promise a class every week. I'd have too many conflicts with work. If you're going to commit to something, especially for children, you have the responsibility to be there."

"That's very honorable, but some ancient history would be better than none for those boys." She pulled the duvet tighter around her breasts. "Just think about it."

A flash of heat flared in his eyes and he hooked a finger in the duvet where it stretched over her cleavage.

"Nope," she said. "I have to get ready for Stratus."

His expression darkened. "I wish you didn't have that job."

"That job pays the bills," she said, trying to pull away from his touch. He feathered his fingertips over the swell of her breasts, making tingles dance over her skin, before he removed his hand.

She realized she was going to have to drop the duvet and walk to the bathroom naked since he was stretched out on top of the bed. She was less worried about being exposed than she was about Will persuading her to be late for work. But she'd just have to be strong.

"I need to shower." She threw him a saucy smile. "To wash off the smell of kitchen spices and satisfied woman."

"I'll scrub your back," he said, his eyelids heavy with seduction. He shifted to prop himself up against her pillows, hands behind his head, long legs stretched out on the duvet and crossed at the ankles so she could see the dog bones on his lavender socks. She was afraid that, from now on, she would imagine him there on her bed, looking like sin incarnate, every time she walked into her bedroom.

"I'm pretty sure you'd end up scrubbing more than my back, so I'll say no to that kind offer." She threw off the duvet and strode toward the hallway.

As she walked out the door, she was followed by a long, appreciative wolf whistle.

Will didn't want to leave. Kyra's bedroom was like a cozy cocoon that he could wrap himself in. A floating sense of well-being permeated his body while he allowed his gaze to scan over the carefully chosen furniture and knickknacks that showed him the private woman. There were a few photographs he would have to look at more closely, but right now, he just wanted to absorb the atmosphere.

Closing his eyes, he inhaled, parsing the scents he'd drawn into his nostrils. Sex. That made his lips curve in satisfaction. A faint aroma of the casserole she'd cooked today, which was probably as much from his clothing as hers. An old-fashioned cosmetic fragrance that he couldn't place. Perfume or a cream of some sort. That old-house smell that combined wood, furniture polish, and age.

The sounds of New York drifted into his consciousness. Distant sirens, a barking dog, traffic . . . always traffic, and the bang of a dumpster lid slamming down. Closer, he could hear the shower running, which sent his mind off in directions that made his cock stir.

He reluctantly banished the image of Kyra, her long, wet hair clinging to her breasts and back, while water sluiced over her naked body.

The idea of teaching nagged at the corner of his mind. He'd loved studying the classics and their history at Brunell, but he'd never been tempted to shut himself up in a musty archive to do scholarly research.

At the time, that had seemed the only way to continue with his chosen field of knowledge. But passing that knowledge on . . .

It had never occurred to him to become a teacher. He realized now that it was because of his parents' weighty expectations.

If they hadn't lavished both their attention and their money on him, maybe he would have had an easier time thwarting their desires for him. But they loved him in their own demanding, self-centered ways. It was hard to disappoint them.

That unwelcome thought had him swinging his legs off the bed so he could examine the framed photos arrayed on the top of Kyra's blond wood dresser. A faded picture of a young couple holding a baby as they stood on a cement patio must be her parents and her. She'd gotten her luminous brown eyes from her mother and her smile that always hinted at an inside joke from her father. Her father wore coveralls with the Mack Trucks logo. His hair was cut short on the sides and left long and curly on top. Where his rolled-up sleeves revealed his forearms, some serious muscle showed on his wiry frame.

Her mother was dressed in tight-fitting jeans and a denim jacket with shoulder pads, her hair layered and blown away from her face, her lipstick glossy pink, huge triangles of gold dangling from her ears. Kyra was reaching one of her tiny infant hands toward the nearest earring, her face rapt with fascination.

Pride and love shone in both her parents' faces as they smiled for the photographer.

Next he picked up a posed head shot of a young Kyra, one of those photos they took in public schools every year. He guessed she was ten or eleven, like the kids at the center. Despite her braces and the roundness of immaturity, her fresh, innocent beauty struck him in the gut. This was Kyra before life had dumped two dying parents and a mountain of debt on her shoulders.

He stroked a fingertip along her two-dimensional cheek. He wished he could give her back that innocence.

The shower noise ceased and he replaced the photo, quickly skimming over the rest, which were groups of friends at various ages. Until he came to one of himself. Well, there were three other people in the picture, including Kyra, all dressed in Brunell blue and orange as they sat in the bleachers of the football stadium.

Memory surged through him. He'd gotten two tickets to that game so he could invite Babette but she'd been busy . . . probably with a different boyfriend. So he'd asked Kyra to come because she was in the suite when Babette turned him down. Then he'd gotten two more tickets and brought along two other random friends, just so Babette wouldn't mistake his outing with Kyra as a date of any kind.

But the day had been an unexpected pleasure. Kyra knew a lot about football because her father was a Steelers fan, so she kept up a running commentary on the game. All four of them had gotten mildly drunk on the scotch he'd smuggled past the security guards in flasks concealed under his jacket. The booze had swept away their inhibitions so they cheered, booed, and sang along with the spirit band. Things he would never have done with Babette.

They'd all staggered out of the stadium together, their arms linked, singing the school's fight song. The security guards had rolled their eyes but left them alone. Will and his two friends had tried to persuade Kyra to come to the fraternity with them, but she'd refused, saying she had to study.

He didn't remember the rest of the day, so clearly it had gone flat after Kyra left.

As the memory faded, Kyra walked back into her bedroom, a large white towel wrapped around her like a sarong, her hair dried into cascading waves, the way it had been when they first encountered each other in Ceres. Then he'd thought it was sexy, making him want to run his fingers through it or spread it on a pillow around her bare shoulders. Now it signaled that she would be tempting other men with it. Granted, her intent was only to entice them to leave large tips, but he knew exactly what they were thinking when they saw those loose, seductive curls.

He forced himself not to scowl. "I remember that afternoon," he said, lifting the photo to show her. "We drank scotch and made a lot of noise."

A faint blush colored her cheeks. "It was the only picture I had of you."

"I'm honored to be included in the rogues' gallery," he said, setting it back among the other photos with a flare of gratification. She'd framed it because of him.

"You were a good friend at Brunell," she said with a shrug. "Even if you seemed to come from an alien planet."

"Connecticut isn't that far from Pennsylvania."

"Geography has nothing to do with it." She nudged him aside with her shoulder so she could pull open a drawer.

He watched unabashedly as she rummaged through a neat pile of panties, pulling out a solid-black bikini without frills or lace. When she caught him staring, she lifted an eyebrow. "Do you have a lingerie fixation?"

"I'm developing one." He pinched up a wisp of pale blue lace between his thumb and forefinger. "Why don't you wear these?"

She tugged the panties out of his grasp and dropped them back in the drawer. "They're not very comfortable for a long night's work."

He lowered his mouth to her shoulder and licked her just-washed skin before blowing on the spot to dry it. "Maybe you could put them on later, just so I can take them off."

She retreated to the other side of the bed and wriggled into the black panties under her towel. "Seems like a waste of energy." But he saw her smile as she bent over.

He fished the blue panties out of the drawer again and slipped them in his trouser pocket. "Efficiency is overrated." He could picture the way her skin would glow under the sheer cobweb of fabric and how he would taste her through it. He cleared his throat.

She pulled a couple of black garments from her closet and tossed them on her bed before turning her back to him and dropping the towel so she could hook on a black bra. As she shimmied into tight black trousers and pulled on a clinging black top that swooped low over her cleavage, he watched her transform herself into the hot, sophisticated Stratus bartender. Even knowing that it was just a persona she donned for work, he felt himself respond to her in a way that was all about sex.

"You're such a chameleon," he said, wanting to drape a scarf over the too-visible shadow between her breasts.

She stepped into a pair of high-heeled ankle boots and shook her head. "It's just a uniform for work."

"No, it's more. Your posture changes. The way your hips move, the way you look out of the corner of your eye at me, even your voice lowers in timbre." He walked around the bed to brush his open palms down the smooth skin of her arms from shoulder to wrist and back up again. "It makes me want to bend you over the bed, yank your pants down to your knees, and come into you from behind."

Her pupils dilated and her breasts rose and fell with her shallow breaths. "Do it when we get back to your place tonight," she said.

Even as his cock hardened in anticipation, an odd disappointment banged around his chest because she didn't want him to come back to her apartment. Maybe his bed was bigger and his wine was more expensive, but he wanted to spend time in this place where he could learn more about her.

"I'll be happy to oblige," he said, then groaned as she ran her fingers over the erection pressing against his fly.

"Hold that thought," she said, rubbing her palm against his straining cock so a spike of electric arousal lanced through him.

"You make it hard to hold any thought at all." His body was tight with the desire to bury himself in her silky heat.

She stepped back and gave him a sassy look. "We need more mind-less pleasure in our lives." Snagging her backpack, she slung it over her shoulder before he could take it. "Can I hitch a ride in the limo?"

He frowned. "That had better be a rhetorical question."

"I prefer not to make assumptions. Keeps things simpler."

He hooked his fingers into the strap of her backpack and slid it off her shoulder. "I'll make it very simple then. The limo is always at your disposal. I will always carry your bag." He let all his pent-up desire loose in his eyes and voice. "I always want to touch you."

Six hours later, as Kyra racked clean glasses into the bar's storage draw-ers, Will's words still sent shivers through her. Good ones and bad ones.

Good because who wouldn't enjoy a gorgeous god of a man saying that he always wanted to touch you with an intensity that convinced you he meant it.

Bad because she was tempted to believe him about the "always" part, and she knew that was delusional. She needed to protect herself against that kind of fantasy thinking, but Will made it so damned hard to hold her heart at arm's length from him.

In fact, she was pretty sure she had utterly failed because it had twisted so hard in her chest that she could barely breathe. She had been afraid that he would notice, but he'd slid her backpack over his shoulder and held out his hand, saying he didn't want her to be late for work.

The moment had passed, but it had left her shaken.

So much so that she'd forgotten to tell Will that his partner, Greg, was meeting her at the center tomorrow morning to discuss dog food. She was skeptical that she had anything useful to contribute, but he'd seemed genuinely interested. That led to her getting up an hour early to give herself enough time to show him all her research and ingredients. He also wanted to meet Shaq, the pit bull with the sensitive stomach.

She glanced at her phone to check the time.

"You can take off now. I'll finish up," Cleo said. "I know who's waiting for you."

"You do?" Kyra slotted the last brandy snifter in.

"The gorgeous blond in the power suit, right? Your old college friend turned CEO." Cleo waggled her eyebrows. "I wouldn't keep him waiting long because there are a lot of ladies who would be happy to entertain him."

Kyra chuckled. "Thanks, sweetie. I appreciate it." She texted Will that she was ready any time. His text came back three seconds later.

Remember what you asked me to do tonight?

Chapter 14

The next morning, as she pulled the ingredients for Shaq's special food mix from the center's refrigerator, Kyra tried not to think about how it had felt when Will drove himself into her from behind. Last night he'd picked her up in the limo, kissed her once, and then moved to his corner so they couldn't touch. But he'd watched her from the shadows, the city lights occasionally flashing over his face and showing how his eyes burned. She'd gone along with the performance because it fanned her own arousal.

Once inside his house, he'd pulled her into the first room with a chair, bent her over it, and had done exactly what he said he'd been fantasizing about. She had come so hard that she was sure she'd pulled a muscle. But somehow Will had made her come again in the bedroom.

Now her body hummed with a mixture of satisfaction and yearning. She felt it like waves of heat that ran over her skin before they seeped inside to settle between her legs.

"Focus!" she snapped at herself. "This is business."

Powell, the security guard, called from the front desk, "You okay in there, Ms. Kyra?"

"I'm talking to myself, the first sign of insanity," she called back as she opened a can of pumpkin.

"I done gone right over the edge then," he said with a chuckle.

She heard the door open and the rumble of male voices before Powell appeared at the kitchen entrance with another man.

"I'm Greg Ebersole," the man said, advancing with his hand held out. Her quick survey pegged him as a decade older than Will, with a focused gaze, dark hair liberally sprinkled with gray, and a tailored blue suit stretched over wide shoulders. He had the build of a stevedore and the grip of one, too. She surreptitiously rubbed her hand to restore the circulation when he released it. His gaze skimmed over the kitchen with sharp, professional interest. "This is where you make the dog food."

"Luckily, the dogs don't care if their chicken is cooked on a Viking range." To a real chef, her secondhand appliances would seem sad and inadequate.

But he laughed. "A point in their favor that I hadn't considered before." He leaned his hip on one of the high counter stools. "Talk to me. What's your proposal?"

"Proposal?" What the hell had Will told Greg? She didn't want to make her lover look bad, even if he was the head honcho. "I think we've gotten our wires crossed. I thought this was just a fact-finding mission."

"Okay." Greg gave her an assessing look. "Tell me what you know about dogs with sensitive digestive tracts."

She gave him a quick summary, showing him the ingredients and the final product. "This is a fresh batch because Shaq is going home for the weekend with his owner. It's a new program our director started. Doggy slumber parties."

"May I meet the famously queasy pit bull?" Greg straightened away from the stool.

While she stowed the dog food back in the fridge and walked down the stairs to the kennel, he peppered her with questions about her research and shared some of his. His market analysis made her think this could be a viable product, and excitement for the center fizzed in her chest.

The moment she opened the basement door, the dogs greeted them with everything from Shaq's deep rumble of a bark to the ear-splitting yip of a Chihuahua mix. The kids were working on the "quiet" command, so Kyra walked in front of the crates where the dogs could see her and said "quiet" in a loud, firm voice while she held her finger to her lips. The volume dropped slightly and she rewarded the dogs who'd listened to her with a treat from one of the baggies that were kept handy in the kennel.

"Sorry," she shouted to Greg over the remaining chorus of greetings. He shook his head with a smile. "I've had dogs myself."

"Quiet!" she said again. Most of the dogs settled down, probably more because the original excitement of seeing humans had worn off than because of her repeated order. But she gave them treats anyway.

Unhooking a leash from the rack on the wall, she opened the door of Shaq's huge crate and clipped the lead on his collar before signaling him to join them. He strode out with his rolling bowlegged gait and leaned his shoulder against her thigh to encourage some head stroking.

"He's well named," Greg said, his eyebrows rising as the big dog's weight made Kyra do her usual off-balance dance step. "A 'Big Fella' indeed."

"But a total sweetheart," Kyra said, kneeling to scratch the sides of Shaq's big jaws. His eyes closed in an expression of doggy delight.

"Will mentioned marketing possibilities using the center's K-9 Angelz program." Greg showed his dog skills by letting Shaq sniff the back of his hand before he petted the huge creature. "I'm starting to see why. Kids, rescue dogs, a pit bull with a heart of gold." He was smiling but Kyra could see the wheels turning in his business brain as he glanced around the spotless but bare-bones kennel.

"Let me show you the doggy playground," she said. "We'll take Shaq out with us. That will make his day."

The dog waddled up the half flight of steps that led out the back of the building. Turning left, Kyra opened the chain-link gate to step into what was once known as "the empty lot" and had brought together Max and Emily in a romantic fairy tale that made all the staff members sigh. Now the staff referred to the lot as "paradise."

The front third of the yard closest to the street was dotted with the raised beds for the kitchen gardens, empty at the moment. Next came colorful play equipment for the children. Where she, Greg, and Shaq stood was the dog park, with toys and homemade agility equipment to entertain the critters and the kids.

"You should see the kids work with the dogs," she said, unsnapping Shaq's leash so the pit bull could amble around the yard. "They're so patient and loving, but still firm. And they have a sense of humor about it that some adult dog trainers could learn from."

Shaq lifted his leg on a fake fire hydrant. "He's a walking cliché," Greg said. Again he examined his surroundings with careful attention. Kyra felt a swell of pride when he said, "This place is impressive."

"You should speak with our director, Emily Wade, about the marketing tie-in," Kyra said. "I'm not qualified to comment on that."

"When children are involved, we obviously have to be very careful, but it could benefit the center in a substantial way," Greg said. "You've given me a lot to think about. Let's go inside and talk further."

Shaq was lying on his back in the sun, legs sprawled in a very undignified manner. "Hey, boy." Kyra bent to attach his leash but the dog just lay there until she gave him a gentle tug. "Time to go."

With a moan, Shaq rolled over and got to his feet, his expression one of reproach for cutting short his sunbathing.

"What a character!" Greg said. "I definitely want him in our ad campaign."

"You hear that, Shaq? The nice man wants to make you a celebrity."

The barking rose again when she opened the back door but she didn't attempt to quiet it. She returned Shaq to his crate and led Greg back to the kitchen.

Greg slid onto a stool. "Tell me about your background," he said.

"What do you mean?"

"Your résumé."

"I'm not sure I understand what that has to do with dog food," Kyra said.

"I want to hire you to work on this project. You've got the food. You've got the contacts." He swept his hand around to indicate the center. "You've got the passion. You're the obvious person to spearhead it."

Kyra sat down hard on a stool. She knew nothing about launching a product for a corporation. "I don't think I'm qualified."

"Talk to me," Greg commanded again.

She told him about having only two years of college, about working part-time in the local restaurant in Macungie, about bartending at Stratus, and cooking for the center. "So, you see, I don't have any corporate experience."

"I didn't either when Will and I started Ceres." He shrugged. "You learn. Sometimes the hard way."

The mention of Will sent a flash of comprehension rushing through her. The dog food was a front. He'd set this up because he felt sorry for her. He wanted to give her some kind of cushy, figurehead job with a salary she didn't deserve so she could pay off her debts. He was throwing her a bone—she winced inwardly at the pun—in order to fool her into believing it was a real business. He'd recruited Greg to throw her off the scent. Dear God, she had to stop with the dog metaphors.

But they kept her mind off all the implications of the job offer that she didn't want to deal with in front of Greg.

"I'm really flattered, but I'm not the right person for the job."

"Think about it." Greg took a business card out of his pocket. "Call me with any questions."

Kyra took the card but she didn't believe a word he said. She didn't have any of the skills required for such a position. "Thank you for the vote of confidence. I'll be in touch."

His gaze rested on her face and he managed to look sincere. "Don't turn it down. You'll be an asset to the project."

Friday night was always busy at Stratus but Kyra didn't remember a single customer she'd served for the last eight hours. Her attention had been focused on examining Greg's job offer from every angle. Will had texted a couple of times with sexy quotations, but she'd brushed him off with a "too crazy busy to text." And he'd left her alone after that, something she should give him credit for.

Except that she was too upset. He'd changed everything between them. Before this, she could fool herself into believing the differences between them didn't matter. Will fit into her world so effortlessly that she'd forgotten that she couldn't move in the opposite direction. She didn't belong in the executive offices of a corporation or on a Connecticut estate that reminded her of a theme park. She had ignored the warning signal of Betsy Chase's contempt for her.

But this job offer threw a harsh light on the vast gulf between them. Will could wave his magic watchband and create a job out of thin air just so his current girlfriend could pay off her debts. She had to give him credit for generosity, but the thought of him having that kind of power knocked the breath out of her.

On its heels came a gut-wrenching realization: she'd fallen in love with him . . . again. And she would have to give him up . . . again.

When the limo cruised up in front of Stratus at 1:30 a.m., Kyra was waiting on the sidewalk under the watchful eye of their late-night doorman, Pete, who wouldn't leave until the last female staff member had departed in what he judged to be a safe means of transportation. It always gave Kyra a little glow of comfort to know Pete cared.

As Will unfolded his long body from the car, she couldn't help it . . . she hurled herself at him, wanting to feel all of him against her for the last time.

"Now that's a hello," he said, his arms going around her without hesitation so that she was wrapped in him. She buried her nose in his chest, inhaling the smell of skin-warmed cotton and beautiful, golden Will. Trying to absorb the memory of how this felt so she could carry it with her when he was gone.

When she clung to him longer than usual, he took her shoulders and held her away so he could see her face, his own clouded with concern. "What is it?"

She shook her head and stepped out of his grasp. "I'll tell you in the car."

His eyes went hard and he gave poor Pete a look that would have reduced him to cinders if he'd been guilty of anything. "Who upset you? Tell me now and I'll deal with them."

She shook her head again and climbed into the limo, but not before he had tugged her backpack off her shoulder. *I will always carry your bag. I always want to touch you.*

She swallowed against the tears. This was going to be hell.

As soon as Will closed the door, he reached for her.

"Not yet," Kyra said, scooting into the corner. Which reminded her of their role-play the night before. She nearly moaned out loud as misery lanced through her.

Will's face was a study in mixed emotions: bafflement, concern, and uneasiness. He sat with his back to the door so he could look at her straight on. "I'd like to hear it now." It was not a request.

"I met with Greg today," she began. "He offered me a job."

Will nodded. "He told me when he got back to the office. He also told me you seemed reluctant to accept it."

"Because I don't accept charity." Her gaze was locked on him so she caught the tiny flinch, even though his expression didn't change. "I'm not qualified to launch a new product. You're just trying to give me money in an underhanded way."

"Or maybe Greg is trying to pay you because you'd do an excellent job," he said. "Keep in mind that *he* wanted to hire you. He makes his own decisions and they are always for the good of Cronus Holdings."

His voice carried a conviction that almost made her waver, but she'd seen that tiny reaction to the word "charity." "Okay, let's say, for the sake of argument, that I would do a decent job. You realize that I'd be working for you. What happens when people find out we're sleeping together? That's not going to look good for either one of us."

The streetlights on the side street were dim, so she couldn't see his face. "There's no reason they would know unless one of us tells them." He made a gesture of impatience. "Not to sound arrogant, but the CEO doesn't spend a lot of time with product managers, even ones on new projects. You'd report to Greg, not me, so there would be no reason for people to connect us."

Kyra sighed. "Don't be naive. Someone would see us together somewhere and talk."

"So what?" Now he sounded every inch the aristocrat that he was. "Our private life is *our* business. Our relationship will not affect how we do our jobs."

"Not true. I would have to work three times as hard as my colleagues to convince anyone that I had been hired for my abilities in the office, not the bedroom."

"You would work three times as hard anyway. That's who you are. That's why Greg wants to hire you."

"I know your intentions are good, but you can't just upend my life." Kyra hesitated before she asked a question she didn't want the answer to. "What happens when our relationship ends? Do I have to find another job?"

He shifted restlessly. "You won't hold the job because we're in a relationship. You'll keep it because you're good at it. Or lose it because you're not."

"It would be awkward to meet around the conference table or in the elevator."

"I'm sure we could handle it like civilized adults," he said with a shrug. Then he leaned forward. "Why are you so sure our relationship will end?"

"Oh, Will, come on. Let's not kid ourselves." She tried to sound cool and sophisticated but a huskiness had crept into her voice. Maybe he wouldn't notice.

"About what?" He peered at her through the dimness, an occasional flare of light catching his intent eyes.

"You're you. CEO. Billionaire. Connecticut aristocracy. College graduate. I'm me. Bartender-slash-cook. In debt. Blue collar. College dropout." She shrugged. "We've got nothing in common except great sex."

"You don't really believe that." Hurt and anger rang in his voice. "The sex is just icing on the cake."

She didn't want to be honest but she owed it to him. "No, I don't believe that."

"Thank you."

"Here's what I believe. We are too unequal. The fact that you could and would offer me a job I have no qualifications for demonstrates that in spades." She looked down at her hands. "I was trying to fool myself into thinking it didn't matter. It's the twenty-first century. A commoner can marry a future king. Blah, blah, blah."

She curled her fingers into fists. "I just want to love you as an equal. A simple exchange of emotions. But the equation doesn't balance. It can't."

The limousine glided to a halt and the chauffeur's voice announced that they were home. Will ignored him. "Go back a couple of sentences. What did you say?"

"We're too unequal to work."

"No, you said you want to love me. What does that mean?"

"It seems pretty clear." She gave up on maintaining her pride. "I fell in love with you. I didn't mean to. I knew it was a mistake. Now I have to deal with it."

"You didn't tell me."

"It seemed . . . irrelevant." She flexed her fingers open. "Why don't you just let me go home?"

"No." He reached across her to push open the car door. "I want to see your face."

She noticed that he hadn't declared his love for her. Not that she'd expected it, but a girl could dream crazy dreams.

Resigned, she climbed out of the limo and trudged up the steps to his door. He did the hand-waving thing and they were inside. When he indicated that she should precede him into the formal living room with an angry jerk of his head, she contrasted it with last night's welcome. Yep, there was the chair he'd positioned her over, a cube of black leather cushions held together by a shiny steel frame. She hadn't really had a chance to look at it before, given that she'd been distracted by their more interesting activities.

Will paced over to a built-in bar, slamming open a cabinet door and plunking a rocks glass down on the marble countertop with a noticeable thud. "Would you like a drink?" he asked, even as he poured scotch into the glass. "Because I sure as hell need one."

"No, thanks."

He tossed the contents of his glass down in one gulp before turning to her, his jaw tight with anger. "Let me understand this. You are not going to take the job. And you are not going to continue our relationship because you think I made it up. And you neglected to tell me that you are in love with me."

He turned back to the bar to splash more scotch in his glass. Kyra realized that she had never seen Will furious before this. He was a little scary in his intensity.

"Yes."

"That's all? Just 'yes'?" he snapped. "I think you owe me more than that." He put the glass back on the counter and crossed the room to tower over her before he took her by the shoulders and yanked her against him. Bending down, he took her lips in a punishing kiss as his hands moved over her. He kneaded her bottom hard, then shifted one hand around to cup between her thighs, pushing against her clit through her trousers. With his tongue, he explored her mouth aggressively, not asking but demanding.

She curled her hands over his shoulders and held on, letting him set her body on fire. Her panties grew damp as he rubbed against her. He must have felt it through the outer fabric because a growl of satisfaction rumbled in the back of his throat. He released her lips and raised his head enough to scan her face. "Tell me you don't want me," he said, his fingers still stroking and pressing while his other hand gripped her buttock to hold her against his erection.

"I've wanted you since college," she said, her voice a breathless rasp.

With a crow of triumph, he bent and swung her up in his arms, walking down the hall to the elevator.

She twined her arms around his neck and let him. One last time. It couldn't make their good-bye any more painful.

As they rode up in the elevator, he curved his long fingers over her breast, tweaking the hard nipple so that she felt an answering pulse between her legs.

The door slid open and he strode over to the bed, lowering her with surprising gentleness before he came down on top of her. He pinned her wrists over her head with one hand and went back to work on her breast. His hips were cradled between her thighs so his cock pushed against her clit.

She arched against him for more friction there, and he lowered his head to the side of her neck, sucking hard enough to balance on that erotic edge between pleasure and pain.

"I want you here in my bed," he growled against her skin. "Every night. All night. Until morning."

Kyra threaded her fingers into his hair and pulled his head up so she could look into his beautiful eyes. "Once more."

"We'll discuss that in the morning," he said.

They stripped each other's clothes off in a mad tangle of arms, legs, and fabric before he rolled on a condom and sank himself into her in a hard, claiming thrust. He braced himself over her on his forearms, his eyes locked on her face as he flexed his hips and withdrew before driving back into her. "You. Want. This." He chanted a word on each thrust.

"Yes," she answered as he came into her each time. "Yes. Yes."

He would not bring either one of them to orgasm, keeping his rhythm just below the pace where they would come, lowering his mouth to suck at her breasts, sending streaks of pleasure down to where his cock filled her. And then, without warning, her muscles convulsed and she arched up into him, gasping out his name as her climax broke over her again and again while he continued to move inside her.

As her shudders eased, he pushed deep into her and went still before her name seemed to wrench from him, a full-throated shout of pure physical ecstasy, while his cock pumped within her. She opened her eyes to see his head thrown back, sweat-darkened strands of hair clinging to his temples and neck.

The sight sent another ripple of response through her, making him groan and stroke in again.

He let his head fall forward to hang between his shoulders, his breath blasting over her skin as he panted, his hips pinning her pelvis to the mattress as his cock softened inside her. Her knees were still bent, feet braced on the bed, to offer herself to him, and she slowly let her feet slide downward beside his calves, feeling the slight tickle of the hair dusted over the hard muscles.

Yes, she wanted this in ways that frightened her. This exquisite melt of utter satiation, the masculine weight of him, the warmth of his skin, the beat of his heart against her breasts, the scent of sexual perfume, the knowledge that she had driven him to a desire so intense that he forgot all his well-bred self-control.

But she also wanted the teasing literary texts, the shelter of his body when the helicopter rotors whipped up the wind, the flash of laughter in his eyes when they met hers at a stuffy party, the seductive choreography of working beside him in the kitchen, the wonder on his face as he talked about the kids.

She wanted to share the journey he was about to embark on because she saw it happening in him. The longing to be fully himself, to no longer allow others to define him.

But he could make that journey without her. And maybe he needed to.

It struck her that the job offer might have been his way of taking care of her in the future when they were no longer lovers. Maybe he didn't even realize it, but he was foreseeing the end as well. And being Will, he felt responsible.

As he slid out of her and rolled away to remove the condom, she felt a choking sensation of loss, both physical and emotional.

But he came back to snuggle them both under the duvet, legs intertwined as he cradled her on his wide, hard chest. "I didn't mean to be that . . . abrupt," he said, stroking her shoulder with a touch so light that it almost tickled.

"I told you yes and I meant it," she said, feathering her fingertips over his pecs in return.

His chest rose and fell on a deep breath. "Kyra, I care about you. Deeply. But I—"

She lifted her finger to his lips, laying it across them to shush him. "I don't expect you to love me. I didn't even mean to tell you. It slipped out because I was being honest."

"Your honesty is one of the things I admire about you." The stroking stopped. "I'll be honest with you in return. I thought I loved Petra. You know what happened."

He didn't trust his own feelings anymore. She could understand that. "She's charming and dazzlingly beautiful, and she had your parents' seal of approval. That's a powerful combination."

He shifted under her and she knew she'd been too honest, but he surprised her. "It's almost a relief to hear that. I wondered why I had been so wrong about her." His fingers began to move over her skin again.

Exhaustion rolled over her like a billow of fog, hazing her mind and making her eyelids heavy. The day had been long. The emotions had been intense. She was tired of being mature and understanding and self-sacrificing.

All she wanted was to savor this last night in Will's arms, in Will's huge bed, with Will's body pressed against, and maybe later, inside hers. "No more talking," she said. "I'm wrung out."

He settled her more comfortably, his lips against her temple. "Sleep as long as you want. Tomorrow is Saturday."

The luxury of that thought floated with her into the temporary oblivion of slumber.

Will lay awake, staring at the shadowy ceiling twenty feet over his head while Kyra slumbered in his arms. The curves of her breasts were soft against his side, her even breathing whispered over his chest, the silk of her hair cascaded across his shoulder and arm.

He'd behaved like a brute, while this incredible woman had shown a patience and understanding he didn't deserve. The anger that had blazed through him when she said they were finished had been uncontrollable. Where the hell had that come from?

Guilt. He'd failed to help her because he had underestimated her integrity. He'd been so enamored of his role as knight in shining armor that he hadn't thought through his plan with any clarity. Of course, she would see all the ramifications, because she was smart. That was part of her attraction for him.

But what an asshole he was to vent his anger on her. It was his fault, not hers.

God, it had been hot sex, though. She'd been right there with him, her orgasm exploding around his cock. He closed his eyes to relive the memory. He'd had her tight nipple sucked in between his lips when he'd felt the first clench of her muscles. Her fingers had dug hard into his shoulders as she pushed up underneath him with a power that blew his mind. He'd held off his finish as long as he could, wanting to feel every one of her contractions, driving her to more.

His cock began to stir, but he wasn't going to wake her. Yet.

He opened his eyes again. He was avoiding the thing he didn't want to deal with. That she loved him.

He should have lied. Should have said the words she wanted to hear. How hard would that have been?

A silent groan formed in his throat.

It was impossible. He'd accused Kyra of being a chameleon, but she'd always been open and direct with him. He had to answer her with the same respect.

What he'd felt for Petra was a steady flame. His feelings for Kyra were a furnace blast that verged on obsession. He texted her between meetings, digging up quotations to coax her into a reply. He accepted dinner invitations that he used to refuse just to fill the time until Kyra got off work from Stratus. During the dinners, he fantasized about how he would make love to her.

Tightening his grip on her, he tried not to count the seconds ticking by.

If he asked her to stay with him, she might. He could use her love as leverage if she thought he needed her. But this intense infatuation would inevitably burn itself out, and he would once again find himself having to hurt a woman he cared about.

And that would damage both of them in profound ways.

As a moonbeam painted a stripe of silver across the duvet, Will faced the fact that he'd never before had to give up anything he truly wanted. Was that a testament to his determination or to his selfishness? Kyra might be able to tell him, but he sure as hell didn't know himself.

So he was going to let her walk out of his life tomorrow morning without telling her that she was ripping his guts out.

Because she deserved to go with a clear conscience.

Chapter 15

Light pulsed against Kyra's eyelids and she tried to yank the covers over her head, but some weight was pinning them down. A big warm body beside her. Will. For a moment her lips curved in a smile but as sleep withdrew its comforting veil, memory surged in a flash of misery.

Her muscles actually twitched in protest as she realized this was the last time she would lie in bed with Will's arm thrown over her waist, his palm grazing her breast, ready to cup it persuasively when he woke up.

She couldn't see a clock but the sun was strong, so it must be midmorning.

Not surprising since they'd gone to sleep late. Then sometime in the middle of the night, one of them had awakened the other—she couldn't really remember who. They'd made love so slowly and sensually that it seemed they had all the time in the world. Really, though, it was a long, wistful farewell, as though they were trying to memorize every contour of each other's bodies for when they were apart.

She'd thought maybe they would lose themselves in each other one more time in a pale dawn glow, but exhaustion had clearly overpowered them. Somehow the bright glare of full daytime made her feel it was past time to go.

Will's arm was still relaxed in sleep, so she lay there, torn between wanting to get their parting over with and not wanting to give up the feel of his body wound around hers. Suddenly, silent tears flowed down her cheeks. She had to hold her breath to keep from sobbing. This was not how she wanted to say good-bye to Will.

"Kyra?" Will's voice was gruff with slumber. She must have moved in spite of herself.

She swallowed hard and turned her face against the pillow, trying to blot the tears. "I'm sorry I woke you."

He moved his hand carefully away from her breast, tucking it between her rib cage and the mattress so she was held against him even more firmly. "I'm not."

She was going to cry again if he said one more nice thing to her. "I need to go."

"It's Saturday."

"I don't want to drag this out."

He jerked as though he'd just remembered the night before himself. "I see." Then the weight of his arm was gone and she felt him roll away from her.

She grabbed the corner of the sheet to swipe it surreptitiously over her cheeks. Then she scrambled off the bed. Turning to face him when she was naked was difficult. But he lay on his back, gazing at the ceiling.

"It's hard enough to say good-bye," she said.

"Right," he said, his face still turned away from her. She'd never heard Will so monosyllabic.

Suddenly, he threw off the covers and swung his legs over the side of the bed. She allowed herself one last scan of his long, muscled body before she began the search for her clothes. They'd tossed them every which way last night, so she had to hunt around the bed for the dark puddles of fabric.

"These are yours." Will's voice yanked her attention to her bra and panties dangling from his elegant fingers.

"Thanks." A ridiculous sense of modesty made her turn her back to wriggle into them.

She heard the hiss of fabric against skin and glanced around to see Will pull on his jeans without benefit of briefs. The sight sent a spear of heat through her. She scooped up her own trousers and tugged them up. Her top was missing in action. Getting down on her hands and knees to peer under the bed would be the perfect addition to the awfulness of the moment.

But Will rescued her by rummaging around among the sheets and pillows to pull out both their shirts. "Apologies for the wrinkles," he said with a tight smile.

This time she didn't bother to hide as she slipped the crumpled black top over her head while he did the same with his shirt.

They faced each other. She noticed that several golden strands of Will's hair stuck out from the side of his head and that one side of his collar was turned up while the other was down. His face was shuttered, nothing showing except for shadows moving in his eyes.

The five feet of air between them vibrated with all the words they held back.

"I hope you consider teaching," she said. "You should give yourself that gift."

She saw surprise in the way his eyebrows lifted. "Not the main thing on my mind right now." He broke eye contact as he glanced down to shove his foot into a loafer.

She'd forgotten she was barefoot and looked around for her boots. One lay on its side right next to Will's other loafer. She dodged around him, keeping the same five feet between them, and scooped up her shoe.

He bent and then pulled her other boot from under the bed. As he handed it to her, their fingers brushed, making her suck in a breath. She plunked down on the bed to hide her reaction from him—and from herself.

As she zipped on her boots, she tried to formulate a farewell that hit all the right notes: genuine regret, appreciation for what they'd had, a wish to remain friends but only at a distance. When she got up, she caught Will standing with his hands in his pockets, staring at the floor. She had the odd thought that he was also trying to find the right words, even though he was usually eloquence itself.

He must have felt her gaze because he raised his head. "You have my cell number. If you ever need anything—anything at all—call me. I mean that. I wish—" He shook his head.

"Me, too." She walked over to lay a hand on his shoulder and rise on her tiptoes, brushing a kiss over his lips. "I'd prefer that you not come with me in the limo. Too many memories. Good ones."

When she stepped away from him, she saw a cloud of hurt darken his face. A feeble spark of pleasure flickered inside her. He'd wanted to ride home with her. That would be something to hold on to.

She hit the down button on the elevator and stepped inside as the door opened.

His mind had gone blank. No, that was wrong. His mind had gone hollow. Echoing. Dark.

The elevator's hum ceased, so he knew Kyra was walking down the hall to the front door. He should be there to hold it open for her, but he couldn't make his feet move.

Why the hell was he standing here instead of spending these last few minutes by her side?

Because she wanted to leave without drama. He could give her that since she'd given him a whole night to say good-bye.

As the loss hit him, he folded slowly down onto the bed, his elbows braced on his knees, his head hanging.

Why couldn't he love her?

Chapter 16

Kyra woke up Sunday morning with the kind of hangover that meant you'd broken up with your boyfriend the day before. Dragging herself out of bed, she stood in the shower for twenty minutes before she could open her eyes more than a slit. As she dripped on the bathroom tiles, she swallowed three painkillers. Then she looked in the mirror.

And winced. The shower had cleaned off the streaks of mascara she'd seen in the restroom mirror last night after she'd cried on Cleo's shoulder for an hour. She hadn't intended to spill her guts to her fellow bartender, but she'd bought Cleo a drink after closing to celebrate the giant tip a couple of businessmen from Peoria had left Kyra. She'd joined Cleo, and the alcohol had made her feel so much better, she had a couple more. That was when the crying started.

However, the exhausted circles under her eyes weren't coming off with soap.

She really wished she'd never run into Will in Ceres. Oh God, now she wouldn't be able to go back there, just in case he showed up on another tour of inspection. Another misery to chalk up to his account.

No, that wasn't fair. She'd done it to herself. Which made her feel worse, not better.

She toweled off, threw on flannel pajama pants and a T-shirt before dragging herself into the kitchen to drink a bottle of water. She should have done that last night before she went to bed.

Now she had a whole day off to wallow in how alone she was. She could throw herself a solitary pity party because there was no one here to care what she did. This was one of the times she really missed her mother. Even if she didn't understand Kyra's ambitions, her mom loved her and would comfort her when she cried.

Kyra thought about asking her landlady for a home improvement project to take her mind off Will, but Gloria was too sharp not to realize that Kyra was upset about something. And she wouldn't hesitate to ask if it was Will. Not to mention Kyra's head was pounding in a way that made concentrating difficult.

She could try to read one of the books that were piled on her bedside table, but she suspected the words would swim around on the page in front of her bleary eyes. At least the hangover caused so much physical pain that it masked the emotional pain of Will's absence. Sort of.

She pulled another water out of the fridge and shuffled into her living room to try watching television as a distraction. As she settled onto the sofa, she heard the ping of her cell phone coming from the backpack she'd dropped in the hallway in last night's drunken stagger to the bedroom. It wasn't Will, so why bother to get up? But she heaved herself off the sofa to retrieve it.

It was a text message from Emily. Sorry to bother you on your day off but we have a situation with Felicia and Shaq. Could use your input, if you wouldn't mind coming in for a powwow at noon.

Emily never disturbed the staff on their days off, so this had to be bad.

I'll be there, she responded, glancing at the phone's clock. She had an hour to clear the haze out of her brain.

Time for coffee and burnt toast.

When Kyra walked into the director's office at the center, Emily gave her a sharp look but didn't comment on her pallor or general air of desolation. Kyra was grateful but even more worried. She lowered herself gingerly into the chair in front of the desk. "What's going on?"

Emily clicked a few times on her laptop and then turned it around for Kyra to look at. The photo was of a child's bloody forearm and wrist.

Kyra winced. "Ouch! Please tell me that's not Felicia. It looks horrible."

"Davina Gibson sent it, claiming that Shaq attacked Felicia. She's at the emergency room now. I wanted to go be with her, but Davina says she doesn't want anyone from the center near her daughter. She was pretty upset, and who can blame her? Poor little Felicia."

Kyra glanced at the photo again and wished she hadn't. She could see the tooth marks now that she knew what she was looking at. One wound was so deep that bone showed through. "I can't imagine how much that must hurt."

"Diego somehow persuaded her to let him get Shaq from their neighbor and take him to Dr. Quillen's," Emily said. "He's distraught about the whole thing. He thinks it's his fault because the kids wanted to take their dogs home like he does. That breaks my heart, too."

Kyra frowned, fighting her way out of the hangover fog. "I just can't believe Shaq attacked Felicia. That dog is a lover, not a fighter."

"Diego says the same thing, but he's a kid and biased by his love for the animals. I wanted to get your clearheaded take on Shaq." Emily's usually serene expression was grim. "He might have to be put down."

Kyra gasped at the idea of the big, affectionate dog being killed. "How soon?"

"I'm not sure yet. We've arranged to have Dr. Quillen kennel him until further notice, so he's no longer with the kids. His junior kid, Min-joo, is going to be heartbroken, but I can't let her even visit him."

Emily squeezed her eyes closed for a second. "This is my worst nightmare come true. We try to vet the dogs so thoroughly, to make sure this wouldn't happen, but I knew it was a possibility. You can't predict the behavior of animals. I shouldn't have allowed such a big dog in the program but he seemed so gentle. Felicia fell in love with him at the shelter and pit bulls don't get adopted much, so I thought . . ." Emily spread her hands in a gesture of regret.

Kyra thought of Shaq lolling on his back in the yard while she chatted with Greg Ebersole, of Shaq leaning against her thigh for a head scratch the first time she'd ever met the dog, of Shaq wearing a bow tie at Max's induction party. "There's no way Shaq would attack Felicia. There's not a vicious bone in his body. I need to talk to her."

"Her mother has pulled her out of the center," Emily said with a shake of her head. "She made it very clear that none of us should come near Felicia. She says she's hiring a lawyer."

"That doesn't sound good."

Emily massaged her temples. "Max wants to hire the big law firm his company uses, but I don't know if that's a good idea. Our insurance company should deal with this."

Kyra frowned. "Don't insurance companies usually settle to keep legal expenses down? Some people would see that as an admission of guilt on the part of the center, so I think that could endanger the K-9 Angelz program. Not to mention that it wouldn't save Shaq."

"Max is concerned about the program—and Shaq—as well." Emily turned the laptop back around and flipped the top down. "I hope that Davina will calm down once her daughter has been treated. I hope even more that she'll let us know how Felicia is doing. I hate to think of the child in such pain." Emily's eyes brimmed with tears.

"Where's Diego?" Kyra wanted to reassure the boy that he wasn't responsible for the catastrophe.

"At Dr. Quillen's with Shaq. He's worried the dog will feel abandoned. He took your special dog food with him." The tears spilled down her cheeks. "He's such an amazing, compassionate kid."

"Especially considering what a piece of scum his father is." Kyra had been astonished the first time Emily had told her about Diego's background.

"That's why these kids are so incredible. They overcome all the odds stacked against them." Emily grabbed a tissue to wipe away her tears. "I want the K-9 Angelz program to continue because it means so much to the children. They need the unconditional love the dogs give them."

Kyra leaned forward to lay her hand on top of Emily's. "We'll find a way to get through this." Not that she had a clue how, but they had a lot of good people—staff, trustees, parents, and kids—who cared deeply about the center. Together they could solve any problem.

But Monday morning brought more bad news. Davina had indeed hired a lawyer, and not just an average one. She'd retained Titus Allen, a darling of the media because he represented high-profile, high-drama cases with big payouts. Which baffled Kyra. The Carver Center didn't have the kind of money Allen usually went for.

Then she remembered that Max had just joined the board of trustees. And he was engaged to the center's director. Would that make Allen smell money?

They were going to need one hell of a tough lawyer to win this battle.

Kyra understood why Emily didn't want to have Max hire his law firm. *Billionaire Board Member Fighting Single Mom.* That was a headline they didn't need.

Kyra perched on a kitchen stool and stared at her phone. She knew someone who knew tough lawyers. He'd said to call if she ever needed anything. She would never ask for herself, but the center was a different matter.

But she'd better run it by Emily first, so she hiked up the stairs to the director's third-floor office. Emily was frowning at her laptop when Kyra walked in and closed the door behind her.

"I might be able to get us a really good lawyer," she said, taking the bright orange chair in front of the desk.

Emily lifted her gaze from the computer and waited.

Kyra shifted in the chair. She'd forgotten that she'd need to explain to Emily that she and Will were no longer together. "Will's father is the senior partner at Chase, Banfield, and Trost. Since Will is a big fan of the center, I'm sure he'd be able to get a top-notch lawyer to work pro bono. That way Max won't be connected to the law firm."

"But you will be," Emily pointed out.

"Will and I broke up over the weekend." Kyra tried to say the words without inflection but her voice cracked the tiniest bit midsentence.

Emily stood up and came around the desk to give Kyra a slightly awkward bent-over hug. "I'm so sorry. I know he was a friend first, so that makes it doubly hard to lose him."

The hug was surprisingly welcome, and Kyra curled her hands over Emily's arms to give her a grateful squeeze. "It was bound to happen. Probably better sooner rather than later, so it doesn't hurt quite as much."

Emily straightened. "It would be painful for you to be in contact with him again. I wouldn't ask you to do that."

"I'm offering." Kyra swallowed. "We both know it's going to take a lot of legal clout and skill to face down Titus Allen. The man is a master at trying the case in the media. We need someone equally savvy."

Emily was silent a moment and then knelt in front of Kyra. "Look me in the eye and tell me you won't be upset by talking to Will again so soon."

"I'll be upset, but I'm a big girl. I've broken up with men before." Never a man like Will, though. She'd never fallen in love with anyone else, probably because she had never given them enough time or attention. "The center needs a big gun. I can get one."

"Max could get one, too. It's just that . . ." Emily turned her palms out in a gesture of indecision.

"Let me do this."

The director studied Kyra's face a moment longer before she rose to her feet and nodded. "Thank you."

"I may not be able to reach him right away. CEOs tend to be busy." She gave Emily a wry look.

"Just let me know when you hear from him."

Kyra walked slowly back down the stairs as she formulated and discarded conversational openings. Finally, she decided to text him as her opening salvo, so that he knew exactly why she was getting in touch.

She sat on the kitchen stool and pulled out her phone.

You said to ask if I needed anything. The Carver Center needs a good lawyer. You know some. Please call me when you have a chance.

She stared at her message, trying to imagine what Will would think when he read it. After all, she was asking him to go to his father for a favor. But she'd seen how Twain Chase looked at his son at the party. She was sure his father would be happy to offer any assistance that Will requested, just for a chance to have a conversation with him.

She could even pretend this was a way to bring father and son together. But Will might not see it that way. It might make him angry to be obligated to his father.

However, she couldn't back off now since she'd committed to Emily.

The worst that could happen was that Will would say no. And hate her for making him do so.

She hit send. And then pulled out ingredients for the most elaborate meal the kids had ever tasted.

Her phone lay silent on the counter for almost half an hour before a ping echoed off the stainless steel.

She yanked her hands out of the giant bowl of ground meat she was mixing and washed them at high speed, drying them on her apron as she approached the phone.

Her heart was thudding and she had to think about sucking in air as she swiped the text message open.

In a meeting. Will call in fifteen.

Greg was giving Will a beady-eyed stare. He must have caught Will checking his phone during the meeting. Will had waited until he thought everyone was looking in the other direction, but it was tough to fool his COO. About anything. Greg had already asked him what the hell was wrong with him today. Will had brushed him off but Greg wouldn't give up until he had an answer.

Will preferred not to face the inquisition just yet. He needed some time to come up with answers himself.

Will realized he was bouncing his heel against the floor with impatience and forced himself to be still. Why the hell couldn't they draw the obvious conclusions and wind this up? The prospect of hearing Kyra's voice again was making it impossible for him to concentrate anyway.

Finally, he couldn't wait any longer. "Caitlin, I'd like you to head up the market research on the pet food. See what locations we should start looking at. Should we stock it in existing restaurants or open separate storefronts? That kind of thing." He looked down the conference table at Greg. "You know more about the rest of this than I do so I'll let you finish up. Excuse me."

That would earn him a virtual torture session with his COO, but he didn't give a damn. Kyra needed his help. Why that took precedence over a high-level meeting about the new pet food project was something he didn't want to examine just now.

Striding into his office, he closed the door and hit Kyra's speed dial. It took two rings before she answered.

"Will, thanks for getting back to me so quickly."

He listened as she described the situation with the girl, the dog, and the mother. When he heard the name Titus Allen, he grimaced. The man would splash the Carver Center all over the media in the worst possible light.

"I thought your father's law firm might have someone who could stand up to Allen. Schuyler mentioned that they're always looking for noncriminal pro bono work." She sounded uncertain. "I'm sorry to ask you to go to your father for a favor."

"Schuyler is also a partner at the firm. She'll know the right person for the job." He thought he heard Kyra sigh and briefly wondered if she thought this would somehow bring about a reconciliation with his father. "I'm glad you called. The Carver Center should be allowed to continue doing its impressive work."

"I knew you'd feel that way." But she sounded relieved.

"Kyra . . ." He ran his hand over his hair as he stared out the window at the boats on the river. He wanted to say something personal, something about them, but . . . "I'll call you as soon as I've contacted Schuyler."

"Great. Thanks." She fell silent and he had the sense that she, too, was searching for some more intimate words, but she said, "I've got to finish cooking the snack. Talk with you soon."

He stood in front of the window, tapping his phone against his palm as disappointment hollowed out his chest.

What did he expect?

He had no right but he wanted more.

Ever since Kyra had walked out Saturday morning, he'd felt like his skin didn't fit him. He'd fought it by exhausting himself in his home gym, then running numbers on the pet food project until Greg had told him to get a life and refused to return his e-mails. That sent Will out on an informal tour of more Ceres locations, although he avoided the one where he and Kyra had met.

Greg's retaliation was to organize a high-level executive meeting about the pet food project on Monday morning. Will had to give him points for an excellent payback.

But now he had something real to do for Kyra. He swiped Schuyler's private cell number.

"Yo, bro," his sister answered immediately, somewhat to his surprise. "To what do I owe this extreme honor?"

"Aren't partners supposed to be too busy billing hours to answer the phone themselves?"

"Don't be an ass. You called my private cell. Besides, *you're* the CEO with multiple executive assistants."

"It's good to know that I will never get any respect from my sister." Then he turned serious. "Sky, I need your legal assistance."

"I'm pretty sure Cronus Holdings has an entire legal department of its own," she said.

"Not what I'm looking for. I need a lawyer who can outmaneuver Titus Allen."

"Are you kidding me? What the heck did you do to get that tiger shark hunting you?"

"Not me. The Carver Center." He repeated Kyra's summary of the situation.

"So this is for your girlfriend." Schuyler sounded oddly disappointed.

"It's for a place that does a hell of a lot of good. And she's not my girlfriend."

"Could have fooled me. I saw the steam on the car windows."

His sister wouldn't let it go until he told her the truth. "Former girlfriend."

"Oh. Sorry. That sucks."

More than she knew or he expected. "It's not relevant. Farr and I already looked at the center for funding by the Thalia Foundation. It's a worthy cause."

"Okay, put me in touch with the center's director, and I'll get started." Schuyler was back in legal eagle mode.

"You?"

"Isn't that why you called me?"

"I thought you'd pass it along to a colleague."

"You think I can't handle Titus Allen?" Her tone was challenging.

Will smiled for the first time since Saturday morning. "I think Allen won't know what hit him. Keep me in the loop, sis."

He disconnected and immediately dialed Kyra's number.

"That was fast," she answered.

"Schuyler happened to answer her phone. She's taking the case."

"Your sister?"

He heard dismay in her voice. *Why?* "She's an excellent lawyer and very tough."

"Oh, of course, I didn't mean . . . I was just surprised that she would handle it personally."

He didn't mention that he had reacted the same way. "Schuyler likes pro bono work, so it's right up her alley." Now that he thought about it, his sister's involvement might give him an opportunity to see Kyra again.

Which he shouldn't want to do. *Former* girlfriend.

The hell with it. He liked Kyra, always had. It made sense that he would still want to see her.

"She's going to contact Emily right away," Will said.

"Wow, thanks so much. I just hope"—her voice hitched—"Schuyler can save Shaq. Not to mention the whole K-9 Angelz program. It means so much to the kids . . . and to Emily. It doesn't deserve to be shut down. And poor Felicia. God, what a mess this is! I feel like we should all be able to sit down and work it out instead of dragging it into court."

A strange pleasure expanded in his chest because she had confided her worries to him. "Schuyler will do her best to keep it out of court, and her best is damned good. Allen should be very, very worried."

"Thank you for being willing to bring your family into this. It's really generous of you and Schuyler."

"We'll get this straightened out." He spoke with conviction. Because he desperately wanted to help her.

"Right. Thanks again. Um, good-bye."

Before he could say anything else, she had hung up. He slammed the phone against his thigh in frustration.

Kyra sent Emily a text, explaining that Schuyler Chase would be contacting her, if she hadn't already. Then she dragged a stool into the pantry, closed the door, and let the tears roll down her cheeks.

Hearing Will's voice had ripped the bandage off the wound of their parting and set it bleeding again. She wished she could blame a hangover for the agony pounding through her today.

She didn't just miss his company . . . and his body. She missed the feeling that someone else in the world cared enough about her to put her needs first. Will had made her feel that way, even though he didn't love her. And now he had drawn his sister into Kyra's problems. It felt so much like love that it devastated her to know that it wasn't.

His kindness teased her, seduced her into thinking she wasn't alone when she really was. She hadn't expected their brief fling to weaken her defenses so much. It was that old friendship that had fooled her into lowering her barriers with him, as if they were back in the ivory tower of college, where real life differences didn't matter.

Now she was going to have to reconstruct her tough shell. She couldn't afford the luxury of unrequited love. She needed all her strength to survive.

Stripping the plastic off a new roll of paper towels, Kyra wiped her eyes with the rough material and stood up.

No more contact with Will.

A couple of hours later, Emily Wade walked into the kitchen. Instead of her usual mug of coffee, she carried a cardboard box bearing the logo of a bakery a couple of blocks away. "The world's most decadent chocolate cupcakes," Emily said, flipping open the box. "For comfort endorphins. We both need them."

Kyra put down the knife she was using to chop carrots. "It's that bad?" She grabbed two plates and slid them onto the counter. "Would you like tea or coffee?"

"I've had so much coffee I'm vibrating, so herbal tea would be wonderful," Emily said as she set the cupcakes on the plates. "Even the caffeine in the chocolate will probably make my hair stand on end, but I need it. And you look like you do, too. I'm so sorry about Will."

Kyra kept her gaze on the teakettle she was filling at the sink. "It was a rough weekend, but it's over. You've got the bigger problem." Setting the kettle on the stove, she busied herself with getting out cups, saucers, spoons, and tea bags.

Emily waited for Kyra to sit before she laid a hand on her forearm. "You care about Will. I have to say that I think he cares about you, too, since he got his sister to take on our case."

Kyra sighed. "That's the kicker. He does care about me. Just not as anything more than a friend with benefits." Kyra looked down at Emily's comforting hand and felt the glow of a budding friendship. "I feel more for him than he does for me and that doesn't work for either of us."

"Well, crap." Emily sighed. "Maybe he just doesn't recognize how he really feels about you."

Kyra met Emily's eyes. "Let's face it . . . his world and mine are so far apart they might as well be separate planets. It would take a heck of a lot of feelings to bridge that divide, especially since his mother thinks I'm poor white trash."

"I believed that about the differences between Max and me," Emily said. "But it turns out that the problem of money can be overcome." She made a comic face. "His mother I can't help you with."

"His mother is just a symbol of the biggest divide. I'm blue-collar Pennsylvania and he's blue-blood Connecticut. College sort of smooths out those kinds of differences. You all live in the same dorms. You all take the same classes. You all go to the same frat parties. Some people dress better than others, of course. But it's more of a meritocracy. If you're smart, you're accepted. That's one reason I loved it so much."

The teakettle whistled and Kyra got up to pour the tea.

"I never went to college," Emily said, her voice wistful. "I took classes at the county extension, but that's not the same. I envy you."

Kyra didn't remind Emily that her higher education had lasted only two years and led to nothing but debt. At least she had been given the experience Emily had missed, so maybe she should feel some gratitude. "Brunell was like the best dream I'd ever had, except better because I learned so much."

As Kyra sat down, Emily picked up her cupcake and held it toward Kyra as though it were a glass of wine in a toast. Kyra touched her cupcake to Emily's. "Here's to the healing powers of chocolate!"

Kyra bit into the pastry and closed her eyes as the flavor and aroma of rich, dark sweetness filled her senses. "Oh my God, who needs a man when you can have this cupcake?"

Emily giggled. "Men are less fattening."

The giggle was infectious and Kyra found herself joining in. Even though their laughter was pure release of tension, it felt good to be silly and girly while they savored their cupcakes. Kyra had so little free time that she'd never been able to build close friendships with other women. Cleo at Stratus was probably her closest female friend, and that relationship rarely extended beyond work because they were both so tired at the end of their shifts.

Kyra had always seen Emily as the center's director, not someone she could relax with. But maybe Emily could be a friend. Kyra certainly needed one.

Once the chocolate confections were devoured, the giggles stopped.

"I don't think you should give up on Will," Emily said, wiping her sticky fingers on a paper towel. "After all, Max was all set to move to Chicago before he met me. Look where he lives now."

Still in New York City. Rumor had it that he'd spent a lot of money to rewrite his contract with the corporation to which he'd sold his business. He'd done it because Emily wouldn't uproot herself or her daughter from the community they were such a part of. That was true love.

"You're a lucky woman," Kyra said. "Will made his choice and I need to respect it."

Emily took a sip of tea before she settled her gaze on Kyra. "I should warn you that Isaiah has invited Will to his K-9 Angelz adoption ceremony on Wednesday. Evidently, Will helped him choose the dog's name. I know that I've asked all staff members to be present for the event, but I'll excuse you if you want. And, of course, Will may not come." Emily sighed. "I'm not even certain we should hold the ceremony, in light of Felicia's situation, but Isaiah would be heartbroken. I just can't do that to him."

An unwelcome thrill of excitement ran through Kyra at the possibility of seeing Will until she remembered the effect of just one phone call from him. For her own emotional protection, she needed to find a way to be out of the center when he came. But the adoption ceremonies were important events in the kids' lives at the center. She refused to miss one because she was a coward.

"No, it's not a problem. I'll be there." Kyra spoke in a firm voice, trying to convince herself. She had to change the subject. "Have you spoken with Schuyler yet?"

Emily nodded. "She's terrific, very reassuring. She's going to set up a meeting with Davina and Mr. Allen tomorrow. We may be able to save Shaq, but I don't think he can come back to the center. Once a dog has bitten a child, he's considered dangerous."

"That dog is less dangerous than I am," Kyra said, putting her teacup down so hard the saucer rattled.

"I wish I knew what had made him go after Felicia," Emily said. "But I guess it doesn't really matter." She sipped her tea. "I want to make sure Felicia gets all the medical care she needs, including the plastic surgery. I've asked Schuyler to see if Davina will let Ben Cavill look at her daughter."

Dr. Cavill was a high-end concierge doctor who used the fees paid by his wealthy clients to fund a free health-care clinic in South Harlem. He worked there as much as his schedule permitted and recruited other doctors to donate their time to the clinic as well. The Carver Center's nurse thought Ben Cavill walked on water.

"Will the center's insurance cover the medical bills?"

Emily sighed. "The essential medical ones, yes. The plastic surgery? I don't know yet. But we have to make sure Felicia is able to heal completely and have full use of her arm, so we'll figure out some way to make it happen."

"How about the K-9 Angelz program? Will it continue?"

"That's still up in the air. I don't know how the parents will feel about this. They may decide it's too dangerous for their children, and I have to respect their wishes."

"Maybe you could just eliminate the K-9 slumber party experiment."

"That's already done." Emily stared into her teacup, her expression one of regret. "The kids loved the idea. It made them feel like they truly owned the dogs."

Now it was Kyra's turn to lay her hand on Emily's. "The parents know how much the K-9 Angelz program means to the kids. They'll support it."

"There's always been a small group of parents whose kids don't like or don't want dogs. Until now, those parents didn't have any concrete reason to object because we always gave those kids a dog-free space. Now . . ." She waved her hand in a helpless gesture.

Kyra saw tears standing in Emily's eyes. "I'll talk to Gloria. She'll rally the troops."

Her landlady was one of the center's trustees and a moving force in the neighborhood. When she got behind a cause, she was virtually unstoppable.

"Let's wait until we know more about how the case will shake out. I don't want to stir up any more trouble than we already have." Emily smiled. "It means a lot to have your support."

After the snack had been served, Kyra was in the kitchen rearranging the jumbled flatware in the dishwasher when Diego walked in. "Hey, Ms. Kyra, need some help?"

"Thanks, but I'm almost done." She retrieved some forks that had fallen out of the baskets and slotted them in place again.

"You said you got more food for Shaq?" Diego said.

Diego knew where to look for Shaq's food, but Kyra said, "It's in the green fridge, as usual."

The boy still stood with his hands shoved in his jeans pockets, staring at his sneakers. "Ms. Kyra, you been around Shaq. Do you think he bit Felicia?"

Kyra rinsed her hands and turned to face the boy as she dried them on a paper towel. "I think if Felicia says he did, then we have to believe her. She loves Shaq and wouldn't want to blame him for something he didn't do."

Diego shook his head. "Something ain't right about this. I need to talk to Felicia direct."

"That's not a good idea right now, buddy," Kyra said. "Ms. Gibson is suing the center and doesn't want anyone here to have contact with Felicia."

"That's what Ms. Emily said." Diego gave her a sly, sideways look. "But I'm just a kid. I don't work here or nothing."

"Or anything." Kyra corrected him automatically.

"Yeah, or anything."

Kyra sat down and gestured for him to do the same. "Seriously, you shouldn't do this. It could complicate an already complicated situation. The center has a terrific lawyer representing us, so let her do her job. Although I understand your concern."

"Ms. Emily say that Shaq can't come back here. That ain't fair if he didn't do nothing . . . anything wrong. He'll go back to the shelter and pit bulls don't get adopted easy."

"Can you be patient, Diego? There's a meeting tomorrow between everyone involved. Let's see what happens. Then we'll discuss our options."

He ducked his head once in assent. "You know, Ms. Emily be all nice and worried, so I can't talk to her like I can talk to you."

"Is there a compliment in there somewhere?" Kyra asked, but she felt honored that Diego would confide in her.

Diego laughed. "I don't mean you're not nice, too, but you're more . . . like tough, street-smart."

"That's a compliment for sure." She reached out to ruffle his hair, and this time he didn't avoid her touch. "Don't worry. We'll find a good home for Shaq."

Even if she had to adopt the dog herself.

Chapter 17

"When was the last time you darkened the door of my office?" Schuyler stood up from her desk as Will strolled in late Tuesday afternoon.

He leaned across the huge mahogany surface to kiss her on the cheek. "Nice greeting, sister o' mine."

"Seriously, I'm honored you came here," Schuyler said. "A real live CEO in my humble place of work."

Will made a rude gesture as he sat in one of the leather armchairs in front of her desk. "You meet with CEOs all the time, so don't bullshit me."

"Yeah, but I have to go to them. Want a drink?" Schuyler walked over and touched a hidden switch in the built-in bookcases. One section of shelves swung open to reveal a well-stocked bar.

"Scotch, please." Will scanned the room, noting the view of the Empire State Building and the small but separate seating area. "You've come up in the world, officewise."

"When I got promoted to junior partner, Dad decided I could have a better office without it looking like nepotism. Of course, the other junior partners have offices twice the size of mine. Not that I care, honestly. This one is fine."

She handed Will a glass and dropped into the chair beside him, turning it so she faced him. "Cheers!" She touched her glass to his.

While he sipped his scotch, he examined his sister with the same attention he'd given her office. "You look tired."

"Thanks, bro." She made a wry face at him. "I have a big corporate case that I'm working on at the same time as this Carver Center situation. Burning the candle at both ends."

"Pass the Carver case on to an associate," Will said, as guilt pricked at him. "That's what I expected you to do."

Schuyler shook her head. "The Carver case is what makes the corporate case bearable." She took a swallow of her drink. "You came to hear about it, didn't you?"

"How'd the meeting go?" Schuyler had set up a meeting earlier in the day with Davina Gibson, Titus Allen, and Emily to see where they all stood on the case.

"Better than I expected." Schuyler leaned back in the chair but her face was alight with satisfaction. "It's pretty clear that Titus jumped into the situation without doing his homework on the Carver Center. When Emily started talking about the K-9 Angelz program and what it meant to the kids, the man looked like he'd eaten a rotten egg. He seemed to believe it was some sort of private school that had billionaires on its board of trustees. But he's not going to back down now. Too much ego."

"Damn." Hope had flashed for a moment.

"Another thing. When Emily said that Shaq might have to be put down since he'd bitten a child, Davina looked horrified and asked Titus if that were true. He spluttered something about the dog only having bitten once and being given a second chance. However, Emily said that even if they didn't put Shaq to sleep, he'd have to go back to the shelter in the hope of finding another home. Davina wasn't happy about that."

"Sounds like no one did their homework."

"Here's how I read it. Davina just wants Felicia to get the best medical care possible. Insurance pays for the basic costs but not the fancy stuff like plastic surgery. Titus thought he was getting a high-profile case with a big payout for his client and himself. So he aims for the negligence angle to invoke pain and suffering, which he has to prove by dragging the Carver Center's reputation through the mud. Now that he knows what the true nature of the center is, he's afraid that will make him the bad guy instead of the white knight."

"That gives you some leverage," Will said.

"Which I already used by subtly suggesting that he not splash this all over the media." Schuyler smiled the toothy smile of a well-fed shark. "He subtly agreed."

Will smiled back. "That's the sister I know and fear."

Schuyler snorted and stood to refill her glass. She returned to lean her hip against the desk. "I think money would make this all go away. Emily offered to get this hotshot doctor Ben Cavill to examine Felicia, which made Davina very happy. If the center can find a way to pay for the plastic surgery, I think Davina will tell Titus to drop the case. He'll negotiate up the payout to save face, but he'll be relieved to get out of this. Problem is that the center's insurance won't foot the bill and Emily is adamant that her billionaire fiancé not pitch in, even though he is more than willing to do so."

"I'll pay for it," Will said without hesitation. "Anonymously. Just figure out a way to make it happen."

"That's a pretty open-ended offer. We're talking tens of thousands of dollars at least." Schuyler gave him a searching look. "I know you can afford it, but why?"

Will tugged at his tie to loosen it. "Does it matter?"

"You're my brother, so yes."

"I owe Kyra and this is the only way I can help her."

"What do you owe her?"

Will met his sister's gaze. "More than I can give her."

"You need to be more specific." Schuyler put down her glass and crossed her arms.

Will forced himself to take a slow sip of scotch. "She wants me to feel something for her that I don't. I care about her, but not in that way."

"She's in love with you and you believe you're not in love with her." Schuyler picked up her own drink but swirled the liquid around in the glass. "It's none of my business, but are you sure?"

"About which part?"

"You're stalling," Schuyler said. "Seems to me that you're going out of your way to help her, which is an indicator of strong feelings on your part."

Will pushed up out of his chair and stalked over to the window. "Let's just say that I don't feel about her the way I did about Petra."

Schuyler barked out a short laugh. "Considering that your relationship with Petra didn't survive one trip alone with her, that strikes me as a positive not a negative."

Will huffed out an irritated sigh. "I'm not an idiot. When things were good between Petra and me, I felt differently."

"Ah, bro, but half the reason you loved Petra so much was that Mum and Dad approved of her. This was something you could do that made them happy. That created the whole rosy glow."

"I know how I felt about her," Will snapped. But his sister's words seeped into the crevices of his mind, watering the little seeds of doubt Kyra had sown. He'd seen Petra as a sort of orchid, exotic yet familiar, fragile but comfortable.

Whereas Kyra challenged his assumptions about himself, about his world. She made him think. She made him want more.

Schuyler held up her hand in surrender. "If you say so."

"Goddamnit, Sky, what does that mean?"

"It means I've said my piece and now you need to chew on it awhile before you admit that I'm right." His sister grinned.

"You can be a real jerk, you know." But Will put no heat in his words.

Schuyler's grin faded. "Did you know that Petra and Farr are dating?"

A jolt of shock ran through him. "When did that happen?"

"A few days ago. Farr actually called me to ask if I thought it would bother you. I said I thought you'd dance a happy dance. Was I wrong?"

Will rubbed his hand over the back of his head as he considered. "Why the hell didn't Farr call *me*?"

"To ask permission to date your ex-fiancée?" Schuyler shook her head. "Put yourself in his shoes."

"*Ex* being the operative prefix. I have no claim on Petra anymore." Relief was his overwhelming reaction. He might not be engaged to Petra, but he'd still felt responsible for her happiness in some odd way. Now Farr had taken on that responsibility. He had a bad moment when he realized that he wouldn't feel relieved if he found out Farr was dating Kyra. "I didn't know Farr was interested in her romantically."

"He was, but she wasn't. He didn't want to push it, but something changed recently."

"I'm just . . . surprised." He grimaced. "And a little guilty. Right after our split, I said some unkind things about Petra to Farr." Now that he thought about it, Farr had never agreed with him, just listened in the way a good friend would.

"Farr would expect you to be upset given the situation," Schuyler said.

"I knew Farr squired Petra around sometimes but I thought it was just a convenience for both of them." Will shook his head. "Farr and Petra. I'll be damned."

"People can surprise you, in ways both good and bad." Schuyler joined him by the window, cradling her glass in her hands as she scanned the Manhattan skyline. "Are you happy, Will?"

"I'm going to assume that means you're not," he said, watching her profile.

"When I get a case like the Carver Center, I realize how little I like corporate law." Schuyler sighed. "Davina and Emily are both good people who are trying to do the right thing. My challenge is to find a way to help both of them. That's what I like to do. Not look up obscure, convoluted statutes in order to bury the other side under an avalanche of paperwork."

"You'd rather be a mediator than a lawyer."

"I'd rather be a lawyer who makes a real difference in people's lives."

"Then do it. You've given Dad six years and made it to junior partner, which is more than I did." Will touched one of the hands she had clenched around the glass. "You don't owe him any more than that."

Schuyler turned to face him. "You didn't answer my question. Are you happy?"

"I know why you're a good lawyer. You never give up." Will sipped his scotch as he considered her question. "I accomplished what I set out to do."

"Which was?" His sister kept her gaze on him.

"Build a business from scratch. Make it a success." Will gave her a tight smile. "Shove it in Dad's face when I did."

"And now what?"

"I've got a company to run." Although he was taking the next afternoon off to attend the K-9 Angelz adoption ceremony at the Carver Center. He'd been honored and touched that Isaiah would invite him, but he'd accepted for the least noble of reasons: he hoped to see Kyra there. "What would you think about me teaching ancient history?"

"Teaching? You?" Schuyler's eyebrows rose, but then she shrugged. "You always loved that stuff. Gods throwing thunderbolts. Greeks fighting Persians. Romans building aqueducts. You used to go on and on about it on school breaks."

"Was I a dead bore?"

"No, and that's why you might make a good teacher. I used to ask for more of your stories, remember?"

She had, but he'd always put it down to boredom when they were at home, away from their school friends. Now he felt a sense of possibility.

"Of course, Mum and Dad would hate it," Schuyler continued. "Which is why you should do it."

"We're a fine pair, aren't we?" Will couldn't keep the edge out of his voice. "Still thinking about our parents' approval."

"Mum and Dad are pretty overwhelming personalities," Schuyler said. "And they care more about how we reflect on them than on what we really want."

There was a perfunctory knock on the door before it opened and their father strode in. "Hello, Schuyler."

"Speak of the devil," Will muttered under his breath.

Twain Chase's stride hitched as his gaze fell on Will. "Well, here's a happy surprise," he said with what seemed like genuine pleasure. "What brings you here, son?"

He held out his hand to Will, who shook it. "Consulting with Schuyler on a legal matter, sir."

Their father's eyebrows rose. "I wasn't aware that Cronus used our firm's services."

Will shook his head. "Not for Cronus."

"It's the pro bono case I mentioned," Schuyler said.

"Right, right," Twain said. "Some nonsense about a dog bite." He waved a hand in dismissal. "Although it brought the three of us together here, so I can't complain. I see you've been enjoying the bar so I think I'll join you."

"I'll get it, sir," Will said, heading for the bar. "What would you like?"

A look of hurt crossed his father's face. "Scotch, straight up. Just like yours."

"I wasn't sure if that was still your preference," Will said, to reassure his father that he hadn't forgotten they shared the same taste in alcohol. "Schuyler stocks good scotch so I should have guessed, since she prefers rye."

Twain accepted the glass Will brought over. "Sit with me. Both of you," Twain said, settling himself on the couch. "Tell me what you're doing these days."

Schuyler sat sideways in an upholstered chair and slung one leg over its arm. "I'm racking up the billable hours, as usual, Pops. Nothing new here."

Her father winced at her casual nickname but didn't complain about it. "I hear you want to take on the Winslett divorce. That's an ugly one."

"I think I can help Bethany Winslett receive her fair share of the assets. It's going to take some fancy footwork, though."

Will flashed her a questioning look and she nodded back. This must be another of the cases where she felt she could make a difference.

"If anyone can beat that bastard Frank Winslett, it's you," Twain said.

Schuyler looked surprised. "Thanks for the vote of confidence, Dad."

So their father didn't hand out compliments any more freely now than he had when they were children.

"How are things at Cronus?" Twain asked. "Any new projects?"

Will smiled. "Dog food, in fact. Fresh, hypoallergenic, gourmet dog food."

"Well, why not?" Twain said. "Your mother loves those dogs of hers. She'll probably be your first customer."

Will and Schuyler looked at each other. Their father hadn't pooh-poohed the dog food idea as ridiculous and a waste of money.

"That would be . . . gratifying," Will said. "However, it will only be offered in affluent urban areas, at least for the initial release period."

Twain nodded. "Makes good business sense."

Will felt himself relaxing with his father for the first time in years. Now that he had the time to look at his dad as a human being, he realized with a shock that Twain's hair was more white than blond and his jowls had the sag of an older man. Even his formerly square shoulders appeared rounded.

Will had been so busy battling his father that he hadn't noticed the changes. Sadness and regret hollowed out his chest. He thought of Kyra, who had no parents left, and he knew what she would tell him to do.

"We should meet more often," Will found himself saying. "Next time, you both could come to my office. I'll make sure the bar is stocked with rye." He met Schuyler's astonished look with a sardonic twist of his lips.

Twain's face lit up. "I'd like that. Next week?"

Will nodded, the look on his father's face affecting him in a way he hadn't expected. "Let's get it on the calendar." He stood. "I have a dinner meeting so I must bow out now."

"Of course," Twain said, but disappointment laced his voice.

"I'll see you to the door," Schuyler said, rising from the chair.

Will refrained from pointing out that he'd found the door just fine on his way in when she fell into step beside him, accompanying him past her assistant's desk and into the hallway.

"What the hell has gotten into you?" his sister hissed. "Suddenly, you want to have family gatherings in your office. When did we turn into the Waltons?"

"He's gotten old," Will said. "I didn't notice until just now."

"Trust me, he's just as sharp and critical as ever during the work-day," Schuyler said.

"I find that reassuring. But maybe we need to give him a chance to be less sharp and critical as a father."

Schuyler shrugged. "It'll get me out of work earlier if we're trekking over to your office, so who am I to argue?"

"Maybe after a few more meetings, he'll be receptive to our new career directions," Will said.

"Go ahead and dream your unicorn dreams," Schuyler said. She surprised him by throwing her arms around his neck and hugging him fiercely. "I'm getting maudlin like Pops, but I'm glad you stopped by."

Guilt slashed through him. In avoiding his parents, he had avoided his sister, too.

He held the hug, even as she loosened her grip. "I should have done it sooner." He let her step away but cupped her shoulders. "No more letting parental pressure push us around."

"You say that now because Pops is feeling mellow." Schuyler gave his forearms an affectionate squeeze. "But I'll try, big bro."

"I'll have your back."

Chapter 18

Kyra checked the kitchen clock, an old Timex promotional item that someone had donated to the center. She had two hours before the adoption ceremony began . . . and Will would be there.

Isaiah was so excited about a CEO attending at *his* invitation that he'd shared the news with everyone. Evidently, Will had also promised to finish his interrupted history lesson about the Spartans versus the Persians.

In fact, the three boys he'd started with had gathered a whole crew to hear the rest of the story. Kyra couldn't help feeling a sense of satisfaction at the thought of Will holding a group of preteen boys spellbound with a tale from a couple of thousand years ago without a single video game in sight. It just proved that she was right. He should be a teacher.

The satisfaction faded as she wondered what he would do and what she would feel when they saw each other again. She had already scoped out a hidden corner from which to observe the ceremony, but, as Isaiah's guest and a potential donor to the center, Will would have a position of honor. How hard would it be to watch him from across the room, knowing he was forever out of her reach?

She closed her eyes as anguish ripped through her. That answered her question. Maybe she should embrace cowardice and hide in the pantry until Will was gone.

But forty hungry kids were counting on her for their snack, so she opened her eyes and forced herself to focus on that task. Cooking had gotten her through the hard times with her parents. It would get her through losing Will, too.

As she sprinkled cheese over the veggie and meat pizzas, Diego came through the door, slinging his backpack onto a stool. "Hey, Ms. Kyra. You said you had some good news for me," he said. "I could sure use some. I got my chem test back today and it sucked."

"Oh, no. What happened?" Diego was taking every science course his school offered so he would be prepared for a pre-veterinary major in college.

"The teacher is a douchebag. Sorry about the language," the boy muttered. "At least he's curving it, so I won't get a D."

"That makes it better, right?"

"He put stuff on the test that was like a footnote in the book. Stupid stuff. That ain't . . . isn't right."

The teacher really did sound like a douchebag. "Let me cheer you up, then." Kyra took a deep breath, knowing that once she made this commitment to Diego, she couldn't go back on it. "If Shaq can't come back to the center, I will adopt him."

Once the thought had crossed her mind, she'd become convinced it was the right thing to do, despite the expense. She might even be excited about it.

Diego's frown eased but he didn't jump right on the news the way Kyra had expected. "You for real? I didn't know you even liked dogs."

"I like Shaq. And he's gotten a bum deal." The big pit bull had turned her into a friend when he'd leaned against her thigh and practically knocked her over in search of a good ear scratch.

"Don't you work a lot of hours at night?"

"I do and that's where you come in. My landlady, Ms. Woods, will let Shaq out during the day when I'm here and you're in school." Gloria's house had a tiny fenced yard in back where Shaq could do his doggy business. "But I need someone to take Shaq out at night." Someone who could walk the dark streets without anxiety, whether alone or with the pit bull. Very few people in the neighborhood would bother Diego because of his size, and who his father was. "I spoke with Violet and she says it's okay with her, if you're willing to take on the job."

She'd asked Emily first and received her blessing before lining up all the other members of the support network. It was a patched-together solution, but she knew everyone involved would do their best to make it work.

"I won't be able to pay you much," she warned. Shaq's food alone would cut into her debt payments, but she was tired of making all her decisions based on financial obligations. It might take longer to retire the debt, but at least she'd be living her life for more than money.

Diego nodded. "Shaq's my man, so I'll do it for free."

"No way. You're helping me out, so I'll compensate you for it," Kyra said, but she was moved by the boy's selfless offer. It made her feel ashamed about hesitating to rescue Shaq because of her money problems. "I'll give you a key to my apartment once we find out when Shaq can be released to me."

Diego's eyes widened. "You're gonna give me a key?"

"It makes the most sense." Kyra picked up another handful of cheese to sprinkle.

"To *your* place." She looked up to see what was making Diego so slow to grasp the concept. Amazement was written on his face. "You're giving me a key?"

"How else would you get in?" She dropped the cheese when Diego launched himself at her, wrapping her in a bear hug that squeezed the breath out of her.

"Thank you, Ms. Kyra," he said. "Ain't nobody but Aunt Violet ever trusted me with a key to their place before. And that don't count because I live there."

Kyra felt tears brim in her eyes. Such a simple thing to her but such a huge validation to Diego. That was why she loved working with these kids so much. You never knew when you were going to do something so right that their reaction made you cry.

She hugged Diego back. "I'll give you two keys since it makes you so happy," she joked to cover her emotions.

Diego stepped back and cleared his throat. "Min-Joo will be real pleased about this. She been so worried about Shaq."

"How's he doing at Dr. Quillen's?"

"He's missing his people and his buddies here. When I take him out of his crate, he always look around like he's expecting someone else."

Kyra's heart twisted. She'd tossed and turned last night as she debated whether she could handle the responsibility of a dog. But her time with Will had given her a taste of having love and caring in her life. Maybe Shaq couldn't quote Shakespeare, but at least he would love her with all his big pit-bull heart. That sounded pretty good to her right now.

"I solemnly promise to give Shaq the best home I possibly can," she said, crossing her heart with her finger. "I'll take him on long walks and find him a nice dog park to play in."

"He may not be allowed in a dog park. Pitties ain't . . . aren't always welcome. It's tough when you look big and mean."

She had a feeling Diego spoke from experience, and that twisted her heart even more.

Will stood beside a fidgety Isaiah at the front of the lounge. The boy was dressed in a bright pink polo shirt and new jeans to honor the occasion. On Isaiah's other side, Diego held the about-to-be-adopted Khonsu by his leash.

Emily Wade faced their little group and gave Isaiah an encouraging smile. The kindness and caring in her expression made Will understand why she was the perfect director for the Carver Center.

Behind him, he could feel Kyra's presence. She probably thought she was well camouflaged in the far corner of the lounge with a sea of kids in front of her, but he'd spotted her the moment he'd walked into the room. Everything and everyone else had faded into a blur when he found her, her ponytail falling in dark waves over her shoulder, her lips curved in that near smile he found so intriguing, as she listened to the woman standing beside her. He'd forced himself to turn away, even as his entire focus locked on her. He'd hoped the intensity of it would lessen but he craved her even more. The depth of his hunger shocked him. For both their sakes, he would respect the fact that she wanted to avoid him . . . unless his craving overpowered his self-control.

Emily spoke, her voice clear and solemn. "We're here to celebrate Isaiah Ford and his new K-9 Angel, Khonsu."

The cheering was raucous and jubilant with Khonsu's excited barking adding to the volume. Emily made a gesture of pushing down with her palm, which made the kids—and the dog—go quiet almost instantly.

"As we all know, having an Angel requires a commitment, so we ask you, Isaiah, to affirm your willingness to take on all the responsibilities of caring for a dog."

Isaiah nodded. "Yes, Ms. Emily. I be down with that."

Will caught the twitch at the corner of Emily's mouth, even as she maintained her serious expression.

"Good to hear, Isaiah," she said before checking the note card she held. "I'm going to ask you a series of questions. I want you to answer them honestly."

Isaiah nodded again and Will saw that the boy's fingers were knotted together. He dropped his hand to Isaiah's shoulder and gave it a light squeeze of comradeship. The boy glanced up at him with a nervous grin.

"Will you always be kind and patient with Khonsu, whether he's being a good dog or a bad dog?"

"Yeah, I will," Isaiah said.

"Will you spend as much time with him as you can whenever you are at the Carver Center?"

"Yeah, 'cause he be my homie."

A murmur of approval went around the room.

"This is an important one, because you should never feel alone or worried that you don't know how to handle your K-9 Angel. And Khonsu should never suffer because you are afraid to seek out help," Emily said. "Will you ask for help with Khonsu if he seems sick or sad or angry?"

"I promise," Isaiah said.

"And this is the most important question," Emily said. "Will you love Khonsu with all your heart?"

"I already do," the boy said, tweaking something in Will's chest.

Emily lowered her note card. "Diego, please pass Khonsu's leash to Isaiah."

Diego's huge hand dwarfed Isaiah's as he ceremoniously presented the looped handle of the leash to Khonsu's new master. "You picked a real good dog," Diego said.

Isaiah looked a little worried as he took the leash, but Will figured that was a good thing. It meant the boy understood that he had a significant responsibility now.

Emily picked up a white box and flipped it open. Pulling out a small gold pin shaped like a paw print with wings, she fastened it on to Isaiah's collar. "Congratulations on becoming the newest member of the K-9 Angelz," she said.

The cheers erupted again, and Will could swear he heard Kyra's voice among them.

"Congratulations on your new dog," he said as he offered his hand to Isaiah.

"Hey, thanks for standing with me," Isaiah said, shaking enthusiastically. "That was poppin'."

Khonsu began to bark again, so Isaiah dropped to his knees and quieted his dog with a hug. Khonsu's tail was wagging so fast it blurred as he licked Isaiah's face and ear, making the boy laugh with sheer joy.

A sudden certainty flowed through Will. He needed to be part of this, not as a guest but as an integral participant. He wanted to work with these kids, not just write a check. To help them succeed in the paths they dreamed of taking.

The audience began to converge on the newly minted K-9 Angel, so Will stepped back to stand beside Emily.

He watched Diego, the kid Kyra had told him was loading up on science courses so he could become a veterinarian. And Isaiah directing traffic around his dog to keep Khonsu from being overwhelmed by the crowd. Maybe the boy would become a historian since he liked the Spartans so much.

Then his gaze swung to the corner where Kyra had been lurking, but she was no longer there. Amazing that he hadn't felt her absence, but too many emotions were buffeting him at once.

"Excuse me," he said to Emily. "I'll let Isaiah bask in the glow of his initiation a little longer before I start the history lesson."

"You were so good to take time out of your workday to be here," she said. "Isaiah was walking on air when you accepted his invitation."

Just his presence made a kid happy. *He* felt a new buoyancy in his step as he wove his way through the lounge to the stairs.

Because there was only one person who would understand.

Kyra hadn't had quite enough time to finish kitchen cleanup before the adoption ceremony began, so she scrubbed melted cheese from the last of the baking sheets before slotting it into the drying rack. She wasn't in a rush to get out of the center since she figured Will would be tied up for at least another hour with his history lesson.

She pinched the bridge of her nose as the pain of seeing him again flared through her. She'd tried to brace herself for it, but when he had walked into the lounge in a navy suit that made his blond hair glisten by contrast, her knees had nearly buckled underneath her. She'd seen him start to scan the room, so she'd quickly started a conversation with another staff member, giving her a natural reason to look away.

But she couldn't ignore him once the ceremony began. He stood a head taller than everyone else in the room, even Diego. Her heart had squeezed when Will put his hand on Isaiah's shoulder and gave the boy a reassuring smile. She'd had to close her eyes to keep the tears at bay.

As soon as Emily had congratulated Isaiah, Kyra had fled back to the kitchen. It was killing her to see Will without being able to touch him or even talk to him.

She heard footsteps coming down the stairs—heavy, masculine ones. She knew she'd tarried too long as dread and nervous excitement did a tango in her chest.

"Kyra." His voice held a strange mix of elation and hesitation.

She took a moment to steady herself before she turned from the sink to find him standing in the kitchen doorway. Now that he was so close, her longing was intensified.

"Hey, Will." Incredible that she could sound so casual. "To be honest, I wasn't supposed to be here. I'm running late."

She grabbed her backpack from the stool, expecting him to take the hint and move out of her way.

Instead he stretched his free hand partway toward her before dropping it in an indecisive gesture that was unlike him. "I hoped . . . but you're late."

She knew it was a mistake but she couldn't stop herself. "I have a couple of minutes." After all, he'd co-opted his own sister to fight the center's legal battles. "Did you need something?"

He closed the distance between them, so she had to look up at him. She took two steps backward and hit the edge of the kitchen counter, but at least now she wasn't inhaling his clean, male scent with every breath. His jaw tightened when she retreated, although he didn't follow her. He ran a hand over his hair, rumpling it in a way that brought back memories of early mornings in his bed. Not good.

"I wanted to tell you . . . I'm going to give it a try." He nodded. "Teaching."

He'd listened to her. Satisfaction warmed her, as well as genuine happiness for him, but she kept her response to merely polite. "I'm glad. You'll be an inspiring teacher."

"You're the only person I knew who would be happy about it," he said, his gaze locked on her face.

"Your family will be, too, once they see how much it means to you," she said, although she had her doubts about his mother.

"You freed me to do this," he said.

"You freed yourself when you refused to go to law school," she said.

"That felt more like rebellion. There's a difference."

She got it. "You were still reacting to their expectations, not finding your own road. But it was the first step. And now you're taking the next step. Congratulations!"

As she swung her backpack onto her shoulder, a disturbing thought struck her. "You don't plan to teach here, do you?" she blurted out.

All the animation vanished from his face, replaced by a stricken look that made her feel as though she'd kicked one of the dogs in the K-9 Angelz.

But Will stood his ground, his gaze still burning into her. "We were good friends before. I miss that."

Kyra shook her head, even as temptation plucked at her heart. "We already had this conversation. I can't do it, Will. Not with the way I feel about you."

He jerked as though she had struck him. "I don't know how to change that."

"You can't. I can't either." She kept her hands fisted by her thighs to stop herself from pressing her palms against the warmth and solidity of his chest. Not even because she wanted to kiss him but because she wanted to take comfort from him. "I was in love with you at Brunell. Seeing you again in New York brought it back to life." She tried for a smile. "You should be flattered. Most college crushes don't survive the fifth reunion encounter."

"I'm the one who screwed this up with the job offer. I want to make it right." His voice was surprisingly raw.

"It wasn't right from the very beginning. It couldn't be. The job offer just made that crystal clear. Don't blame yourself. It's just as much my fault."

"No!" He chopped his hand through the air in denial. "There is no fault in loving someone honestly. I'm the one who's missing something important that keeps me from loving the most extraordinary woman I know."

She squeezed her eyes closed to shut out the passion lighting his face as he called her "extraordinary." If she listened to him any longer, she would stop caring whether he loved her or not and let him draw her back into his life. Until he found someone who could reach his heart.

The agony that seared through her at the thought of Will lighting up in the presence of another woman ripped away the haze of temptation. She opened her eyes and slid sideways so she had a clear path to the door.

Then she braced herself to meet his gaze. "I'm not strong enough to be friends with you. No matter how much I'd like to be. For my sake, please don't ask me again."

She watched the struggle on his face. Will had never given up easily but his innate gallantry would make it impossible for him to refuse her request. What she hadn't expected to see was the cloud of loss in his eyes.

He stepped aside in a movement of chivalrous acquiescence, the slight lowering of his head pure elegance. "My apologies. I understand your position. I wish . . ." He shook his head. "I wish you all the best."

"The same to you. Always," she said, finding it hard to force the words past the fist squeezing her throat.

She felt him in every molecule of her body as she walked past him, knowing she would never again be able to claim him even as a friend. She had cut the ties between them with a finality that felt like a sword slashing through her heart.

Will watched Kyra walk out the door, her backpack swinging from one proudly squared shoulder in a way that somehow signaled how firm her decision was. How many women would have the bone-deep honesty to admit to loving a man who couldn't return that love? How many more would be able to say it and then walk away? Her strength knocked the breath out of him.

He heard the front door close with a solid thunk that cut him off from her forever. An ache of loneliness rolled through him, almost worse than what he'd felt Saturday morning because then he had still hoped for her friendship. Now that had been taken away.

He slumped back against the counter, his hands braced beside his hips.

How had she become so important to him in such a short time? If he'd thought about her half a dozen times since college, he'd be surprised. They'd met again by pure chance, yet she'd somehow shifted his whole perspective on his life. She'd challenged him, shaken him out of his rut, made him smile, according to Greg, and heated up his nights in a way he hadn't realized he was missing. She'd even changed his relationship with his father.

"Mr. Will?" Isaiah appeared in the doorway, followed by Jayden, Zion, and a couple of other kids. "I put Khonsu in his crate, so we ready to hear about the Spartans."

Will must not have straightened away from the counter fast enough because Jayden asked, "You okay?"

He had to look like crap if an eleven-year-old kid would ask him that. He put some steel in his spine and smiled. "Just a tough day at the office. Let's go back upstairs where the chairs are more comfortable."

"My brother got me a DVD of *300* but my mama say it's too violent, so I can't watch it," Zion said as they headed for the stairs.

"How does your mother feel about you reading a book?" Will asked.

"She always trying to get me to read stuff."

"Well, I brought some books for you, so you can read all about the Spartans with her blessing."

As they trooped up the stairs with the boys chattering about Leonidas and the Persians, Will felt a thrill of exhilaration about his new future.

But without Kyra, it seemed to echo in the hollow spaces of his chest.

Chapter 19

For Thursday's meal, Kyra had chosen a dish that required her to chop onions. That way she could blame her red-rimmed eyes on the pungent fumes instead of a night spent crying over Will. Emily wasn't fooled, but no other staff members had looked at her with pity, so her camouflage seemed to be working.

She'd been second-guessing herself ever since the day before, wondering why she couldn't find the strength to be friends with Will. She'd done it in college. But Babette had provided a handy barrier to her feelings, so she'd been able to tamp them down to a manageable level. With nothing to stop her now, she'd plunged into love with him without a moment's hesitation. Stupid move.

She picked up another onion and whacked the ends off with more violence than necessary.

"Ms. Kyra?" Diego looked around before he slipped into the kitchen as though he didn't want to be seen. "I gotta talk to you. In private."

Kyra wiped her sleeve across her eyes to dash the onion tears away. "How private?"

"I need you to come somewhere with me," he said. He'd ducked into a corner so no one could see him from the hall.

Kyra put down the knife. "What's going on?"

He shook his head and gave her a pleading look. "Can you just come with me?"

She scooped the onions into a plastic storage container and shoved them in the fridge before washing her hands. She should probably get Emily involved but Diego seemed in a hurry. "Do I need my bag?" she asked.

"No. It's not far." He checked the hallway before leading her out past Powell.

"We'll be right back," Kyra said to the guard, since Diego seemed to want to keep this outside jaunt under the radar.

Powell nodded and went back to reading something on his cell phone.

Diego checked both directions on the sidewalk before turning right and practically jogging down the block. Kyra had to trot to keep up with him.

"In here," he said, veering into a narrow walkway between two buildings. They dodged around several garbage cans and a ramshackle shed. Behind it, Felicia sat on a plastic crate, her bandaged arm cradled on her lap. When she looked up, her thin face was streaked with the tears welling up from her brown eyes.

"Oh, sweetie, what's wrong?" Kyra said, dropping to her knees by the child without a thought about the dirty cement. "Is your arm hurting you?"

Felicia shook her head. "I mean, yes, it hurts but that's not it. I heard Mama talking to Mr. Allen and she say Shaq gotta be put down because he bit me. I can't let my dog die. He didn't do nothing wrong."

"He bit you," Kyra said gently. "But he probably won't have to be put to sleep since it's the first time. He won't even have to go back to the shelter because I'm going to adopt him." Why hadn't Diego told her that?

Relief and hope flared in Felicia's face, then faded. "But I won't ever get to see him again."

"Do you want to after what he did?" Kyra asked.

"You gotta tell Ms. Kyra what you told me," Diego said. "You can't let Shaq take the blame no . . . anymore."

Felicia shook her head. "If Ms. Kyra going to adopt Shaq, he'll be okay."

"You know that's not right," Diego said, his voice stern.

"I can't. My mama . . ." The girl dropped her gaze to her arm.

"It's okay, sweetie," Kyra said. "I'll take good care of Shaq."

"It's not just Shaq," Diego said. "It's the K-9 Angelz. They might have to shut it down."

"We don't know that," Kyra said, noticing that Felicia's shoulders were shaking with silent sobs. "I'm sure Ms. Emily will find a way to keep it going."

"I heard Doc Quillen talking," Diego said. "When a dog bites a kid, it's real bad."

"He didn't bite me," Felicia muttered so softly that Kyra barely heard her. "Another dog did. One from down the hall."

"Are you sure?" Kyra glanced up at Diego, hoping he hadn't persuaded the child to make up a different story.

Diego evidently guessed what she was thinking. "I kept my promise to you, Ms. Kyra. Felicia came to me after school. I didn't make her say nothing . . . anything."

Felicia took such a deep breath that her shoulders rose and fell. "I went to Mrs. Galvan's apartment to get some arroz con pollo she made for me and Mama. I was carrying it back when Axel got out of the elevator with his big mean old German shepherd, Chopper. Chopper's mean 'cause Axel makes him that way. I'm scared of both of them."

Kyra put a comforting hand on Felicia's small knee. "I don't blame you."

"Axel lets Chopper off his leash when he's in the building, even though he's not supposed to." Tears started down Felicia's cheeks again. "I guess Chopper smelled the food because all of a sudden he ran at me and clamped his teeth on my arm and started shaking it. I dropped the dish and it broke all over the floor. So Chopper let go and started eating. He probably got glass in his mouth."

Diego made a strange noise in the back of his throat, and Kyra knew he was feeling bad for the dog.

"My arm hurt so bad and was all bleeding so I started yelling for Mama. She came out and she and Mrs. Galvan took me to the hospital. I don't remember a whole lot about being there 'cause they gave me some kind of medicine to make it hurt less and then I got anesthesia."

"I don't understand. Why did you say Shaq bit you?" Kyra asked.

Felicia stared down at her hand again. "Mama told me to say it. She say our insurance don't cover all the stuff that my hand needs and Axel ain't got insurance. But the Carver Center does, so if I say Shaq bit me, their insurance will pay." She threw Kyra a quick glance before she started to sob again. "But he didn't do it. He was barking and scratching at the door. He wanted to come protect me when he heard me yelling. He's a good dog."

Kyra sat back on her heels, wondering how to untangle this mess. She understood Davina's dilemma. As a mother, she wanted her child to get the best possible medical care. But this was going to require great delicacy to resolve.

"Thank you for telling Diego and me the truth," Kyra said. "You're very brave."

"Mama won't get in trouble, will she?" Felicia asked.

"No one will get in trouble," Kyra soothed, although she couldn't figure out how to avoid it. But Schuyler Chase might have a way. "I have to share this with Ms. Emily."

Felicia started shaking her head.

"She won't tell anyone else at the center, I promise," Kyra assured her. "Diego, will you see Felicia home safely?"

The boy nodded and Kyra stood up and offered her hand to help Felicia. The little girl jumped up and flung her arms around Kyra's waist. "I didn't want to lie to anyone but Mama said I had to. She was scared and sad."

"Your mama was just taking care of you," Kyra said, gently encircling the girl's thin shoulders. "She did it because she loves you so much."

"I love my mama," Felicia said, releasing Kyra and wiping her own cheeks with the back of her uninjured hand, "but I love Shaq, too."

Kyra accompanied them back to the sidewalk and watched the big, hulking boy take the little girl's unbandaged hand in his as they walked away. Tears brimmed in her eyes at the protectiveness of his gesture. God, all she did was cry these days.

Kyra sat beside Emily at the director's desk teleconferencing with Schuyler. Will's sister had listened to the beginning of the phone call and decided they needed to be able to see each other as well. Behind the lawyer was an imposing credenza of some dark wood, filled with weighty-looking tomes, their gilt titles made shiny by the subtle up lighting. Kyra wondered what Schuyler thought of the background behind them, which consisted of some fake-oak filing cabinets and artwork by the center's kids.

Schuyler took notes as they talked. "So Felicia said the dog who actually bit her was a German shepherd. We should be able to take impressions of Shaq's teeth and show the bite marks on her arm don't match his."

Kyra interrupted the flow of legal strategy. "How are you going to keep from revealing that Felicia told us all this? She's terrified of getting her mother in trouble."

Schuyler put down her pen. "I had an associate canvas the apartment building for witnesses. Word of that will have gotten around. We didn't actually find anyone who would admit to seeing the incident, although a few said they might have heard it." Her lips curved in a sly smile. "However, Allen doesn't know that. All I have to say is that a witness came forward. Since I don't expect this to go to court, I'll never have to identify or produce the witness."

"Allen won't ask you who it was? Or how credible they are?" Emily asked.

Schuyler's smile turned sharper. "He can ask. I don't have to answer." Kyra liked this woman more all the time.

"Honestly," Schuyler continued, losing the smile, "I think Titus is looking for a way out of this suit. I don't expect him to even ask for the bite-mark match. He'll know I wouldn't request it if I didn't have proof."

"But the center's insurance won't cover Felicia's plastic surgery," Emily said. "How will you get him to drop the case?"

"We're taking care of that," Schuyler said with a wave of her hand. "It's part of the pro bono work."

"You mean the law firm will pay her medical expenses?" Kyra asked, knowing she sounded skeptical.

"Something like that," Schuyler said. "You don't need to worry about it. What I require from you and the entire staff is radio silence on the whole situation. Don't involve any more people. Make sure nothing is said in front of the other kids. I'm going to force Allen—and Ms. Gibson—to sign a gag order as part of the settlement. That way the center doesn't get its reputation dragged through the dirt. You can keep the K-9 Angelz program up and running. And Shaq can return."

"If you can do all that, you're a miracle worker," Emily said, but Kyra heard the hope in her voice.

"I've never been called that before." Surprise and gratification rang in Schuyler's voice. "But don't jump the gun. I've got some delicate maneuvering to do yet."

The lawyer's image winked out as she signed off the call.

Kyra pushed her chair far enough away to see Emily's face. "I don't think the law firm is paying for Felicia's medical expenses," she said.

Emily closed the conference window and flipped down the laptop's screen. "You think it's Will, don't you?"

"Yes, but I don't know what to do about it."

"Nothing. He's doing it for the center." Emily's tone was firm. "You should have seen him yesterday, surrounded by a circle of kids that kept getting bigger and bigger as he told his Spartan stories. He finally had to stand up so everyone could see him as he thrust and parried with his imaginary sword and spear. The kids were fascinated, but Will—" Emily smiled reminiscently. "Will was on fire with the thrill of sharing his knowledge with the kids. I could see how happy it made him. He really should teach a class at business school or something. He has a true gift."

Kyra nodded, but she didn't feel she could share Will's decision with Emily. That was his news to announce in his own time. "Maybe he'll find a way to teach part-time."

"I hope so. The world needs more teachers who can inspire the kids." Emily looked guilty. "I shouldn't be singing Will's praises to you."

"No, I appreciate it. Now I don't feel so guilty about my suspicion that it's his money being used for Felicia's treatment. Even more important, the K-9 Angelz program is safe now," Kyra said, standing so she could carry her chair back in front of Emily's desk. She wished she felt more excited for Emily's sake, but she just felt tired.

"And Shaq. I guess you won't need to adopt him now."

Disappointment sifted through Kyra. She hadn't wanted a dog, but now she felt lonely without one.

Chapter 20

As Will finished reading the financial analysis of the new dog food project, his assistant informed him that Nathan Trainor wanted a minute of his time. "Of course," Will said, although he was surprised. Nathan didn't generally drop in on him.

Will came around his desk as Nathan walked into the office, carrying a small black case. "Thanks for seeing me without an appointment," Nathan said, shaking hands. "I took a gamble that it was late enough in the day for most meetings to be over."

"It's always good to see you. Would you like water or something stronger?"

Nathan hesitated a moment and then nodded. "Something stronger. I have cause to celebrate."

Will crossed to the built-in bar. "Champagne or scotch?"

"Scotch. Single malt, if you have it." Nathan put the case down on Will's desk and accepted the glass of caramel-colored liquor from Will.

Lifting his glass, Will said, "Here's to good news."

Nathan returned the salute and took a taste of scotch. "Excellent stuff. Worthy of the accomplishment." Setting the glass down on the desk, he flipped open the multiple latches on the case and lifted a streamlined cube of brushed stainless steel out of the custom padding. The elegant object had rounded corners and measured about seven inches on each side. Several black rubber insets dotted the shiny surface.

Nathan placed the device on the desk and stepped back. He swept his arm toward the cube and said, "This is a prototype of the TE-500 battery made portable."

"But we use the TE-500s for our refrigerator backups," Will said, thinking he'd misheard. "They're twenty inches across and weigh forty pounds each. We have special racks for them."

Nathan's gaze was fixed on the unassuming cube. "We've been working on how to downsize the TE-500 without losing any power." He looked at Will with a grin of triumph. "It took a lot of hours in the lab but we did it."

Will ran his finger over the smooth metal case. "That's damned impressive."

"It is." Nathan picked up his drink and sipped it while contemplating his latest invention.

Will envied the deep-seated satisfaction Nathan took in having solved a complex technical challenge. What radiated from the other man could only be described as joy, a quiet exultation that he had used his talents to the fullest.

Nathan flipped open one of the rubber flaps. "This is the charging input. The others are for different kinds of plugs—including USB—so the battery is versatile."

"How did you do it?" Will let the admiration sound in his voice.

"Ah, that would be giving away patented secrets," Nathan said with a smile. "Besides I don't think you'd understand my jargon."

Will chuckled. "Very true. I know more about ancient Sparta than modern technology."

"You're no slouch in the tech area. That's why I knew you would appreciate it." Nathan ran his palm over the top of the battery. "This handsome little box has some revolutionary stuff inside it. Not even your average engineer would understand it."

"How do I get my hands on one?"

"Your name is already on the friends and family list."

Surprise swept through Will at Nathan's easy inclusion of him as a friend. "I'm honored."

Nathan nodded. "It may take a couple of months. We have some work to do on the production and financial side of the project but you'll get one of the first batteries off the assembly line."

"My hearty congratulations." Will felt guilty that he had to force the note of enthusiasm into his voice, even though he was genuinely pleased for his friend. "Reports of your genius are not exaggerated."

Nathan patted the box. "This was a team effort. I've got some amazing minds in my R and D department."

"But you work shoulder to shoulder with them, as any good general does."

"It's not work for me," Nathan said. "It's pure pleasure to forget everything but solving the problem in front of me. Chloe will tell you that I lose track of time when I'm in the lab. She sometimes has to chase me down there."

Nathan's gray eyes lit with affection when he spoke his wife's name.

"How did the baby shower go?" Will asked, remembering their dinner.

"I was informed that it was a success." Nathan leaned one hip against the desk. "Chloe asked the guests not to bring gifts but a few did, of course. When she showed me the tiny little clothes, it socked me in the gut. I'm going to be responsible for a brand-new life." He stared down into his glass. "I know that I don't want to raise a child the way I was raised, but that leaves a lot of open territory. What kind of father *should* I be?"

"You'll be all the things you wanted in your own father but didn't get. That's a good place to start." Will understood Nathan's doubts, though. He had no role model he would want to work from either. "And you have Chloe to guide you. She won't let you be anything but stellar."

"That's what gets me through the terror," Nathan said with a wry smile. "Chloe has far more confidence in my parental abilities than I do." Kyra had confidence in Will's ability to teach. Was that what it meant to love someone? To believe in them?

"What made you realize you loved Chloe? I mean, loved her to the point where you wanted to spend the rest of your life with her."

Nathan's attention focused on Will. "Are you asking for a friend?"

"No." Will made a restless gesture. "I think I've screwed up."

"I screwed up, too." Nathan took a sip of scotch and stared out the window. "I let her go and the world turned gray. So I went out and got drunk with Gavin Miller, who can be an ass but is also a keen observer of human nature. He asked me what I would do if Chloe walked into the bar at that moment and said she had made a mistake and wanted me back." Nathan brought his gaze around to Will. "That clarified everything for me. Maybe ask yourself the same question and see what your answer is."

Without meaning to, Will turned toward the empty doorway. He imagined Kyra walking through it, dressed in her sexy bartender's uniform, giving her hips that extra little swing she adopted for Stratus. A ripple of heat shuddered through him, stirring his groin but also making his heart clench with longing. "I would be happy to see her. Very happy. Is that the right answer?"

Nathan shrugged. "If you're desperate enough to ask me for advice, I'd give it serious consideration." He set down his empty glass and picked up the battery, fitting it back into its case with great care. "I'm going home to show this to my pregnant wife, who will probably cry over it because her hormones are on a rampage." He flipped the latches shut. "But that's a sign of true love, too. She cries over a cube of metal filled with power cells, fuses, and circuits simply because I developed it. Think about that when you're answering the question."

Would Kyra cry? He couldn't picture it. She would examine whatever he had created with focus and attention before giving him her clear-sighted opinion. Then she would tell him that he should keep creating because he had that desire in him. And she would support him in whatever endeavor he took on.

"Will?" Nathan stood with the case in his hand. "Still trying to answer the question, I see." He held out his hand. "Good luck. When you've decided, bring her by so Chloe and I can meet her."

"You seem to know my answer already." Will shook the other man's hand.

Nathan shook his head. "Just hopeful."

Then he was striding out the door, leaving Will alone with his thoughts and his scotch. He stood in front of the window, considering Nathan's question. He knew what he wanted his answer to be but he'd been so wrong before.

He couldn't do that again . . . declare his love only to find out he had grossly misjudged his feelings. Or that they had changed. Maybe there was some essential piece missing in him, the emotional element that allowed a person to feel deep, lasting love. He swallowed the last of his scotch in an attempt to wash away the throat-gripping fear that he was defective.

Kyra didn't need to be hurt by a man who didn't understand his own heart. She deserved someone who could declare himself to her without reservation or doubt. A man with the courage to answer her statement of love with one of his own, untarnished by past failure or fear of the future.

She deserved a hell of a lot better than Will Chase.

As he considered refilling his glass, his cell phone buzzed. A flicker of hope that it might be Kyra made him pull it out of his pocket. Instead Schuyler's name came up on the screen. His mood was so bleak that he wasn't sure he should inflict it on his sister, but he wanted to nurture the new relationship growing between them, so he answered.

"Congratulate me," Schuyler said, her voice vibrating with excitement.

He winced at the contrast to his feelings but injected an answering appreciation into his own voice. "Consider yourself congratulated. But what's the happy occasion?"

"I routed Titus Allen. He agreed to every term of my contract, including the total media silence, which must about kill him. No crowing about how he singlehandedly saved an underprivileged young girl from a lifetime of disfigurement and pain." Satisfaction rang in Schuyler's words.

"You are magnificent, sister o' mine. How did you bring about this total surrender?"

"Well, your money helped." Schuyler's tone had gone dry. "And a witness who said Shaq wasn't the dog who bit Felicia."

"You found a witness?"

"Your ex-girlfriend found one. Sorry, maybe I shouldn't have mentioned her, but I like to give credit where credit is due."

Kyra. Of course she would find a way to help. Another wave of loss broke over him, sucking the oxygen out of his lungs. He had to take a breath before he could say, "I'm not surprised. She's very resourceful."

"The director, Emily, called me a miracle worker. You know how great that makes me feel?"

"I can hear it through the phone."

"Thank you for bringing me in on this," Schuyler said. "It's helped me make a decision. I'm resigning from the firm. I want to do this kind of law . . . miracle-working law."

Will grimaced at the storm this would unleash in his family, but he spoke with total conviction. "I'll back you every step of the way."

"I'm going to need you, big brother." He heard a hitch of emotion in her voice.

He thought of Nathan's bone-deep satisfaction in his battery. Of Schuyler's excitement about her triumph over Titus Allen. Of Isaiah's, Jayden's, and Zion's rapt faces as he told the story of the Spartans.

He was ready to reach for the same feelings.

"We're going to need each other, Sky," Will said. "I'm leaving Cronus to become a teacher."

"Whoa! That's a big step. Don't you want to ease into it by teaching a class once a week or something?"

"No." In this, at least, he could be worthy of Kyra's faith in him. "I'm done here. It's time to admit that Ceres was Greg's dream. I just went along for the ride." His partner would not be happy, but he would understand. "Greg will take the company into the future."

"Wow." Schuyler went silent for a long moment. "You worked mighty hard to realize someone else's dream."

"Haven't you worked hard to become a junior partner?"

Her sigh came through the phone. "Point taken. At least, it's in the same field, though."

Will shrugged, even though she couldn't see it. "For me, it didn't matter what field I went into as long as it wasn't law."

"Right." Schuyler paused. "When do you want to break the news?"

"After Sunday dinner at the farm," Will said.

Schuyler snorted. "I can't remember the last time you came to Sunday dinner."

Guilt nipped at him. He'd left all the parental pressure on his sister's shoulders. "You're tougher than I am."

"Ha," Schuyler said before she blew out a long breath. "I can't decide who it's going to be worse for: you or me."

"The heat will be on you," Will said. "I've already disappointed them."

Chapter 21

On Sunday morning, Kyra stood in the cat room of the same animal shelter that all the K-9 Angelz came from. Now that Shaq didn't need rescuing, she had no reason to adopt a pet. It was an expense that would only delay paying off her debts even longer.

But Will had made her realize that her life was missing the same thing so many of the center's kids were: unconditional love. Her apartment seemed cold and gray, no matter how much spring sunshine poured in through the windows. For so long she'd shut everything out of her life except scraping together money, but now . . . now she wanted more.

So she had decided to adopt a cat.

Hysterical laughter bubbled up in her throat as she compared the down-on-their-luck cats in the shelter with Will's patrician good looks.

Shantay, the shelter volunteer assisting her, gave her a quizzical glance, but said, "Let me know when you find a cat you'd like to take out of the cage."

Kyra nodded and walked up to the small, barred cubicles that lined two walls of the room. As she scanned the shadowy recesses where cats crouched, slept, or lolled, a yellow-and-white leg poked out between the bars to pat her on the thigh with a softly padded paw. She squatted to see who wanted her attention.

A matching-colored face with long whiskers peered out at her. "Hello, Malcolm," she said, reading the tag on the cage. Malcolm meowed loudly and stretched his paw farther so he could pat her cheek. "You're a very insistent fellow," Kyra said, her heart squeezing at the cat's gentle touch. She checked the fine print on the tag. "And a man of mystery. A broken leg, a guess that you're about four years old, and nothing else."

"He probably got hit by a car," Shantay said. "You want to take him out?"

"Will it hurt him?" Kyra could see the cast on Malcolm's right front leg.

"Just handle him carefully and it will be fine." Shantay swung the door open and gathered Malcolm in her arms. "Besides, getting him adopted is more important than some brief discomfort."

Shantay transferred the cat to Kyra. He was lighter than he looked, so she suspected he was undernourished under all his long hair. As soon as she had him settled in her grasp, he butted his head against her hand, and she stroked his soft fur. Loud purring vibrated through his little body.

"He likes you already," Shantay said with a grin.

"I'll bet you say that to everyone who picks up a cat," Kyra said, but she was smiling, too. Malcolm's enthusiasm for her touch was endearing.

Shantay shrugged. "Do you want to take Malcolm in the playroom to spend a little time together?"

Kyra gave her a sideways look. "I think you already know the answer to that."

Shantay chuckled. "Because of his broken leg, there will be some extra work required, just to warn you."

"As long as it's not hourly, I can handle that," Kyra said, although inwardly she winced at the additional expense for medical care. Malcolm snuggled his head just under her chin while he made a trilling sound of contentment. "Okay, let's not pretend any longer. He's coming home with me."

A few hours and a couple of hundred dollars spent at the pet store later, Kyra poured clean kitty litter into Malcolm's new box in her apartment's bathroom. The cat sat on his haunches watching her. He hadn't left her side from the moment she let him out of the cat carrier in her apartment, surveying all her cat-prep activities with interest and the occasional meowed comment. While his cast made him limp, he didn't seem to be bothered by it otherwise.

As soon as she smoothed out the litter and leaned back on her heels, Malcolm stepped into the box and did his business.

"What a very smart and considerate gentleman you are," Kyra said.

Malcolm scratched around in the box and then jumped out, coming over to plant his good forepaw on her thigh so he could stretch up and lick her chin.

"You act more like a dog than a cat," Kyra said, ridiculous tears starting in her eyes. She scratched behind his ears and gathered him up in her arms before she stood. "Let's give you a little treat for using your litter right away."

As soon as Kyra sat on her sofa with a book in hand, Malcolm curled up on her lap. She found herself paying far more attention to stroking the cat than to reading the novel she'd picked out. Malcolm purred almost continuously, shifting positions in order to offer different parts of his furry little body to her touch. Occasionally, he would flick his little pink tongue out to give her a sandpapery slurp.

A bone-deep contentment radiated through her, muffling the constant misery that thrummed through her over losing Will.

She supposed she should be grateful to him. Before they'd met at Ceres, her focus on earning the money to pay off her mother's debts had narrowed to near obsession. He had shown her how much more there was to life. He had made her feel again—to the point of agony—but it was better than letting her heart shrivel up to a money-grubbing husk.

Loving meant sowing the seeds of loss. She knew that, but it made her sad that she'd never had Will's love in the first place. Crazy of her to aspire to that, but the heart didn't listen to reason.

At least now she had Malcolm's purring to get her through the loneliness.

"Don't be ridiculous! You can't walk away from a billion-dollar company or the family law firm," Betsy Chase said, calmly sipping her coffee as she sat at one end of the mahogany dining table.

Will and Schuyler exchanged glances across the polished wood between them. They'd made their respective announcements over the raspberry-and-rhubarb sorbet.

"Bets, I think they intend to," Twain said from the head of the table. Will noticed that his father's shoulders were so rounded that they no longer spanned the back of the heavy dining room chair. His tone was resigned.

"Nonsense," Betsy said. "They just need a vacation."

Schuyler sighed. "Mum, I've tried it your way. Now it's my turn to decide where my future lies."

"What's *your* excuse, Will?" his mother said, turning away from her daughter. "You did what you wanted to do right from the start."

"I proved that I could succeed by the standards of your world," Will said. "I have nothing else to prove."

"You know I was a classics major, too," his father said, surprising Will. Twain sounded almost . . . nostalgic.

"That was because lawyers use Latin," Betsy said.

Twain shrugged. "Maybe."

Betsy put her coffee cup down with a clatter. "I can't believe this. You two are throwing away brilliant careers to do what? Be a bleeding-heart pursuer of justice and a schoolteacher."

"I thought Ceres was no better than a burger chain," Will said, unable to keep the edge out of his voice.

Betsy waved her hand in dismissal. "My friends' children all eat at Ceres."

"And that makes it acceptable," Schuyler said, her expression pure exasperation. "Instead of making more money that we don't need, we're putting our skills and talents at the disposal of people who can use the help."

"Oh, for goodness' sake, stop trying to make me feel guilty," Betsy said, taking a gulp of the wine she'd abandoned earlier. "What am I supposed to tell my friends?"

"Tell them your children are following their passions," Twain spoke up, his voice strong. "That's something to be proud of."

This time Will's and Schuyler's gazes met in astonishment. Had their father not only taken their side but also claimed he was proud of them?

Betsy sniffed. "All this folderol about following passions. We did what our parents told us because they knew what would make us happy in the long run."

"Are you sure of that, Bets?" Twain asked. "Or did they just want us to keep their world going the way it was so they could be comfortable?"

"Let's not get philosophical," Betsy said. "This is about our children's *lives*."

"That's exactly right," Will said. "Because you are our parents and we love you, we are giving you the consideration of letting you know first. However, our lives are our own and we will make our own decisions."

"This isn't about you, Mum," Schuyler said gently. "It's about Will and me."

"You're my children, so it affects me, too. I don't want to see you make a terrible mistake." But the certainty had faded from her voice.

"Bets, they're adults," Twain said. "Let's wish them well, and hope they find joy in their new paths."

His father's words were both gentle and yearning.

"We appreciate your backing, Dad," Will said, his astonishment receding under the warmth of his father's support.

"That means a lot," Schuyler agreed.

They turned to look at their mother. She picked up her coffee again. "You know your father can't hold a place for you at the firm," she said to Schuyler. "And I hope this doesn't mean you're going to marry that woman you brought to the Spring Fling," she sniped at Will.

"I'd be fortunate if she'd have me," Will said, fighting to control the fury that flared at his mother's tone.

"She didn't fit in, dear," his mother said. "That dreadful cheap dress."

"She was dressed more appropriately than some of my friends were," Schuyler said.

"Furthermore," Will said, letting ice crust over his anger, "the fact that she could dress so well on a limited budget is more impressive than your friends spending thousands of dollars to look fashionable."

"Oh, dearest, you know what I mean," Betsy said, unruffled.

"You're a terrible snob," Will said. A horrifying realization seared through his brain. He'd been guilty of snobbery himself. He'd thought that his mild affection for Petra was more "appropriate" than his intense longing for Kyra. He hadn't trusted his feelings for her because they seemed so sudden, so irrational, and so out of place in his life. Since his emotions about Kyra knocked him off-balance, he looked at them as suspect. When he felt a bonfire instead of a gentle glow, he had labeled it as something else: obsession, fascination, infatuation, anything other than what he identified as love.

He heard a tearing sound from his lap. He had twisted his linen napkin so hard that he'd ripped it. Tossing the mangled fabric onto the table, he pushed back his chair and rose. "I've made a serious mistake that I need to fix."

"Will!" his father said, standing as well. "I'll walk you to the door."

Will could only nod because his jaw was clenched so hard at the anguish of knowing how much damage he'd done to Kyra. How could he have been so stupid and blind?

As they passed out of the dining room, his father said, "Forgive your mother. She loves you so she worries."

"I don't doubt her love," Will said, adjusting his stride to match his father's slower gait. "It's her perspective that I question. Schuyler and I are no longer ten years old."

As he said it, he felt the last chains of parental control fall away from him. Kyra had been right. On some deep level that he hadn't been aware of, he was still seeking his parents' approval. That had contributed to his blindness about his feelings for Kyra. He nearly groaned out loud, but he wouldn't show that weakness.

"I know," Twain said, "but it's hard for your mother to let go. She had rather domineering parents herself." His father made a wry face. "Sometimes I wonder if she married me because they told her to."

Will stopped in his tracks. "I thought you fell in love with her when you saw her win a sailing race at age seventeen."

"Oh, I fell in love with her, but it took a while to convince her that she was in love with me."

Will had won Kyra's love but he'd thrown it away. He'd thought they should be just friends. What an ass he was.

Twain put a hand on Will's arm. "I won't say that I haven't enjoyed building the law firm, but I'm glad that you and Schuyler are finding your own directions now. I knew she wasn't happy with the corporate cases." His eyes twinkled. "I thought about firing her for her own good, but she needed to make the move herself."

"It would have helped if you'd said something," Will said. "She feels like crap about this."

"If I made it easy, she wouldn't be sure this is what she wants to do."

"You're a bit of a bastard, Pops." But Will understood. He'd put his heart and soul into building Ceres because he had to justify walking away from the family business.

"So my opponents say," his father said with pride. "But don't let me keep you from wherever you're rushing off to. I suspect it has something to do with Kyra."

Another surprise. His father remembered her name.

"I screwed up, and I guess I have to thank Mum for making me realize that." He started to shake his father's hand, then pulled him in for a hug. "Tell Schuyler what you told me. We're past the need for tough love now."

"It's a hard habit to break," Twain said, returning Will's hug. "Good luck, son."

"I'm going to need it."

Chapter 22

Kyra's arms were buried up to the elbows in a giant bowl of chopped fruit when Isaiah peered around the doorjamb from the Carver Center's hallway. "Oh, good, you alone," he said.

"You *are* alone," she corrected, but Isaiah had vanished. "Yeah, I'm alone," she muttered as she mixed the salad with her bare hands. A piece of loose hair fell over her forehead. Without thinking, she used her wrist to brush it back, smearing fruit juice over her forehead and in her hair. At least she didn't have to look good later for bartending. "And who knows? It might even be good for my hair."

She smiled. In less than twenty-four hours, she'd gotten into the habit of conversing with Malcolm about whatever she was doing in the apartment. He was a very chatty cat, so he often responded with trills, chirrups, or an occasional ear-splitting yowl. She'd have to watch her impulse to continue her external monologues at the Carver Center since the kids might think she was going crazy.

As she redistributed a clump of diced apple, she heard footsteps that sounded noticeably different from the kids or the staff. Each thud was sharper and heavier. Somehow she wasn't surprised when Will appeared, framed in the kitchen doorway, looking like pure temptation in a tailored gray suit, his jewel-green eyes and golden hair glinting in the kitchen's harsh light. Only he could look good under fluorescent bulbs.

She squeezed her eyes shut to battle the longing that threatened to choke her.

"Kyra, please hear me out." His smooth, deep voice sent ripples of yearning through her as his footsteps came closer.

She angled her head downward, so when she opened her eyes, she was staring at the multicolored fruit. "Will, I told you that I can't be your friend."

"I don't want to be your friend," he said.

That made her look up, bracing herself for the familiar perfection of his face. "Then why the hell are you here?"

"I missed you."

She sucked in a breath as the simple words battered her self-control. "Yeah, well, life's tough all around." Her harshness was an attempt to stop the conversation in its tracks.

"Please, Kyra . . ." Will stretched out his hand, palm up.

She heard whispering outside the door and suddenly Isaiah, Jayden, and Zion poured in from the hallway, lining up in front of Will. Isaiah nodded and Jayden stepped forward as the other two began to beatbox. "Hey, Ms. Kyra, don't be on his case," Jayden chanted. "'Cause he's our homie, Mr. Will Chase."

The other boys repeated, "He's our homie, Mr. Will Chase."

"He know he done wrong so give him a break," Jayden rapped. "Let him say sorry, he make a big mistake."

"He make a big mistake," Isaiah and Zion said, busting out some moves as they got into the swing of things.

Kyra glanced at Will's face to see that his jaw was slack with amazement as he watched his young supporters.

She pulled her arms out of the fruit and planted her hands on her hips, picking up the rhythm of Jayden's words. "You tell

Mr. Chase that he better make it good, 'cause I don't want things to be misunderstood."

"To be misunderstood," the chorus chanted.

Will took up the challenge. "See, Ms. Kyra, I gave it lots of thought, especially the thing that happened on the yacht."

Kyra's gaze flew to his face as heat flared through her. His eyes danced when the boys repeated, "That happened on the yacht."

She glared at him and shook her head, but she could feel his hands on her as though they were back on board the *Royal Wave*.

"Okay, boys," Will said, his voice commanding. "You've broken the ice for me and I appreciate that, but I need to talk with Ms. Kyra alone now."

"We hear you, Mr. Will," Isaiah said, giving Will a fist bump. "You got this." He led the trio out into the hallway.

"Completely alone." Will pivoted to swing the heavy door closed and shot the ancient, pitted bolt. He stood with his head down and his back to her for a few moments before he turned. "I didn't know they were going to do that."

Kyra wiped her sticky, wet hands on her apron. "I figured that out."

"I told them you had good reason to be mad at me and I had to apologize. I guess they decided that I would need some help," he said with a rueful grimace. He stood in front of her, his gaze roaming her face as though he were trying to memorize every detail.

Kyra wiped her hands again because she didn't know what else to do. "Could you just say what you came to say?"

He walked forward until only the kitchen island separated them. The air seemed to vibrate with his presence.

"Kyra, I didn't trust myself to know what love should be. I questioned my own judgment because with you it was so different . . ." He shook his head and took a deep breath. "I was afraid of how you make me feel. It's crazed and intense and unsettling. But it's also brilliant and exhilarating and makes me want to do handsprings." He spread his hands at his sides. "I kept calling it something other than love because it burns so hot. When you walked away I thought I would get past it, that the craving would fade without your presence to fan it, but"—his voice rasped as though it was hard to force the words out—"my life has no joy without you."

Too many emotions were crowding in her throat, making it hard to push speech past them. But she needed more. She swallowed hard. "What does that mean?"

His knuckles went white as he gripped the edge of the stainless steel island. "It means I want you to spend every night with me, to make love to you, to wake up together every morning and have breakfast. I want to take you sailing and seduce you on a secret beach. I want to take you to parties . . . and to Paris. I want you to get to know Schuyler and my parents better."

Kyra held up her hand, trying to stem the rush of images his words were painting. Hope bubbled through her like champagne and she felt drunk on it, which wasn't conducive to cautious, rational thought. "You know your mother doesn't like me."

His smile had a strange edge on it. "Thanks to you, I've gotten past my need for parental approval, so I don't care." His smile turned warm. "But once she gets to know you, she'll change her mind."

"You're sweet," Kyra said, "but I can't picture it."

"I want to kiss you. Badly," Will said, his voice gritty with restraint. "But I won't do it without your permission."

She wanted that badly, too, but she forced herself to stay on her side of the island.

"What is it?" he asked when she didn't answer him.

It was hard but she looked him right in the eye. "I believe that you don't care what your mother thinks, but there are other people in your world. I'm so different from them."

His jaw went stiff with anger. "I live in the same *world*"—he emphasized the word irritably—"as you do. You mingle with CEOs and politicians and brain surgeons at Stratus."

"I don't mingle. I serve them."

"You charm them, challenge them, make them feel attractive and witty, while you mix drinks for them. That's not serving. Hell, I mix drinks for people who come to my office at Cronus."

"But I do it for money."

"So do I," he said with a flash of a smile. "Just *more* money."

She gave a weak laugh at that.

He flattened his palms on the island and leaned in. "The only person who believes you are less is you."

"Except your mother," she said. Will didn't acknowledge her lame attempt to avoid the real topic, and she had to consider the truth of his words. Neither Farr nor Schuyler had ever treated her as inferior in any way. Even Will's father appeared to view her as just a date Will had brought to a party. At least, he didn't look at her dress with scorn.

She'd let Will's background and one person's disapproval intimidate her. "But you're a billionaire," she said.

"Yes, I am. I can buy helicopters and yachts. So what?"

"So I can't even pay off my college loans." She knew she sounded bitter.

The anger came back into his face. "Because your mother, who should have helped you, instead saddled you with her problems. In fact, you are all the more impressive because you refused to walk away from the obligation. Many people would have."

Somewhere inside her, a weight seemed to slide away. Or maybe it had just shifted onto Will's powerful shoulders, but she no longer felt crushed under it. She had considered herself a failure for so long that it made her giddy to see herself from Will's perspective.

"You always did have an answer to every argument," she said.

"Annoying, isn't it?" he said, one corner of his mouth kicking up.

"No, it's wonderful." She allowed herself a real smile. "When I see myself through your eyes, I look very different. I'm going to try to believe in that vision, because I want to be that person for you."

"You're already everything for me. I love you," he said, his voice rumbling low with emotion.

Kyra thought her heart would explode right out of her chest. "Say it again."

He fixed those amazing eyes on her and drew out each word. "I. Love. You. Will you forgive me for not recognizing that truth sooner?"

Kyra bolted past the island and hurled herself against him, wrapping her arms around his neck without regard for the fruit crud she was smearing on his expensive suit. His body felt even better than she remembered it, warm and solid, permeated with Will's delicious scent. He brought his mouth down on hers with a tenderness that surprised her, his eyes closing as their lips touched.

"I was afraid I would never do this again," he said when he pulled a fraction of an inch away. He angled his forehead against hers. "I've been such an idiot. I don't deserve you."

"True," Kyra said, tears welling up and streaking down her cheeks. "But for some reason, I can get past that."

"Now I need to hear *you* say it," Will said, his fingers whispering through the hair on either side of her face. "So I can do what I should have done the first time."

She knew what he meant because his feelings were clear on his face. "'Doubt that the stars are fire, doubt that the sun doth move his aides, doubt truth to be a liar, but never doubt I love' you," she said, borrowing the Bard's eloquence.

His smile was pure joy. "'For where thou art, there is the world itself, and where thou art not, desolation.' I love you. It's so good to hear those words and feel how right they are."

She could barely breathe as happiness rioted through her. When he lowered his head and took her mouth in a kiss that held all his pent-up feelings, she felt light-headed and swayed into him.

His arms tightened around her and he lifted his head. "Greg's taking over as CEO and I'm phasing out of Cronus and Ceres to be a teacher. You gave me the courage to do that."

She laughed for no reason except that she couldn't contain all the emotions ricocheting around inside her. "I found out that I can finish my college degree part-time. You inspired me."

Will smiled down at her. "We make each other better when we're together."

"That seems like the best kind of love." Kyra brushed back a stray strand of his shining hair. "Oh, I hope you're not allergic to cats."

"Not that I know of." He raised his eyebrows in a question.

"I was lonely after we split up, so I adopted Malcolm."

"You replaced me with a cat." Will's eyes were alight with laughter.

"Yep, I have another blond guy in my life."

He pulled her close again, stroking her hair down her back. "I can't believe my good luck in meeting you at Ceres that day."

"Do you believe in fate?" she asked, resting her cheek against the steady beat of his heart. "I never did."

"I believe you make your own fate," he said. "You choose who and what to love and that shapes your character and your life. But maybe I started Ceres so that you would walk back into my life."

"That's a heck of a lot of work when you could have just done a search on Facebook."

"And this is why I love you," Will said.

"Because I'm a smart aleck?" But his words burrowed deep inside her, spreading sparkles wherever they touched.

"Because you're smart."

He ran one arm around her shoulders and one around her waist to bring her against him. "As much as I enjoy talking, there's a more concrete way to show you how I feel."

He angled his head so that their lips met perfectly, the kiss beginning as a slow exploration but quickly turning into a scorching demand. Desire slid through Kyra like a draft of fine vintage brandy, pooling low in her belly with sensual warmth. Will's hands moved over her back, rubbing the fabric of her T-shirt against her skin, sending flutters of sensation dancing along her nerve endings.

He seized her bottom and lifted her onto the kitchen counter, standing between her thighs, his erection pressed against her sensitive center. Skimming his lips down her neck, he licked at the skin where it joined her shoulder, making her shiver with pleasure.

When he brought his hands up to cup her breasts, she leaned away from him. "I'm afraid your posse is lingering outside the kitchen door, so we can't go any further."

Will groaned in agreement. "You made me forget where I was." He flicked her aching nipples once with his thumbs, making her gasp and arch. Then he pressed his palms flat on the counter on either side of her thighs. "If I don't stop now, I won't be able to."

She could hear the raggedness in both of their breathing. "Those boys are not stupid. They're going to have a good idea of what we've been doing."

"Ah, but my conscience is clear because we stopped short." Will put his hands around her waist and lifted her down from the counter. "Tonight, however, there will be no stopping until—"

Kyra put her hand over his mouth. "If you say any more, I'll drag you into the pantry and sully your conscience in a big way."

She grinned as Will's hands curled into fists of frustrated lust. When he nodded, she dropped her hand and went to the door to unbolt it and swing it open.

Sure enough, the three boys were perched on the bottom steps of the staircase, their heads swiveled in her direction.

"Did you and Mr. Will get right?" Isaiah asked.

Will appeared beside her and slipped his arm around her waist. "We got right," he said, smiling down into her eyes. "Very, very right."

And then he bent his head and kissed her, right in front of their audience. She heard snickers and a snort of disgust, but she didn't care. Because the man she'd thought she could never have was kissing her as though he would never stop.

Epilogue

Six months later

Kyra stood at the front of the gathering of spectators on the sidewalk outside the first Ceres for Canines and Cats. A ribbon in Ceres's trademark deep green was stretched across the storefront, twisting slightly in the October afternoon breeze. The store's facade featured several heights of drinking fountains for dogs, as well as poop bag dispensers and fake fire hydrants set in beds of bark mulch. The store designers had taken their job seriously.

But what made her grin was the assemblage of Carver Center kids with their K-9 Angelz. Will and Greg had made the product launch publicity all about the original inspiration for the new, fresh pet cuisine.

Shaq, his collar decorated with a green bow to match the ribbon, was front and center with Felicia, whose arm had healed successfully, thanks to Ben Cavill's medical expertise and connections. Even Davina Gibson had joined them and stood off to the side, her eyes on her daughter while pride glowed on her face. She had written a letter of apology to Emily. Of course, Emily had accepted it and welcomed Felicia back to the center. But they'd learned some valuable lessons from the experience.

Diego hovered over another half-dozen kids and dogs who were being wrangled into place by the Cronus marketing team, petting the dogs even as they directed them.

Kyra smiled to herself. Malcolm would have loved to be a part of this, but today was about the K-9 Angelz program. In fact, Will had tried to get her into the photo op, arguing that she was the original inventor of 3Cs, as the marketing people had already nicknamed the food for the customers' convenience. But she would have felt ridiculous taking credit for the simple recipe she'd put together, so Will had settled for making sure she was at the front of the audience.

He stood in the background, talking with Greg as they watched the kids and dogs. He'd gone low-key, too, wearing a white button-down shirt with khakis. He was even letting his hair grow a little longer, although far from ponytail length. As he brushed back a stray lock behind his ear, Kyra decided she needed to persuade him to grow it even longer so she could twine her fingers into the golden silk of it.

Her breathing hitched as she pictured it curtaining the sides of his face while he moved over and inside her.

Her X-rated reverie was interrupted when a television van drove up, discharging a reporter and cameraman from a local New York station. That was the cue for the ribbon-cutting ceremony to begin.

Will and Greg strode forward together, but when the crowd quieted, Will spoke first. "I'd like to introduce Greg Ebersole, the cofounder of Ceres," Will said. "He will be taking Ceres and all of Cronus Holdings into the future as the new CEO. There is no one with a greater passion or vision for the company we've built together. With Greg at the helm, the sky's the limit."

Applause rippled through the audience, and the reporter's face went from bored to intent at this new angle on what had seemed a routine story.

"Thanks, Will," Greg said, his voice gruff. "Before we started working together, I'd never seen a preppy sweat, but you impressed me because you weren't afraid to get your khakis and polo shirts dirty."

The spectators chuckled.

Greg turned serious. "I'm aware of the trust you have placed in me, and I will do my best to be worthy of it."

The two men's hands met in a way that showed their business partnership had become a deep friendship. Nostalgia, confidence, and anticipation were written on their faces as Will publicly transferred the mantle of power to Greg's wide shoulders.

Will released Greg's hand and stepped back into the group of Ceres staff.

Greg gestured Felicia and Shaq forward and addressed the spectators. "Please welcome Felicia Gibson and Shaq from the K-9 Angelz program of the Carver After-School Care Center, a program that brings together kids and the rescued dogs who need their love." Greg knelt to put his arm around Shaq's substantial shoulders and gave his enormous head a rub. "If you can believe it, this big, handsome fellow has a sensitive stomach."

Laughter rose from the crowd.

Greg stood again. "Which prompted the school's talented human chef to develop a recipe of fresh ingredients that wouldn't trigger food allergies or digestive upsets in dogs like Shaq here. When we heard about it at Ceres, we thought it was the perfect complement to our human restaurants that emphasize fresh, organic ingredients." He gestured toward the Ceres restaurant adjacent to the 3Cs store. "We were fortunate to be able to find space right next to one of our premier locations right here in Manhattan."

A marketing person handed Greg an oversized pair of scissors, which he then offered to Felicia. "So we are celebrating the launch of Ceres for Canines and Cats today with the opening of our first store. Go for it, Felicia."

The girl opened the scissors wide and sliced through the fabric with a loud "snip," letting the ribbons flutter to the ground. Then she held the scissors over her head like a trophy, her injured arm looking as strong as the other one.

The marketing staff swung open the doors and first invited the kids and dogs inside, then the press and VIP guests, and finally, the public. The reporter rushed up to Will and held a microphone in front of him. He smiled and shook his head, gesturing toward Greg. Once the reporter moved on, Kyra strolled up and gave Will a quick peck on the cheek. "That went well," she said.

Will slid his arm around her waist and snugged her up against his side. "Wait until they see the buffet at the human café. Everyone loves free food."

They'd closed the Ceres restaurant next door for a private party to celebrate the launch. To keep uninvited but hungry customers happy, Ceres staff members stood outside the restaurant, passing out ten-dollar gift cards to be used for either pet or human food at a future date.

Will drew her to the entrance into the café. Everyone from the Carver Center had been invited, so the kids and their parents were scattered around the tables, chatting and scarfing down food.

Emily stood near the door with her fiancé, Max, as she nibbled on a shrimp brochette. "Congratulations on the successful launch," she said to Will as she waved her skewer. "And thank you for inviting everyone. The kids are so excited to be here with their parents."

Max shook hands with Will. "I hear you're joining the Carver Center board at the beginning of next year. It will be good to have you with us."

"I should be pretty well free of any obligations to Cronus by then. Greg has taken over my job with gusto." Will's lips slanted in a wry smile. "We all like to think we're irreplaceable but it's just not true."

Max laughed. "I learned that when I sold V-Chem Industries. They barely noticed I was gone."

"Because you still work for them," Emily said. "Just not in Chicago."

A glance passed between them that made Kyra want to melt into Will as the air vibrated with emotion.

"I'm only a lab rat now," Max said.

Kyra knew that Max was a brilliant researcher, currently doing what he loved instead of running a corporation. It made her believe Will would also be happier when he had disentangled himself from Cronus and started his master's in education in January.

"Sorry I missed the ribbon cutting," Schuyler said, dashing up to them, her coat billowing out behind her. She kissed Kyra and Will. "But I got the final divorce agreement signed between Bethany Winslett and her jerk bastard of a husband. She'll never have to worry about money again."

"Isn't that your last official case with Chase, Banfield, and Trost?" Kyra asked.

"It is!" Schuyler threw her arms in the air. "So celebrations all around." She let her hands fall to her sides. "Of course, you're a step ahead of me, Kyra. How's it feel to be an undergrad again?"

"Like trying to get a drink of water from a fire hydrant," Kyra said. "I love it."

"I'm getting an education, too, because she's so excited that she shares it with me," Will said.

Kyra nudged him in the ribs with her elbow. "Don't worry, I'll let you practice your teaching techniques on me when the time comes."

"I don't want to hear about what techniques my brother uses on you," Schuyler said with a smirk.

Kyra felt a flush heat her cheeks, but Will laughed. "You have a gutter brain, Sky. Go get yourself some food and stop embarrassing Kyra."

"Sorry, but you guys are so lovey-dovey that it gets kind of nauseating sometimes." Schuyler grinned and spun away to grab a plate from the buffet.

"*Lovey-dovey?*" Kyra sputtered.

Emily smiled. "It's wonderful to see you together. You're so engaged with each other."

Will's arm was like a steel bar around Kyra's waist. "Since I almost lost her once, maybe I hang on more tightly now."

"If that's what she means by lovey-dovey, I'm okay with it," Kyra said. "But we're not sappy."

"Never sappy," Max agreed, but his eyes were amused.

Greg strode up and cast a quick glance around them before saying, "If I have to smile and be polite for one more second, my face is going to crack." He looked accusingly at Will. "You didn't warn me about this PR garbage when you convinced me to take over as CEO. I may resign and force you to come back."

"Not a chance," Will said without a second's hesitation.

"Yeah, you've got better things to do," Greg said, giving Kyra a kiss. "And I don't blame you for wanting to do them with this lovely lady."

"Is this National Embarrass Kyra Day?" Kyra asked, but she hugged the newly promoted CEO. She and Greg had bonded over their blue-collar backgrounds and then joined forces to tease Will about his life of privilege. "You did a great job of projecting CEO mightiness today."

"I noticed you bowed out of being in front of the cameras," Greg said. "You should have been front and center since you started the whole 3Cs project."

"All I did was throw together a few basic ingredients after an hour's research on the Internet," Kyra said.

"And convince our former CEO to invest in the whole idea," Greg said.

Will waved a hand in dismissal. "Will you ever stop bringing that up?"

"Nope." Greg grinned. "Because it bothers you every time." He turned to Emily and Max. "He doesn't like to be reminded that he allowed love to affect his business judgment."

"Not true," Will said. "I don't like being reminded that I let business affect my love."

Kyra's heart did a little cha-cha in her chest, and she gave his back a quick rub of gratitude.

"I'm going to eat some of our food before the TV people finish it all," Greg said, following in Schuyler's footsteps.

As soon as Greg moved away, Davina Gibson approached them. She looked as though she wasn't sure she wanted to be there, but she managed to smile. "I wanted to thank you for letting Felicia cut the ribbon. She was so proud she could do it." Davina swallowed. "Especially with her arm and all."

"She was the right person for the job," Will said, his smile pure charm.

Davina beamed at Will before she looked at Emily. "That nice reporter said she'd like to do a follow-up story on Felicia and Shaq and the K-9 Angelz program. I'd be happy for my daughter to be part of that, if you say it's all right." She nodded for emphasis.

"That means a lot," Emily said, her pleasure shining in her eyes. "Why don't we go talk to the reporter to see what she's planning?"

As the three of them walked away, Will bent to murmur, "How do you feel about leaving now?"

"Now? Don't you want to bask in the glow of accomplishment?"

"This is Greg's accomplishment. And as he pointed out, I have better things to do with you." His voice dropped to a seductive rumble.

Anticipation fluttered through Kyra, sending little ripples of sensation over her skin. They'd found some interesting ways to enjoy themselves in the limo.

Will caught Greg's eye across the room and angled his head toward the door. Greg nodded and mouthed something that might have been "Lucky bastard," but Kyra couldn't be sure.

"Don't you want to say good-bye to Schuyler?" Kyra asked, looking around for Will's sister.

"She'll understand," Will said, seizing Kyra's wrist and towing her toward the door.

The limo glided to a stop by the curb, but the drive had been too short to reach Will's house. Actually, now *their* house. She'd agreed to move in with him two months earlier because he had pointed out that it was selfish to deprive Gloria of potential rental income when Kyra spent almost all her nights at Will's. That happened right after Will had convinced her to let him pay off her mother's credit card debt. He'd made the argument that the debt wasn't actually Kyra's, so she shouldn't feel obligated to handle it by herself when he could easily take care of it. She had tried to find the flaw in his logic, but he'd kissed her the moment she'd appeared to weaken and her mind had turned to mush. At least she had clung to her pride about dealing with her own college debt.

As Will held the door, Kyra realized they were in front of the Ceres where she had sat down at his table on that momentous day. As with the Ceres they'd just left, several members of the waitstaff stood outside distributing gift cards because the doors bore a sign that said "Closed for a Private Event."

Kyra was baffled. "Is this another 3Cs opening?"

Will pulled her across the sidewalk. "No, it's more private than that."

She couldn't see into the restaurant from outside. As the door swung open for them, Kyra realized why. Heavy blue curtains were hung on tall rolling frames in front of all the windows as well as the door. Will pulled one aside to usher her into the interior of the restaurant.

"Oh, my goodness!" She put her hands to her cheeks in astonished delight. All but one of the tables had been moved to the edges of the room. The last remaining table was placed in the center, surrounded by tall silver candelabras that stood on the floor. Although the table was the same size and shape as all the others, it was covered with a white linen tablecloth and a dazzling array of gleaming china, crystal, and silverware. The basic Ceres chairs were draped and tied with deep blue fabric that matched the curtains.

"Is it our six-month anniversary or something?" she asked, trying to recall the date.

He laughed and offered her the crook of his arm. "Such a romantic. No, you missed that by a month or so."

"Then . . . what?" A little whisper of excitement tiptoed through her.

"You're rushing me, woman," Will said, pulling out a chair for her.

"You can't set all this up and expect me to patiently wait for whatever it is you brought me here for."

Will pulled a bottle of Dom Pérignon out of the silver ice bucket set by the table. "At least, let me open this so we can celebrate. I hope."

Kyra tried to stop herself from smiling but it was a lost cause. She tucked her hands under her thighs to keep from fidgeting as Will drew out the cork with a soft pop and filled two flutes with champagne.

"And now," he said, dropping fluidly to one knee beside her and then looking exasperated. "May I please have your hands?" he said, his palms held out. She pulled her hands out and laid them in his, loving the feel of his strong fingers.

He took another deep breath. William Peyton Chase III was actually *nervous*. Her smile widened.

"Would you stop grinning at me like a demented clown?" he said irritably. "This is a serious occasion."

"Are you going to ask me or not?" Kyra said, trying to tame the unruly corners of her mouth. But they just kept curling upward.

"I had intended to tell you how much I care about you, what a lucky man I am to have found you again after all those years, and how sorry I am for taking so long to understand my feelings for you."

Kyra nodded.

"But I should have known that you would want to get to the point right away." He smiled in a way that sent her heart into her throat. "And that's one of the many things I love about you."

Kyra blinked as tears prickled behind her eyelids.

"I love you," he said, his grip tightening on her hands. "Will you marry me?"

That the normally eloquent Will Chase spoke such short, simple words touched her heart as no flowery declarations could have. She yanked her hands out of his and threw her arms around his neck, burying her face against his shoulder as she sobbed, "Yes, yes! Yes, I will. I love you so much."

"Thank God," he groaned, wrapping her in a hard embrace. "I was afraid you would think it was too soon."

"Are you kidding me? It's been ten long years." Kyra lifted her head and buried her fingers in his golden hair, savoring one texture of the man who was going to be her husband. What a marvelous thought that was.

He laughed. "Maybe that's why I didn't want to wait any longer."

He loosened his hold on her and reached into his trouser pocket to produce a small velvet box. "This was my grandmother's," he said, flipping it open and removing the ring before she could see it. Once again he held out his palm. She gave him her left hand, fingers extended, and he slipped on an exquisite emerald-and-diamond ring in an antique filigree setting.

"It's amazing." She smiled at him and the glittering ring through a haze of tears. "And the color matches your eyes, so it will always remind me of you."

"I would hope so," he said with a chuckle, "since it's our engagement ring."

"You know what I mean," Kyra said, happy laughter burbling up in her throat. "Your knee must be killing you, so stand up and 'give me a thousand kisses.'"

"Quoting Catullus to a classics major? That's gutsy," he said, his eyes lit with amusement and a love that made Kyra's breathing go shallow. "I'll answer you with Shakespeare. 'A thousand kisses buys my heart from me.'"

He stood and swept her to her feet along with him. Lowering his head so their lips almost touched, he whispered against her mouth, "But you already own me, body and soul." And his lips met hers in a kiss that claimed her for the rest of their lives.

ACKNOWLEDGMENTS

A novel holds an entire imaginary world within its pages, so perhaps it's not surprising how many people—and animals—are involved in the making of one. I am very fortunate to have an incredible team to support me in ways both professional and personal. My heartfelt thanks to:

Maria Gomez, the dazzling and talented editor who takes such loving care of my books from contract to publication and beyond.

Jessica Poore and the magnificent Montlake team, the incredible folks who work tirelessly and with superb skill behind the scenes to support my work in every way.

Jane Dystel and Miriam Goderich, literary agents beyond compare. I've said it before and I'll say it again: you are the world's greatest agents.

Andrea Hurst, my sensitive, splendid developmental editor, whose instincts I trust implicitly to make my books shine.

Scott Calamar and Erica Avedikian, my focused, meticulous copyeditor and proofreader, who catch all my many mistakes and make my prose so much more polished than it started out.

Letitia Hasser, my gifted, creative cover designer, whose artistic flair captures both the book and the reader's attention.

Miriam Allenson, Lisa Verge Higgins, and Jennifer Wilck, my awesome critique partners, who know about everything from gang colors to commercial food prep, with a lot of grammar and subtext in between. You are so important to me in every way.

Betty Pappas, food industry pro, who shared her expertise and sent me down the right path for my characters.

Cathy Genna, my wonderful author concierge, whose creative ideas and in-depth knowledge of what readers want makes her such a great resource, as well as a pleasure to work with.

Rebecca Theodorou, dedicated veterinary student, whose generosity in sharing her knowledge of touchy canine digestive systems made Shaq's problem and cure so much more authentic.

Carol van den Hende, whose smart, insightful presentation on millennials sent this book in a whole different direction.

Pie, my beloved and much-mourned little gray cat, whose soft fur and purring got me through all but the last two months of writing this book. She is no longer by my side but forever in my heart.

To Jeff, Rebecca, and Loukas, my amazing family and my strongest supporters. You make my life rich.

ABOUT THE AUTHOR

Photo © 2015 Lisa Kollberg

Nancy Herkness is the award-winning author of the Wager of Hearts, Whisper Horse, and Second Glances series, as well as several other contemporary romance novels. With degrees in English literature and creative writing from Princeton University, she has earned the New England Readers' Choice award, the Book Buyers Best Top Pick honor, and the National Excellence in Romance Fiction Award, and she is a two-time nominee for the Romance Writers of America's RITA Award.

Nancy is a native of West Virginia but now lives in suburban New Jersey with a goofy golden retriever. To learn more about Nancy and her books, please visit www.NancyHerkness.com or find her on Facebook at www.facebook.com/nancyherkness, Twitter @NancyHerkness, and Pinterest at www.pinterest.com/nancyherkness.